MW00627612

# Town Under

### The First Book in a New Apocalyptic LitRPG
### The System Apocalypse – Australia

**By**

# Tao Wong & KT Hanna

# License Notes

This is a work of fiction. Names, characters, businesses, places, events, and incidents are either the products of the author's imagination or used in a fictitious manner. Any resemblance to actual persons, living or dead, or actual events is purely coincidental.

This book is licensed for your personal enjoyment only. This book may not be re-sold or given away to other people. If you would like to share this book with another person, please purchase an additional copy for each recipient. If you're reading this book and did not purchase it, or it was not purchased for your use only, then please return to your favorite book retailer and purchase your own copy. Thank you for respecting the hard work of this author.

Town Under

Copyright © 2021 Tao Wong and KT Hanna. All rights reserved.
Copyright © 2021 Sarah Anderson Cover Designer

Published by Starlit Publishing
PO Box 30035
High Park PO
Toronto, ON
M6P 3K0
Canada

www.starlitpublishing.com

Ebook ISBN: 9781990491450
Print ISBN: 9781990491504
Hardcover ISBN: 9781990491511

# Books in the System Apocalypse Universe

## Main Storyline

Life in the North

Redeemer of the Dead

The Cost of Survival

Cities in Chains

Coast on Fire

World Unbound

Stars Awoken

Rebel Star

Stars Asunder

Broken Council

Forbidden Zone

System Finale


## System Apocalypse - Relentless

A Fist Full of Credits


## System Apocalypse - Australia

Town Under

Flat Out

Bloody Oath

## Anthologies and Short stories

System Apocalypse Short Story Anthology Volume 1

Valentines in an Apocalypse

A New Script

Daily Jobs, Coffee and an Awfully Big Adventure

Adventures in Clothing

Questing for Titles

Blue Screens of Death

A Game of Koopash (Newsletter exclusive)

Lana's story (Newsletter exclusive)

Debts and Dances (Newsletter exclusive)

## Comic Series

The System Apocalypse Comics (7 Issues)

The System Apocalypse Graphic Novel: Issues 1-7 (limited edition hardcover)

# Contents

*To Tao, for obvious reasons*

# Chapter One:

# Timer

Usually, the stars gleamed through Toohey Forest at night, twinkling through the glass to remind me why I loved my work. Tonight though, the glare of the non-fluorescent lights reflected off the window and back to me, like it was trying to blind me. I hurried through my tasks as fast as I could trying to get the sample kits prepared before everyone got to the labs bright and early the next morning.

"Mum. Are you done yet?" Jackson's bored voice broke through my contemplation as I juggled several ecological sample kits. He was lucky I didn't drop them.

"You didn't have to come. I told you you could babysit." I kept my voice as soft as possible, knowing that Wisp was asleep over on my office chair. Jackson rolled his eyes at me but went back to whatever he was tinkering with on his laptop. It was true, though; he'd just turned thirteen. I figured he could babysit for a few hours, but he surprised me by insisting they come with.

Almost eleven at night. Just over another hour and it would literally be tomorrow. I would have been so much faster if I hadn't brought them with me, but sometimes I think they just liked to be near me. Not that they'd tell me that, of course. That wouldn't be on the cool scale at all. I stifled a chuckle knowing my newly minted teenager would assume I was laughing at him. I wasn't even close to in the mood for teenagerisms.

"Not too long. Just keep an eye on your sister while I check the progress on a few of these experiments and we'll head home. Just got to make sure the grafts are taking."

Jackson didn't answer but shifted in his seat with a wry grin. He always said I treated plants like they were kids too.

Glancing at the array of kits I still needed to check over, I couldn't blame him. After all, it wasn't difficult to get lost in my work. Ecosystems were an amazing thing, and helping them thrive when they'd almost been wiped out gave me tingles up and down my spine. With the amount of drought Australia went through on a regular basis, finding rare plants and trying to rejuvenate their habitats was everything I'd ever wanted to do. There I went again . . .

One more quick scan over the gear I'd gathered together so the field trip could leave in the morning and help gather the next round of samples we needed. Done, which meant I could check on the few running grafts I had percolating. I managed to suppress the sheer joy I felt at grabbing my clipboard so I could jot down my observations. There was this one fascinating plant graft that I'd had to use very specific soil mixture for, not to mention lugging back its native water source for testing—

The lights flickered, and I frowned.

That was odd. I was sure there hadn't been any storm warnings, not even an electrical storm. I'd have known, and I definitely wouldn't be in here for one of those. A few seconds passed. The entire university campus had back-up generators just in case. Turning around to comment to Jackson, the lights flickered again, and while I only had a brief moment to adjust as darkness engulfed us, I clearly saw a wave of bioluminescent air hit me in the chest.

My entire body tingled, and the power remained off.

"Mum. What the . . ." But Jackson didn't get any further, and my brain didn't have an answer for him anyway.

Blue flashed across my vision again, but this time eerily like the blue screen of death I'd grown up fearing as a child.

*Greetings, citizen. As a peaceful and organized immersion into the Galactic Council has been declined (extensively and painfully, we might add), your world has been declared a Dungeon World. Thank you. We were getting bored with the twelve we had previously.*

*Please note that the process of developing a Dungeon World can be difficult for current inhabitants. We recommend leaving the planet till the process is completed in 373 days, 2 hours, 14 minutes, and 12 seconds.*

*For those of you unable or unwilling to leave, do note that new Dungeons and wandering monsters will spawn intermittently throughout the integration process. All new Dungeons and zones will receive recommended minimum Levels. However, during the transition period, expect there to be significant volatility in the Levels and types of monsters in each Dungeon and zone.*

*As a new Dungeon World, your planet has been designated a free-immigration location. Undeveloped worlds in the Galactic Council may take advantage of this new immigration policy. Please try not to greet all new visitors the same way as you did our Emissary; you humans could do with some friends.*

*As part of the transition, all sentient subjects will have access to new Classes and Skills as well as the traditional user interface adopted by the Galactic Council in 119 GC. Thank you for your cooperation, and good luck! We look forward to meeting you soon.*

*Time to System Initiation: 59 minutes, 23 seconds.*

"Mum?"

This time, Jackson sounded scared, and if there's one thing I've learned about my two-week-strong teenager, admitting he was scared was no longer a thing. So much for vaguely hoping he'd played a practical joke. With his programming knowledge and penchant for fiddling with electronics, I was fairly certain a part of his brain was already trying to figure this shit out.

"It's okay. Probably just a gimmick of some sort." Even I didn't believe that lie, but he had the good grace not to harp on it. "Check on your sister for me."

I tried to keep my voice steady, not to give away that I might be freaking the hell out. That blue wave of whatever hit my chest had left a glowing residue behind in the project I'd been checking on. My fingers even felt like they'd been saturated, like they were swelling. The soft blue glow was our only light, because as I glanced at my phone, it was nothing but a glass and metal brick. Nothing I tried to do switched it on.

Breathe. I had to breathe. Maybe. What if the air was suddenly toxic?

This was the same old, though. What I'd done every day of my life for the last thirteen years and two weeks. My kids needed me. I couldn't and wouldn't panic right now. Later, when I'd figured out things, I could go somewhere and scream into a pillow, but right now I needed to gather my shit together and figure out what was happening and why the damned back-up generators hadn't kicked in yet. The samples, the supplies, the research . . . all of our work was going to die if their environments weren't maintained.

There was a part of me, though, that knew that screen wasn't a good thing, that knew I should probably swipe it back in front to read through again, and that knew none of our usual concerns mattered anymore.

Only the moonlight and stars shining through the massive, double-glazed windows illuminated the room now—like it mocked my earlier thoughts. I gazed around the room, past the desks to where Jackson stood watching over Wisp who was, somehow, still asleep.

"I . . . Mum, this is weird." Jackson kept his voice low, his words hurried, even if I could sense a hint of excitement underlying his tone. "It's like something beamed a video game into our heads."

My first response was to tell him not to be stupid and to take this seriously, that now wasn't the time for games, but since he couldn't legitimately beam anything into my brain and I had definitely read that weird shit only moments beforehand, I took another breath. A blue screen I'd basically swiped left on.

"What do you mean?" It was all I could do to fight that flight response, especially as I could have sworn that the soft blue glow in all of the testing tanks was rippling, moving, alive.

"Wave your hand, like you're using that VR rig dad got me for my birthday."

Yep. There was definitely excitement oozing out of his voice now.

I humored him, still wrestling that thing called panic. Surely, I could spare two minutes to indulge my slightly delusional son. Except maybe he wasn't imagining things. There, in the corner of my vision, was a golden glow, like it was trying to get my attention. Fine, then. My panic could just wait and sulk in the corner I'd relegated it to originally.

*Congratulations! You have been spawned in Australia, Griffith University, Nathan Campus, Brisbane.*

*Australia is an exception under the Dungeon World Development Schedule 124.7.5.2. Just for being in the Down Under of Australia, not to mention being brave enough to eat Vegemite, you are assigned one Small Perk. Aren't you lucky? You'll need it.*

*As per Dungeon World Development Schedule 124.7.5.2, inhabitants assigned to a region with a recommended Level 25 or more (+25) will receive one Medium Perk.*

*As per Dungeon World Development Schedule 124.7.5.2, inhabitants assigned to a region with a recommended Level 50 or more (+25) will receive one Large Perk.*

*As per Dungeon World Development Schedule 128.9.6.2, inhabitants recognized as parental units must allow their spawns access to the System before they can have full use of all assigned Perks.*

*Your spawns awaiting approval are:*

*Jackson Kent—13 years. Enabling Jackson's interface allows him direct access to his Perks and abilities. Any choices will require your approval before being applied.*

*Whisper (Wisp) Kent—8 years. Warning: Wisp is only 8 Earth years old. It is highly recommended that she does not have full access to the System yet per Dungeon World Development Schedule 133.4.2—Protection of Youth Potential and the Abuse Avoidance Scheme.*

*However—Wisp will have one Small, one Medium, and one Large Perk at her disposal. You are responsible for choosing these. Please select them wisely.*

*Caution: As per Dungeon World Development Schedule 142.4.2.8, certain Skill sets are recognized as having abilities sympathetic to the System. Not applying these would be a grave violation. Swipe to let us know you're ready to choose a Class, upon which your life and the lives of your offspring will depend.*

What. The. Actual. Fuck.

"Don't pick anything yet," Jackson urged, and he didn't have to tell me twice.

Maybe I was asleep; this was too surreal to be, well, real.

"Sure." My voice even sounded dull to me, and I reached down to stroke Wisp's hair behind her ear.

She was still wearing the leotard she'd been in when I picked her up from training. Silly thing, she'd get cold and only reluctantly put on her warmups. It was turning to winter out there . . .

"Mum. Pay attention. You need to allow me access to my abilities or I can't help you." His voice was soft, gentle even, like he was trying to take care of me.

What a shit-tastic thing for me to do to my son in what appeared to be an end-of-the-world scenario. "Sorry. Okay, give me a moment." Crap on a stick, Kira, what the fuck are you doing making your son be the adult?

This time I stood there, determined not to let him down. I thought at it, wanting it to show me how to give him permission.

*Your spawns awaiting approval are:*
*Jackson Kent—13 years*
*Whisper (Wisp) Kent—8 years*

With a thought, I activated his ability to choose himself. He knew more about stats and abilities in games than I did. Well, nowadays anyway. It had been years since I'd played seriously. Kids, post-graduate degrees, doctorates—they all ate right into that leisure time. Right now, I had a gut feeling that I was going to need Jackson's help at least as much as he'd need mine.

*Parental Notifications. Do you wish to receive notifications when your spawn wishes to make adjustments to their Class, not restricted to abilities, Levels, and equipment?*

Another hasty yes and I was done. I watched him as he clearly looked through whatever list of abilities he had in front of him, and I glanced at the notification and advisement about Wisp. I chose not to activate hers, especially since they were advising me not to. She was eight, and I was her mom. I didn't have time for any of that other crap right now. We just had to get to the damned carpark and get out of here so I could figure out what to do, before that glowing stuff in the terrariums blew up and took us all with it.

Jackson looked up at me, and I could see that excitement about a new game tempered by having no idea what was happening. Me too, kid. Me too.

So I did what any good mum would do: I told him what to do. "Grab two of those sample kits over there and we'll get one of the tents and ground sheets out of the lockers on the way out."

I quickly tallied what we had in the Jeep. Thank everything I grew up in America with a prepper for a dad. I turned to figure out how to carry Wisp, but just as I went to pick her up, she raised her head, bleary eyes blinking rapidly in the dim moonlight.

"Mummy . . . why are the tanks glowing like that?"

Wisp was a good kid. But just after eleven at night, after a full gymnastics session and a nap, she was still in the middle of waking up groggily. Balancing her on my hip, I had one of the rationed backpacks on and carried a tent and supplies in my free hand. The halls were dimly lit, but if nothing else, humans adapted well, and my eyes could make out shapes and doorways, enough that we didn't walk into walls. I okayed the choices Jackson had made so far without paying much attention and just hoped I wouldn't regret that decision later.

No lights were visible anywhere on campus that I could see even though the science area was a little bit further away from the main portion of the campus, close to the trees, letting us study our ecosystem in fitting surroundings. But the lab creeped me out, the glow of the tanks and their movement seriously giving me *run now* vibes. I had this urge to just move away from there, to get away as fast as we could. My watch wasn't working, our phones weren't working, and for the first time ever, my son hadn't even blinked when he packed the laptop.

"Could it have been an EMP?" I asked Jackson. For all his young age, technology was his gift, in a way anyway. Gifted technological understanding, obsession with gadgets, disassembled everything whether or not he knew how to put it back together . . .

He hesitated. "It acts similar, but I don't think that's what it was."

Almost at the exit, I felt like a lifetime had passed since we left the ecology lab. I glanced out the corner of my vision, noticing yet again that there was something flashing there and realized it wanted me to make choices for myself. But I needed more information and time to go over them, so I didn't screw this up. For some reason, I didn't think I was going to be able to respec in this apocalypse.

I refused to make uninformed choices if the information was available to me. Whatever this screen in my vision shit was had the potential to be really scary and dangerous for my kids. And it would be just plain irresponsible of me to rush any decision that could impact my children's survivability.

Survivability. We needed to survive this. And while a quick choice on my behalf might help us in the short term, I didn't plan on dying any time soon. Important decisions were going to have to wait.

Shit.

I wished Mason wasn't traveling for work again. Maybe if he'd had the kids this weekend. . . Taking a breath, I shook my thoughts away from my ex-husband. Right now, I had to analyze what was happening.

Had the apocalypse really come? I tried to push open the entry doors and groaned. They were controlled by electricity. Shit.

"You two, around the corner. Wisp, stay with your brother." It probably added to the gravity of the situation that Wisp didn't even argue as I lowered her to the ground.

Glass fucking doors weren't going to stop me. I walked over to one of the displays. This month was for ecological awareness and highlighted the dangers of construction close to protected habitats. There were several bricks scattered around it. I remember thinking it was a bit gimmicky, but now I had never been so glad of a promotional tactic in my life. Hefting one of the bricks in my hand, I took aim, heralding back to that one season I played softball, and heaved the block right at the glass next to the doors.

The noise would have woken the dead if any had been around. Oh no, had I jinxed myself now? Were zombies going to appear too?

Breathe, Kira. Just breathe.

Shit.

I get it, brain—things are confusing. But I needed to get myself together and stop with the panicking. As the last of the glass clattered down, I turned and beckoned the kids. Wisp was properly awake now, her pale face scared but determined. She clung to my hand, gripping it like I was a lifeline.

"We have thirty-five minutes left, Mum. We have to get your Class chosen. We have to pick our Perks."

Jackson was just quietly urging, but it was all I could do to not snap at him. I knew I had to, even if the whole concept sounded absurd. Since when did the entire world turn into a bloody computer game?

Twenty-five minutes ago, my helpful brain offered.

We stepped onto the path outside the science building. The wrongness of the air and of the bush around us hit me immediately. I could feel something, the same way I could tell a bushfire was coming before the smell reached me. Only this was different; this was more dangerous, altering, devastating.

We needed to get to the car as soon as possible, which meant cutting through the campus and around to Park Road.

"Any guesses?" I asked the question quietly to buy time, and Jackson obliged with an answer.

"I don't know. I've never seen a game like this, and frankly, if it can insert itself into our minds, I have to think it's not just a game. I have to think we've been taken over by aliens." His expression didn't change or twitch.

He was dead serious, and I knew deep down he was also right. Maybe. The idea of aliens was insane. Then again, so was the idea of a game System world. Either way, this was outside of any game visuals I'd ever seen.

I nodded, not trusting myself to speak and still be strong enough for my kids right now. Half an hour left of this System initiation. Maybe I could get us back home and we could all just sit down in the safety of our own four walls and figure this out.

We wove among the buildings, along the paths, the breeze blowing the gum leaves in such a way I could smell the scent strongly. If I strained my ears, I swore I could hear the teeth of the koalas as they chewed their food, but that was just my overactive imagination.

All of the buildings held soft blue glows, even down to the fountain close to the quad where the students preferred to eat on sunny summer days. There were koi in there, but I wasn't particularly interested in taking a peek. No one else was here this late. I hadn't even glimpsed Steve or Jane. They'd usually be on rounds about now.

A shadow passed us on the path we were taking. Rodent-like yet larger than it had any right to be. My breath tried to stick in my throat, and the look Jackson shot me told me I hadn't been seeing things.

I'd always loved the campus for its place in the middle of the bush, yet as we neared the carpark and more creatures began to slither or creep close to us, I wished I'd taken that job at the uni in the city instead.

# Chapter Two:

# Flying Bugs

## 15 Minutes Post-System Onset

Adrenaline faltered as we rounded the bend, and I could see our car sitting there in the carpark. Wind whipped the trees above us, and I felt like we might just make it to safety so we could figure this all out. At least things would have been okay if a massively mutated flying cockroach hadn't chosen that damned moment to sit on my head and hang its mandibles into my eyes.

There was no part of me that wanted to scare my children, but there was equally no part of me in enough control of my faculties not to scream like a banshee as I shook my head trying to dislodge it.

Have you ever seen a cockroach? Their legs have tiny hairs on them, but this one was about the size of a small cat, on my head, and about to make me throw up with panic. Jackson yet again came to my rescue, knocking it off with the backpack he was carrying. I saw his eyes in the moonlight, wide and scared, but he did it anyway. It was what I needed to buck up. It fell to the ground, and I stomped on it. My boots squished its tail end with a sickening crunch; white innards exploded outwards and luckily missed my boots.

The squeal it let out hurt my ears it was so high pitched, and I hoped to whatever god this System had brought with it that it wasn't calling a flock of the flying fuckers. I hit it over and over and over again with the tent bag. Those metal rods were the only thing I could think of that would do enough damage to kill it as dead as I could. Cockroaches have to be torn apart. They can and have survived nuclear fallout.

Flying cockroaches are nutters. I hate them. I never wanted to speak of this pet-sized creature again, but I had yet another horrid feeling that this was just the first of many.

### Experience Gained +183 XP

*You have gained Experience. The Experience will be stored until you have chosen your Class and it can be applied. Please do so shortly as experience gained will decay. Great job with that cockroach. It's amazing how much harder they are to kill when they can fight back.*

*Note: Due to high Level difficulty in Dungeon Continent: Australia, all kills within the first 24 hours will receive bonus experience.*

We stood there, panting as the thing twitched in death throes, looking around fearfully for the next attacker. Wisp clung to my jacket, hiding behind me and the wave of fear that swept over us all, making me gag. This was real, and I had no idea how to deal with it.

"Hey, my brilliant son. What did you learn from all those games? What do we do now?" I asked, not liking having to depend on my son. "What are the things we have to pick and figure out in this game interface?"

We were at the car, the car which luckily was unlocked, because apparently no electronics were working at all. And lo and behold, my few-years-old car mostly consisted of electronic improvements. Focusing on that was all that kept hand steady and the scream in my throat from escaping it. My son looked at me and nodded, and I noticed his hands *were* shaking.

Here, in this deserted carpark where we'd been attacked by a monstrous insect, my little boy had saved me. I pulled him into a hug, gripping Wisp around into it too.

"We've got this. We just need to stick together and we can figure this out." I had to say it just to help myself believe if nothing else.

Their eyes told me they knew I'd keep them safe. They were my kids, and we'd been through a lot already in their short lives. Divorce, while pretty amicable, had still been hard on them. After we got through this onset, maybe I could figure out how to find Mason. We'd kept the kids mostly upbeat, and they loved their dad time when he was in town. I'd be damned if I'd let a stupid apocalypse stop us now.

"Ask it for options. Speak to or think quietly at the game. It's all there, all ready for you to use. But look through your options. Don't take the first thing it offers to you. Give it directions and be firm. I think it takes things very literally." He squared his jaw like it had almost caught him off guard.

We didn't have the time I wanted. But that was partially because of how I deal with things. I need plans, I need actions, and I need to follow those specific lists every step of the way until I reach a conclusion. And research. I need to research so I know that what I'm buying—or, in this case, choosing—is the best possible option for me. Only now that wasn't possible. Direct the System, he'd said.

"Access previously suggested Classes." I spoke softly, and it complied.

The blue screen, complete with that blocky Courier script that hurt my eyes, flashed in front of my vision again. I only gave the new Skills a perfunctory look before frowning and shaking my head. These had nothing to do with my current occupation. And my patience was wearing thin. First and foremost, because I didn't want to be a surveyor, sap harvester, or whatever that option that looked suspiciously like a cook that the System offered up. Nothing in there would help me keep my kids safe. And I was a horrendous cook.

*Calibrating. Retrieving previously parsed information.*

*Caution: As per Dungeon World Development Schedule 142.4.2.8, certain skill sets are recognized as having abilities sympathetic to the System. Not applying these*

15

*would be a grave violation. Swipe to let us know you're ready to choose a Class upon which your life and the lives of your offspring will depend.*

*Would you like to view applicable Classes now?*

"Yes," I snapped, feeling oddly uneasy talking to myself. I could feel the minutes ticking away. I wasn't sure what it entailed for the System to finish the initiation period, but I didn't want to be in the heart of this bushland when it did. If the cockroach was anything to go by, I didn't want to see what it could do to koalas and magpies.

*The following options are open to you:*

### Basic Class: Cleaner of the Land

*Due to your unique understanding of what makes the creatures and plants around us evolve, you are tasked with cleansing the environment. This ability allows you to launder Mana emissions, distilling Mana down to a System-acceptable form. However, due to high Mana contamination levels inherent to the passive abilities in this Class, you will deal damage to individuals in your presence.*

*Class Abilities: +3 Intelligence per Level +1 Constitution and Willpower.*

*+4 Attributes per Level - unusable in Intelligence and Charisma*

*+20% Mental Resistance*

*+50% Elemental Resistance*

*+20% Mana Regeneration rate*

Well, that one was bullshit. Couldn't be around my kids? Not going to happen.

***Basic Class: Pest & Pathogens Unit: Microbiologist / Plant Pathologist / Entomologist / Hydrogeologist / Molecular Biologist - Abbreviated as: Ecological Chain Specialist***

*Your life's studies have led to this path. Yay for you. You will continue to deepen your studies and understanding of the surrounding ecosystem even with its Mana-mutating wiles. Eventually, even this new Earth will help you when needed. If you make it that far.*

*Class Abilities: +2 Intelligence per Level +1 Constitution, Perception, and Willpower per Level.*

*+3 free Attribute points per Level*

*+22% mental resistance*

*+35% Elemental Resistance due to your ecological affinities. This will increase as you Level.*

*Warning: Nature is powerful. Always remember that.*

Cryptic warnings were cryptic. I raised an eyebrow, wondering if this System thing could see me. It's like it plucked my actual job description from my HR file and went with that. Still. It sounded better and didn't appear like it would make me persona non grata like the other option. Going with what I already knew seemed like the best plan, so I chose it, gulping as I did so.

***Congratulations!***

*You have chosen your Class and are Level 1. Your stored experience has been applied.*

*Would you like to choose your abilities now?*

Sure.

*You may choose one (1) of the following Class-specific Skills:*

### Tier One
### Earth Barricade (Level One)

*Earth Barricade allows you to command the earth beneath your feet for the purpose of defending yourself and your allies.*
*Effect: 100 HP shield created, within a 3m × 2.5m region (shapeable).*
*Mana Cost: 20 Mana*

### Mana Attunement (Level One)

*Using your affinity for the world around you, you can tap into the earth and coax it to warn you of any incoming threats. Radius and specific information increases with Skill Level and Level of caster's awareness. Mana Regeneration reduced by 5 Mana per second permanently. This is a passive Skill.*
*Effect: Adds an additional seismic sense to user which can detect ground-based movement. Degree of sensitivity dependent on distance and degree of earth disruption.*
*Range: 200 meters*

### Blood Transfer (Level One)

*Due to your devotion to understanding the world and mechanics of biological evolution, you are able to tap into the blood of your opponents and redirect that damage to heal yourself. Beneficial effects only usable on self.*
*Caution: Best targeted on enemies. Self-heal only.*
*Effect: Drains and transfers 5 HP per second. Target must have blood.*
*Mana Cost: 5 Mana per second*

I read them, and then reread them. If my ability to comprehend English hadn't taken a hit, then Mana Attunement was the best choice for now. While having a barricade and self-heal could be useful, I'd like to think being forewarned of danger was the better option, especially at the beginning. Choosing these options let a surreal wave of nausea wash over me. That one sensation didn't feel like a game, even if everything else did.

*Please be aware you have 1 Small Perk, 1 Medium Perk, and 1 Large Perk to spend. Would you like to allocate Perks now?*

Jackson was kneeling down to his sister's height. She wasn't really short for eight, but she definitely wasn't tall. I'd never met a kid with less fear, but I think the darkness and massive cockroach didn't really qualify as normal.

I quickly checked over what he'd chosen and frowned. He'd chosen something called Techzard.

*You have a penchant for all things technical, and your weird affinity with power sources has led you to seek out alternative Mana friendly methods. Be aware—Mana and power go hand in hand. Don't let yourself be corrupted.*
*+3 Intelligence, +1 Willpower, and +1 Constitution*
*+3 Attribute points per Level*

I shrugged. It definitely sounded like something he'd resonate with. He was done with his Class choices.

"Almost done." I spoke softly to try and reassure them both. Steeling myself, I attempted another request, this time in my head. *Please show me something I can protect my family with.* I didn't like the high-pitched tone to my inner voice. Not even I could tell if I was begging or panicking.

*As per Dungeon World Development Schedule 18.4.7.6.8(a) (the Amendment to Family Unit Perk System), as the head of your non-colony-based familial unit with two (2) or more dependents in close proximity, you are granted one special Perk equal to one Large Perk. Perk choices will be limited to those that benefit the protection and on-going survival of your family as a whole.*

*Attempts at contravening or amending this Perk to contravene the intent will result in additional penalties, including experience defrayment, limited Class upgrades, and potential, additional reputation amendments.*

A list so long it made my head hurt scrolled up my vision, and I narrowed my eyes. I felt like this System was a more typical teenager than my son. One of the Perks it showed, one of the ones I could actually decipher, had prerequisites I knew I wouldn't have yet.

"Uh. Thanks. Show me the strongest option I can use and purchase with this special Perk that will allow me to protect my kids."

I swear I could feel this entire System thinking. Maybe it was just my way of coping with the shitstorm that hit us, but I remained firm. The damned thing interpreted my words exactly. But I wasn't about to look a gift System in the electrodes.

Several things flashed up this time, much more manageable. In the end, I narrowed it down to a couple of options.

### Cost: 1 Large Perk
### Ability: Quantum Shift Shield

*The QSS allows the friendly target(s) to be placed in a secure and unreachable dimensional pocket for a duration not exceeding ten minutes.*

*While active, the target(s) cannot be harmed by conventional means. Requires time to recharge once depleted. Recharge time based off Galactic-standard Mana density— 1 hour 8 minutes.*

I frowned at it. It seemed pretty awesome, but did I really want to drop my eight-year-old or my thirteen-year-old in a dimensional pocket? Wasn't there mythology suggesting that might be where vampires allegedly came from? Speaking of which, what if vampires were actually an intergalactic race?

I mean, not that I believed in vampires, but until forty-odd minutes ago, I hadn't thought aliens existed either.

I shook my head. As much as I liked the look of the Perk, something about it kept me from choosing it. So I went with the other, hopefully safer option.

**Spell: Shield of Power**

*This shield can be activated on a family member regardless of distance between them. It can absorb up to ten times the caster's hit points trading each hit point for ten shield points. Castable once per hour.*

*While active the ally is locked inside and cannot disperse the shield before the caster allows it, or the caster dies.*

*Cost: 25 Mana + Hit Points traded for Shield*

*Note: Shield of Power is limited to a maximum of 200 Hit Points at current level of Skill*

Perhaps a bit more morbid than necessary. But at least Wisp would be safe while protected, and in a pinch, I could use it on Jackson too. There was a momentary pause before a screen showed up again. "Status Screen," it said while the System asked me more questions.

*You have three unspent Attribute points. Would you like to allocate them now?*

| Status Screen | | | |
|---|---|---|---|
| Name | Kira Kent | Class | Ecological Chain Specialist |
| Race | Human (Female) | Level | 1 |
| **Titles** | | | |
| | | | |
| Health | 100 | Stamina | 100 |
| Mana | 220 | Mana Regeneration | |
| **Attributes** | | | |
| Strength | 9 | Agility | 12 |
| Constitution | 10 | Perception | 16 |
| Intelligence | 20 | Willpower | 19 |
| Charisma | 12 | Luck | 12 |
| **Class Skills** | | | |
| Mana Attunement | 1 | Leadership | 1 |
| Analysis | 2 | | |
| **Combat Spells** | | | |
| Shield of Power | | | |

*Please be aware you have 1 Small Perk, 1 Medium Perk, and 1 Large Perk to spend. Would you like to allocate Perks now?*

Here we were in the middle of a carpark in the middle of the freaking night like sitting ducks. There wasn't time to sit down and sort through the likely thousands of perks I could choose from. How was I supposed to do that now?

Shaking my head, I directed the System to save the rest of the Perks and the Attribute points until later and closed down the interface even as I glanced at the countdown in the corner of my vision. Seventeen minutes left. Right then.

*You have forty-seven hours and seventeen minutes left to allocate your Perks, your daughter's Perks, and affirm Jackson's Perks or else they will be lost. Would you like to set a reminder?*

I stopped myself from snapping in irritation and simply answered it. "Yes."

That was all it needed to bugger off for a while. First things first. Get kids and myself to safety. Make sure to bolster said safety with other humans so there was a higher probability of protection. And then I'd sit down and work on my family's damned Perks.

My Jeep wasn't going anywhere. But we hadn't removed our bikes since our last outing a couple of weeks ago, and at the very least, those didn't have any electrical components. "Grab the bikes."

I began to secure the tent to the backpack I had on, rummaging through the back seat to locate the first aid kits and the three small prepper packs I always carried with me. Some food, cooking implements, special heat sheets, water filtration straws, and more first aid. Couldn't be too careful.

"You know. Everyone always laughed at your grandpa and his prepping habits." I nudged Jackson who was starting to look like he might faint as the reality of what was happening hit him.

"Really?" He perked up a bit. Jackson and my dad were a pair. "I always thought it was kinda cool."

"Yep." I brandished one of our prepper packs as I finished shoving them all in. "And yet here we are in an apocalypse all set."

This time, Jackson smiled and some of that tension left his shoulders. I had to admit, it left mine too. Good ole dad. They were in Tasmania right now. Damn, I hoped they survived this.

"Right. Wisp." I crouched so that I could make eye contact with her somber green gaze. Her dark brown hair was pulled back in two French braids and tied at the nape of her neck just like she preferred it. "We think an EMP hit. Nothing electrical is working. We need to get out of here and to the highway. Can you bike on your own?"

A grin spread over her face, and I suppressed my sigh of relief. My little daredevil. She'd probably outpace both her brother and me, now that she'd had a brief nap.

"I'm awake enough, Mum, if that's what you mean." She tugged on her braid, and her lips pursed. "Can I bike on my own . . . what a question."

She dove into the car to retrieve her backpack and pulled several pairs of leggings and autumn jackets into it from under the seat in. Apparently, she had some tricky hiding places everywhere, including my car. She grabbed one of the prepper packs from the top of my pack and shoved into hers.

On top of it all, she placed her bunny, very carefully, before zipping it up and pulling her bike away from her brother. That dang stuffed bunny had been glued to her side every night since she was two. Worse for wear, he was her constant companion. Riding into the apocalypse with her toy rabbit—only my Wisp. The look of determination on her face reflected in the moonlight gave me a lump in my throat.

The bikeway wasn't far. One of the best things about Brisbane was the constant presence of bike tracks and how they wove in and out of the city like the non-motorized traffic method needed. First destination locked in. As soon as the wheels began to move, our friction-based headlamps began to glow. Though I was thankful for being able to see my kids as I brought up the rear, I couldn't help thinking that maybe the light would draw massively oversized moths our way.

*Time to System initiation: 8 minutes 34 seconds.*

Damn it. There wasn't enough time; we still had to weave our way out to the intersection, and I swear the leaves in the trees above us sounded restless. Naturally, it was probably my overactive imagination, but right then, I couldn't help but brainstorm for what type of creatures were about to leap out of the trees and divebomb us.

At night. While on bikes.

We had to make it to the Klumpp Road and University intersection. The only way I could see us getting to safety was to hunker down with other people, and even this late at night, I couldn't help but reason that Brisbane city center was probably the best place to do that. But it was about fifteen clicks out. We'd done longer bike rides before. But not at night, and not with a timer looming over our heads.

And not with more cat-sized flying cockroaches on the horizon.

The insects skittering across the path were already larger than usual. Some possum sized, others more like cats or small dogs, but from the number of legs they possessed, we weren't looking at any friendly household pets, either. Jackson led the way, constantly glancing behind to make sure we kept Wisp in between us.

Part of me wanted to pinch myself just in case this was a dream, but the memory of cockroach hairs against my face made me reconsider. This wasn't a dream. It was fucking weird and surely there had to be a logical explanation for it, but it definitely wasn't a dream.

"Watch out!" Jackson called as he swerved suddenly to avoid something on the path. Wisp had good enough reflexes that she avoided it, and I'd enough warning. But as I passed it, I didn't like the look of those remains. Even the brief glimpse I got didn't remind me of any insect or animal native to these parts. Which left the possibility of interloping creatures. Perhaps there'd even be in-the-flesh aliens. Seriously, though?

Maybe I wouldn't find logical explanations in any of this.

The trees began to thin out, and the path led to the traffic lights. Jack braked sharply, and Wisp almost ran into him. But I could see why he'd braked, and my brain was having difficulty processing the images in front of us.

The EMP hadn't just shorted out my phone, it had done the same to all vehicles whether they were stationary or not. Even though it had been almost midnight, even though it was lucky that it hadn't happened in peak-hour traffic.

Cars mashed together at the intersection, crushed further by a couple of large trucks that must have gained some momentum coming down the slight incline of Klumpp Road. I could hear coughing, crying, and one of the piled-up cars had the distinct sounds of a crying baby emanating from it.

"Stay with your sister." I spoke sharply to Jackson, the commanding tone in my voice brooking no argument. He was a good kid at heart, and I know he'd done his own assessment of the mess in front of us.

Leaning down, I gave Wisp a quick hug. "Be good for your brother, okay? Stay here. Don't come out after me. There could be sharp metal and still falling glass that could hurt you."

I gestured up at one of the precariously leaning streetlights and saw Wisp take that in. She nodded solemnly. What a weird turn of events when leaving my kids at the side of a busy intersection was something I considered safer.

I walked past two cars crushed beyond recognition, barely able to discern colors in the dim light of the moon. Wind whipped my hair around my head, the chill of autumn calling me out like a warning. First aid kit solidly in hand, I approached the first car where I could see a limb sticking out.

No part of me was a medical doctor. I didn't have the stomach for blood that required, not like my twin brother. He took care of people; I took care of the planet. Great trade. But I needed to squash that unease for a bit because I was still whole enough to actually do something.

I crouched by the car, aware that the crying baby had stopped and unsure in all of the forty-odd vehicles around me, where it had come from.

"Hey. Are you okay in there?" I asked softly, not daring to hope.

A cough, very wet and raspy answered me. "Yeah. Arm's fuckin' gone, mate. This pipe won't come out."

I cringed, not knowing what I could do to help the man. The way the pipe was lodged through his chest and arm made me think he should already have been dead. Since he wasn't, maybe something in this System was preventing death, but I had no idea how to check.

"I don't have any pills for that." The words came out, and I realized

27

how insensitive they were, but the man inside the vehicle laughed, finishing with a gurgle.

"All right, mate. Help others if you can." He sounded resigned to his fate, or whatever this was. Soft blue clouds wisped around the man, like it was trying to help, and I fought the urge to pull the pipe out of his chest. The worst that could happen was that he died, right?

"Want me to pull that out?" I couldn't hesitate; time was ticking.

Fear passed through his gaze, but he clenched his teeth and nodded. "Worth a shot, right?"

I just leveraged my leg against the car door and counted. "One, two..."

But before I hit three, I yanked it out. A gruff scream tore from my patient's throat, and cold sweat beaded his brow.

It didn't exactly slide out—there were bones and muscle in the way—though the tug I gave it was strong enough to remove it, but it felt like it took hours to exit. Those blue clouds dissipated—well, not quite. It was more like they were sucked into his body and vanished inside. I refused to believe I was seeing things.

"Thanks." He panted, his face pale as he batted around and picked up a shirt from next to him. "Name's Mike."

"Kira." I nodded, glancing around, feeling the urgency bite at my heels as I tried not to focus on him staunching the blood flow with the shirt. Reaching into my pack I grabbed some gauze. "This might help too. Take it easy."

I couldn't dwell.

"I'll come back if I can." I breathed the words out, not trusting myself and not believing myself. But I'd had to say something.

I turned and moved further into the graveyard of vehicles and didn't look back. If he survived, he survived. I'd done what I could.

28

"Fuck."

The expletive came from off to my right, and I frowned, turning to head toward it. An actual word was a lot more to go on than heavy breathing and crying. The sound came from behind one of the massive semi trailers where the driver was clearly dead. Two cars lay crushed beneath it and had slowed its head-on roll. They were equally as irretrievable.

I could see how it had gone down in my mind. Brakes failing as power steering gave out and electronic motors and failsafes burned out in the onslaught of the EMP or Mana wave. Hydraulics failing without electronic controls . . .

As I rounded the rear of the trailer, my eyes found it difficult to pick out live and dead bodies from the mangled remains of torn metal.

I could see him there, on the ground, crouched over. The coppery tang of blood was too overwhelming around me, too much death. But I didn't think it came from the man in front of me.

He was tugging at something. Quite gently, with this quiet desperation that made my heart ache. I didn't want to alarm him as he worked what I thought was the seat from the car, but maybe I could help.

"Can I do anything?" I asked, my voice as gentle as I could manage.

He turned to me, and I could tell even in the dim light that his face was partially covered in blood. "I can't get her out."

He sounded bewildered and probably had a concussion. I couldn't hear another person there with him. I moved closer cautiously. There was a strong urge in me to help, but I also had two kids to keep alive. Caution needed to be my middle name.

"Let me help." I crouched down next to him and realized what the problem was.

Trapped behind the seat was a beautiful golden retriever. Her golden eyes glinted in the moonlight, the fear plain to see. She had a bad gash on her side, if the blood soaking her fur was anything to go by, but didn't appear to still be bleeding. She was stuck though, behind that seat, wedged in.

Her owner fell back, sitting on his butt, his head between his knees. I worried the dog might have a broken limb and would need to be put down in this strange new world.

Maneuvering the seat was more difficult than I thought but not as bad as I expected. She pushed out finally, favoring her right front paw like she was testing if it could bear weight. Then she turned to me, sitting like a good girl. She was much bigger than any golden retriever I'd ever seen, and I swear the wound on her side looked like it had disappeared, but I was no expert at seeing in the moonlight.

"There we go. Got her out," I said gently, and her owner looked up, blinking as the dog ran to him. "Get somewhere safe," I said before moving on to try and help some more of the pile-up survivors.

There was movement over to my left near the underpass, and squinting my eyes, I could see several people gathered in a makeshift group. They were alive, able to help others. Relief washed over me. Frankly, right now I needed to be more concerned with my kids. I turned to go back the way I came, making sure I circumvented that massive dog and her owner before I headed back to my family, but just as I got going, a notification flashed briefly in front of my eyes. So quick I almost missed it, even as it sent chills down my spine.

**System Initiation Complete**

# Chapter Three:

# Free For All

## 1 Hour Post-System Onset

From the murmuring around me, behind me, and coming from the direction of the kids, I knew everyone received that notification. The more I discovered about how this thing in my head worked, the surer I was it was a game. Come on, Kira, think. I played games through college, hell, through my masters and even my PhD. Who needed sleep when you had to work off nervous energy? Killing and destroying shit without any repercussions was one of the finest and cheapest forms of therapy.

So? What did I need to do? I needed spells, I needed to be able to locate my brother, and I had to be able to protect my kids. Skills, that's right, I'd chosen that Skill what seemed like hours ago.

"Bring up Skill list," I muttered to myself.

Lo and behold, it worked.

### Mana Attunement (Level One)

*Using your affinity for the world around you, you can tap into the earth and coax it to warn you of any incoming threats. Radius and specific information increases with Skill Level and Level of caster's awareness. Mana Regeneration reduced by 5 Mana per second permanently. This is a passive Skill.*

*Effect: Adds an additional seismic sense to user which can detect ground-based movement. Degree of sensitivity dependent on distance and degree of earth disruption.*

*Range: 200 meters*

Great. Okay. How did I do that, then? Tap into it? If it was passive, was it already working? Or did I have to do an initial activation?

I took a breath, not liking the strange sensation, the warning I could feel in my stomach like something that had nothing to do with my digestive system was about to explode. *Activate Mana Attunement.*

All at once, a spell of vertigo swept over me, disorientation so wild it took me a few precious seconds to orient myself again. I was almost back to Jackson now, but I had to pause, bending down to grab at my knees and steady myself. The sensation was surreal. Closing my eyes, I could see, like an overlay of a map, this web of life, of the planet and plants, and blue shiny wires darting everywhere which I assumed was "Mana." Much stronger than the occasional strands I'd seen up until now. Guess this was just how things looked now.

It was all around us, flooding the area, flooding each of us, trying to steal us and our entire world. It wasn't a huge space, two hundred square meters or something, but I could tell there was something coming from the forest. Something from the trees that I hadn't considered.

"Come here!" I raised my voice slightly beckoning to the kids, fully aware of the ripples of power that one movement and sound set loose around me. Subtle shifts, Mana compensating for my vocal emissions. Jackson had my bike, but I didn't think they'd do us any good right now. Not if the swarm of bat like creatures really was on its way.

I pulled up his abilities briefly, knowing I had access to what he'd chosen, and hadn't yet peeked. We had to use those perks, but I needed more time to study them. We all needed more time.

### Light (Level One)

*Effect: This ability creates a ball of light illuminating a five-meter radius brightly.*
*Caution: Can be blinding if used at full modulation as a surprise attack in order to confuse or misdirect an enemy.*
*Mana Cost: 5 Mana per minute.*

32

I frowned. It wasn't a bad Skill, but for bats, as long as these mutations had maintained their sonic navigation, something louder would have been better. "Jackson. Leave your bike here and come with me. Wisp—hip."

My daughter rolled her eyes, but she was smart enough not to question me as she jumped up so I could carry her on one hip. "Get that light out, soft glow only. There are people under the underpass, and we're going to need their help."

The sense of urgency trying to choke me made me want to run, but I still felt like it wasn't the best choice. It could arouse something else that might not be aware of us yet. I couldn't think about the bodies, the corpses lying in these cars, squashed under these trucks. I only hoped that baby had been rescued or else died a not-too-painful death. There was a distinct feeling hanging over me that this would get much worse before it got any better. Approaching the bridge, I walked carefully. Not only because my daughter relied on me, but because the sensation of moving with my Mana Attunement whatchamacallit was disturbingly difficult.

"What do you want?" There was fear in the voice that called out softly to me, tinged with a side of hope as if they didn't dare feel the emotion because underneath all they had was endless sadness.

It made me wish I could allay their fears, but I didn't have a clue what was actually happening either. "We were up at the uni. Got away just now. I . . . Have you seen the . . ."

Words weren't working for me. I didn't know what to call this shit. Player interface?

"Interface," Jackson provided helpfully, unless he could also read my mind, but I'd figure that out later.

"Yeah," The person who stepped forward was spattered in all sorts of

33

blood, the glow of the light Jackson held showing it in more detail than I wanted Wisp to see.

"Head down," I whispered to her, even though I was fairly certain she was about to be dropped in the middle of bloodshed far more graphic than that cockroach we'd squashed.

"I'm Dale. My family—" He cut off a choke, and his eyes told me he wasn't quite with it yet. "My son and I survived, but he was badly hurt. Seems fine now though. There are about twelve of us here. Alive. Half of us were pretty badly injured . . ."

His voice trailed off, like he didn't expect me to believe they'd been injured in the first place. But I got it, the little blue lines and clouds, the ambiance around us that suffused the earth and our bodies. It enabled us to see those screens in our vision, it enabled everything this apocalypse had brought about.

A sense of urgency swept over me, like the force of the earth was trying to get me to shut up and take care of shit. My stomach tried to heave, and I barely managed to stop myself from dropping Wisp. She jumped down and rubbed the small of my back like I'd done so many times for her in her way-too-short life.

Fuck.

"Introductions if we survive this. Have you seen any of the . . . mutations?"

Dale cocked his head to one side, and I sucked in the irritation I was about to expel. It wasn't his fault. It was none of our faults. What we had to do was survive and then we could sort out whatever this crap around us was. All we had to do was make it to daylight, even if it was like six and a half hours away.

"As far as I can tell, in a few minutes a flock of some weirdly mutated bats are going to come flying out of the wood beyond the intersection. We need to be ready for them." At his skeptical look, I just barreled ahead. Either he believed me and helped me try and kill this stuff, or I'd just have to attempt it myself with all of my totally not combat anything. "We chose Classes. My son and I."

"Dad." A tall boy of about fifteen pulled at Dale's arm. He was thin and gangly in that way that told me he'd only just gone through a growth spurt. "Told you to pick. We have to. You have to let me pick mine. Do it."

There was a sense of urgency in the boy's tone, like he knew something his dad didn't, or perhaps he believed all his favorite games had just come to life at once and was excited about adventure. Kids were resilient, but this would be a test.

"It's probably a good idea. We have, like, maybe five minutes. Try to ask it for specific things. It seems to work much better when it's given direction, so it doesn't have to guess. In your head or out loud. Both good options." That was all the advice I had for them.

Frankly, it was more than I'd had to go off. The warning signals were trying to tear my gut apart, like I'd eaten some particularly bad food along the way or something.

Five minutes was pushing it. I'd have to figure out a way to use this ability without making myself sick. The constant movement of the . . . Mana made me feel like I had motion sickness. Queasy and ready to throw up at a moment's notice. Practice made perfect, right?

Dale spoke to the other people hiding under the underpass. I got it, though, totally got it. Apart from the one vehicle that appeared to have broken partially through the railing above us, it currently felt like the safest place to be.

Feeling the sense of immediacy growing around me, the presence of the creatures flying toward our very spot like they could smell our blood, all the blood, or were being directed here . . . I didn't know what to do.

"Activate Shield of Power on Wisp." I spoke under my breath and hoped that was all I had to do. Vertigo washed over me for a moment, and I felt like I'd been smacked in the stomach.

I don't know what I was expecting, but I probably should have forewarned her. A short scream tore from her throat before I crouched down in front of her.

"Sorry, Wispy. That's a shield I got to protect you. I want you to hide in the shadows of the underpass, and I want you to stay there until I come and get you. Understood?"

She glowered at me briefly, but I knew she could tell just how serious this all was. It wasn't the time for her to make an "I'm older than I look" stand. She nodded briefly, and I watched her go as the shield around her skin glinted slightly in the moonlight.

Dale handed out a few baseball bats and offered me one. Considering I didn't have any offensive capabilities, I grabbed it, raising an eyebrow.

He shrugged a little self-deprecatingly. "Baseball coach."

Yet there was something so sad in his voice as I heard it hitch. He was being a strong dad, the dad his son needed. I knew how he felt. There'd be time for him to mourn later.

And then there was no time to think.

I'd thought these were going to be bats. I'd even been prepared for that. But these things looked like a nest of flying cockroaches had smooshed together with a nest of fruit bats and gone for a nighttime jaunt.

Their cockroach-shaped wings were a leathery, bat-like texture, and their antennae appeared to be some sharper modification of teeth protruding from their heads. All along, I was tapped into the Mana Attunement, feeling the rumbling of the Mana deep beneath our feet as it got ready to bubble and boil and infect the rest of the planet.

Thanks to Jackson's foresight, we had his subtle ball of light so we weren't totally blind, and he stuck to Dale's son whose name I'd not caught, but who seemed to be armed with an offensive spell. Mage-type Class like I'd hated playing back in the day. Always running out of Mana. Bloody glass cannons, the lot of them.

I hefted my bat and swung with all my might at the first creature that came shooting in my direction. The cool night air made my grip on the bat almost painful, and the breeze whistling through the underpass behind me didn't help the atmosphere around me.

The bat-monster was bigger than I'd thought. Easily half my torso size. Not that I was huge or anything, but I hadn't been training as hard as I used to the last couple of months because of work commitments. The divorce didn't exactly help either. Looked like that was all going to change now. Not the divorce, though. Even though I was worried about him, our marriage was much better off over.

The bat made solid contact with the main portion of the creature's body, but it wasn't soft like I'd been expecting. Instead, the metal bat crunched into the harder carapace adapted from the cockroaches into whatever this thing was.

Instead of blood, the gooier liquid cockroaches were known for came exploding out of the wound, but I couldn't take time to scream at the ick factor as another of the creatures approached me on the right. The damn thing dropped out of sight onto the ground while I swung—and missed—

the new mutation flying at me.

In passing, it left a stinging welt across my face, claws tearing a line even as I flinched away. The sheer number of these creatures would have made me balk if I had time to assess our situation properly. They kept coming, flying in and out of the light, under the overhang pass and at the survivors and my pick-up group. Wow. Pick-up-group. That was a flash from my gaming days.

Before I knew it, I couldn't see anything but them.

Cricket and baseball bats made thudding sounds against the bodies of our attackers all around me. Screams ricocheted off all the metal and concrete surrounding us. And as I was distracted by all the new sensations, a stinging pain hit me in the leg.

The stupid creature that dropped to the floor and successfully dodged my bat swing had bitten me, or else . . . leveraged one of its legs through my own. A screaming yell tore from my throat as I dislodged it, pushing desperately away and stomping it with my completely useless sneakers. Combat boots, when had I stopped wearing damned combat boots?

Its cockroach guts sploshed all over the pavement, and its wings fluttered ineffectually as I continued to bear down on it. This was insane. I realized I couldn't just stop to take care of one creature like this, because too many more were swarming toward us all.

Nor did I have time to pay attention to the screams around me as they cut off abruptly. Regardless of how much the sounds battered at my mind, trying to instill fear, I was in survival mode. Protect-my-kids mode. I had to get through this. So I kept swinging and stomping, splattering guts everywhere. It spattered on my clothes, into my hair, all over my skin, and I still kept at it.

My backhand with a bat had never been great, but I was desperate, and determined, and bloody hell, I wasn't going to get taken out in my first fucking Level. Part of the reason I stopped gaming was my obsession with having to be better, do better, and get stronger. This was the first time it would be a boon.

Pain erupted along my leg again, perilously close to where the previous wound had been, and I looked down to see one of the monsters trying to crawl up my body this time. Its tiny, warped claws filled with minuscule rigid hairs dug into my thighs, its pincer mouth biting into my hip. I screamed while bringing the back end of the bat into its head again and again till it fell off, tearing skin and cloth off my leg. I did the two-step on its head, then ducked as another shitty monster tried to take my head off.

Then I got back to swinging.

Flying cockroaches had always instilled this strange fear into me, and now, with them fifty times their usual size and their wings having leathery bat like texture, it felt like I was going to piss myself at any moment.

I didn't have time to keep an eye out for anyone other than myself and my son. Even then, neglect gnawed at me like I'd just received the Worst Mother in the World trophy. But I had to trust that Wisp was safe. That shield thing had to be keeping her safe.

Not to mention the guilt I felt at not being good enough, not knowing enough about all this to help others. Bet that was my twin inside my head. He'd always been the more personable type.

I choked down a laugh. Getting hysterical wasn't going to help, but I could feel it beckoning me. Beckoning even as my face split into a manic grin, driven by adrenaline and lack of oxygen. That and the roiling mess of my guts as another shift occurred in the ever-changing, ever-churning sense of Mana in the earth.

I glimpsed others out of the corner of my eyes, as I battered more monsters aside. Some of the survivors were on the ground, unmoving, as the flying cockroach bat things tore into their bodies en masse. Each thought, each sound seared into my mind. The smell of blood only helped cement the death around me, the sudden change in the world, the way the lines between life and death had narrowed significantly.

It wasn't just the survivors under the overpass that were being torn into. Not just the ones who'd been too slow to move and start defending themselves.

No, out in the distance, out among the wrecks, I could hear flesh tearing, muted screams echoing down the road, that made my stomach recoil whenever they cut off and Mana surged into the atmosphere. The latest, a particularly intense burst of rushing Mana disoriented me, totally ditching my concentration.

Falling to the ground as white-hot pain seared through my calf, I rolled over on the ground, through the mushy and leathery remains of our attackers, oblivious to how vulnerable that made me.

Then, a cool wash of blue energy filled me, reducing the agony.

"MUM!" Jackson screamed, but I didn't have time to think about him. Not as I swung the bat one-handed onto the creature still worrying my leg. More of a flail, really.

I smashed it to the ground and then rammed another cockroach-bat into the side of a car, using my greater mass to hold it still when it tried to kill me. Held it there as I struggled to my aching feet, not wanting to die on the ground.

Jackson shot another burst of electricity at one of the creatures coming around me, and I pushed away from the car, letting that body fall to the ground. In one hour, Mana had already transformed creatures to this degree. I didn't want to think about what it'd do in a day, never mind a year.

I kept swinging till there wasn't anything left to swing at nearby. I wasn't sure how much time passed since the attack began, nor how many of the creatures I'd managed to pulverize, but I could sense that the surges of Mana around us had calmed.

I panted and spun around, searching for more threats in the air, on the ground.

Nothing.

Slowly, I began to realize we'd survived. That I was woefully out of shape. And that there we'd already lost like half of the survivors from the System Onset, their corpses splayed across the ground, parts of them much further from their bodies than I'd care to really measure. I checked on my health, on Wisp, grateful to see the shield was still working.

Still. Shit.

Glancing over at Jackson, I noticed he was fine. His ball of light was gone, but at some point, my eyes had readjusted. We were just lucky the moon was out and friendly tonight. He looked as exhausted as I felt, and I noticed my wounded thigh was no longer smarting.

Odd.

*Congratulations!*

*You have helped kill a swarm of basic Level 4 fresh {designation to be confirmed— base lineage: fruit bat}.*

*What an accomplishment in your first hours. Your share of this experience is 125 XP times 87 mutations.*

*That's 10,875 XP.*

**Congratulations!**

*You have successfully helped the survivors of Klumpp Road Pass not all die. Careful, compassion can get you killed.*

*Hidden Quest Completed.*

*2,500 XP gained.*

That was a lot of experience. Especially for their first day, hours . . . whatever. I glanced around at the rest of the group. Out of the dozen or so I'd roughly counted, there were maybe nine adults standing. I hoped that didn't mean the rest were dead already. Maybe there were kids hiding back at the underpass with mine.

**Congratulations!**

*You have been granted the Down Under-specific quest: Survival 1*

*Objective: Keep yourself and your spawns alive for the first 24 hours after initiation.*

*Reward: Doesn't really matter if you die, but it'll be something cool.*

*Warning: Projected survivability on extreme Dungeon continent less than 6% total occupation.*

I gulped, but its notifications didn't stop there.

**Level Up\*2**

*You have reached Level 3 as a Pest & Pathogens Unit: Microbiologist/Plant Pathologist/Entomologist/Hydrogeologist/Molecular Biologist - Abbreviated as: Ecological Chain Specialist*

*Stat points automatically distributed. You have 9 free Attributes to allocate. 1 Class Skill point available.*

Okay. Okay. This was so much. I had to check on my kids first and then figure out what we were going to do. I waved the information away, confident I could recall it again later, and ran over to check on Wisp. Jackson had been talking to Dale's son, so I knew he was okay, but Wisp, she'd done what I'd told her, and I couldn't be sure everything was fine.

But she was there, right where I'd left her, under the overpass, tucked into a corner where no one could see her, still covered in every iota of that damned shield.

"Worth every fucking Perk," I muttered at the System in a way I hope it could hear and pulled her into a hug.

The panic nipped at my heels again, but it had to wait, so I pushed it down while checking my Mana Attunement for ripples, but it seemed calm, at least for now.

"Everything okay?" Dale didn't appear to be worse for wear as he came over to where I stood with Wisp. I nodded, making sure I could speak without screaming first. "Jackson did well with his light thing. Hope your leg is okay now."

"You healed me?" I reached down toward where the wound had been, feeling a surreal conflict in my mind as though it had never been there, but the rips in the fabric were still there. The skin underneath though was smooth and unbroken. So that worked like a game too? That made absolutely no fucking sense.

"Yeah. Sort of. Whatever is mutating everything seems to repair us gradually. But EMT is, or I guess was, my real job. Baseball coach to pay my kids' sports fees." A hitch caught his voice, like memories had settled over him again.

I wondered if it was just his wife he'd lost.

Then he looked up and grinned at me, even though his face was half shadowed by the overpass. "Your Class title is really something."

"Class title?" I wasn't sure what he meant.

"You can inspect other people apparently. Darren told me how to get that Skill." He gestured toward his son, and I finally had a face to put with the name. Though, if I was being honest, I had no idea how much longer I'd see these people. "It's called Analyze."

"Thanks. Gotta check on Jackson." I nodded to Dale and ushered Wisp with me, needing to see for myself that Jackson was okay.

Before I made it to him, Mike, the man I'd pulled the pipe out of, stopped me. Well, at least that wound healed, I guess. I needed to figure out exactly what the Mana of the System was capable of. It seemed otherwise mortal wounds weren't necessarily going to kill us anymore.

"Hey, Mike. Good to see you." And it actually was.

I knew the amount of people who'd survived had already begun to diminish, and it was only a question of how much time before we were attacked by more mutations. The more of us who survived, the higher the possibility we'd continue to do so if we stuck together.

"Thanks." He appeared out of breath, and I got the feeling he'd been trying to find me. "For earlier. I'm glad you survived this."

He gestured at the bodies—not all of them mutated creatures—that littered the ground around us.

"Me too. Gotta check on my kids." I didn't mean to fob him off, but my mum-dar was in overdrive.

Without a word, he moved with me. Not in a creepy way, or in a must-save-a-damsel-in-distress way, but more of a what-the-fuck-is-this and I-should-stay-with-the-partially-stable-person-I-found way.

There was more sticky cockroach blood and guts than I recalled as I moved toward my son. He was talking animatedly with Darren. Even in the midst of all of this, he'd made a friend. He was the outgoing one, the goof with a heart of gold who did his best to hide his intelligence a little too often. Though that didn't appear to be a problem for this new friend.

I let myself heave a sigh of relief. With the whole "permission needed" for him to choose his spells, I knew I would have received a death notification, but I was still getting used to this shit. So many dead bodies around us, warped and mutated creatures, humans. I hurried over to free Wisp so we could retrieve our bikes, luckily far enough away from the carnage to still be usable. Somewhere along the way, Mike found Dale, leaving them chatting together.

I noticed a mother with a small baby in her arms and a blood-streaked toddler by her side. Shit. Whatever this System thought it had done, it had a lot to fucking answer for. Part of me wanted to go over and help, but that was it. Just want.

This attack had shown me that whatever had happened to our world, it wasn't the same. While I might have been compassionate yesterday and helped this lady get to where she was going, doing so now took on a whole world of responsibilities. Energy I had to reserve for protecting my kids. Still, though, the entire thing was fucked.

Speaking of energy . . .

Checking that I had my Mana Attunement on and ready to read the area if another attack was incoming, I finally pulled up my stat sheet to do what needed to be done.

| Status Screen | | | |
|---|---|---|---|
| Name | Kira Kent | Class | Ecological Chain Specialist |
| Race | Human (Female) | Level | 3 |

| Titles | | | |
|---|---|---|---|
| | | | |
| Health | 160 | Stamina | 160 |
| Mana | 280 | Mana Regeneration | |
| Attributes (6 Unspent Skill Points) | | | |
| Strength | 11 | Agility | 14 |
| Constitution | 16 | Perception | 19 |
| Intelligence | 26 | Willpower | 22 |
| Charisma | 14 | Luck | 12 |
| Class Skills | | | |
| Shield of Power | 1 | Mana Attunement | 1 |
| Combat Skills | | | |
| | | | |

*You have 6 Attribute points to allocate. Do you wish to do so now?*

Couldn't do much if I was dead. So I needed Constitution. I couldn't add to Mana, so that made it easy. But I could add to Mana Regeneration, which was Willpower. Charisma would help if I talked to people. I'd never had much Luck and wasn't sure which way the stat skewed, so I was unwilling to risk putting points into it.

I ended up with two into Constitution, one into Agility, two into Strength, and one into Charisma. I'd work on the other stats next time. But I needed to see my Skill tree since I had a Skill point left, so I pulled it up again. First tier choices, huh? Wonder when I unlocked the rest.

| Earth Barricade | | Mana Attunement | | | Blood Transfer |
|---|---|---|---|---|---|
| Water Siphon | Mud Slide | Rockslide | | | Mana Transfer |
| Treesong | | Top Soil | Planted in Place | Implantation | |
| Vine Defense | | Stone's Throw | | Blood Dispersion | |
| Cocoon | | Ecological Outreach | | Mana Dispersion | |

Okay. So . . . it would be cool to heal myself, but I didn't think I could use it on others from what the description said, so the better thing to get for now would be something that could shield myself, the kids, and anyone who chose to travel with us.

### Earth Barricade (Level One)

*Earth Barricade allows you to command the earth beneath your feet for the purpose of defending yourself and your allies.*
*Effect: 100 HP shield created, within a 3m x 2.5m region (shapeable).*
*Mana Cost: 20 Mana*

It wasn't much, but it was something. Way more than I'd had to fight the cockbats with. Yeah. Cockbats. That was a better name.

# Chapter Four:
# Not a Game

## 2 Hours Post-System Onset

Change of plan. The city center was a good few clicks away, and I was pretty sure there'd be carnage on the freeway. Initially, I'd assumed there might have been more damage done during peak hour, but the traffic at that time was often bumper to bumper. At eleven at night, the vehicles were spaced and could cruise at the speed limit.

Which meant vehicles hitting each other while traveling faster, and my imagination did not need reality to boost what it already knew.

I didn't even want to imagine the feeling of dread when the EMP took out all electrical systems, because it seems that the hydraulics of the brake systems failed too. Most people wouldn't have even been able to open their doors to even roll out of the car in time before impact.

Since most of our traveling was likely to be done on foot, heading to the city might not have been the best idea. My prepper parents had never been the bunker type, but the food-and-tool-and-water-filtration sort. Sure, they'd toned down when we moved from the States, but they'd never fully left it behind.

Dad always joked that if the world came to an end, he knew where we'd meet up. The more I thought about it, the more sense it made.

Garden City was a massive shopping center that was close to where we were but in the opposite direction from the city center. It would have been closed when the wave took over, so hopefully there was little if any destruction inside the actual complex. The way there, however, was either along Logan Road, or else the freeway. And both of those were going to be piled high with death.

Still, it was a shorter route than the city, and we didn't have to cross a river to get there. I might have loved swimming, but drowning was not a way I wanted to go. All my Mana Attunement gave me from that direction was darkness, foreboding. Not to mention there was a slight chance that my brother might remember Dad's constant joking too. Twins were connected, I guess. I was quite certain Kyle was still alive, just wished I had that same inner knowledge of Mason. They might not have asked about their dad yet, but the kids were bound to soon, and I had nothing for them.

Dale approached me cautiously. "Mind if we tag along?"

There was a layer of uncertainty in his voice that I instinctually knew wasn't directed at me, but at all of this. He was barely holding it together and only just managing for his son. Those emotions were all too familiar to me.

The lady and her two small kids, as well as Mike, lingered behind Dale, like they were using him as a bargaining chip.

I nodded, raking my gaze over the ragtag bunch of survivors. The area around us seemed almost too quiet, making my shoulders ache with tension. Darren appeared skittish, but he was a teenage boy, and sometimes that went with the territory. I could use another set of eyes and muscles who knew how to swing a baseball bat, and I wasn't about to say no to an EMT and Healer, considering all the creatures we were likely to come up against.

Even if the System itself healed us at a decent rate, I knew it sometimes wouldn't be able to compensate on its own.

As for Mike, his arm had repaired itself, and he'd survived the swarm. I sighed. If this woman had managed to protect herself and her two small kids? Who was I to judge?

I nodded at her. "Kira."

She let out a breath, like she'd been holding it, and shifted the smaller child to the other arm. "Jessica."

50

I wouldn't have expected her to come through the swarm unscathed. Prejudging people was a bad habit and one I tried to steer clear of. But her long, black hair had probably been luxurious before cockbat guts covered it. She could obviously kick ass and take names. Something we definitely needed more of.

The other survivors milled around the underpass. I couldn't just leave them all standing there. They seemed so lost. If our most recent encounter was anything to go by, the Toohey Forest wildlife was about to severely diversify. Damn that compassionate streak of mine. Though, if the System hadn't mentioned how it might get me killed, I probably wouldn't have been as hesitant.

"Hey," I called out, hoping I wouldn't end up regretting the decision.

There were reasons I chose my profession. Plants were a hell of a lot easier to organize and talk to than humans, especially when the latter panicked.

Most of the adults swiveled their attention around to me, their worry barely hiding the panic just under the surface. It wasn't going to help anyone right then. There were so few of them now. Humanity's population was plummeting right before my eyes. Nothing about this was okay.

"There'll be more like those cockbats." I used my handy little nickname.

I hadn't expected the partially hysterical giggles that greeted me. Some of the tension eased a bit, but there was more of it lying underneath.

"Yeah. Cockbats are the least of our worries. Cockroaches, cane toads, huntsmen, magpies . . . you name it, think of how they're going to mutate." Shudders even ran down my back. "It's probably best to stick with people you trust. Get somewhere big, barricadable, and safer."

Dale stood next to me, nodding, like he was reinforcing my words despite the fact that he still looked green in complexion and like he'd throw up at any given moment. Mike and Jessica were almost hidden behind him.

Some of them looked doubtful, others angry at being told what to do—by a woman no less. Others looked at the corpses about and nodded hastily. A few began to speak, but I tuned them out, not wanting to get further involved. I carefully dropped my gaze and turned to my children, ushering them onto their bikes.

Dale and Darren pulled two of the bikes from the rack at the back of a totaled car. It was pretty clear that the vehicle had been his. Then he pulled a little cargo trailer, the ones kids ride in as well, and grabbed the other large bike. I could see his bottom lip quiver, but he refused to look through the glass to the death inside.

Jessica took the bike and the little trailer wordlessly, not even making a sound as tears rolled down her face. Her grim look of determination as she attached the trailer and settled her two kids inside made me think nothing stood a chance against her.

I wasn't sure where Mike got his bike, but there were enough cars with bike racks in the pileups. Brisbane's bikeways made some of my favorite teenage memories. Our parents dropped us close to a bikeway entrance so we could jump on our bikes and pedal all the way to the beach at Southbank. Those were the days.

Maybe that's what Mike was thinking about when he snagged some wheels. After all, the dead couldn't use them anymore.

The feeling of something approaching tickled at the base of my brain, prickled like I was being stung by nettles. It wasn't imminent, but the longer we didn't move, the closer it'd get. We really needed to get going now.

Glancing overhead at the destroyed guardrail with a car most of the way out, I took a breath. I had small torches in each of our survival kits and extra batteries, but I'd save them until we moved away. Wasn't sure they would work anyway. In the dark, weaving our way through streets of stalled traffic was going to be difficult.

"Should—" Dale began, glancing behind him at where others were still trying to pull themselves from their shock. Some were already arguing with one another; a few were just staring around dumbly. I even noticed someone trying to break into cars. "People can be so unpredictable."

I knew what he was trying to say. To be honest, I wouldn't have been reacting so clearly if it wasn't for the kids. They had to come first. If I made myself concentrate on them and their safety, nothing else mattered. It was probably how Jessica was surviving too.

"True. Freeway is probably the better way to go. Fewer people and potentially less panic," I said and nodded toward the off-ramp to our right. It wasn't like it was "Wrong Way Go Back" now—there were no vehicles to be cautious of.

Dale let out a breath, a sigh of relief. He needed to push on. Standing around near his dead family members probably wasn't helping. No one moved toward us, and I was done waiting. I'd given what advice I could.

With a backward glance at the rest of the group, some of whom were watching me intently in a way that I was beginning to dislike, I motioned for the kids to get on their bikes. We cycled up the Klumpp Road offramp and onto the freeway, leaving the others behind to fend for themselves.

Jackson rode next to Darren, carefully. Those little friction lights gave us some illumination but fortunately not enough for Wisp to see the full gruesome details if she looked up from trying to navigate her way. With the amount of glass on the road, it was only a matter of time before we'd have to abandon the bikes anyway. I didn't have enough spare tubes for that.

I was glad that the others didn't seem to want to talk. I was too busy focusing on our surroundings and trying to hear oncoming danger. Mana Attunement didn't work as well when traveling by bicycle. Perhaps because I wasn't in direct contact with some form of the earth. Still, it was there, active even if the strands of blue that interwove with everything were barely visible.

### Congratulations!

*Through your natural affinity with the world around you and your chosen Class, you have gained the ability Mana Sense. Those blue, swirly things you can see are Mana doing its thing. The more you use the Skill, the stronger it will get and the more you will understand.*

*Mana Sense has reached 2.*

*Quest activated!*

### What is Mana?

*Due to your Class and your natural affinity for Mana resulting in Mana Sense, you have been granted the Quest to figure out just what Mana is. Good Luck.*

*Rewards: ??? The benefit of knowing?*

I suppressed a groan, pushing the notifications aside to worry about later. There was too much I had to be cautious of right then.

It was easy to get caught up in the surrounding sounds, and I almost stacked it before I realized everyone else had stopped. Lucky for me, I narrowly avoided smashing into everyone. Thanks, reflexes.

Right in front of us, a semi trailer had careened sideways and blocked almost the entire side of the freeway. Not even the median strip had managed to stop it. Wisp was starting to flag, and I guided her away from the cab of the truck. It wasn't a pretty sight in there. Broken glass, blood, and pieces of goopy flesh. I couldn't begin to imagine the force required for that.

For us, the silver lining came in the form of being able to traverse to the other side of the freeway through the now-broken guardrail.

Standing still, I focused on the one security alarm I had. There were constant rumblings, sensations that turned my stomach and made me nauseated. I could pay that price, though. Nothing imminent as far as I could tell, but everything around us was unsettled, collapsing, gurgling, recreating itself. The entire area that I could sense felt like lava just waiting to burst through the Earth's crust.

"What do we do?" Dale seemed tired, and his eyes were filled with about as much fear as I was ignoring.

He just wanted someone to tell him how to get through all this. I couldn't blame him. Jessica with her two small children in tow didn't seem to say much, but her jaw set told me she was ready to go.

"We keep going. We should be able to jump over to the busway and through to Garbo soon." I glanced around at this side of the road, waves of intensity flowing underfoot like something was coming.

Wish it would list out the potential incoming threats or something. How not to be useful.

"It's the only plan I have," I added, trying not to let the strain show in my tone.

This side looked worse, but there was no getting around the crashed semi. I didn't have those sorts of skills. So many more cars on this side. I fished out a torch and held my breath as I depressed the switch. It turned on, but its light was weak and barely made a difference. I handed it to Wisp, and she grabbed it with a brave smile.

"Better than my wait-until-the-nightmare-is-over plan and pinching myself until it works." Dale's humor was forced, but I appreciated it nevertheless. After all, I was fairly certain his other option was to scream. And boy, could I feel that.

"Excellent." I glanced at Wisp, who was attempting to hold her bike up while she was juggling the torch. Frankly, it was doing more of that than she was, and its tires were flat as a tack. I grimaced. "I think we have to ditch the bikes."

"I've been riding on rims for a while," Dale agreed and motioned for the boys to come over.

Mike laughed softly. "Haven't been bike riding in way too long. My arse is killing me."

Jessica laughed, and I could hear an edge of fear to it as she dismounted from hers and leaned in to fetch her sleeping kids. Mike grabbed the larger one. He was a sturdy guy, and there was no way Jessica could hold both her sleeping kids. I watched as her gaze followed his every move, debating whether she could trust her precious cargo with him. In an instant, she nodded a thanks and scooped up the other one.

We hadn't made it nearly as far as I'd liked. Constant car crashes, navigating broken glass, broken bodies, and climbing over car bonnets was slow going. So far though, there'd been a few empty cars, which meant more survivors, only I didn't have the energy to look for them right now. There were shadows that constantly moved, my senses speaking of monsters in the darkness. I could only hope the survivors got to safety or, if not, that we were in a place to help them if we encountered them.

I really hadn't thought it would take us this long to traverse a couple of kilometers. Rather than worry about it, we kept moving ahead. The only good news was that whatever this System was, it had buffered our healing

56

and stamina, allowing us to keep moving even if we should be exhausted.

Going on foot was way worse than being on the bikes. The scent of gum trees wafted down to us from the heights, an odd sensation in the presence of so much coppery blood. It was still early enough in autumn for it to be cold at this time of the morning, and the strange sounds of crying, screaming, and battle that drifted over to us made my skin crawl. Sometimes, I could almost make out actual words.

But we had our own battles to fight.

The monsters kept coming out to attack us, scavenging beasts hoping to take down one of us while we weren't watching.

Thankfully, Mana Attunement and Mana Sense together gave us enough warning time. Best. Skill. Ever. Even if it did make me nauseated when a new wave of energy appeared. I let the group know whenever I sensed a threat, pointing it out or calling out the direction.

Scurrying spiders the size of my head, blasted by our casters, mopped up by Dale and my super bat-wielding skills. Sarcasm made me hit harder, I swear. Mike had a set of skills that defied my expectations. He shot what appeared to be metal pylons at the creatures. They rose from underneath them and exploded their bodies as they hit. I really needed that Analyze Skill.

There was no doubt we looked like a hot mess as we figured out how to work without accidentally impaling one another. We needed time to hone skills, but for that, we had to survive—messy as it might be.

I was pretty sure the last lot had once been bull ants, but I wasn't going to dissect their corpses. The only good news was that we kept getting experience for each of the kills.

❖

I'd lost count of the number of surprise attacks we'd dealt with or how much ground we'd covered. But a sudden shot of fear plummeted down my spine and I took a breath. Something was coming. We needed to get to the busway. The route was only for buses, making public transport quick and effective, even if it was a chunk overpriced. As we got closer to Garden City, its walls were high, protective. Most of the buses would have been on their last route of the night, so there shouldn't be too much carnage. It should be safer there. It had to be.

"Something new's coming," I said, trying to sound matter-of-fact as I hoisted Wisp up on my hip and tossed her backpack at Jackson.

Mike continued to hold one of Jessica's kids, but he swung a baseball bat in the other hand. It was difficult to orient myself and figure out where the warning was coming from. It was close. Behind or in front—there was something brewing, and if I had spider senses, I'd say they were tingling.

Dale picked up on my alarm and ushered Darren closer as we began to pick our way through the car wrecks. A couple of Holden Utes were smashed beyond repair, Fords, Nissans . . . even Subaru Outbacks, which, incidentally, were not an Australian car.

Just up ahead there was a break in the partition giving us a way into the bus lanes. Relief hit me harder than I expected, and it was only as I climbed over the next car, fueled by adrenaline and the need to get to our goal, that I realized the warning came from up here.

I stared around, trying to take in the ever dim surroundings. It wasn't like it was last time, and I didn't know how this all worked well enough to know what it was trying to tell me. The sensations were larger this time, rippling right through me and tugging at my gag reflex. At the end of our path to the far left, I could see people stumbling about and a soft glow emanating from the ground, the color of the initial wave back in the lab when

I was checking my samples.

The brief blue glow and gut-wrenching pain were all I got as my ability warned me a split second before the massive swell of Mana appeared. It flowed across the bitumen like bright blue magma, lighting up the night in a gorgeous way even as it chewed through the cars and remains exposed to the liquid, melting them into it seamlessly.

**Congratulations! You have activated your Mana Sense Skill.**

*Due to your natural affinity for, and your innate sense with Mana, you can see all Mana flows within your immediate vicinity. The more you access this ability, the more information it will give you, and the higher it will level. This is a passive Skill.*

Oh, fucking fantastic. Hadn't it already mentioned that? I gestured it away irritably. There were far bigger things to think about right now.

Then, slowly, almost as if in time-lapse, spiders begin to crawl out of the hole the flow came from. Or I thought they were spiders at first. Instead, their limbs shone like Christmas lights until they hit the pavement next to the fount of Mana lava. Their limbs were long and spindly like a huntsman spider, but the bodies appeared thicker, armored, almost like a scorpion. You know, except they were about the size of a medium-sized dog.

Huntsman spiders were bad enough when they appeared next to my head in the middle of the night on the wall. Armored versions were so not my cup of tea. Neither, apparently, were they the cup of tea of survivors who were still in or next to their cars.

Why hadn't the idiots moved yet?

It couldn't be injuries. The System seemed to fix those, like it didn't want its toys breaking or something. Two screams echoed toward us from the survivors directly around the hole. Their fear froze them, and I felt momentary guilt at not having made it in time despite the fact that we weren't trying to be heroes.

Mana static shot through my brain, like white noise on acid as Jessica's power welled around her. A beam shot out from her extended right hand toward the survivors, enveloping them momentarily in a bright, white light. Then the Mana noise in my head receded and so did the well on the ground until it disappeared like it had never been there.

Except for the stunned survivors and the angry baker's dozen of armored, Mana-fueled creatures skittering toward us.

❖

Their blood was purple. No matter how many we killed, the light from Jackson's spell never failed to illuminate it. Perhaps the Mana affected more than just mutating the creatures far beyond their original form.

It had a pretty undertone to it, a stark juxtaposition to the creatures trying to tear my face off.

"These things are smart," Dale huffed out as he caught another one of them in a sharp, rising swing with his metal bat.

I had to agree, I just didn't have the spare energy to voice it. It wasn't like the cockbats. These didn't travel in a massive flock but in a small pack. And they seemed to communicate together. They backed each other up, feinted, moved as a unit like they'd been trained somehow. The Level ups we'd previously gained were our one boon. So long as we kept an eye out and had our backs to one another, we could help each other. Backed up against a pair of cars, the kids stuck behind us. Jessica and Mike stood on the cars themselves while Dale and I tried to fend off the monsters on the front lines.

Even then, these creatures were winning. We'd managed to injure a few, and they'd taken their turn to tear at us. I needed to get my kids out of here. But as much as I wanted to get away, to leave the other survivors to deal with the monsters, the creatures wouldn't let us.

We needed to adapt our strategy.

Reaching out with my Earthen Barrier, I wasn't sure what I was expecting when I willed it into being. I pulled at the earth beneath us, through the bitumen, determined to help us somehow. This whole wielding an ability fueled by Mana was surreal and oddly ungainly.

The loud cracking and shifting of the ground nearly sent me to my knees, and my first thought was for Wisp, tucked away behind me and covered in our family shielding.

Bats weren't the best weapon, but with the Skills we'd gained, my Barrier allowed us to cut down on the amount of space we had to cover. It shrank the circle, giving Mike and Jessica a chance to aim. It drained a chunk of Mana though.

From what I could tell when I had a moment between blocking the huntsman-spider mutations and beating them over the head, my Mana Regeneration happened faster than I'd anticipated. I needed more information. I needed time to actually pay attention to our choices and pick our Perks.

But this environment was barely giving us a chance to get somewhere safe. Maybe we all should have just run to a house—but I had a gut feeling Garden City would be far more defensible.

Either way, it didn't matter. I'd run out of Mana all too soon, if one of those stabbing legs didn't impale me first.

I caught another attempted stabbing with my trusty bat, smacking the creature into the earthen wall. It sank deep into the earth, trapping the spider for a second. That was enough time for me to wind up with a rising strike with the bat, catching it in its mandibles, cracking it open and splattering the area with more purple blood.

Something screamed, high pitched and painful to my ears. That moment of distraction was enough for another leg to sink into my side before Dale hit it, tearing the leg off the creature and my wound open.

Pain welled in me even as the tiny heal spell Dale was capable of using hit me, and I smashed in on that huntsman mutation with all my might until it twitched in death throes. I looked up and gasped.

There were four more of them.

Even with Dale healing us, we were down to about half health each, and the boys' Mana was mostly non-existent now. Darren had a fire spell from what I could tell, and Jackson one that appeared to resemble electricity. So they had some offensive capabilities at least. And Mike—he had that strange concrete-looking pylon attack that the stupid spiders kept dodging.

I'd bitten my lip somewhere along the line and could taste blood in my mouth. The baseball bats didn't do as much damage to the carapaces of these opponents as they did back then to the cockbats. These were hardier—like they'd already learned to adapt. I shuddered at the thought.

Each hit carried a heavy thud. Each slug from all of us only chipped away at their health like we were throwing pebbles at windowpanes.

I dropped to one knee when dizziness washed over me just as my son fried the last of the creatures. He fried it. With a Skill that was probably one of the flashing notifications at the corner of my periphery. I'd waved the intrusions away. I needed to be more invested in the direction he was taking, but I didn't have the time.

None of us did.

"Shit." Dale's tone was higher pitched than usual, you know, for the whole few hours I'd known the guy.

Seriously. Invading us in the middle of the night? Bloody brilliant plan. Half of the city was still asleep. I didn't want to think about how many were already dead.

"This is so cool!" Darren smiled, excited by the prospect of more adventure, of more real-life computer gaming.

Maybe it was the best way for him to deal with the death of his family members. Focusing on surviving himself. Disassociating.

Speaking of which. I had messages waiting for me to open them. More experience, no doubt. But right now, there were several people walking toward us. Perhaps "stumbling" was a better word. I had to remember that not everyone had been totally coherent, sober, and working on an ecology experiment when the Mana wave hit, when this System Apocalypse happened to us.

Some of these guys were exhausted after a day's work. Coming back from a baseball game. Or perhaps going to the night shift. I could tell the people approaching us were like everyone else I'd encountered—already exhausted.

Just from the way they walked, supporting each other, their eyes wide and scared, there was no way they'd realized what the System was when it flashed across their eyes in all its blue glory. They didn't have their Classes and probably had no clue what they were doing.

All in the same boat there, then.

Worst of all, the exhaustion wasn't physical, it was mental. Because even several minutes after the attack, I was already raring to go—body-wise, anyway. Considering how fast wounds seemed to heal, I felt like the System wanted us healthy so we could fight? Made me wonder if this whole

Dungeon World thing was being televised for entertainment.

My screens were going to have to wait, and I was just going to leave Wisp in her protective cocoon for a few. I pulled up my big-girl pants, got my friendly smile on my face, forgetting for a moment that I was mostly covered in the remnants of cockbats and the pretty splash of huntsman Mana spiders' remains. They needed as friendly an encounter as they could have, and I needed for them not to lose their shit.

I wasn't sure if I was imagining it or not, but their expressions crinkled in that fearful—or was it disgusted?—way.

Without their presence distracting, pulling away some of the huntions, as I'd decided on a whim to call them, we'd be dead. Like more of their companions. I was so grateful, I felt a wave of emotion roll over me, and I had to take a deep breath to calm myself.

And then it hit me.

The drawback about the pretty purple blood was that it stank to high hell.

# Chapter Five:

# Slowly Does It

### 3 Hours, 27 Minutes Post-System Onset

We were getting closer to Garden City. I couldn't help but take in a deep breath of putrid air and try to calm myself down. We had a group of six survivors with us, all that was left of the much larger group from before. Their corpses were, thankfully, out of sight in the darkness, but their scattering had bought us time. Dale walked the remaining members through how to choose their Classes, how to activate their Skills, and what we surmised had happened.

Most of them listened to him, their eyes dull in the dim light, like they thought this wasn't real yet somehow knew it was. The healing cuts on my body said otherwise, and in a few more minutes, any proof of what this was would be gone from me. Or maybe that in itself was the proof.

There was one survivor sitting down and muttering to herself. Jackson and Darren had Wisp off to the safest corner I could find before we crossed over through the Mana-eaten barrier and hopped onto the busway. Best thing the city council ever did. A highway specifically and only for buses, with stops along the way and interchanges at every major shopping center throughout the Brisbane area. Not that the walls were impenetrable. Just one of those simple, woven-metal noise reduction ones. Nothing to prevent an uncontrolled semi crashing through.

At least we didn't have to pay exorbitant public transport fees to use it right now—I mean, silver linings, right?

"Hey," I said as I sat down next to the muttering woman, hoping that I'd judged her correctly and that she hadn't completely lost it.

She turned her head to me and stared for a moment before taking a deep breath and holding out a shaking hand. "Evelyn."

"Kira." I offered my own hand, hoping she hadn't activated some sort of leech effect of her own.

What? This was a new world—a new, gamified world.

"Sorry. This is a bit crazy. You know? I develop games for a living, but this is insane." Her eyes held a haunted look, and I was fairly sure she'd seen the screamers die before we got to the creatures.

"My son is better equipped to deal with this than I am. All the games I played were cartoonish 3D." My joke came out dry and honest, but Evelyn chuckled softly anyway, even if the sound did quiver.

"Yeah. I don't think gamers wanted *actual* reality. Virtual was more than fine." She fiddled with her fingers and picked at her nails for a moment. "So do we just use these Perks or whatever?"

Great. Now I was an instructor. But if I hadn't had Jackson there insisting I needed to choose things, I probably would have meandered around it for a while or chosen something in panic to regret later. After all, whose first instinct is it to go "Oh yeah. It's a brain game. Let me just activate shit"? Unless you get lucky and someone in the know, like, tells you what to do.

"Yeah. Make sure to instruct it like it's a tricky genie. Be very specific in what you want to see and to know. It takes everything literally. Think at it or speak to it. Sometimes saying shit to it out loud makes me feel better."

Evelyn nodded, some understanding flashing through her eyes, like she just needed a push in the right direction.

She had the right idea. I didn't even know where to start expanding this Class thing I had. Couldn't do anything without checking the System though.

### Congratulations!

*You have helped kill a pack of Level 8 Huntions.*

*What an accomplishment in your first hours. Your share of this experience is 248 XP times 21 mutations.*

*That's 5,208 XP.*

I knew that wasn't all. It never was. There I went, speaking like I'd been doing this for longer than a few hours.

### Level Up*2

*You have reached Level 5 as a Pest & Pathogens Unit: Microbiologist/Plant Pathologist/Entomologist/Hydrogeologist/Molecular Biologist - Abbreviated as: Ecological Chain Specialist*

*Stat points automatically distributed. You have 6 free Attributes to allocate. Level 5 Class Skill available.*

Level 5 Class Skill. I could deal with that, right?

I glanced over what else I had on the first tier, realizing there was only one left that I hadn't chosen.

### Blood Transfer (Level One)

*Effect: Due to your devotion to understanding the world and mechanics of biological evolution, you are able to tap into the blood of your opponents and redirect that damage to heal yourself. Only usable on self. Caution: best used on enemies. Self-heal only. Mana cost, damage and heal amount dependent on Level of spell and caster.*

*Mana Cost: 25*

*Please note: You still have unspent Perks. 1 small Perk. 1 medium Perk. 1 large Perk. Your wards also have unused perks. Would you like to allocate those Perks now? Reminder: They will expire in forty-four hours and thirty-seven minutes.*

I pushed the prompt away irritably. Of course, it was right that I had to choose my Perks, but it reminded me of computer updates constantly harping to be applied. Stubbornness and I got along just fine.

I refused to be rushed. Making sure I chose the best possible Perks available to us was essential to survival. All I needed was a chunk of downtime.

Evelyn cleared her throat. "It's offering me options I don't like."

She frowned, her eyes focused on the screen I couldn't see.

"Tell it exactly what you want to see. Ask it specifically. Something like: show me options that use my personal skills. I asked it to show me options that utilized skillsets I'd already developed. Sort of." I was clutching at straws, but it had given me my very weird option, and maybe others had to dig around for something they had an affinity to.

A couple of seconds later, while I was still digesting my new ability, a faint blue shimmer activated over Evelyn, and she gave me a half smile.

"Don't suppose you and your husband need another?" she asked making a rather uncomfortable assumption.

The twelve-year-old in me tried to make me giggle out loud, but I stuffed her back in her place. Didn't have time for that right now. "Dale isn't my husband, he's another survivor. My ex is . . . hopefully still on the Gold Coast. But I can't help feeling that the more the merrier. Safety in numbers and all that."

Evelyn smiled fully this time, even if her eyes flickered slightly at the mention of Mason.

"Right," she said, and a bow appeared in her hands. It glowed with that blue light, blindingly upon first appearing. I cringed at the sight and only belatedly realized that she stared right at it without hesitation.

Maybe I was the only one seeing all these traces of magical energy—with this Mana Sense. I extended my awareness momentarily into my Attunement ability, locating my children, Dale, and Darren. I needed time where I could sit down and figure out exactly what these Skills I'd been given could do. There was so much I didn't understand, yet until we reached Garbo, stopping for a few like we just had was a luxury I didn't think we could afford. I refused to answer my brain's insistent question about what we'd do if Garden City was already destroyed.

My one hope was that most people were asleep. It was close to 3 a.m. by now, and all I knew with certainty was that this magical blue Mana stuff was suffusing everything. Morphing everything, mutating anything with cells. It crept around, lighting up creatures, binding them together, blowing massive chunks of bitumen out of the ground. My fingers tingled with the need to study it, to understand how it worked.

"All right. Anyone who wants to join us can." I nodded at Evelyn, and she gripped that magic bow tightly.

Idly, I wondered what us having a ranger might mean, but I chastised myself for contemplating gaming stereotypes. After all, fighting from a distance with weirdly mutated creatures had to be ten times better than getting stabbed in the leg by pincers while swinging a baseball bat.

A few of the stragglers joined us. Red and Barry were brothers. The former was tall and lean, sort of like an Aussie rules player, while Barry was more my height and stocky. Better suited to Rugby League.

Jules and Gemma were college friends who'd been coming back from their part-time jobs. And here we all were, traversing the busway with its high walls and dearth of buses. We'd only left a couple behind who were still shell-shocked. I couldn't force people to come even if I wanted to. They'd only endanger us more.

All I could hear was our footsteps and the whispered conversations that the wind snatched away before comprehension could set in. Paranoia knocked against my mind, trying to coax me to believe that these people couldn't be trusted. Maybe it was right, but I'd always been one to choose kindness over myself. You just never knew what someone was going through. Being kind never hurt anyone—not truly. Not to mention that more bodies meant more distractions and focal points for mobs of mutations.

I'd throw any of them to the wolves at the moment if it meant saving Wisp and Jackson.

This was a new world. And it was far too quiet for my liking.

Even in the moonlit night, I could see the silhouette of the massive complex over the top of the barriers. Nothing other than us made a sound except the wind as it whistled through the corridor. Not even a cricket's chirp.

To me, that said danger. I could see a bus up ahead, just before the home stretch. It wasn't moving at all, as if it was deserted. After all, if anyone had survived, it was already four hours after the EMP hit. There was no way they'd have just stayed sitting in the bus. Especially with the tunnel back to Garden City right behind them.

"Mum." Wisp's tired voice caught me in my thoughts, and I reached down to pick her up without thinking much. My shoulders protested, already carrying a fair chunk of stuff in my backpack, but I couldn't imagine how much worse it would be if my profession didn't entail a lot of hiking.

"What's up, buttercup?" I asked as I lodged her on my hip without breaking stride.

She rested against my head, and I could practically feel the fatigue dripping off her. "I'm scared."

Hugging her fiercely, I side-kissed her forehead. "I know, buttercup. I know."

She clung to me for several moments, and the group began to slow down as we got closer to the bus. It was one of the newer ones, flashy and sleek, pretty much completely made up of electronics. The front of it had plowed into the concrete portion of the barrier. Luckily, with its proximity to the bus interchange at Garden City, it likely hadn't been moving at its top speed.

"Close your eyes," I whispered to Wisp. Not that I needed to—I think she was half asleep.

The driver was slumped over the wheel, blood dripping from a pretty bad head wound from what I could see. Or at least I hoped it was blood because it was dark against pale skin. Newfangled buses had huge windows, and it was easy to see inside without actually going in there. Several bodies were strewn about, but the back doors had been pried open, so at least someone had managed to escape the big metal coffin.

"Lost cause?" Dale asked as he stopped beside me.

"Yeah." A pang of loss hit me in the gut unexpectedly, and I had to stagger to get my footing back. I could feel nothing but quiet stirs of Mana inside there—none of it attached to anything living.

Dale raised an eyebrow. "Everything okay? Do you want me to take

Wisp for a bit?"

Sure, I did, but I also didn't. I'd known the man for like five hours at this stage. I wasn't about to give him my kid. So instead, I smiled and lied through my teeth. "Nah, I think she'd wake up."

He nodded, understanding in the glint of his eyes. Evelyn joined us, her bow drawn, and I really wanted to sit down and talk to her about how she moved around with that thing like it was an extension of her arms.

"We're almost there, right?" she asked, her eyes not settling on me as she surveyed the surrounding area.

She was highly alert, something I'd not have expected from her, but it seemed like a good thing for all of us.

"Yeah. Probably another couple of hundred meters, navigate the tunnel, some stairs up out of here, and we should be able to force the doors open on the upper level." Wisp stirred, and my shoulder ached.

Shit. I couldn't afford any type of injury. None of us could. Hopefully, Dale could heal this too. Or maybe it'd heal gradually like everything else seemed to.

Jackson meandered over, his little light ball giving off a warm glow. "Hey, Mum. Isn't it too—"

"Don't you even think of saying that!" I almost fell over my words to stop him.

From the alarms sounding through my Attunement ability, I was pretty sure he'd already tripped that trigger. Well, not really. If it was going to happen, his words wouldn't have made any difference.

"We have enemies approaching." I sighed, and the rumbling began shortly thereafter. Jackson paled further and grimaced.

"Sorry." He sounded like he'd never regretted anything more in his life.

"Probably a coincidence," Dale said, his voice steady.

"What do we do?" Red asked quietly. It was the first time I'd really heard him speak.

"We fight, we survive, and we make it to safety," I said as confidently as I could.

"I'm just a cook. A baker, even. I picked what it suggested. I have no idea how to fight this shit." Fear made Red's voice rise, and his gaze darted all around like he was trying to figure out where the rumbling in the ground originated from.

I was about to speak, but Dale put his hands on Red's shoulders and looked him square in the eyes. "It's okay. You've got this. You're not alone."

Red calmed visibly, and I sent a thank you out to the weirdly warped world that it at least had the foresight to let me cross paths with Dale. I could momma bear my own panic down, but EMTs were obviously better equipped to deal with other people.

"They're coming from there." I gestured to our left, where I knew a carpark was located above the barrier. We were essentially beneath the suburbs, and I didn't relish what was about to come over that wall.

Jackson and Darren stood off to the side, their young faces serious with determination. From the way blue lines flickered around them, I could tell they were getting ready to use whatever spells or abilities they'd gained. It was like the power just wanted to be used. And if it couldn't find the people to use it, it would infect anything in its way.

Mike and Jessica curled her older kid up in the cart and pushed it against the back wall, as much out of harm's way as they could, while the younger one rode in a carrier on Jessica's back. The kids were exhausted and had been champions so far. Maybe they thought they were dreaming. Evelyn was poised and ready to go, and I hurried to gently unload my little girl and seal her away in her shield.

*Unavailable. It has been less than an hour since you last used Shield of Power.*

Fuck. It's okay. I could still keep her safe. I had to. Trying to stamp down on the panic in my mind, I ushered her over to the cart too. I gripped the baseball bat from where I'd strapped it under my backpacks and divested myself of the latter, trying to use them to obscure Wisp from view.

Not a moment too soon.

The first creature landed on the far side of the busway, too close to the kids for comfort. At some point it had probably been a Doberman. Gorgeous dogs. Regal even. But right now, slime dripped down from its jowls, and its eyes glowed with that shimmer I was coming to fear. It was larger than it should be. Its head would have reached almost to my shoulders if I was stupid enough to stand that close. Cold certainty wrapped around my guts, telling me that hitting them with baseball bats wasn't a good option.

Earthen Barrier. Could help, maybe just to protect the kids. I wished it was more useful.

I also knew instinctually that all the dogs who spent nights outside had likely broken free from their yards and were congregating in packs. Because of course. What post-apocalyptic game wouldn't have a bunch of savage, roving dogs?

It raised its face to howl, and a thunk sounded, right as a thick arrow shaft jutted out of its neck and dropped it to the ground.

It took me a couple of moments to register the fact that the pack scout had fallen. Evelyn stood next to me, breathing heavily, her eyes wild as everyone looked at her.

"What?" she asked somewhat defensively. "I've got a bow. I've been carrying it for a while now."

But I could tell she was using a bit of bravado there. She was shaken. I couldn't blame her. There was a big difference between accepting this all as reality and actually, proactively taking part in it.

Sadly, the reprieve came to an end when about twenty more dogs jumped down to join us. A couple of them let out yelps as they landed awkwardly, too small to take the impact as they collided with the bitumen. Their howls turned to pain as broken bones ripped through flesh. More horrifying though was when the others turned and devoured their dying pack members.

The slurping and growling, yipping and howling were enough to cover the noise of our attack.

Evelyn let loose two arrows, taking down two of our larger attackers before they could launch themselves at us. I really wanted a bow. Darren fired some sort of bolt that flashed through the air, skewering two of them.

Gemma threw what I thought were knives, sinking them accurately into the dogs' necks, while Jules managed to surround us with a faintly glowing blue barrier that I only hoped meant we'd take less damage. Mike launched his pylons, the metal ripping through the air to explode chunks of dogs. His ability seemed to do less damage now, or perhaps the monsters were stronger, but it wasn't a sure kill anymore. Jessica hung back, shielding the children and watching our flanks, lacking any long-range attacks.

Like me.

Jackson gave us light and threw an explosion of power into the middle of the fray that hit the pack with some sort of damage over time. It was small, but the creatures moved slower, and it took them far longer to turn around to us than it otherwise would have.

That allowed Evelyn time to nock an arrow again. She stood there, silhouetted in the golden light, pulling back her arm with practiced precision that I was sure she hadn't inherited from the game. Then she let two arrows fly in quick succession, leaving us to face six dogs by the time they finally reached us.

Most of these mutations weren't as large as the first, but they were definitely bigger than they should have been. On recount, it appeared there were seven. Although the one in the back appeared reluctant to come near us. There was also no blood on its pale gold muzzle, so it hadn't partaken of the feast.

Gripping the baseball bat in my hand, I didn't have time to worry about the psychology of cannibal dogs. These weren't some cute, fluffy household pets anymore. They'd been mutated by the Mana like all the other creatures we'd seen, warped and set to kill.

But even telling myself that, my stomach rebelled against the idea of smashing any of them with a baseball bat. Even as I swung, I hated it. Even as I fought, I gagged. Even as I cracked skulls, I could feel tears welling. What sort of fucked up System took loyal and beautiful pets and turned them into terrifying, teeth-gnashing horrors of the night?

It made me angry, it made my blood boil, and it made me so focused on what I was doing that I didn't realize the pale golden fluffball had moved. Not until I glanced back at Wisp and saw her sitting there, petting it.

# Chapter Six:

# Doodle Dandy

**4 Hours, 20 Minutes Post-System Onset**

I froze as the others continued dealing with the remaining couple of canines. I'll never know if it was my inaction in those seconds that cost Jessica her life. But she screamed as one of those dogs jumped at her, hurtling itself with full force on top of her, sending her crashing to the ground, where she landed on her smaller child who'd been riding on her back. Her head snapped backward, slamming into hard concrete with a sickening crunch.

I don't think anyone else saw it, but I screamed and had to use everything within me to not run to her side to check. She wasn't moving, and the child wasn't crying. Worse, the damn creature was savaging her body, tearing at her throat, which pumped weakly before stopping even as the monster burned with that sickly blue glow.

I didn't have time to compute it all though, not as my bat connected with the dog's skull, ending in resounding thuds of finality as I let hopelessness fuel my anger.

She'd survived the damn cockbats only to go down here. I didn't want it to be real, but it was.

Mana distorted the dog's features, making them look more feral and less pet-like. It probably helped us all. It was far easier to kill slightly alien-looking dogs than pets we liked to cuddle. At least it gave me an enemy to focus on for all the senseless killing and death.

The blue that surrounded them was frazzled around the edges with a gleaming, off-colored tinge I couldn't quite place.

But when I turned back to check on Wisp, that fluffball dog was still sitting there with her, its tongue lolling out of its mouth and its tail beating a rhythm into the bitumen so loudly I was surprised it hadn't left indents.

"Mummy. Can I keep him?" Wisp's eyes were barely open, but she'd buried her nose in the soft, fluffy coat of the creature.

I kept my bat raised, inching closer so as not to startle the creature. It wasn't behaving like the others; from the lack of blood on it, I'd subconsciously already realized it wasn't as crazed. Instead, it sat there, enjoying scratches and visibly getting larger right in front of me. It bent down and licked Wisp's hand gently, never blinking once as it held my gaze.

What the hell?

"That's different," Evelyn said, her hand gripping her bow tightly but holding it at her side as she cocked her head and looked at the dog. "I think it likes your daughter."

"You don't say," I mused snappily.

Then I took a breath. It hadn't eaten its friends, and it hadn't attacked us. Not to mention it hadn't done anything when it could have while I was preoccupied with my useless revenge on the mutt that killed Jessica.

Which led me to wonder why it had been with the pack in the first place. Perhaps it was more intelligent and realized safety in numbers was best. Still keeping an eye on the creature, I looked up to see Mike standing over Jessica and her baby, the older man finished smashing the dog into a pulp. When he saw me looking, he shook his head, and I had to wipe at my eyes hastily. I'd known she hadn't made it, but I'd still hoped in a way.

When I looked back again, the dog still hadn't hurt Wisp. As for Jessica's remaining kid—Steven, I thought it was—he was rubbing his bleary eyes, and I knew nothing had sunk in yet. Mike was there instantly, a wall to lean on. It hurt my heart, but I didn't have time.

"I'm not sure what to do about it." About the dog attaching itself to my daughter, about Jessica's death and leaving her remaining child with us . . .

about anything, really.

The tunnel was up ahead, and it was even darker in there. How could I be sure this fluffy dog wasn't going to try and devour the kids?

It barked softly in its throat, its eyes still never leaving mine. Soft blue ropes of Mana wound around its muzzle, but its eyes remained clear. Call me crazy, but I swore it felt like I could trust it instinctively.

"Fine," I said, more to it and myself than anything else.

I'd just have to keep an eye on it. Maybe take my mind off the fact that we were already losing allies we'd saved. On the bright side, it seemed to have invigorated my daughter's energy levels. When she crashed, she was going to crash hard.

"Hey, Mum." Jackson spoke softly to my left. "Our bags are full. You guys are going to have to start looting now too."

I blinked at him. "What?"

Evelyn laughed on my right, though it was strained. I noticed she was avoiding looking at Jessica's body or her kid. I didn't blame her.

"Wow. I didn't even think of that. I'll help loot," she promised Jackson solemnly.

He nodded, with a slight eyeroll in my direction. "Thanks."

"Loot. You know, even in those silly, cartoonish games, you still had to loot the monsters you killed so you could get crafting materials, upgrades, stuff like that." A light went on in my brain as she spoke, and it took all my willpower to stamp the anger out.

"So, just like in a game, we have to gather materials. What, does it pop up in like a windowed blue screen or something?" I mean, it made sense, but at the same time, I was furious our lives had come down to gaming mechanics. What a fucking shitfest.

Evelyn shrugged, like she'd simply accepted this all and was adapting.

Meanwhile, here I was super angry about things I very likely couldn't change. It looked like we were going to be looting corpses now.

"Just hold your hand over the corpse and think *loot*," Jackson instructed.

I obliged with one of the smaller dogs and didn't want to think if anyone had done the same for Jessica.

Surprisingly, it had several things like claws and a couple of teeth that it offered me. I wasn't really on board with taking them, but anything to sell right? It plopped them right in my five-by-five inventory, and let's just say I had no intention of going into that either.

"Thanks." I gave my son a squeeze and looked at the looming bus tunnel ahead of us.

We could do this. We had to.

"Through the tunnel, then?" Gemma spoke up, a little more confident in the way she carried herself after having landed her abilities and actually using them in combat.

She had a killer punch reinforced by some sort of green glow. Maybe it was poison. And those knives? Her aim with them was spectacular, and I could only assume it came from the Skills themselves.

I nodded, and Dale moved forward, while I gathered my kid and her new pet, glancing back to where Mike stood holding Jessica's older child, who was asleep in his arms. The pain on his face, the lack of acknowledgement by everyone else, it was all coping mechanisms. He glanced over at me, and I nodded, though not fully sure why, and he began to make his way to follow us.

"We'll stay with her." Jackson almost made me jump, but I managed to stop myself and turned to thank him.

Darren and my son took over walking on either side of Wisp and the animal.

80

Even without this Mana apocalypse, I would have been cautious about stray dogs, but this one gave me feelings of trust I didn't understand. Even the seismic sensing around it was calm, confident. No trace of malice.

And we needed to get to safety as soon as possible, so I was just going to have to trust that gut feeling. After all, my guts had saved our lives a few times already this night.

Moving ahead, the tunnel loomed in the darkness, like some sort of massive monster that might swallow us whole. Sure, in functioning society, it wasn't dark but well-lit and an easy way for the buses to bypass the traffic on the roads. But right now, it seemed hella creepy, and I wasn't sure anyone had time for that. Except we had to. I couldn't see a way for us to scale the walls and get up to the other level. And backtracking just wasn't an option.

It was wide enough for us all to fall in next to each other. It felt like the safest way for us to travel. After all the tunnel was what, three hundred to four hundred meters long? No problem there.

"Anyone know what's going on?" To his credit, Barry managed to keep the fear I was sure most of us felt down to our bones out of his voice.

His face filled out, and the smile spread easily, unlike his brother Red who appeared opposite—a bit frail and thin.

"I have a theory." Jackson's voice echoed slightly through the tunnel as his excitement got the better of him. His golden light made our shadows dance against the walls and lent a warmth to the situation that I wished I could feel personally. At least for the few meters of vision it provided.

I should probably be happy that at least he didn't seem scared, but the last couple of generations had seen a lot of video games, so most of us had an inkling. Yet this wasn't a game. We'd passed at least hundreds of lost lives that testified to that.

Gemma swapped places with Jules and nudged my son. "Me too. Let's hear yours first."

I could see his hesitation. Gemma was an inch or two taller than him, and her sun-freckled face and sun-bleached brown hair augmented by the mage light made her softly attractive. My just-hitting-that-teenage-stride son wasn't really used to talking to girls.

But then eagerness got the better of him. "Some sort of alien conglomerate has taken over at least our country, probably the world, and Earth is changing with the magic they've used. We have to change with it." He smiled, but nerves were visible behind it.

"That's . . . pretty much what I was thinking." Gemma grinned. Maybe she was younger than I first thought. She could be a first-year uni student.

"I mean just look at your stats," Darren added as the boys gained confidence. "Mana and hit points. Strength, Dexterity, Luck, Charisma. All of the tried-and-true roleplaying methods."

Red let out a sigh, his voice shaking with nervousness. "And I panicked and chose a damn cook."

"It's okay, buddy." Dale gave him a light tap on the shoulder. "We're going to need to figure out food somehow. If we don't have electricity, frozen shit, meat . . . it's not going to last long. Everyone will always need food, and there'll be plenty of room for discovery in this new . . . whatever it is."

That seemed to brighten Red's mood, and for a moment, his anxiousness fell away and he resembled Barry far more than previously.

The only bad thing about Jackson's light, and our weak-ass torches, was that they didn't reach more than a few meters in front of us. So the bus beyond our light was more of a surprise than I'd expected. Or I should have said buses. Two of them. It wasn't uncommon for them to be traversing the tunnels at the same time. But it had been late, where the time between buses was longer and close to the last bus service of the night.

Our chatter disguised one thing though. Low moans came from one of the vehicles. Survivors. It cut off our conversation immediately, and I could almost see the change come over Dale as he switched into EMT mode. He stood straighter, and his concentration immediately kicked it up a notch, fully alert as his training kicked in.

We neared the buses carefully, dimming the light and walking as softly as possible. There was no way to know what it was ahead of us, and my Attunement Skill didn't give me enough information yet to tell anything more than living creatures were in there. Not with the metal of the bus in the way of direct sensations from the ground. I hoped I could upgrade the Skill in the future.

Soft blue light emanated from inside the bus. I was pretty sure by now I was the only one of us who could see that. Barry planted himself outside of the bus, his jolly face masked with determination. Jules and Gemma joined him.

"We'll stand watch," Barry said.

There was a grim resolve about him, so all I did was nod and plant my kids and Darren behind them, pulling the protective Shield over my daughter now that it was finally usable again. Mike fell back, watching our backs, for which I was grateful, but I knew the older man did it partially because of Steven.

The bus at the rear had its face smashed in, and none of the doors were open. The noise didn't seem to be coming from there, not that an empty bus but for the driver was unusual at this time of night or anything. Dale and I moved into the first bus, relying on the dim light Jackson's spell gave us to let us see.

I wasn't sure what I was expecting, but the woman was only a few seats in and had obviously been thrown when the bus crashed. With no seat in front of her to stop her due to the wheelchair allowance, she'd plowed straight into the wall ahead of her. Right into the luggage rack. Her leg was broken at an odd angle yet seemed to be healing very slowly, and all wrong. Very unlike the System-induced healing we'd experienced up until now. It had to be something else that was stopping it. She had a nasty gash down the side of her face that didn't appear to be healing at all.

Slime trails appeared all around her, but I couldn't see an actual creature anywhere.

A small child huddled in the corner next to her, and that's where the whimpering came from. Her mother was barely conscious.

"Jackson. I need more light in here. Red, come in here and help me. Jules I'm going to need that regeneration shield." Dale snapped out the orders. He wasn't being a dick about it, but he needed to get shit done, and the best way to do that was to issue commands.

Red stepped in, his nervousness almost tangible through each step he took. Jules, the quieter of the two girls, maintained this soft confidence about herself. Complete juxtaposition to Red. I knelt down to coax out the whimpering little girl so Dale would have room to work.

"Hey, honey. Can you come over here so my friend can help your mum?"

Her eyes were wide with shock, silent tears running down her cheeks as she looked up at me through messy black hair.

"Hey, Dog!" I called out, able to feel the animal through my awareness. Kids loved dogs. Right?

Lo and behold, it came to me, those understanding eyes focused first on myself, and then on the kid. It then trotted up to her mother's side and sat down, wagging its tail. The little girl's eyes lit up with recognition.

84

"Puppy!" she said, and practically dove across her mother's body to fling her arms around the fluffball in what seemed like desperation. She couldn't have been more than five.

I glanced up at Dale, but he was fully concentrating on the mum. Her breathing seemed shallow, and if I knew one thing about broken bones that looked like that . . . Since it seemed to be healing slowly and incorrectly, he was probably going to have to rebreak it before he did anything else. Her sickly pallor made me think poison. Not to mention the green slime trail.

And that was definitely something I noped out of.

I got up out of my crouch, fully aware that my shoulders were starting to ache. Not only was I overloaded with backpacks, but swinging that baseball bat wasn't something I was used to. If I didn't keep moving, I wasn't going to be able to. Whatever was recovering our stamina seemed to have a limit—or maybe I had a limit. Or it just hadn't played itself out fully. Who knew? I certainly didn't.

Glancing back, the gash on the woman's face had me worried, and I could see Dale didn't like it either. It almost looked like the flesh was rotting away. Fanfuckingtastic.

I made it outside the bus, leading the little girl and the dog who promptly sauntered over to where Wisp slouched on a couple of jackets. The little no-name girl ran after it and curled up with the fluffball and Wisp, whose skin was still bound with my shielding.

If we could just make it to the shopping center, we should be good. Our house was even further out in Wishart. Trying to get there right now wasn't in the cards. But Garden City should have everything we'd need, if it hadn't already been raided yet. Given the time of night, I thought it unlikely.

I had a sneaking suspicion that all of the survivors we hadn't met yet would be there. Or maybe it was just desperate hopefulness.

Noise came from inside the bus, startling me.

"Think they're making a stretcher?" This time, Barry's voice held fatigue so great it didn't hide his fear.

Poor kid was just as unsure as the rest of us. And yet, he still managed a smile, a pleasant expression, like he didn't want anyone else to worry.

"Probably. She didn't look too good," I murmured, glancing around in the practically nonexistent light. Maybe it was one or two hours before sunup. Before people would really begin waking up for work.

I glanced at my watch out of habit.

"Hey." Gemma cleared her throat. "Um, Miss . . ." She looked thoroughly embarrassed.

I took pity on her and grinned. "Dr. Kent. Kira Kent. But you can just call me Kira. And no, not that type of doctor."

Gemma smiled with relief. "Sorry. Just so much is going on and I've never been good with names."

"Totally understand." Hell, I wouldn't remember names if I didn't have to know them, in case I needed to shout at someone to protect my kids.

"Kira. Do you think we'll be okay?" She asked me the question like I was the preeminent source of all information on the subject. Her eagerness shone in her brown eyes, and I could imagine she was the perfect student, always making sure she'd done the work.

So I did what any responsible adult would do. I told her the truth. "I have no idea. All I know is that we're safer in numbers and that we need to get somewhere we can establish a safe base for everyone."

Dale and Red carried the makeshift stretcher. I was mildly impressed by it. Dale had jimmied two of the seats he'd ripped out together and taken the standing poles out as well, attaching them with zip-ties to make a very crude stretcher.

"Will she be okay?" I asked, glancing at the little girl who gripped Wisp's hand tightly.

Dale nodded. "Yeah. Probably. Magic is far cleaner to heal shit than surgery or emergency tourniquets. Her leg will probably be fine, but she has some bad gashes on her cheek and her left arm that just don't want to heal. They seem to be getting worse. I wish I had something to combat the poison, but that's not in my Skill tree for a while yet."

I nodded, pushing down the slightly panicked laugh I could feel bubbling in my throat. It didn't matter though, because the end of the tunnel was in sight, and I could let go of the irrational fear that somehow a group of mutated moles were going to tunnel out in the middle of it with their concrete shredding claws ready to cut our throats.

Yeah. I needed sleep, and I needed a damned massage. Neither of those looked likely for me right now.

The blue glow around us started to grow thicker the closer we got to the exit, and by the time we crossed back out onto the open portion of the road where we could see stars once again, I felt like I was wading through seas of Mana.

It sparkled and rose up into the atmosphere like a blue glitter mist that clung to me uncomfortably. But we'd made it. Just like fifty more meters or something. My legs tried to buckle underneath me, but I grimaced and locked my stance for a moment.

"Mum?" Jackson reached out and squeezed my hand, and for a second, I wasn't sure whose comfort he was doing it for until I realized it was for us both.

His sister hung over his back in what looked like a very uncomfortable version of a piggyback, at least for my son. But he didn't seem to mind. Five years' difference and he'd always seemed to love his little sister. Dog trotted between Darren and Jackson, like it was guarding both of its little girls. We'd see about that, but I was even more inclined to trust the creature now, especially after it retrieved our patient's kid safely.

Finally making it up to the bus interchange felt like I'd hiked to the highest peak in the world. There were four deserted buses in the station that I could see and probably many more along the bulk of the busway. I wondered if this happened worldwide, and just how other countries were faring. The stairs up to the main level and potential salvation were an aching reminder that I needed to get in more cardio despite my nature hikes for work.

It was slow going because of the stretcher, but at the same time, at least this section wasn't lift only. The air around us began to warm up a little as the night got ready to make way for the sun. Our winter was approaching, and while I wasn't fond of the cold, I'd hate to live somewhere where I had to deal with sub-zero temperatures on a regular basis. Here in Brissie we could get away with fleecy trackies.

Just a little ways more and we'd make it to the glass doors that opened into the Timezone gaming center and main section of the shopping center. If Wisp were awake, we'd never be able to get past the library.

I was ready to get to one of the department stores, find a bed, and sleep for days. Or maybe that was a better option once I'd managed to figure out this whole System and just what we needed to choose from. I didn't want to be rushed, because I had a feeling whatever Classes and Perks we chose, they were going to be important for however much of a life we still had.

Reinforcements, scouting out what we needed to protect. Perhaps there were already a heap of non-security staff in there too.

What I hadn't expected was that some moron hadn't known how to release the glass doors and had simply thrown a metal trash can through them.

Shit.

# Chapter Seven:
# Ready or Not!

I paused, staring at the shattered entrance, and suppressed a groan, already trying to recalculate what we could do. There'd be ways to figure it out. We'd probably be able to use some of the gates from the inner stores or something to rig a makeshift door.

The rest of my traveling buddies milled around me, as if they too were uncertain what to make of this new set of circumstances. Garden City sounded like such a great idea, and it still was. After all, I was doubtful how long glass doors would have held any of the monsters we'd encountered so far at bay.

This was just one of the many entrances to the massive, hundred and forty thousand square meter shopping center. Everything we could possibly need to tide us over until we figured all the rest of this System shit out—well, it was in here.

Multiple grocery stores with plentiful aisles and storerooms full of dry packaged good. Since the fresh stuff would be bad in the next few days, it was dry goods we had to focus on.

Shops filled with clothes and shoes, camping and sports items, things we could use to adapt to our environment without all the techy advantages we were used to. Beds, mattresses, chairs, tables, garbage bags, disinfectants . . . all of it. Garden City was as close to hope as I could get for now.

Renewed optimism flooded my system, but I clamped down on it and chose one of my twin's mantras. Don't get ahead of yourself.

"Hope you've all got shoes," I muttered.

The thing was, I wasn't sure what to expect once we got through there, and since this had been my brilliant plan all along, I forged ahead, willing to take the brunt of whatever was waiting to meet us head on, though I ushered my kids behind me. They weren't made of brunt-taking material.

Glass crunched underfoot and, still, I was just glad to make my way inside somewhere that didn't appear to be torn apart. Food and shoes, beds and bedding, there might even be showers in here. If plumbing still worked, which it technically should for a while, I wasn't sure how long it would last. I almost groaned, because I hadn't thought of having to take a shit yet.

I held my breath as I crossed the threshold, but nothing new assaulted me. There was no other sound other than the breathing of the people behind me and the crunching of the glass beneath our feet.

The dog. I turned to see Dale carrying the fluffball who sat in the EMTs arms like it was a throne and belonged there. Maybe it was part cat. Yeah. I think Dog was a good name.

Having all made it through the broken glass, it was silent around us now as we moved cautiously into the hall. The tiled ground always got me; it was so pale I had no idea how they managed to keep it as clean as they did for as long as they had. I mean, even with machines that scrubbed it every night or something, surely it should have had more wear and tear.

Idle thoughts to distract me from the fact that I was in the shopping center after dark, without permission. I'd grown up coming here for late-night shopping on Thursdays. It was one of my favorite places to eat, have coffee, or just spend hours mindlessly window shopping.

"I think"—Dale put the dog down as we all stopped to look at him. Well, mostly anyway—"That door wasn't smashed in. It was smashed out."

He gestured back the way we'd come, and he might have been right.

I frowned. "You mean security felt the need to escape?"

He shrugged. "Maybe? There's no electricity in here, none of the phones would be working, none of the monitors have a display. I mean, would you want to stay in here if the world had gone dark?"

"Yes," I answered without hesitation. "Yes, I would. There's survivability in here. So much we can use, ration, or adapt."

Dale shrugged. "Not everyone has an anchor helping them keep a hold on their faculties."

His tone was soft, but I knew exactly what he meant. And he was right.

"True." I glanced at Evelyn, who was slowly scouting out around us. She moved with such precision, her bow held like an old pro, that very subtle glow underwriting everything she did.

"Not even the arcade would have been open late tonight. Nothing. Maybe there's some people in the courtyard. Most of the restaurants might have been closed, but some could still have had staff there." She gestured out past the sushi place, and I wondered if I'd ever get to have my favorite food again.

I mean, fish would survive, right? But would the mutated versions stay the same or were we going to get a three-eyed fish scenario?

No one moved, and I realized they were looking at me. It took most of my willpower not to snap out at them and ask what they wanted. Because I knew what it was, it was what I'd wanted to do but didn't have the choice to. It was the reason why I'd clung to that old joke my dad told all the time when we were growing up.

If the end of the world happens, meet at Garden City. So that was my whole plan, and I hadn't thought about it past getting here. Past getting my kids somewhere I could maybe keep them safe and figure out what the fuck I was doing and how this System fit into everything.

These people had followed me because I looked like I might have an idea.

It was almost laughable. But they deserved more from me than that. Because I really had dragged them with me. I hadn't told them all to bugger off or anything. We might even have kept each other alive. There was a certain level of commitment that sort of camaraderie deserved.

"First things first. Let's find something we can barricade that exit with. Then maybe see if anyone else is in here." I don't think I sounded like a leader, but I did sound like a mum. That whole tone of voice was ingrained in every child and former child's system.

Red motioned to Jackson and Darren and the three began to move off.

Mike nodded at me and gave me a wink that felt out of place. "Don't worry, we've got the door."

Then Barry and Mike moved to join the others as they headed toward the food court. Probably to grab tables or something. I didn't give the wink too much thought. There were more important things for me to think about. Like how I mentally tried to avoid the math of how long we had until the entire upper level smelled like rotting food.

The kids needed to sleep, and we all needed to get our own stuff figured out. Dale transferred the injured woman to one of the benches and checked up on her, his frown deepening. "She needs more supplies than I have. Things I don't have with me. I don't get it, though. Up until now the System has been repairing us all steadily in the background. There must be something in her wounds that's interfering with it."

I pointed to the corner we'd passed where a very well-stocked pharmacy stood. "We can probably jimmy that door open and get some supplies there. They'll have medicine too."

He followed my gaze and shook his head. "Let's see if we can find the concierge. They should have a med kit there, I think. Might be easier for now. Perhaps quicker."

"It's next to the evil coffee place." I sighed. Coffee. Damn, I could go for a cup right now. Hell, could I mainline it? IV right into the heart? Or perhaps snorting it might work.

"You mean St—" Dale started but I placed a finger over his lips.

"No. We don't speak the incantation when the lack of electricity means I can't make a nice hot cuppa." There, I'd startled him into a laugh. Always good as a tension breaker. "Come on. Can you watch the kids?"

Gemma nodded. Frankly, she looked like she was about to kip over from exhaustion herself, but she was being stubborn and protective. Good thing too, because I was pretty sure Jules had fallen into a doze from the way her head rested on her friend's shoulder.

Evelyn smiled tightly. "I'll try to get into the pharmacy. We'll need those supplies eventually anyway."

The information center was only a few shops down, across from the top of the escalators, near a jewelry place. Pretty granite adorned the top of the counters. I undid the latch and stepped inside.

A blue screen stopped me short. I couldn't see around it, and I couldn't dismiss it.

*You have entered the newly formed control hub for the town: Garden City*

*Current Direct Occupancy: 37*

*Current Potential Extended Occupancy: 7,852*

*Current Land Occupied: 0%*

*Mana Saturation Levels: 487%*

*Warning: This hub teeters on the brink of collapse. Its ability to act as a Safe Zone is currently limited.*

*Please locate Settlement Orb to gain control of Garden City.*

Pros and cons. See, that was a list they should have given me. The more I thought about it, the more I realized this Galactic whatchamacallit didn't give a flying fuck about what we thought, or what information we required. It had acquired Earth and wasn't giving it back. Thirty-seven people inside here meant there were twenty-six other people.

It wasn't going to be easy to find them in a center this big. Hide and Seek on acid. Unreal.

If I didn't locate this Settlement Orb, did that mean Garden City would cease to exist as a Safe Zone? Meaning that we'd have to take the injured woman with us when we ran to find somewhere else we might be able to establish a base?

From how it was phrased, I was fairly sure we didn't have cities. All we had were small locations, if this town listing was anything to go by. Which, don't get me wrong, Garden City was pretty massive for a shopping center. Not for a town.

"Kira?" Dale sounded irritated and made a swiping motion in front of his face. "I need to get in to find the first aid kits."

"Sorry." I bit my lip, still trying to make my decision, and tried to move slightly to my right, at which point he squeezed past me. "Just contemplating that notification."

"Ah. Well, I'll do the first aid shit." He stepped in and began rummaging through things under the counters.

Thing was, I had no idea where to find a stupid Settlement Orb. Shouldn't it be here in the control hub? We needed a damned Safe Zone, a place where monsters wouldn't attack us—or at least, that's what they were in most games—and if this was the only way for us to get one, then I was going to have to find the bloody thing.

Taking a deep breath, I threw caution to the wind and spoke up. "Hey, I've got to go find that thing."

Dale paused and looked up at me, squinting like he wasn't entirely sure what I was talking about. "Is it safe to go alone?"

I choked back a laugh at anything being safe in our current predicament and nodded instead. "I've got a good idea of where it is."

He nodded, before turning back to amassing first aid supplies.

❖

What I needed first was to find that damned Settlement Orb.

It had to be in the library, right? That's where the hub of knowledge was in this center, I guess. It was where the notary stayed during the times they were available. The things we learned when filing divorce papers. If it wasn't there, I was going to be shit out of luck.

Luckily, it was located just down the path from where we'd originally entered the center. It was a nice thought that if we could get this all sorted, we'd have some form of literature to preserve. I walked past the rest of the group lying half asleep on the ground, past the news agency, and straight to the library.

The glass doors weren't open, because of course they weren't. I sure as hell didn't feel like smashing them, but my lockpicking abilities were fumbly, almost non-existent, and required an extensive use of bobby pins, of which I had none with me.

Staving off the exhaustion I could feel trying to creep up on me wasn't that difficult. It was as if the System didn't want us to rest, so it made it easier not to. I leant against the door, which swung open with my weight. I barely managed to avoid faceplanting the floor, but that knee was going to bruise. Or not. I mean, it was pretty quick to heal us when we weren't poisoned. Silver linings everywhere.

Guess the library *was* open, or it had been when the shift happened. Of course! It had been open until midnight. Which meant there could be people in here, so moving cautiously was my best bet in case they thought I wasn't human.

Mana Attunement flared in the direction of the offices, maybe even the staff kitchen. Either there were blobs of solid Mana there, or else there were people.

As I crossed the threshold, I glanced around, noting the blue tinge to everything around me. Subtle shades of Mana floated through and suffused everything. It was everywhere, about to devour the world around it. I had to find that orb.

Taking a deep breath, I made my way back. Across the brown and blue floor, made even deeper in color by the ever-present glow of power. But I didn't make it to the kitchen. There was a hum coming from one of the main offices. The head librarian's. The glow of blue emanating from underneath the door could have blinded me if I didn't shade my eyes.

Steeling myself, I reached forward and opened the door, stepping into the room.

The Settlement Orb hung there, barely floating above the small desk, in front of the now-useless monitor. It was so pretty, so full of life and Mana that I reached out before I could seriously think and touched it.

### *Congratulations! You have become a Settlement Owner*

*As the first sapient individual to come in contact with the Settlement Orb, you have become the Settlement Owner for the Garden City Township. The current location (Garden City Shopping Center and included carpark) is a limited Safe Zone. Mana flow is stabilized, and random spawning is neutralized in Safe Zones. Full access to administrative controls is limited or restricted until specific prerequisites are fulfilled.*

*Current options available include:*

~~*Shop (restricted until Quest completion)*~~

~~1.     -Land Purchases (restricted until Quest Completion)~~

2.     *Settlement Defenses (limited until Quest Completion)*

*This Settlement Orb must be purchased from the System within 13 Earth days and 17 hours.*

*Cost: 100,000 Credits—bonus available for early completion.*


*Congratulations – you have received bonus experience for being the second Settlement Owner on this System-forsaken continent.*

*Bonus: 5000 XP*


### Congratulations! Quest Granted: Gather Survivors

*Gather the survivors into a defensible position to help increase overall survival rate of the Dungeon Continent Australia. You will need to gain additional aid to survive, unless you're an insane loner with a death wish.*

*Requirements: Gather 1,000 Survivors within the bounds of the temporary Safe Zone*

*Time Limit: Ten Earth days from Initialization.*

*Rewards: 100,000 Credits—Coincidentally as much as a Settlement Orb!*


### Quest Received: Trade Hub Creation

*The Coefficient Crafting Cartel have utilized the Trade Lock Skill, locking the Settlement Orb of the Garden City Township from utilization of the Shop functions until a trade hub around the Settlement Orb is created.*

*Requirements: The Garden City Safe Zone must be fully activated, including full administrative control.*

*Rewards: Full access to the Shop, 20% discount for 5 years for all contributors to the quest and a Galactic trade hub.*

There were popups trying to inundate my vision, yet all I could think about was how bad this all was. Not even eight thousand people left in this direct area? If what the information center told me was true, more than three thousand people were already dead. I was sure Upper Mt. Gravatt used to have at least eleven thousand people.

How much life had already been lost in the area surrounding this complex? Did the update in the information center only include Upper Mt. Gravatt or had it also meant Browns Plains and MacGregor? Panic tried to creep into my lungs, and my breath came fast. Forcing myself to calm down took more effort than I wanted to admit.

I had to figure out where this "town's" boundaries were supposed to be. Three thousand lost was so much life, but if it included the other suburbs, I'd probably throw up.

Memories of empty cars, blood splatter I refused to look too closely at, even the ever-present hum of Mana mutations, they threatened to make a lie of my optimistic thoughts. I refused to listen, not now.

All of that was only to distract me from the real problem gnawing at my heart. If twenty-five percent of the local population was already gone in fewer than ten hours . . . what did that mean for the whole city?

The sheer loss of life was already staggering. It took so much willpower to push down the dread trying to rise up and choke me. All that loss, all those lives lost. Brisbane's extended population had been close to three and a half million.

Now how many were there?

# Chapter Eight:

# Tick Tock

## 6 Hours Post-System Onset

I spent far too long trying to figure out things in the library. At least I found the poor librarian who'd been left there to close up for the day. She was sobbing uncontrollably in the kitchen. I'm not even sure if she recognized me as human at first.

Her relief was palpable. "I thought I was seeing things," she whispered.

"Nope. Not a mirage, Bella." I handily got her name from her badge. She followed me eagerly, like a lost puppy. She seemed young, barely out of college, if at all.

By the time I got back, it was well into the early hours of the morning, just hitting five. Didn't look like I was getting any sleep.

Dale had already begun work on the mum. She didn't seem coherent, and the Mana around her was frayed at the edges, tinges of purple like blood on the delicate fringes. Her life force wasn't healthy; it was draining. And I had no idea how I knew that.

At least her daughter was still asleep. Maybe the medication and ointments we'd found would help combat whatever that slime trail had done to her.

I looked up to see my son and the rest walking back after having barricaded the door. Or, at least, I assumed they had since they looked mighty pleased with themselves.

"Hey, Mum." Jackson spoke under his breath from next to me. "Door's done, but how do we keep monsters out? It's just a barricade."

"For now? This is a temporary Safe Zone. It has to mean something," I guessed. The System told me that the continued protection of this hub was totally dependent on us shepherding enough people within its boundaries within the time limit. "We have a Quest to fill this place up enough to make it a town."

He eyed me suspiciously for a moment, suddenly a lot older than his age. "You're taking this awfully well. Why aren't you freaking out?"

I raised an eyebrow as I watched the woman on the bench writhe in pain, unsure how both of the girls slept through the noise. "Why aren't *you* freaking out?"

Jackson actually laughed. "I'm thirteen and love video games. Even though I know this is more real than I would have chosen, the fact is, that it works just like some of those games in my VR rig . . . well, you know, except for that whole death thing."

He fell silent, as his gaze slid toward his sister and her makeshift bed on the floor.

I pulled Jackson away from the spectacle of Dale working to save this unknown woman, though I was fairly certain it was in vain. The Mana around her looked sick, poisoned and unhealthy. I motioned to the rest of our little group.

They joined me several feet away. I wasn't feeling confident about the information I had to give them. I knew we weren't invincible. There was no God Mode here. But I also knew this Mana, this blue that suffused the entire world now, it had already healed cuts and scrapes, wounds I knew I'd received. Like they'd never happened in the first place. I wasn't even sure what the implications of that were.

"Garden City is now considered a temporary Safe Zone." I thought I'd start with the good news. After all, we needed some.

"But?" Evelyn crossed her arms. "You have 'but' face."

I suppressed my nerves, refusing to give in to my inner twelve-year-old.

"There is most definitely a but. There are thirty-seven people here in the complex already. That includes us. We need to find the rest of them and try to work together. I found the settlement core, but right now I'm limited to what I can do. So our Safe Zone is conditional on turning this into a town."

"Conditional? Why is it only conditional?" Barry's usual cheer was present, but I could tell panic lurked under the surface.

I shrugged. The System had its reasons, and it wasn't about to change them because we were scared. In fact, it was more likely to make them more difficult. Its total disregard for human life clued me into that. "We have to gather more people."

"But we're in Brisbane City . . ." Darren's voice trailed off, full of confusion.

I was about to speak, but Evelyn did instead, her arms crossed and tone sincere. "Safety in numbers. For ourselves and for them. There are bound to be more of us out there. We just have to find them."

Barry nodded, his mouth pursed thoughtfully, his previous angst gone. His smile lit up the room and made even me feel relaxed. "I'll take Jackson with me, and we'll scout out the complex. Right, mate?"

Jackson preened a little, obviously happy to be considered one of the guys.

Evelyn tapped her foot and Barry grinned at her. "Guess the ranger's comin' too."

She rolled her eyes.

I'm not sure why I didn't feel worried, but I thought Jackson would be safe with Evelyn and Barry along. "Good plan. Get everyone in the center together, post guards at the entrances close to us, and maybe take a brief nap. We need to be fresh to find survivors—better sooner than later."

For some reason, I was hesitant to let them know we had to fill the center with at least a thousand people. It could make them panic; it could even make them give up. I didn't know them well enough to make that call yet.

I could have mentioned that around three thousand people from this suburb had already died if the numbers the System listed were correct. It had no reason to lie. I refused to do the mental math of what that might mean for the death toll nationally, especially considering the greater Brisbane city area had around one hundred and ninety suburbs. Calculating shit like that would only lead to madness.

"Okay." Evelyn smiled with grim determination.

Subtle shades of power flowed from her fingers and along the bow. Barry and Jackson readied their own abilities; the same blue coating suffused their bodies too.

I wondered what they were doing, what Skill they activated. Must be a buff of some sort, because the Mana flow was steady. Maybe.

"Right. We're off, then." Barry tipped an imaginary hat at me, a massive grin on his face.

There was such an air of happiness about the kid, man. Maybe he was treating this a bit too much like an adventure. Even so, his parting quip brought a smile to my face.

"She'll be right, mate." I gave him a wink. No one questioned why I wasn't going with them to look, and while I didn't really want Jackson to leave my overprotective circle of care, I also knew that he wasn't about to stand for any malarkey. He'd leveled up as much as I had, and he still had a couple of Levels on the others.

My son gave me a brief hug before departing, his face set in that typical teenage defiant determination, and it made me feel oddly safe. It let me switch my focus to Wisp and the little girl who was curled up next to her.

And beyond them to the mother who moaned in pain as Dale continued to work on her.

Mana was everywhere. Through the plants in the center that I knew I'd have to take care of, to the way it shimmered in the moonlight that came in through the skylights in the ceiling. Everything was coated in magic.

Mana. Whatever you wanted to call it.

It left me wondering why this felt like a nightmare instead of enchanting. Nightmarish or not though, I needed to take some time to sit down and figure out these Perks that I hadn't used yet. Not just for me, but for my kids as well. I'd learned enough about the world that I felt I would make a more informed decision now anyway.

Time, though? Did I really have the time to delve that deeply into the possible advantages I could get for us yet? Our safety in here was precarious at best.

I wanted to run the choices past Jackson, too, and he was already off scouring the center for hidden people. If these Perks weren't something that was available at all times, then they were obviously important, and we needed as deep an understanding as we could get.

Those damned Perks. May as well study them. Small, medium, and large, I believed, recalling the windows so I could double check. Yep, right on. So not like a coffeehouse. No Latin or French names here for the sizes.

Small . . . small. I knew it could hear my thoughts. Show me what small Perks are best related to complement my current chosen Class.

There. That should do it. Had to treat it like a five-year-old. At least if I was completely clear, it shouldn't be able to misinterpret.

It took a moment, sort of like the three little meatballs that used to blink at you in DOS . . .

**Applicable Small Perks - 1 Available**

*Increased Mana Awareness—this will heighten your already-peaked awareness of the Mana around and inside you. Requires a Mana Sense ability for full compatibility.*

*Increased Item Drop Chance earned—this adds a minuscule percentage (0.005%) increase to the value of items formed from System loot.*

*Analyze (Skill)—enables the ability to see another being's name, statistics, Class, and abilities to certain extents. May conflict with other Skills and abilities.*

*Note: Medium Perk may be used to allow Perk to be offered on a familial level.*

Analyzing others felt like the right choice. If I knew their Class and their abilities beforehand, I could figure out just how much of a threat they might be. Adding my Mana Attunement onto that, everything made sense. Analyze it was.

Small Perk choice made. Tick that one off the list.

That left the medium Perk. The tension around me was distracting. I didn't deal well with my or others' pain well at the best of times. Blocking it out helped me focus on what I wanted to see. Just one more choice and I could move on to figuring this all out.

"Show me what medium Perks are best related to complement my current chosen Class, as well as those that will allow me to best protect my family." I directed the thought at the System and hoped to high hell that it wasn't sick of me yet.

What if the System was really a group of beings laughing it up at the humans scrambling beneath them?

Those dots flickered at me again, very briefly this time before my vision was inundated with three different windows popping up simultaneously. I swear I could practically feel the reluctance on behalf of the System.

**Medium Perks available: 1**

*Esoteric Chance—Roll the die and see where your luck leads you. Luck stat increased by 100 when activated. Duration—20 minutes. Cooldown—2 hours.*

Yeah, that one was just asking for trouble. How that would help me or my family remained lost to me.

*Diviner—Sounds better than lie detector. Permanent Passive ability. All Perception-based Skills increase 75% faster. Perception gains a 20-point boost, and you gain the Skill—Sense Motive—at Level 24. This will provide a contested chance (approximately a 50% chance using human subterfuge Skill-Level norms) to know when people are attempting to deceive you. Chance to divine increases with each Skill Level gained. Rather nifty, wouldn't you say?*

That one was tempting. I'd have *two* teenagers soon enough. Knowing when they were lying—or when others were—if they wanted to betray us. Sheesh. Thanks for making this so not easy.

*Mana Well—This is a permanent passive ability that allows your Mana to regenerate faster. Regeneration depends on Level, Attributes, Class, Skills, and Mana Saturation. This added regeneration applies in combat as well. Perk has limited availability to select Classes including Ecological Chain Specialist. This Perk may cause the side effect of being noticed more readily by monsters.*

Now that was a pretty ability, but the side effect made me nope out of it. And it appeared targeted toward my extremely specific Class. Like, was someone hiding behind something with a camera ready to load me onto the net? I'm sure they had something like recording devices in the rest of the universe that didn't require electricity.

Esoteric Chance felt like a complete and utter waste of a perk. I wanted Diviner, wanted it so badly . . . but what were the odds of me running out of Mana? In any game I'd ever played, I skulled Mana potions like they were going out of style.

Know what? Diviner it was. After all, more Mana wasn't going to help me right now when I didn't have any decent spells to use it up with. If it was only available to my Class, then odds were at some point, I could find it, pay for it, or worst-case scenario, just run out of Mana faster.

As I accepted Diviner, a weird sensation washed over me. A clarity of vision. It made all of the Mana lines I could see that much crisper. The way they intricately wound around and through each person. How it was present in everything around us.

High perception apparently made me more observant too. Suddenly I felt cold. The way the Mana seeped into everything made me think that this whole alien Dungeon World thing was even worse than I'd originally thought and the impending doom battering at my head made me nauseated. For just a second, the air tasted like a week-old forest fire, scratching the back of my throat with its potency, and for that same moment my skin lit up like I'd been flash frozen.

And then all of those sensations vanished, leaving me empty and more vulnerable than I'd realized.

❖

The great thing about being a mum? When your kids call out to you, you have this total ability to just switch off whatever was about to send you into a panic—and go to them. You push everything else aside and be mum. Pain, illness, arguments, irritation—that's just what it was. That's how I avoided the breakdown I'd felt was imminent only moments earlier.

Wisp was awake. The little girl we'd picked up still clung to her hand. Wisp is loving and fun, but she's not a morning or immediately-after-a-nap type of person. Especially when she's been sleeping on a cold, tiled floor with only a flimsy baby blanket to ward off the chilly bite, and with someone she doesn't actually know clinging to her.

"Mum!" This time she was awake enough to insert some irritation into her voice.

I was only a couple of strides away, and the sky was lightening through the skylights. Maybe she was a bit scared as well. At least she'd had a bit of a powernap.

I couldn't blame her. I could still feel the coil of dread in the back of mind, waiting for the next shoe to drop.

A glance at Dale told me he was sure the woman he'd been trying to help wasn't going to make it. He offered me a half smile, but I knew what it meant almost like I could read his mind. Point to me for making the right Perk decision, I guess.

"You did what you could." Jules leaned over and patted him on the shoulder, finally lowering her damage healing shield or whatever it was.

I needed to know more about what these people could do. We were going to have to depend on each other. It was literally us against the universe as far as I could see.

Analyze would give me information, but I needed to be able to sort and store it. I'd have to do that later when I had the time to sit down and actually use it properly.

Survival meant depending on others, because there was no way I could face this . . . Dungeon World or whatever by myself and hope to protect my kids. It took a village, right? I'd have to make my own. Determination welled up, and I knew that was precisely what I had to do before I could take more time out to pick the rest of my "System benefits."

Dale's return smile didn't reach his eyes. I'd think by now he was numb. Maybe we all were.

"You need to get some sleep, even if it's just a catnap. We all need to raid one of the mattress shops." I tried to sound confident and I squeezed Wisp's hand. "Harvey Norman's down the way even has beds."

Dale nodded and glanced around. "We could go and get a trundle bed or something and transfer her and wheel her back. If we keep her wound dressed and disinfected, I think she could even make it. As long as I can get her to keep the antibiotics down. Whatever this is has caused an infection I can't treat normally—it could even be poisonous or necrotic. Her skin around that wound is darkening rapidly." He shrugged, a sadness overcoming him. "I'm just a bloody EMT."

I nodded, and maybe I should have offered another platitude, but to be honest, I was trying to figure out what we could do when I heard footsteps approaching. But when I looked toward them it wasn't Evelyn and my son and Barry, but Red instead. He had his head down, and barely made eye contact, his anxiety even more prevalent now his more jovial brother wasn't around to temper it.

Wordlessly he held out food for us. I didn't know what it was, and I also didn't care. "Thanks," I said, handing the sandwich to my daughter and taking one for myself as I suddenly realized how hungry I was. Maybe using our newfound abilities did that or something.

Or maybe hiking half the night, while combating weird insect and arachnid mutations and half-arsedly wielding Mana. Yeah, probably that.

110

Red glanced around, realizing half our group was gone. His eyes widened, and he gulped a couple of times before speaking, like he'd had to work up the courage. "Thought we could use food. While it's still good. These fridges might hold up to forty-eight hours if we don't keep opening them. But after that, the food will rot."

He left the rest unsaid and stood there, like he wasn't sure where he should be.

Wisp finally extricated herself from the small girl and looped her hand around me, half hiding from everyone despite the fact that she'd been sleeping right in front of them.

She took a massive bite of her sandwich, and I realized belatedly she hadn't eaten after training last night. Was that like . . . only ten hours ago? It seemed like a different lifetime.

"The others have gone to try and find the other people stuck in here with us. Should be about another twenty or so people." But that was as far as I got because I heard the footsteps behind us and turned to see several new people with our first team.

A sense of relief washed over me. Day was dawning. It was well after five in the morning now, getting close to six. Thousands of people around us would be waking into this new world, facing death from rabid family pets, or mutated pigeons on their roofs.

At least we'd managed to keep some of us safe so far. Now we just needed to rescue people outside our temporary Safe Zone. Looked like I wasn't grabbing that nap after all.

"Hey, Red. Can you grab me some cold energy drinks?" It felt like it was going to be a really long ass day. And we needed to start with the few people we'd scraped from the bowels of the shopping center. I needed some caffeine, stat.

Red's face lit up at the prospect of having a definitive task, and he dashed toward the food court eagerly. I couldn't blame him—this all felt so surreal, like maybe we'd wake up at any moment. Except we all knew there was no waking up from reality.

❖

"I'm a Tank. Warrior, actually. I'll fight on the front lines." Molly's appearance completely belied her statement.

She was five feet tall—and that was being generous—petite, with mousy brown hair and big, grey eyes. And she held herself with a quiet confidence I wished I could replicate.

"Great." I made a note of it to myself and glanced at the person standing next to her.

"Sange. They." Their short dark hair fell over one eye, and while they appeared to be solid, their eyes flickered constantly back to Molly. "I'm a Cleric."

I noticed Molly nod very slightly, as if she was lending Sange strength. Loved that dynamic—they obviously knew each other well enough to work in sync.

"Tank, Cleric duo. That's perfect. Molly and Sange. I take it you'll both want to venture out together preferably?" Even just a hint of mum niceness always put people at ease, and these two were no exception.

Some of the tension dropped out of Sange's shoulders, and they nodded, finally making eye contact with me. "Please. That'd work best."

I'd probably misjudged their ages initially. I'd say they were mid-twenties, not early like I'd originally thought. "Excellent. Rest up for a few, I think we're going to need you here in a bit."

Tank and Cleric, couldn't have planned it better myself. They were the only ones who'd chosen actually useful Classes; the others still seemed to be in shock. Though they hadn't had to fight any damned insect mutations yet, so I didn't know why. It was just a blue screen; surely their imaginations could stretch that far.

Their names all blended together. None of the others would make eye contact, and they answered in monosyllabic tones. I'd deal with them later, but for now, we needed to get out there and find more people. We had to keep our home base—and my kids—safe.

We'd do that by finding more people. When we'd started to build a secure front, I would sit down and worry about the rest of mine, and their Perks.

# Chapter Nine:

# Fetch

## 7 Hours Post-System Onset

It took a lot of effort for me to leave Wisp under the care of Red and the rest back in the center. My first instinct was to keep her by my side, but we'd seen what happened to Jessica's youngest when she did that. Still, my anxiety about leaving her there tried to strangle me from the inside out. Parental guilt wins again.

"Which way do we go, then?" Evelyn asked, her voice low as she stepped up beside me to view Logan Road from the overhanging carpark canopies. The temporary barrier that marked our safe space seemed weak and only ran the literal perimeter of the shopping center, including its carparks. At least from what I could see of the faint blue glow. I'd checked and no one else could see it, so it was very much a Mana thing.

My eyes had trouble adjusting, and it took me a few moments before I could properly answer the Ranger. It wasn't the morning twilight that was causing me a problem but the constant variability of the Mana around the entire area beyond the boundary. My head hurt just trying to keep track of it.

It didn't matter where I looked. Everything was overrun with this Mana Sense. It pulsed in and out of my senses, in time with my heart, the breath of the earth. This Mana that somehow caused our planet to mutate into this Dungeon World. I could feel the time counting down as I stood trying to make up my mind.

I took a breath and finally answered. "Let's start by searching the apartment blocks up and down Logan Road and work from there."

Evelyn nodded and beckoned to Molly and Sange. I was dead tired, but sleep hadn't been an option, and I didn't want to be out here without my kids for too long. Dale and Red seemed trustworthy enough for people I'd known for under eight hours. Good thing I had that Diviner Perk.

Mana Attunement allowed me to narrow in on the Mana eruptions all around us. I could feel the fluctuations running through me like I was a type of conduit, like a continual zinging through my veins.

The concrete jungle of Logan Road as it sloped toward Eight Mile Plains was rife with more piled vehicles. Those accidents had happened seven hours ago now. Anyone left in those vehicles was a corpse. After all, with the exception of Dale's patient, everyone else who wasn't dead on impact had healed quickly.

Still, though, it was quiet around us as we exited the boundary. Far too quiet. I could see the same thoughts reflected in Evelyn's face. I was glad we'd chosen to go this way. Facing the Logan and Kessels Road intersection was a bit too much for me right now.

I could feel it building, in the earth beneath my feet, something powerful and dangerous. A concentration of Mana. My gaze scanned the lightening sky for any signs of trouble, but it remained clear and normal, for now. The power down below me didn't feel immediate but more like it was gathering and waiting, which made me all the more nervous.

"Hey." Evelyn motioned me over to where she was at the lights, about to cross the road, and gestured toward the large, several story high tower of modern apartments diagonally from us.

She didn't need to say anything else.

Light flickered through the windows, more like the intermittent light of a flame than anything magical. Obviously, someone had lit a fire. I only hoped it was for the light, warmth, or to cook by and not to burn down the structure.

The four of us began to move toward the complex when it suddenly struck me. Here we were, a couple of Level 3s and two Level 5s, acting like we knew what the hell we were doing, about to approach an apartment complex with at least one survivor and likely more.

How was I going to keep us safe? Would my Earth Barricade even work if we weren't, you know, touching the earth or something? Did concrete count as earth? My shielding would only fit around me, because I was fairly sure I couldn't use it on someone who wasn't my direct family.

"We need to level scouts up somehow." Evelyn decided to read my mind, or she was just on the same wavelength of practicality.

"Yep." I didn't feel like being too chatty, not when anything could leap out at us at any time.

There was no barking, no cats meowing. Just the dawning of the sun about to crest the horizon and bathe the world in a beautiful orange glow. By sunset, the red hues were likely to reflect the state of life in the world.

We moved slowly. None of the bitumen here had been torn up. Even the trees waving high above the streets in front of us hadn't begun to morph yet. It seemed so peaceful. Like it was any old morning and I was out for a walk before most people had left home.

Except Mana lines hovered around the base of the tree trunks, not yet suffusing the entire plant. I wanted to understand how this whole System worked. Mana was a type of life-giving property, life-altering, really.

As we stepped onto the footpath in front of the apartment complex, I heard a massive bang. Not a gunshot or backfire bang, no, as if something heavy impacted with something else, that sort of noise. I almost shat myself and desperately tried to gulp air back into my lungs.

"What the hell?" Molly gasped.

I couldn't for the life of me figure out what it was either, so I shrugged.

117

"Let's just keep going and see if there's anyone we can help."

Help. Save. I wasn't sure how to phrase what we needed to do. Convince them that safety is in numbers? To come back with us?

Yep. That's all there was to it. Easy as pie.

Sure.

A few steps around the corner and we found just what made that loud bang. To the left of us, hanging over the previously white wall of the complex, was a fresh body, if the blood dripping from it was anything to go by.

Molly retched beside me, and Evelyn turned away, but decomposing bodies had always fascinated me from a purely scientific "oh wow, they fertilize plants really well" standpoint, so I didn't back away like everyone else. A fresh one definitely smelled better.

I looked up toward the balconies slowly, but I couldn't see anyone to indicate that he'd been pushed out. The light wasn't shining on the right side yet. Everything was couched in shadow.

It had to be close to six thirty now from the way the sun was rising—how had this world been a reality for less than eight hours? One of the things being a plantophile meant was that I was highly aware of the time of day so I could monitor samples during experiments better than the ones I'd studied.

"He probably tried to fly," Sange muttered under their breath.

People were stirring now. And those people who hadn't left their houses yet were about to get a very rude awakening.

"Come on." I ushered the others to follow me, my Earthen Barrier ready to rip up concrete if it needed to.

If it could. Why couldn't I just stop time and enter a training montage or something? We hadn't gone far, what with Molly's stomach still heaving, when I stopped short at the sound of a voice I didn't recognize.

"Do you have any idea what the fuck is going on?"

I turned to find a wild-eyed man standing there. Probably late twenties. His hair was disheveled, and he'd buttoned his shirt wrong. Debating what to say, I gave up trying to lower people gently into this. After all, they should have woken up when the System activated and not been so fucking sleepy.

"Have you chosen your Class yet? From the prompts in your head? If not, ask it to show you the best Classes for you. Be specific. You need to choose." I crossed my arms, wondering if this man was safe, or if he'd had anything to do with the body that dropped. Fell. Whatever. "It will take everything you say or think at it literally."

He blinked, his straight black hair getting in his eyes. "No. I . . . what do you mean, Class? Is this a virtual reality test or something?"

At the mention of games his demeanor perked up briefly. He was genuine; I could tell he wasn't putting it on. He had no clue what was happening.

*Successful Skill Use!*

*One off XP Gain – 500 XP*

*You have successfully realized this person is telling the truth. Congrats on actually using your passive Skills.*

*You have reached Level 6 as a Pest & Pathogens Unit: Microbiologist/Plant Pathologist/Entomologist/Hydrogeologist/Molecular Biologist - Abbreviated as: Ecological Chain Specialist*

*Stat points automatically distributed. You have 3 free Attributes to allocate. No new Class Skill points available.*

Great. I'd deal with that later. At least the Skill worked. Couldn't I get Plant Whisperer?

Still, I shook my head at our new recruit, and Evelyn butted in, waving her hand dismissively as she spoke. "Nothing so simple as a VR test. Alien takeover invasion sort of thing that's mutating everything around us."

The guy stood there with his mouth open, blinking at us, and suddenly I felt extremely exposed. Mana reverberated through the ground close to us. And not just because we had to find enough survivors to keep our Safe Zone or we were probably all dead. This System didn't give a shit about our survival rate. It just wanted us healthy enough to battle things, until we couldn't be healed.

"Look. Pick a Class so you're useful and stay with us. We have work to do." I turned around as unease began to set in. This wasn't going to be as easy as I'd hoped.

His expression changed again, firming up, and he nodded. "I'm Ray."

I watched as a ripple of Mana passed through him, successfully anchoring him into the System. He straightened a little, giving me a single nod.

If everyone treated the revelation that way, we might even stand a chance.

# Chapter Ten:
# Smoothing Out

## 7 Hours, 50 Minutes Post-System Onset

That reverberation, the sense of dread that had been following me around since we left the center? Yeah—those were things I needed to pay more attention to in the future.

Ray had barely chosen his little Class when the danger intensified. I could feel it emanating from all around us—the trees, underneath us, looking down at us from every vantage point. Waves of blue began to coalesce around us, buffeting up and down our bodies.

Then the trees closest to us began to warp, and the bitumen just beyond the pavement started to boil, waves of heat and that sticky tar smell suffused the air.

Australia had its own fair share of creepy animals, so it never occurred to me that this crazy game like place might actually spawn things that weren't native to our country, instead of just mutating what was there already. I had a lot to learn.

The bubbling bitumen wasn't just a weird concentration of heat. And I noticed it with an odd detachment as claws emerged first amid a well of bright Mana rushing in toward it, like it was absorbing the power in a rush. Those claws grabbed on, followed by strong, crustacean-like arms that then pulled the rest of the body through. Muscles rippled through the lumpy black liquid.

Tar dripped down the bodies, and I bit back the nervous laughter bubbling in my throat at the sight of them. Monsters from the black lagoon had apparently become monsters from the freshly laid tar roads.

There were only five of them, but they were large and partially covered in what appeared to be hard shells. Maybe that had to do with this being an island or something.

Ray backed up behind both Evelyn and myself. Sange and Molly brandished their weapons bravely, but even I could see the tremble to Molly's hold on her shield. Yep. Nothing like a game.

I reached down, gathering the energy for the Earthen Barrier. Seems bitumen was hard to break through. Pushing with monumental mental effort, I raised a pitiful wall in front of myself and Evelyn. I wasn't sure what Ray's ability entailed, but he'd only just chosen his Class.

Evelyn squinted briefly and let her arrows fly. Some of what she did had to be natural talent. Her aim was impeccable, hitting the joins between plates where the skin was the softest. For me, apart from some more earth flinging, I couldn't do much from a distance.

"Stay here," I said to Ray, not bothering to check whether he listened.

Bat in hand, I was going to need some combat training if this persisted as my offensive line up. With Evelyn providing cover and Molly wading into the thick of it, it left me small openings to move in and whack with a bat.

Therapeutic? Maybe. At least I could take out my anger this way. My first hit made me glad I never locked my elbows. Might not have learned much else from softball, but I had learned that. My aim was slightly off, and the contact reverberated along my arm in a way that aggravated my funny bone.

I winced, happy for the arrow that distracted the creature from me. My next swing crunched, hammering the well-aimed arrow farther into the soft join it bit into. The creature squealed with a noise like a hyena getting caught in a trap. Mana flared around it. Apparently, Mana helped everything heal.

Shit.

Just as I prepared to hammer what was left of that arrow as far as it would go, an icy lance whizzed past my face, plunging in through the creature's chest plate and out the other side.

The thing was as thick around as a stubby, and the tar-crab fell twitching back into the street. I glanced around, noticing that Ray stood, wide-eyed, behind my Earthen Barrier, his arms outstretched over the top, like he had no idea what had just happened.

Evelyn's grin said it all. And suddenly my bat felt a bit cactus. Pretty much useless, but it was all I had.

❖

Molly scowled at her swollen wrist as it slowly healed. All five creatures were dead, Molly was injured, Sange and myself had obtained several cuts, and we'd found out that Ray could only fire two of those icicles in a deadly manner before needing to replenish his Mana, which seemed to take forever.

By the time we were done with our opponents, the apartment block lobby was full of people. They'd been watching us as we dispatched those intergalactic interlopers, or whatever they were. The XP notification called them Crziftuk, but it might as well as be Klingon to me. At least if it was Latin, I'd understand it a little more. So many pairs of eyes stared out at us from behind the glass doors, like they were somehow safe inside despite how easily glass breaks.

To my surprise, Ray, and his entirely new Level-2 self, strode confidently up to the door and motioned madly with his hands for them to come out. Or else to open the doors.

A young girl stepped forward, maybe in her late teens. Probably first-year uni or something. Thing was, her features weren't quite human anymore. I couldn't put my finger on it, but her cat-like eyes and the sheen of pale, silver fur that began to cover her skin lent this whole experience a surreal element of finality.

"Leena?" Ray's voice broke a bit on the tail end of her name, and she just ran forward to hug him tightly.

It took a moment for him to compose himself, but then he raised his head, squared his jaw, and spoke like his voice hadn't suddenly developed a vibrato.

"Right then. Yous—" he paused momentarily before rushing through to the rest. "We gotta bail. Like it's fucked out there."

He glanced at me, and I could feel the tension rising, not only within the building, but all around us as the Mana built its own mini volcanos ready for eruptions whenever it wanted to. Power just waiting to grasp onto any outlet it could find.

"This lot here though"—He gestured to us, and I could see that now his own shock had settled, he was down to Earth and probably honest to a fault—"They saved me. Shouldn't be too bad if we stick with 'em."

Leena looped her hand through her brother's, gripping his arm tighter. Her transformation was still taking place. It was gradual, but thankfully slower than the couple or so dozen people who began to move outside to join us.

From what I could tell, they didn't all have their Classes yet. Which I couldn't really fathom. Perks were one thing, but Class? At least take half an hour to examine what you might be. Still, there was safety in numbers.

The Mana around us wasn't churning like it had been before the last attack. I could only hope to get these guys back to relative safety and have someone give a mass tutorial on choosing Classes if they hadn't done it yet, before we all got killed.

❖

Even though Ray was easily growing into his Ice Lance abilities, moving with this many people had me on edge. More people to fight off shit meant my kids were safer. I just had to keep going and surround them with more padding for a while.

While Ray organized his fellow apartment-building dwellers, the rest of us skirted around it, trying to flush out any remaining residents. It still felt too quiet, but the area was clear.

Except for the massive borer beetle that dropped onto my nose and made me scream like a fucking banshee. Borers are generally tiny, and they like to, you know, bore through plants, hence the name. Weevils, types of moths . . . heaps of different beetles.

This one was the size of a fucking mouse, and I slapped it so hard that it hit the concrete with a squished sound, only to be followed a split second later by my foot as I squashed what was left of it.

Shit. Shit. Shit. My breath came in gasps as I crushed it, and I only looked up when Evelyn began to scream too.

Hundreds, probably thousands of the little shits cascaded down on us. Mouse-sized bugs in our hair, on our shoulders, and I swear one fell into my fucking bra. We stomped and shook and smacked them off each other. Their little heads hurt when they came into contact with our skin, giving us definitive locations for where the buggers were landing.

I couldn't help the sheer alertness the encounter gave me, but for the rest of the way around the complex, and while scouting up the street a ways, I was more vigilant than I'd ever been in my life.

Normal bugs I could handle—System-mutated bugs were a big fat no.

Evelyn grimaced as we made it round full circle to where the others waited. "Imagine how big they'd be in a week if we hadn't squashed them."

"No thank you." Molly shuddered visibly, her tiny shoulders squared. "Not doing that again."

Ray had the rest of the survivors from the complex lined up and ready to walk. "Got most of them sorted into Classes so far. Ready to go."

I gestured toward the center, and Sange led the way. It wasn't far, just up the road, across it, and into the carpark—then we'd already be in the complex.

Leena sidled up to me. I was desperately avoiding the question of why she decided to be a cat person, so I was glad when she spoke first.

"Do you think . . . maybe we should make a sign at a couple of the driveways, entrance-type things?" She seemed a lot younger than I'd originally thought with the way she twisted her hands as she spoke.

"Signs?" I wasn't quite sure what she meant by that.

"Like a 'Survivors welcome' sort of thing." Her voice was even more mouse-like than the first time she spoke.

Dang, I hadn't thought about anything like that.

"I think that might be a ripper of an idea," I said. Probably not something we wanted in our city once others got here . . . if they got here, if that was even how this worked. But it might even help us right now.

It was almost eight o'clock, and the sun was being typically Australian. Still, Leena's face shone with excitement. Maybe she'd just needed to have a task.

I waved down Mike, who stood at the lower entrance to the center, guarding as much as was possible. If something really wanted in, our defenses were currently non-existent. "Got a batch for you. We're going out again for more."

"Got it, boss."

126

He winked suggestively at me, and I groaned internally, quite certain I knew what was coming.

"Can I take you out for coffee one of these days?" Mike continued, his voice on the husky side, though it cracked with the lack of sleep and probably the nerves of hitting on someone in an end-of-the-world scenario.

Called it. I had to laugh. This was an apocalypse, and I had two kids. Couldn't blame him for trying.

So, I winked back and shook my head. "Sorry, love. I like my men older and my women strong and independent."

Mike staggered theatrically like I'd just broken his heart and gave me a good-natured grin. "The kids are safe. Come back soon."

The reality hit me, and I nodded before setting back out with my little team. I needed more people, more protectors. If this had happened pre-divorce, I feel like I wouldn't have been so stuck on things.

It wasn't like Mason was a dick. He just really wasn't cut out for adulthood with responsibilities. And that was okay. He did love his kids— like best friends. He never shirked on contributing, and he was there as much as he could be . . . except now we had an apocalypse, and I didn't even know if he was alive.

I needed more people. A hundred, preferably ten . . . and then my kids would have a buffer of people who could help me defend them. Then maybe I could relax and figure out the rest of this System shit I needed to apply.

# Chapter Eleven:

# One Down

### 15 Hours Post-System Onset

It was quiet upstairs, outside the kiddie play center where my favorite coffee shop was, used to be, whatever. Most of the others were in the department store. It had beds, and I could see the windows from where I sat. The day was marginally successful.

With the thirty-seven people already in the shopping center, and the total of forty-two we'd ended up bringing back, we only needed nine-hundred and twenty-one more people.

Shit.

Most of Ray's neighbors hadn't done anything with their Skills or Classes before we gathered them. He'd taken care of a few out in the field, while Barry took over ushering them through everything once they arrived.

He was so good at it. Almost like a Santa Claus without the beard and belly, and maybe thirty years younger. Mike complemented him well. The jolly old St. Nick and his helpful elf. I watched them for a while, working their magic with people. Kyle could do that too.

The thought of my twin hurt. I needed to find him. Hell, I needed some alone time. This here plant person was getting way too much human time right now.

Jackson, however, had always been blind to when mum needed mum time and sat down next to me. "You know we have to, Mum."

It was as close to an admonishment as he'd ever given me.

"I know. I know. There's just so much information, so many possibilities. What if we pick the wrong things?"

He didn't have an answer for that.

The pair of us fell silent, seated companionably next to one another like we were home, watching TV, rather than scrolling through blue boxes of doom. I'm not sure how much time passed, not with both of us querying the System for more information about availability of Perks, scrolling through options for things we'd heard or seen other people use before he finally spoke up.

"Mum. Seriously. Something to allow us three to communicate with each other just makes sense." Jackson was doing the teenage pout thing. He was also right.

"Fine. I get it. It's only a small Perk anyway. Just make sure the others you take can protect you or help you in some way. Okay?" I needed to know that he was safe. I had to.

He grinned in triumph, and I rolled my eyes. A notification flashed up before my eyes telling me I had access to familial-based chat at Level 1. We could communicate as long as we were within five hundred meters of each other. It wasn't much, but it would do for now.

A bit of the weight trying to suffocate me lifted, and I had to admit that Jackson had been right. If I hadn't been utterly buggered, I might have mentioned it out loud.

"I want to get Wisp poison immunity. That woman we found has some kind of necrotic poisoning, and Dale has no idea how to treat it. She's only still alive because of the System, but even its regeneration is slowly losing the battle." I laid my thoughts out, hoping he agreed with me.

Jackson nodded. "We are in Australia. I mean, things are going to be poisonous, venomous, dangerous . . . deadly."

Okay, so I had Wisp's small Perk done. Frowning, I tried to think of other things to pull up as I received notification of Jackson's medium choice.

### Enhanced Tech Manipulation

*Allows the user to see beyond simple mechanics and manipulate Mana as a source of power.*

I raised an eyebrow at him. "Seriously? How will this protect you?"

"Hear me out." He paused, making sure I was going to let him speak. I crossed my arms and waited. After taking a deep breath, he continued. "It goes hand in hand with my Techzard powers, allowing me to utilize them in ways that can benefit everyone. And I have the perfect protection in the large Perk I want to pick."

"Hm." What was I supposed to do? Discourage him from wanting to help others? Damn it. "Fine. But your large Perk better be a doozy."

I waited, almost scared at what he was going to show me next.

### Dermal Underarmor

*This thin layer of super-strong, under-skin protection can be enhanced and upgraded through Artisan-based Skills, providing a less bulky and always-present layer of added protection equal to 800 physical defense, 250 Mana defense. Can be damaged. Regenerates damage from ambient Mana within the vicinity over a period of thirty-two minutes.*

"Okay. That's more like it." I paused for a moment. So he'd receive a layer of armor that would always be on him. Might give me some breathing space. I accepted the choice for him and sighed. "You better not make me regret that."

"It might seem like a game, but I know it's not. I don't want to die, Mum." Jackson's expression took on a haunted look, and I pulled him into a hug whether he wanted one or not.

"That makes two of us." I ruffled his hair, and he rolled his eyes, but the grin on his face was still my little boy's. Always would be, even when he was thirty.

"So, what about Wisp?" he asked.

I pondered it. Something that would protect her and didn't require her own Mana or hit points to be used was a bonus. That Dermal Underarmor seemed too good to be true. "Do you think that dermal thing would work for your sister?"

Jackson shrugged. "Maybe? It's really just a passive way to protect her. We can't get her active abilities, can we? She's not supposed to use the System yet, right?"

"Will it grow?"

Jackson shrugged and we both queried the System. Thankfully, it seemed like the Perk would grow with the children, something that Jackson seemed relieved by.

I nodded, considering the Underarmor for myself as well. "You'd be able to upgrade hers as well if needed, right? Once you have the Skills?"

He nodded. "I mean, technically. Yes. But she won't have access to all my advantages."

True. We couldn't be sure of anything, no matter how nice the System seemed to be when you were explicit in your needs. "Okay. I'll get her the same large Perk as you. It makes sense. Something she and we don't have to consciously activate."

With Wisp's large Perk chosen, she still had one Medium, and I still had to choose my large one. Medium for my daughter . . . something to keep her from taking damage.

"Mum!" Jackson's excitement pulled me out of my thoughts. "Check out this Bracer of Protection."

I requested it and frowned. An external item that added a shield of five hundred hit points. Rechargeable in fifty-three minutes through ambient Mana. I mean, this way it would take a lot to hurt her, and even if I wasn't there in time to shield her… these things would be able to provide enough protection until I could, right? Probably.

"Good find," I muttered and chose my kid's final Perk. Done. It was done. I'd protected them as much as I could. And it only took me what . . . almost twenty hours to do so? Go mum speed.

"Thanks, Mum." Jackson gave me a hug and sat close to me. "What you going to pick for your large one?"

"Great, ask me the questions I have no answers for." I grinned at him, only half joking. I could take the easy way out and get a Dermal Underlayer. But surely there was something that could benefit more than just me?

There was so much about this I still didn't understand, but I only had forty-eight hours to get Perks chosen, and I'd wasted almost a full day. I was always in danger of being injured; choosing them sooner was logically better. And yet . . .

I really hated being rushed. Call me McStubbornpants.

Mutations happened, and some weird alien shit had birthed itself out of bitumen, but frankly, given our colorful wildlife, I'd been expecting bigger and badder. Maybe it took more time than like, twenty-four hours for the Mana to really soak into stuff.

Where were all of the cockroaches and their mutations? Not to mention the abundance of household animals we had in this area. Birds? I hadn't seen a magpie all day. Everything, from the feeling of the Mana welling beneath my feet, seeping into the bedrock and leaking into everything . . . it just felt like it was waiting for something.

Seventy-nine people. We were all low Levels, practically sitting ducks.

Tomorrow we needed to find ways to gain strength. If we didn't, we weren't going to make it far. There was no way we could help others if we didn't gain strength. And I had to make that large Perk count. I wasn't going to get this chance again.

Suddenly, a notification popped up in front of my sight, interrupting my minor paranoia session.

### Congratulations!

*You survived an entire day! You humans really are an excellent bunch. Only 60% of you died yesterday. We are impressed. Have a cookie. And some experience. Remember, monster spawning will increase over the next week.*
*XP gained: 5000*

*You have reached Level 7 as a Pest & Pathogens Unit: Microbiologist / Plant Pathologist / Entomologist / Hydrogeologist / Molecular Biologist - Abbreviated as: Ecological Chain Specialist*
*Stat points automatically distributed. You have 6 free Attributes to allocate.*
*One new Class point available. One new Class Skill available.*

Level 7. I could handle that, right? Why couldn't this be like an actual MMO and just automatically distribute my Attribute points appropriately? I had another Skill available to me. Better to have all the Skills first and then beef them up, right?

### Blood Transfer (Level One)

*Effect: Due to your devotion to understanding the world and mechanics of biological evolution, you are able to tap into the blood of your opponents and redirect that damage to heal yourself. Only usable on self. Caution: best used on enemies. Self-heal only, damage and heal amount depended on Level of spell and caster.*
*Mana Cost: 25 Mana to activate*

I ran my hands through my hair, glancing over to where I could see Wisp curled up on a huge bed through the glass window of the department store. She was snuggled into blankets with little Kylie gripping her hand tightly. Who were we to usher these kids through this?

Who was this Galactic Council to plunge us into a post-apocalyptic nightmare? Fuckers.

"Mum?" Jackson's tone was filled with concern. I didn't usually go silent on him.

"It's okay. Just one day to go before this large Perk of mine disappears." I smiled at him, but he didn't return the gesture.

"I wouldn't laugh about it. That's an important thing. You may want to protect us, but we need you just as much. Don't forget that." And he hugged me fiercely, like he didn't want to let go. "You can't die either, Mum. You're all we've got."

"I'm not taking it lightly. I promise I will choose something wisely." I couldn't let his seriousness be belittled. He was genuinely worried, and neither of us knew if his dad was still alive.

He eyed me for a moment and then released his hold. "Okay. But you need to tell me as soon as you've got one and let me know what it is. We have the chat function for that."

"Promise," I said and meant it. "Now go chat to the other boys and try to get some sleep."

"Well, I can't promise that. Hey, Mum, can I ask you something?" His tone was hesitant now, like he didn't really want to ask what he was about to.

"'Course, love." I was fairly certain this was coming, as much as I didn't want to deal with the unknown right now.

"Do you . . . do you think Dad made it too?" Jackson gulped back the tears I could see threatening to spill from the corners of his eyes.

I pulled him into a fierce hug, not just because I had no answer for him, but because he was my little boy, and he was hurting. It made me angry, but there was nowhere for it to go. Resting my head against the top of his, I stroked his hair and murmured softly, "I don't know, but I'd like to think he's okay. We all know how dogged he can be."

Some of the tension flowed out of Jackson's shoulders, and he squeezed me back. "Yeah. Don't you say I get my stubborn from the both of you?"

"That I do," I said, smiling softly at him.

As he pulled back, he forced a smile into place. "I'm going to go talk to some of the kids I conned into picking useful Classes like mine." He waved, and I had to take a few deep breaths so I could contain myself.

Yesterday afternoon he'd been worrying at which classes to pick for tenth grade, before he'd even finished a semester of ninth. Normal worries, future concerns, academics.

Now . . . now he had to worry about life and death. What spells could best protect him and his little sister, and just how powerful he needed to be. That was a crock of shit right there.

"Hey. You okay?"

I glanced over at Evelyn, not enough energy in me to jump at the unexpected interruption. "Yeah. Dandy. Level 7 now too. Oooo, fear me."

Evelyn laughed, but it was a dry sound, and it felt like she forced it for my benefit. "Have you figured out the city shit yet?"

I grimaced, all my thoughts jumbling together. "Not really. We need to find a thousand people and bring them into Garden City. That'll at least make it a town and give us access to better defenses and stuff, I think. Other than that? It's a fucking shopping center, right? How did this become a settlement?"

She looked at me, and promptly sat down next to me. "A thousand people?"

Shit. I sighed. "Yeah. A thousand people so we can be considered a town."

I wonder if my distaste for the classification shone through.

Evelyn mulled it over. "So wouldn't it stand to reason that it's not just this one? Wouldn't it be Carindale, Indooroopilly, Chermside as well? The Hyperdome and several others I'd be willing to bet on. They'd all need enough of a direct population I'm thinking, to be considered towns. They're all the outskirts—for something like this, they're almost strategic points for the city itself."

I eyed her. Not just a pretty face, Evelyn was proving to be a fantastic ally. Maybe even a friend or something else . . . I shook my head. Sure, I told Mike I liked my men older, like Mason was, and my women strong and independent, like Evelyn definitely was, but let's be real. Now wasn't the time to even contemplate that shit.

Right now, we had to stay alive and keep the kids alive. Priorities in an apocalypse. Shut up, brain.

Brisbane's population was scattered on a good day. Spread out in a spiraling cascade of suburbs. It basically meant we had to go out and recruit people to come and stay with us so we could all have the protection of a Safe Zone. All it meant was that things wouldn't spawn in it, I think? I needed to learn so much. Maybe there was a beginner's guide?

There were so many other controls and options for buildings, shops, for domiciles . . . everything. But it was all greyed out, and I couldn't even see the individualized possibilities. More people, more Skills, more Levels. That's what we needed.

"You can ask for help, you know." Evelyn wasn't looking at me; she was squinting off into the dark, like she was sure something monstrous was out there.

It was still dark outside. My son and his newfound friends concluded that they needed to Level up in order to perform the tasks they wanted to. Not to mention that they needed to Level up the people he'd coaxed into playing a similar Class to his. His eyes still shone like my eager little boy wanting to play roleplaying games with his father and me. Back before the divorce, anyway. Mason was a big kid and frustrating as hell sometimes, but he was still one of my best friends. Right now, I just wished he could help me keep them safe.

"Kira?" Evelyn sounded concerned.

"What?" I was tired and cringed, pretty sure I'd snapped at her. "Sorry. Feeling a bit overwhelmed over here."

"I've had a nap. Do you trust me enough to go get a few hours of shuteye and let me deal with whatever happens?" She was serious, a sparkle in her eye that told me she knew my real answer but was asking politely anyway. "It's been a day. You didn't sleep last night."

"Fine. Maybe I'll trust you a little bit more if I can think straight."

I got up before I could second guess myself and made my way into the department store so I could fall on one of the beds. It was softer and more comfortable than any bed ever had the right to be. Wisp moved slightly, rolling into me. My worries disappeared as soon as my head hit the pillow and exhaustion took over.

# Chapter Twelve:
# New Reality

## 31 Hours Post-System Onset

The second full day dawned clearer. Regardless of how exhausted I'd been, six in the morning was about my usual waking time. It was actually overcast, but everything was clearer in the sense that we knew this was real now, there was no avoiding it. There was no waking up from it. And the only escape appeared to be death.

"Mum." Wisp tapped her foot impatiently next to me. She'd been trapped inside the center yesterday, and she wasn't the sort of kid to sit still for even a minute. I could almost sense what was coming.

"Mum, I'm better than this. I can help. I'm small and strong, and I can out-chin-up you and most of these people any day. You know it, and I know it."

Her arms were crossed, and her black-brown hair was brushed till it shone and pulled back in her no-nonsense gym bun.

But before I could say anything else, she continued. "I want to go out and find Dad."

Hi there, breaking heart, let me count the ways. Taking a deep breath, I gathered her into a hug. "Dad is probably keeping everyone's spirits up wherever he is by playing his guitar and singing."

She eyed me skeptically. "He was down the coast a few days ago when we last spoke."

Her voice hitched a bit, and I squeezed her tighter. Her big eyes looked up at me, like I was somehow going to make this all disappear.

"Do you think he's okay, Mum?" Her voice dropped to almost a whisper, like she hadn't wanted to ask the question in the first place.

"Yeah, buttercup, if it's your dad, I think he's got to be fine." And I sort of believed what I told her—because I really had to.

"Okay, then. But you let me know as soon as we find out for sure." Even at her age, she knew that we couldn't actually know; he was too far away for that. "Meanwhile, don't treat me like a little kid. I'm tougher than I look."

She had a good point. "I promise. I'll sit down with you and go through what we chose for you. The System won't allocate you a Class or Attributes yet because you're too young, and it stunts growth or something like that. So just bear with me, okay?"

"Seriously?" She scoffed and partially rolled her eyes. "I don't need super abilities from some System. I've already got them. I can jump anything you put in my way, or flip over it, or even ninja climb it. I can fit into places you guys might not be able to get in. I'm not little like Kylie. Don't count me out!"

Ah, that's right. She'd been stuck with the five-year-old all day yesterday. Kylie's mum was still fighting whatever it was she had in her system. I was pretty sure she was going to die, but then I was feeling pretty negative about then. Kylie looked at Wisp like she had stars in her eyes.

"Okay. I promise I won't count you out. And if a situation arises where we need your skills, I won't refuse just because you're my little girl." Those words were harder to say than I thought, but my head was clear. The sleep had done me good. "Besides. Jackson and I chose some protective benefits last night. You're a lot safer now than you were yesterday."

"Pinkie promise, Mum. Gotta keep that trust." She nodded at me like she was eighteen, not eight. "And Mum, I'm almost nine, remember that!"

I watched her stomp away and head back to take care of Kylie. Almost nine. Sure, seven months to go was close to "almost."

"She's so grown up."

I turned to find Jackson standing behind me, his eyes shining with so much excitement that I knew he was bursting to tell me something.

"Go on. Before you explode. We need this building intact."

He laughed and pulled out whatever he'd been holding behind his back. The contraption sort of looked like a battery. Sort of—more like a car battery. Attached to it was a rudimentary fan like the ones that sat on hats or in water bottles.

Biting his lip, he pressed down on the button, and the fan began to turn. Meanwhile, the battery glowed the beautiful and bright blue of the Mana all around us, and I smiled. It was a small achievement, but it was a start.

"Looks like Techzard was a good choice." My smile was genuine, and I didn't let the fact that there was a lot to organize bother me.

I was lucky my kids were alive. Some of these people, like Dale, had literally lost their partners less than thirty-six hours ago, their kid or kids. Despair was easy to lapse into, and I knew my situation was shitty too, but I was so much luckier.

Now I just had to keep them safe. I needed to try and keep everyone safe.

Hellooooo, mantra.

"Crafting is pretty cool though; I'm leveling with it too. Not as much as we got killing those things, but hey, not life threatening. That should make you happy, Mum." He grinned at me, and I barely resisted the impulse to cuff him over the ear.

Cheeky little bugger.

He continued, eyeing me warily like he'd read my mind. "I need some Levels, though. I need some of those Skills higher up in my tree. Most of us are working on the infusion elements we have, but we have to get stronger

141

faster." He frowned for a second, and I knew he was calculating something or other in his head. "Like . . . I don't think whatever this really is will wait for us to get stronger. It's not exactly into fair play."

He had a good point, too. A *very* bloody good point.

"How many people chose Techzard?" I asked, trying to be nonchalant about it. After all, it was Jackson's project.

"Well, technically only one more, but there are three other very similar Classes, it appears, and we have two of those as well." He paused, eyeing me, and I knew something was up. "It would be great if we could take turns going out with patrols to test our crafting as well as get some power-leveling while the rest of us stay and Level slower."

He was determined. I could feel my gut clench; a parent's desire to shelter and protect rose up. He might be a teenager, but he was still my little boy. Not that I was about to say that out loud. I was pretty sure he wouldn't kill me for it, but he would get very angry if he heard me say it.

Then I fought it down. Just like I had fought it down every time he climbed up on monkey bars or scaled a tree too far or when he broke his damned arm. Part of being a parent—part of being a good parent—was learning to let go, to let them make their own mistakes.

"Fine. But only one of you can scout with each group. And you need to be more help than hindrance, got it?" I used my best mum voice, trying to drive home the seriousness of this whole thing. "If not, we will have to rely on the crafting experience until you're all higher Level, got it?"

Jackson just smiled. "You're the best, Mum."

And he ran off to his little group that was sitting in the now-open gadget and toy store across the way, waving his arms excitedly at his friends. It was probably where they pulled most of the wires and soldering stuff from.

"He seems to be adapting well." Dale was sitting at my usual table when

I finally made it to my destination.

"He's a teenage boy. This is like his dream come true. Video games as a way of life." I sighed, casting my gaze around to locate Wisp as well.

She was with Kylie and a couple of slightly older girls who'd come in with us yesterday evening. I wasn't really worried. Wisp could hold her own, especially now she had her dermal shielding, but I was allowed to get protective. Maybe I should have picked children tracking devices as a Perk or something. Hindsight sucked.

"Darren seems to be adjusting too." Dale's eyes appeared to be seeing something that wasn't there for a few moments, and his expression adjusted slightly, enough to see the gaping sadness in there.

He felt alone. He'd lost so much. I couldn't help but want to make it better for him. Yet I couldn't. Nothing could bring them back . . . this wasn't something we could wake up from. This was our new reality.

"He'll adjust. He's young, and there are a few of them in their teens here. We're only going to get more." I paused, watching Dale quietly as he digested everything around him, and I tried to offer some gentle words of comfort. "It doesn't mean he's not sad. It means he's trying to deal with it in his own way."

Dale turned to me and just looked for a long moment before nodding. "You're probably right. There will be time to mourn. Just not now."

Of course I was right. Humans and plants had similar needs. Plants grew over shit in their way, and humans used what was in their way to make them stronger . . . usually.

I didn't say that to him, though. "There will be a time."

I closed my eyes for a moment and felt in my head. That thing where I always knew Kyle was there, even if we were apart. From the time we were kids, I'd never worried about him unless that place, that spot, gave me a warning. I'd know if he was in pain or hurt . . . or even just sad.

So. Nope. Kyle was alive. I just had no idea where the fuck my twin was. But now wasn't the time to think about that. There'd been such a huge loss of life worldwide that we needed to pull ourselves up and conquer this shit before it killed all of us.

I wasn't about to let our species be wiped out of existence.

❖

Dealing with stubborn people, while being an obstinate person myself, was never my ideal. I pinched my brow as Dale and I spoke to a small group of the survivors we'd brought in yesterday.

They'd not picked their Classes fast enough, so the System had, upon being active for a full day, just allocated one to them. They wouldn't even tell us what they were. Now we were trying to convince them that choosing Perks was necessary before they lost them too.

"Why do we have to listen to you, huh?"

Jason stood about six feet tall. He was stocky like a rugby player and stood with his arms crossed as if he was an impenetrable line of defense. I could feel it, though—he wasn't as forceful or confident as he sounded. Good old Diviner Skill spotting a lie at ten paces. He was scared. Not just for himself, but for his girlfriend and their other friends.

And he was young enough to be an idiot about it.

"It's not a matter of listening. It's a matter of standing back and assessing the situation and seeing what our best chance of survival is." I walked over with Wisp next to me. People with small kids rarely seemed threatening. Why, yes, I was using my daughter as a tool. She knew it, too, smiling as cutely as possible for all she was worth.

144

Jason scowled, a stubborn set to his jaw, but he hesitated, like he'd just thought that maybe "you're not my mum" *wasn't* the greatest comeback. His girlfriend pushed to the fore, her face pale, and her dark brown hair didn't help her complexion.

"Sorry. He's just worried about us." Her name was Cherry, and she was sweet, petite, and for the first time I noticed . . . she was also pregnant.

Oh, this just kept getting better and better. I sucked in a breath, hoping they didn't notice, and gave her my best reassuring smile. Plants. I just wanted to sit underneath a tree and breathe. I'd have no trouble then.

"That's what we're all doing. We want to be safe. But this is a whole new . . . whatever it is, and I for one would like to save as many people as possible. So, Cherry, please? Can you tell me what Classes you chose?"

I hated having to ask, but my Analyze Skill hadn't worked properly on them, so I needed to.

She hesitated and then blushed and I realized why Jason hadn't been forthcoming. "We didn't pick so now we just have these Classes and . . . we thought it might be a terrorist attack, or some sort of sabotage. Maybe a blackout . . . I mean, it can't be a game, right?"

She trailed off, and her face took on this sadness I felt like a sucker punch.

"Yeah. I get how it appears." I sighed. "But the system is set up like a game."

Jason scowled. "This is nothing like Rugby League Live. I'm a Heavy Infantry Linesman. Whatever that is."

Trying my best not to grimace, I nodded. From his build it seemed about right, and I turned to Cherry, who suddenly just seemed resigned to everything. "And you?"

"I'm an Apprentice Tailor." She shrugged at me, like she just had no clue.

Well, at least Cherry would be able to Level with some crafting, unlike her partner. At least it would keep her mostly home and safe, once we figured out which loot items could help her Level.

Wow. I really was starting to think in game terms.

I put on my best keep-calm-and-soothing voice. "Jackson knows more than most of us about whatever this is. He'll help you pick Perks that should assist in protecting you. I'll leave you in his capable hands."

Jason started to look mulish again, but Cherry shot him a look, and the rest of their friends fell back in line. At least that was something.

Sixteen people who hadn't chosen Classes and had them allocated automatically by the System. Most of them were young, with two middle-aged couples. Older than me by several years. I wasn't about to admit to being middle aged quite yet. I still didn't understand. It wasn't like you could completely ignore those blue screens even if you minimized them.

I hoped this was just an outlier, that it wasn't going to be normal for only seventy-eight percent of people to choose their Classes before encountering others. All I could hope for was that we got to the rest of them before their Perks' timer ran out. In our current state, Perks were important.

Some had Leveled up on the walk over. Random engorged rats, creeping, slug-like cockroaches. I shuddered at the memory of that one. Ray had been brilliant and already stepped in to help Barry. He'd just hit Level 4, so he was more pro than most of these people. The two of them jelled so well. Barry with his welcoming, automatically likable personality and Ray with his over-confidence. Together they made others feel welcome, and maybe like we weren't all going to die.

We had a Warrior and a Cleric we'd collected yesterday who had obviously played some RPGs and were both Level 3. Even though their

Class names weren't traditional like that, it's what their Classes boiled down to. The others were some sort of casting, stabbing, fleeing Classes that I didn't get. Jackson seemed to understand.

If we sent out Evelyn with a group, and Dale with a group, we had a good chance of bringing back survivors. But I had to make sure enough people stayed at home. How was I already referring to this deserted shopping center as home?

"Mum?" Jackson tugged on my arm, and I realized I must have been zoning out.

"Sorry. What?" I blinked at him, a thousand thoughts running through my head at once, including the way the blue strands of power danced around in the whites of his eyes. I needed to get a handle on Mana Sense so it didn't constantly disorient me.

"So . . . I mean, you can see my abilities, right?" he asked.

"Yes, but I haven't looked at just your Class Skills." Better to come out with it straight up. That way he'd explain whatever tech thing he was about to share with me. I knew my son well enough for that.

He rolled his eyes in that "oh my god, Mum" way that only teens can accomplish and took a deep breath.

"After my last Level up, I think I can sort of help . . . manipulate power into container-type things. Mana as a sort of current? Like, I mean, it powers everything here, right? It's what's mutating the Earth and us and everything around us. So it is a source of power. A type of electricity. That's how I did the battery thing."

He paused for a moment like he was trying to wrap his brain around what he was telling me and get it out in some form of mum-standable language.

"This ability is literally called Mana Empowerment. So. I'd like to

147

request to stay back here instead of scouting so I can work on a few things." He hesitated, and I could tell he wasn't sure if he should ask what he was about to. "Is it okay if I instruct people who have abilities, Classes like mine? Some of the younger guys chose tech-like stuff. We might be able to get things powered, give us back some sense of stability. Like refrigerators, lights, air conditioning and such. Like I don't know if I can do it fast, but I definitely can't do it all alone."

I watched him as he spoke, that life still in him, that complete and utter enthusiasm for finding things he could tinker with and get to work in different ways. My little tech genius. And here he was adapting to a world that shouldn't exist. A nightmare world I was still hoping I could wake up from, and he'd found something he could do that most others couldn't.

"Do it. I have no doubt there are others who love tech as much as you do. Better to have people who will love what they're doing than fight it every step of the way. If you think it'll work, I trust you." And I realized that I wasn't just spouting parental platitudes. I was genuinely proud of him, and I had faith in his intelligence if he thought this was something he could do.

"Thanks, Mum." He gave me a very quick hug and darted back to the group he'd been counseling.

My teenage son had risen to the occasion. It was about time we all did.

# Chapter Thirteen:
# New Order

## 36 Hours Post-System Onset

I pushed myself up from the tables. I'd lost track of how long we'd been sitting there arguing. If we continued to meet here, it wasn't going to be my favorite place to have a coffee for long. Not to mention I was fairly sure the kids would take over with the indoor play area being right here.

Besides, I was probably going to have to go and raid one of the supermarkets for more cans soon. I was going through way too much.

Gemma, Jules, and Evelyn were out scouting for people. I really could have used their backup. Several of our Garden City foundlings weren't happy with the circumstances. They thought it was all an elaborate scam cooked up by the government. They thought it was staged, and they didn't see why they should stay in here—in this safe space with us. The odds of us coming back and finding them gone were fairly large.

I had half a mind to tell them to bugger off and go and fend for themselves. But they wouldn't even choose their Perks. Their Classes were all based off their jobs, and considering most of them had worked in the center, I had no confidence at all in their survivability.

Letting them run off like nothing had happened would be like releasing birds into the wild who couldn't see or fly yet. Even if those people insisted that they'd have no part of the tracking devices we were using. Stupidity had no cure when people insisted on remaining willfully ignorant.

Time would either convince them, or they'd just become another percentage of the death toll.

"Jackson." I called out his name, trying to push myself into a better mood. The sound echoed through the mostly empty shopping center sounding eerier than intended. He came running out of the shop, his brow pinched with worry. I really couldn't complain; his teenage moments were still far and few. "Did you still want your students to come out and earn some Levels?"

I tried not to let the fear show in my voice. Hadn't he mentioned not necessarily wanting to go out himself? There was an area up near Kessels and Logan Road intersection that was proving challenging to cross. Mana hadn't been kind to the animals around there, so we were sending out two teams. "We can take two of you with us."

He nodded, his excitement almost tangible. He needed to calm down or he'd give me a heart attack. In the end, it was him and a boy he called Galen. Not a name I would have chosen, but then I did call my daughter Whisper because I felt like she whispered to me when she was first born, so who was I to judge names?

I would have preferred to take Evelyn and her trusty bow skills and over-confidence that lent me some. But she was still out with Gemma and Jules, so Molly and Sange it was.

Molly, our petite and ruthless little Tank who didn't look like that should be her Class, made me feel oddly safe. Sange with their taciturn manner and on-point heals made bringing that duo something I expected to do often after yesterday's outings.

We dragged Mark and Tasha with us too. They were new additions from yesterday's scouting missions. We hadn't found them inside but instead with blood caked on their wounds as they traveled from where their car had plunged into a traffic light.

They were a young couple who would probably at least fight to keep each other safe. Tasha's Class appeared to be Spellsword Fighter-Mage, which I assumed was close combat with magic? Maybe?

Mark's Class seemed similar to Gemma's, stealth and daggers, high-damage attacks—or at least the potential for them once he wasn't, like, Level 4. They'd been lucky to survive.

Darren tagged along as well, even though Dale was obviously against the idea. Still, he realized his son needed experience to survive, and we were staying relatively close to the entrance anyway.

I'd keep an eye out for the kid. Dale wouldn't survive through losing his only living child, and frankly, right now? We didn't have another true medic. Maybe it sounded callous, but we needed him. Magic was one thing, knowing what the fuck he was doing with his Skills was priceless.

"Come on, people. We don't have all day." I felt like time was ticking, regardless of whether this was a new reality or not—we'd essentially been invaded. And from the sheer lack of people coming here, or visible to us, most of them were hiding or already dead.

The System didn't give us a shielding or anything to mark our temporary Safe Zone. Instead, it had boundary limitations. Safe zones appeared to be areas where the Mana wasn't going wild, or at least that's what my Mana Sense told me.

Mana was a strange beast.

I led the way, going through my own Skills in my head and trying to figure out just how I could use that Barrier of mine to better protect us. And that blood thing, too. Though I guess for now, that was just for me. I'd never played anything like this in games.

Yet this whole Mana Attunement thing was beautiful, especially when we stepped outside of the Safe Zone. I could feel the land beneath my feet, sense the way the animals were being affected, and taste the difference in the air. It gave me this sense of belonging, just like I had when I spent time in nature, studying it, understanding it and how it grew.

Who was I kidding? This Class was perfect for me. Understanding the changes in the earth, what the Mana meant for it, and how it all worked together? If I didn't have this Class, I would have been trying to figure it out anyway.

The carpark was mostly deserted if you didn't count the now useless motor vehicles. I could see the few tall gum trees out near the road, and I knew immediately that those trees weren't included in the Safe Zone. I picked up my pace, falling into a jog and realizing suddenly that the pain in my knee was gone. A remnant of my high school netball days, I'd had that constant pain longer than I cared to admit. What else had the System done? What else could it do?

As we neared the trees, I realized there were more creatures here than I'd anticipated. Rodents of System-induced size, some of those damned flying cockroach things that were my first encounter. Some large dogs and cats crept around the plethora of vehicles in their crashed states on the road itself. The intersection was never pretty, but without power steering and that whole mess of electrical shit that controlled cars now . . .

Cars had crashed into one another, into traffic lights and buildings over the other side of the road. Yesterday hadn't been particularly roasty, but our autumn here in Brisbane wasn't exactly what other places would consider cold. After thirty-six hours of death, I could definitely smell the corpses.

A gentle wafting perhaps, but it was there, just under the smell of petrol lingering on the road. Behind the sounds of flesh being chewed right then by some of those rodents and former pets. Dystopia at its finest. Damn, I wished it was still fiction.

Sange stopped next to me and took a look around before speaking. "We need to stay together."

Wise words. I nodded, and they raised their voice. "We need to stay together. Don't separate for any reason."

Sange was more comfortable giving orders if they didn't have to make eye contact with anyone. I made a note to myself for later, but my thoughts were stopped in their tracks as our flying attackers pounced.

Fucking magpies.

Have you ever been around a magpie? You know how crows like shiny things? Yeah, well, magpies are like crows on acid. Magpies love shiny things, and that includes your eyes. They love shiny things even more if they're building their nests, or hell, if it's a day ending in Y.

Magpies.

They're medium-sized black and white birds with a dive bomb that a B52 bomber would be proud of. They're dangerous. Their beaks can rip out pretty hair barrettes, hair ties, hair clips, earrings, scalp, skin, tissue, eyes . . . you name it.

Now imagine those on the steroids called Mana, and you have Mana magpie nightmares. That's my name for them and I'll call them the MMNs from now on regardless of what this System says.

As soon as they noticed us, they attacked. They swooped down at us, breaking off in ones and twos as they winged around. Darren's Gale of a wind helped disturb their aim, and one of them landed on Molly's sword. The wind pushed the rest away, while a few of us batted at those closest, with most of us missing.

Then they pulled back and circled around, landing on branches or roofs, fluttering wings and preening. The occasional other idiot monster tried to get close, to launch an attack, only to be smacked down by the MMNs.

It took a few seconds for us to size each other up. I had to force myself to breathe regularly, to remember to drag in oxygen without hyperventilating. Not yet. And then, as though there were an unspoken command, they attacked. Not just the magpies but the rest of the swarm too, the creatures choosing to go after the bigger, dumber targets.

Australia is well known for its, shall we say, "colorful" fauna. The System should have just left our continent alone, but the Mana and our native wildlife got on like a house on fire. So here we were.

Magpie beaks as strong as reinforced steel.

Molly positioned herself at the front, her jaw set in determination as she raised her shield overhead and activated some Skill that made the shield appear to extend. The shielding it created spouted out sparks of electricity as it fried birds coming anywhere within a foot of it. She played Tank while the rest of us got ready to get swinging, even as magpies and others attacked.

Jackson and Galen threw balls of light into the air to frighten the flyers back and catch the occasional one on fire, but all it gave us was momentary reprieve, a break in the mass coming at us as they dodged around the flying attacks.

Though like I mentioned earlier, magpies love shiny things, and pecking at the orbs became the next big things. At least they were distracted.

That left the rest of us to get the hits in.

Magpies weren't stupid, though. They backed off once they realized the orbs hurt and let the flying cockroaches get fried by the boys' and Molly's shield. They waited for the rodents to be skewered on swords and be bashed by bats before diving back toward us.

Their beaks pecked at our arms, and our faces, and our arms covering our faces. Their claws tore strips of flesh from our shoulders and scalps as they flew past or launched off. And the occasional grounded one, wing smashed or feathers crisped, they just kept hopping over to peck at us.

Upon closer inspection, their wings were longer, and they were overall larger than usual. Everything about them including their talons and skin had been reinforced.

After the initial rush, I summoned my Earthen Barrier behind us so that at least nothing could surprise us from our flank. Hopefully. I made it twist, pulled it around the front so we had a more controlled entry for ground-based, non-flying, non-gliding attackers.

Sange was a capable Cleric. They kept up with the wounds on all of us and with the more extensive damage that Molly, Mark, and Tasha took. Their heal spell lofted light over each of us to heal injuries, bathing us in a "Healing Aura" or so Analyze told me. I hoped they had enough Mana to keep it up.

The latter two were both close combat. Mark had the Swashbuckler Class, so not exactly the same as Gemma, but still very similar. Tasha's was actually called Fighter Mage and came from an alien race she couldn't pronounce. She used spells and a kitchen knife that brought her in way too close a contact with her targets for my liking. I still had no idea where Mark had found an actual, working, sword.

Me? I tapped into an MMN with Blood Transfer, and even though it seemed to make the creature target me all the more, it helped keep up with my own blood loss, while contributing to the bird's health decline, and taking a bit of pressure off Sange left them open to healing the others. Every once in a while, they'd call out a number, and it kept going down as their Mana disappeared like crazy.

The number of heals they had left didn't fill me with confidence. My worn-out baseball bat was the only thing other than Blood Transfer that could do damage.

On the other hand, magpies made a satisfying crunching sound when they came into contact with a metal baseball bat. Music to my ears.

Glancing at the bat as blood flew from it as I wound up for another hit, I couldn't help remember there were sports supplies galore in the shopping center. We'd have baseball bats for a while at least. *Let's see if I can break this one.*

Except, while I was planning for the future, the magpies showed how intelligent they really were. A series of screeching caws went up around us, and they spread into three groups of about ten each. They flew around, gaining a little space and speed, and while the rest of us finished off the other swarming attackers, they banked and hit us. All at once.

Distracted as I might have been by beating the crap out of the creatures, the others weren't. Molly shifted, taking the first group on the dome of her shield. It staggered her tiny form, made her almost fall before her booted feet caught on the asphalt and she ground to a halt, the repeated strikes no longer moving her.

The second MMN assault team had to turn away from a rush of flames generated by Tasha and Jackson at the last minute, though my son sank to his knees after they peeled away, his face wan.

Unfortunately, no one was dealing with the third group. I tried to bring the barrier higher, but it refused to budge more than an inch, the limits of the Skill a jarring pressure on me.

Time slowed, like a bad action movie. I watched the tiding of magpies approach me, my family, my charges like a series of black and white living arrows: fast, accurate, and with sparkling intelligence in their eyes.

A sudden calm hit me as I felt the waves of Mana beneath me, around me. I let the existing Earthen Barrier go and in the same instant called forth a new one right in front of my feet. I burnt Mana, forcing it to shoot up as high as I could get it to smash right through that flock.

Bitumen split, and pavement crumbled all around us as the earth responded to my command. I felt energy, the Mana I commanded, drain out of me instantaneously as it summoned forth an enormous earthen pillar that caught the tail end of the tiding, smashing several of the birds just before they plowed into us.

With the wall rising and the MMNs shooting down, the impacting crunch of bone meeting earth echoed through my head.

Bouncing magpie corpses and broken feathers plummeted down to the ground around us, and I fell to one knee. Falling saved me from the remaining MMNs, one claw tearing at my hair and leaving a wound on my scalp. The other few slapped and cut the others before their momentum took them away.

Rather than turn around, the last remnants of the magpie flock chose to wield that unnatural intelligence again. The surviving other tidings joined them, and they kept flying away, followed by the rest shortly afterward. Not that the fight was over, since there were remnant cockroaches and rats to deal with, though most had died already.

I didn't really care. My legs were shaking, and checking my Mana levels showed me that I'd pretty much drained everything I had by pushing my ability in an offensive way instead of a defensive one. My head was light and spinning, but everyone seemed intact, even if we all had wounds that weren't quite healed yet.

Notifications flashed at me, but I wasn't ready for blue screens quite yet.

Jackson reached down and helped me stand. "Mum? You okay?"

The concern in his voice almost broke my heart. It should be me being the adult here. But I didn't have the energy it required right now. Just give me ten minutes, right?

"Fine. Just overdid it." I looked up at the pillar, but it was only half there now, crumbling away as I stopped pumping Mana into it.

I staggered to my feet with my son's help, only to watch the last of the pillar fall forward and away from us, like it was still aware enough to be considerate. Around us, the footpath and part of the road were churned up remnants of street and concrete, with roots and earth scattered all around like an explosion.

My stomach roiled a bit, notifications flashed in my vision, and all I wanted to do was go to sleep. But I plastered a smile on my face, grinned, and spoke up. Did my best to lend people energy I didn't even have for myself.

"We did it."

The words sank into the silence that had surrounded us like a lead balloon before. Mark clapped, then looked a bit embarrassed to be caught doing so. It made Darren laugh though, and that was enough for the floodgates.

We'd survived a bombing formation of MMNs. Relief rushed through us all. We cheered at each other, we high fived each other, and there might have been some hysterical laughing in between it all.

The thing was, I knew there were more hotspots like this around the outskirts of our supposed safe space, but if it took this many of us to take out this bunch of forty odd wild animal mutations, then we needed a lot more practice with our abilities.

I checked my notifications as we walked back, the group chatting about their great victory all around us.

**Congratulations!**

*You helped defeat a group of Level 12 Feral Magpies. Bonus 1200 XP*

*Death Experience x 14 Level 12 Feral Magpies = 238x14 = 3,332*

*Death Experience x 24 Level 6 random mutations = 97x24 = ,2328*

*Bonus XP for using your Mana Sense and Class awareness to use Earthen Barrier as a weapon—Bonus 3,000 XP.*

### Level Up*1

*You have reached Level 8 as a Pest & Pathogens Unit: Microbiologist/Plant Pathologist/Entomologist/Hydrogeologist/Molecular Biologist—Abbreviated as: Ecological Chain Specialist*

*Stat points automatically distributed. You have 6 free Attributes to allocate.*

Great. What a reward. I guess I'd have to figure out what to choose when I got inside and nursed this ridiculous headache I could feel coming on.

I motioned for the next blue screen to pop up, really just wanting to collapse, and blinked at what was there. Apparently, I'd changed my ability. Yippee.

### Earth Barricade (Level One)

*Earth Barricade allows you to command the earth beneath your feet for the purpose of defending yourself and your allies. If you pump enough energy and Mana into it, however, you can make it an offensive high-powered wall.*

*Effect: 100 HP shield created, within a 3m x 2.5m region (shapeable)/large earth wall that smites incoming air attacks*

*Mana Cost: 20 Mana/all the Mana you need to make it work.*

All righty, then.

Those MMN pecks on my arms smarted, pulling me back to look at them. It wasn't that they couldn't have been healed faster, but I'd noticed that we all regenerated our health over time anyway, so why waste Mana on it? After all, Sange had drained their own Mana healing us during the fight already, and I had no body to use Blood Transfer on.

Besides, at this rate, we'd all be dead when we failed to find enough survivors to meet the town requirements.

Fuck. I was letting it get me down.

Back the fuck up. I refused to let this beat me. This wasn't a situation anyone ever thought we'd be in. There was no prerequisite for it, no case studies, no work experience. I bit my lip and took in a deep breath. Calm the fuck down, Kira. Forward. Don't dwell, keep marching on.

I glanced at the small group I had with me. "Up for a quick sweep to see if we can find anyone in the shops around here?"

The cheer that went up made me smile. It was at least ninety percent genuine.

❖

We'd found more people. More Perkless people. Including some who'd not chosen their Classes and thus had the System force one on them. Perks I got, Classes . . . how could they have just let it pick for them?

"Hey." Evelyn came and sat down next to me.

I blinked, realizing I'd lost track of an hour or two while I tried to figure out why Red had come and handed me the potential food preservation ideas he'd had. We had maybe a day left before everything in the massive deep freezers began to completely thaw and thus start to rot. That is, unless the kids could figure out a way to convert Mana into energy capable of powering some of those cold boxes.

I'd been sitting here just outside the food court watching as Barry and Ray, Mike and Jules helped the fifty-odd newcomers we'd managed to find today. Their demeanors, their friendly banter—it put everyone else at ease.

Garden City was surrounded by other retail areas, so as of tomorrow we'd need to venture farther out. I was starting to worry we'd never find the people we needed.

Evelyn poked me in the arm with a lone finger. "I know you heard me."

"Sorry. Don't suppose you were a restaurant manager or deep freezer expert while you were studying?" I tried to make it sound like a joke, but it wasn't. I was getting desperate to hand some of this shit off to other people who knew more.

But who was I kidding? None of us did right now. Outside, the plants and creatures were all mutating, developing, feeding off another life source. And in here we were all going stir crazy, cooking up conspiracy theories, or trying to assert a dominance we couldn't use right now.

Jason got into a mix up with someone Cherry was being kind to. Tearing those two young men apart had me wishing I could reach for Earth Barricade and put them both in little cells of dirt to cool off. We didn't need stupid alpha pissing contests right now.

Our little expeditions had fished another fifty-three people from surrounding buildings or off the streets. I wished we could take it slower, but I was on a timer. How were people supposed to mesh well if we came together that fast?

How were humans going to survive if we didn't go faster?

Touché, brain.

I took a deep breath. "Sorry. This is just so . . . vast. Almost two full days and I'm at a loss. How can we do this? Did you hear about the damned magpies?"

Evelyn nodded. "Yeah, we encountered a much smaller pack of those mobs."

I held up a hand to stop her. "Did you really just call them mobs?"

The Ranger hesitated, and then burst out laughing. "I guess I did. The

161

annoying things flee when enough get hurt. Careful bunch. They'll only attack in packs. Safety in numbers applies to everything, I guess. At least it helped us find some more people."

She paused for a moment, rocking her legs back and forth gently as she looked out through the skylights.

"How do you not just sit down and stop?" She asked the question quietly, like she just didn't want this all to be real.

I shrugged, but then I really thought about it. Glancing at my children in their respective groups, being themselves, I knew it was for them, but that wasn't all. "Because I don't want to die. Because I worked hard to get where I am in life. To raise my kids, to be independent, to be a good mum and a damn good person. And I'm not going to give any alien fuckers the satisfaction of taking my life away from me without a fight."

Evelyn blinked at me and sat up straighter. "Too right, mate!"

She grinned at me. And in that moment, I knew that no matter what happened, at least a few of us wouldn't be handing over our world without a fight.

# Chapter Fourteen:

# Denial

**47 Hours Post-System Onset**

The darkness that pervaded the shopping mall abated somewhat as Jackson, Galen, and friends managed to create a few Mana-powered mage lights. I think it helped with morale, and it definitely didn't go unnoticed by the people who trickled into the center. After two days now without the electrical conveniences we were used to, lights where there should be none helped lighten the mood.

Level 8, eh? Pulling up my Skills, I pored over them while Wisp snuggled into me. The fun thing about the System was it didn't matter how dark it was outside my head, I could have a party with the screen lights behind my eyelids.

| Status Screen | | | |
|---|---|---|---|
| Name | Kira Kent | Class | Ecological Chain Specialist |
| Race | Human (Female) | Level | 8 (1479 XP to next Level) |
| Titles | | | |
| Diviner | | | |
| Health | 200 | Stamina | 200 |
| Mana | 400 | Mana Regeneration | 6ps* |
| Attributes | | | |

| Strength | 15 | Agility | 22 |
|---|---|---|---|
| Constitution | 20 | Perception | 46* |
| Intelligence | 40 | Willpower | 40 |
| Charisma | 20 | Luck | 17 |
| **Class Skills** | | | |
| **Mana Attunement** | 2 | | |
| | | Earth Barricade | 1 |
| **Blood Transfer** | 1 | | |
| | | | |
| **Combat Spells** | | | |
| Shield of Power | | | |
| **Skills** | | | |
| Mana Sense | | | |

Eight Levels. I was only Level 8. Spare points allocated. I needed to keep on top of that better. Without taking care of making myself as strong as possible and as *soon* as possible, wasn't I almost as bad as the people who'd left choosing their Classes until the last moment and then lost the choice?

My son was Level 9 thanks to his crafting crap. How was I supposed to protect him when he was stronger than me?

Wisp stirred in her sleep, and I wanted to join her, try to resign myself into oblivion. But I couldn't. I had to pick that damned large Perk. I'd not thought time would run out this quickly, but I'd been wrong. Maybe it was easy to forget to choose your Class with all the shit going on around you.

*List large Perks best suited to my Class,* I thought at the System, trying not to move and wake up my daughter or her little friend. Dog raised his head, looking at me as if to ask if I needed help. He was a good boy, if rather massive now. That was another mystery that needed solving. Why was he fine but not any other dog?

*You have one hour and three minutes to choose your Perk. Please choose wisely.*

*No shit, System,* I thought to myself and busied my mind with going through them.

Dermal Underarmor. Yeah, that was a wise choice, so it was a great backup. Quantum shift stuff that I didn't want to risk using because I had total fear of being stuck halfway into a dimension or brick wall or something.

My eyes scanned down the long list. I kept poking at it, getting it to filter things out, getting distracted by my brain zoning out, and then forcing myself to focus again. In the end, the list I had was all things that required Mana, tapped into Mana, regenerated with ambient Mana.

### *Excess Ambient Mana Regeneration Enhancement*
*When you're lucky enough to be caught near a large influx of ambient Mana, you will temporarily gain an extra 100 Mana to your Mana pool.*
*Warning: If the ambient Mana falls below what is considered excess, your pool of Mana will disappear.*
*Warning: If the pool disappears, placing you into Mana exhaustion, your Mana recovery is halved for a duration of 5 minutes.*

I really liked the thought of that one, except for the Mana exhaustion, and how would I know how much excess was where? There were a lot of what ifs for increasing my Mana pool, and it didn't appear at all reliable.

### Mana Projectile

*You have enough finesse with and understanding of Mana to form small projectiles that can pierce your target and siphon Mana from them to you, while causing minimal damage.*

*Caution: High-powered mages will resist the Mana projectile while in its infancy.*

*Warning: High-powered Mages won't take kindly to your attempts to steal their Mana.*

While it sounded like fun, it didn't really ring like a main Perk to me. Maybe there was more it wasn't telling me, but again, I needed something that would help me survive, maybe even grow with me.

Mana Projectile really sounded like a Skill I might be able to learn or buy or something in the future.

In the end, I came across one that I thought was most suitable.

### Mana Cloak

*This is a passive ability that covers your body with a thin layer of ambient Mana, allowing your ability to sense surrounding Mana surges and mutations with greater accuracy. Works well in conjunction with Mana Attunement. Can serve as a secondary Mana pool (100) if necessary. Full charge requires 2 hours of ambient Mana flow.*

*Note: This Cloak may be modified by the user and have a percentage of Mana regeneration from the user applied to it. The Cloak will upgrade accordingly.*

Mana Cloak it was, then. If there was one thing I'd learned from the day's misadventures outside, it was that I could and would run out of Mana, and it was vital to have more on hand in a pinch that I could count on.

I was tired. Wisp and Dog made the warm bed even more welcome. Despite it all, my brain was too wired to sleep. Magpies on acid, cockroaches mutated with numerous other things, rats feeding on decaying corpses in crashed cars.

It was like the setting for a post-apocalyptic game where I should be climbing out of some cryogenic bunker trying to find the baby they stole from me. Those games didn't really hit up the realism, though—the smells, the sadness.

Rolling over, I curled an arm around Wisp protectively. A few hours of sleep and we needed to tackle the new day. Expand our search circle, find more survivors, create a stronghold we could rely on.

Tomorrow.

Except not all of us woke up the next day.

Kylie's mum didn't make it. I never knew her name; hell, I hadn't even searched for her purse. But Dale greeted me in the dawning light, bags under his eyes. I think he'd thought if he could save her, if he could just help someone else survive, maybe he'd make up for his failure to save his own family.

"You tried." I patted his shoulder, unsure of what to do to make him feel better.

If we hadn't come along that route, if we'd taken a different approach, maybe neither of them would have survived. He didn't need other facts to make him feel better though. So I simply patted his shoulder again and hoped it was enough to know the rest of us were still here.

"I know. I just wish I could figure out why she died, what that slime around her and in the wound was. The System actively tried to heal her. I could see it. But it was two steps forward and three steps back." He frowned, like he was already trying to figure out what it was again. "No machines working, hell, no machines here for me to test with. It had to be a poison, something I couldn't treat by just seeing."

Words failed me again. Plants were so much easier than humans. Patting Dale's shoulder seemed to help a bit. The tension in them lessened.

Jason, the jealous rugby linebacker, came running in from where I thought he'd been on watch overnight. Some of the "tougher" crowd we'd wrangled yesterday took it upon themselves to stand watch. Wasn't a bad idea. I was glad Mike had stepped up to take charge. He'd ended up splitting them into groups and sending them off to guard entrances.

"There are people coming. Like maybe a dozen?"

Mike was out of breath, and I realized we needed to get a training regimen started. Unfit people couldn't outrun or outlast predators. Or did this Stamina thing change too? Did we just need to have people put more points into Stamina and they'd magically get better? Or could we do both and get the best results?

I really wanted a cheat sheet. Or a manual. Or a helpful voice from the heavens.

Something.

Dale and I looked at each other. It was bloody early morning right now, so these people must have traveled through the night. Might have come from the group of neighboring houses and apartments we hadn't got to yet.

"You're sure they're human?" Evelyn asked, and I jumped slightly, not having noticed her creep up next to me.

Jason gave her an odd look, stubborn, sort of vacant. "Why wouldn't they . . . oh."

He realized what she meant, and he paled. I didn't think Jason was equipped for this new world.

"Garden City is an easy and logical destination for anyone who lives close to here. Shops with non-perishable goods, clothing, bedding, crammed full of things we need to survive for a while. Not to mention it's huge and protected from the elements. Don't be so shocked that others would head here." I moved forward, determined to make my way out to greet whoever our visitors were. "Coming with me?"

Dale and Evelyn moved to my side, and Jason joined us on the way back. Cherry's absence surprised me since they'd been joined at the hip before the kerfuffle yesterday.

I felt like I was playing some sort of part, but I didn't know my lines. I should probably see if I could hand over part of the burden for this town in the making right now. Couldn't I at least share this newfound responsibility?

Then again, would I trust someone else with the power over my kids' lives?

Jason was right. There were people approaching the shopping center. They were walking slowly, and from what I could see, some of them were limping. I upped his assessment to about sixteen people. There were two kids in the group being carried on their parents' backs.

My apocalyptic mum senses kicked in.

Evelyn and I pushed out into the dawning light. She held her bow loosely in her hand, trying to make it seem less threatening, but I got the impression she wanted them to know that we did have weapons if they made us use them.

Good call.

It was the same reason my bat was within easy reaching distance, even if it was hidden behind the entrance pillars.

I glanced at the trees while we waited, noticing braids of Mana winding their way up the trunks which seemed thicker, and not quite as gum-tree-like as they'd been yesterday. Gradual morphing. The eagerness to investigate tickled at the back of my mind.

"Stop for a moment, please," I called out in the crisp morning clearly, and waited as they slowed and did so. "What you lot looking for, then?"

This time my tone was softer. The kids couldn't have been older than Wisp, and the rest of them looked pretty beat up.

"We're just trying to find other people."

A lady, maybe a few years younger than me stepped forward. Her dark hair was full of debris and dust, and her clothes were torn in places where skin had since been healed by the System.

"Our apartment block didn't seem too bad a place to hole up. We looked out for one another, like. Neighborly and all. We were all fine in there until last night."

The man who spoke seemed skittish, and his gaze flickered around as if he was searching for something dangerous. He was older, maybe already in his forties, a peppering of grey visible through his light brown dusted hair.

"What happened last night?" Evelyn asked, her tone warm, like she was coaxing them to trust her.

The first woman spoke up. "Monster attack, I think. I mean, the floor ruptured, and there were screams and something very tentacle-like reached through the hole and grabbed onto some of us trying to flee. We could hear the . . . crunch of bones." She gestured to the limpers behind them. "We tried to save them but could only manage a few. Regrowing chunks of leg takes a bit."

There was a catch to her throat, and for a moment I thought she was going to break down in fits of sobbing laughter. But the woman recovered and righted herself.

"No one else made it out of our complex. Then we headed here, hoping we might find others." She was drained, and her voice held little hope by the time she was done.

"Come inside. For now, it's mostly safe in here." I ushered them in with us, my eyes scanning the horizon for signs of anything untoward, for that tentacle monster she described.

Anime, eat your heart out. We were living it.

As I turned to go inside, I caught a whiff that made me gag. The bodies in the cars had definitely begun to rot over the last eighteen hours. This was going to get a lot worse before it got any better.

Names all flowed into one another, and I forgot them as soon as they told me. Apparently, I had an upper limit of identification monikers in my brain, and those slots had already been taken by the people we'd previously added to our group.

Sixteen survivors left out of an apartment block with twenty units. One of them mentioned families, and the kids didn't have surviving parents, but those who'd carried them had known them. They estimated they'd lost about thirty-odd people. It was such a minuscule amount of death in such a vast and encompassing massacre. Yet it saddened me, angered me.

"Dr. Kira?"

I was only used to being called by my title while at work, so it took me a second to give my full attention.

"Kira. Kira is fine," I muttered as I faced the worn-out woman who'd spoken up when we first greeted them.

Jana, I think was her name. Her dark hair was free of debris now, pulled back into a ponytail. Her skin held a deep bronze tone, and I couldn't quite place her ethnicity and didn't want to be insensitive.

"I'll take care of the children. If you reckon that'll help. I'm a . . ." Jana paused, and I could see her fighting with a rising sense of panic, but she knuckled down and kicked it in the 'nads, and voilà, she was back with me. "I teach grade three. Have been in primary schools since I graduated, so I'll be fine with taking care of them for now."

I nodded, grateful that someone else was thinking about the kids for a change, because I don't think I had it in me to mother more than my own. Kylie would be needing guidance, too. "You realize these kids are too young to pick their Classes and Perks themselves, right? The System will require a guardian to take them over, I think. Hell, I'm not even sure they'll have access to the Perks anymore. We'll have to look into that. I'm pretty sure the System doesn't care about shit like that."

Jana seemed shocked by my words, and I hadn't meant to say the latter out loud, but I was pushing down my own panic about our predicament. There was so much more to worry about than just the kids. The bodies outside were going to be ripe very soon. I guess we were fortunate that we were heading into winter and weren't smack bang in the middle of summer. Forty-odd degrees Celsius would have made this just that much worse.

I took a breath, trying not to get ahead of myself. "Thank you for offering. I'll take you up on that. Making sure the kids are okay is important."

Jana seemed relieved. She hesitated, but then words tumbled out of her. "I know I picked my Class first thing. It felt like the right thing to do. Not that Knowledge Seeker is going to help much in the long run, but I figure it'll help with kids. The flashing in front of my eyes was being pretty insistent. If people didn't pick a Class, something went wrong."

"Yeah. It wasn't subtle, was it?" I laughed. Seriously, laughing was a lot easier than crying.

"No, ma'am." She laughed with me; maybe she knew what I meant even if I cringed at her honorific for me.

"Just Kira, please?"

Jana nodded, her face solemn once again. "I'll get that nice lad Barry to help me set up one of the restaurants as an interim place for me to keep the kids out of the adults' hair. Don't you worry. We can do this."

She left, going back to the group of kids she was gathering around Barry.

Village it was, then.

That made me breathe a little easier.

"Mum!" Wisp flew toward me and jumped into my arms, giving me a massive bear hug as Dog the miniature golden pony doodle stood at my hip like he was guarding both of us. I wasn't entirely sure why he'd attached himself to us, but I'd bet it was mostly because Wisp loved dogs, and I hadn't killed him on sight. Got to take the wins you can in this situation, even as a dog.

"Hey . . . why the greeting?" She usually missed me. Still at that age where Mum didn't embarrass her, but this was a little clingier than usual. Although I guess we were also experiencing an apocalypse, so there was that.

She shrugged and then squirmed to be let down. "More people, huh? Do you . . . do you think the rest of our family is okay? Like, you know, not just Dad?"

There was a slight hitch to her voice, and I knew she was putting on a brave face. She worried about everyone she loved, constantly. Her dad, my brother, her grandparents. I couldn't lie to her, but since I didn't have irrefutable proof that they were dead, I was going to let her go with hope. Bloody oath, we could all use some of it right now.

"I'm sure they are doing their best, just like us." I pulled her to me and gave her a fierce squeeze, checking her over to make sure she had her Bracer of Protection on.

"It's fine, it's fine. I promise. I'm taking it seriously." Her gaze wandered over to where Kylie stood listening to some of the other kids, while Jana organized them all.

My kid seemed thoughtful. She'd seen death close up now. I hugged her closer.

"I'm always here, love," I said quietly, giving her one more squeeze before she took off, Dog trotting easily behind her. Made me wish I could talk to animals.

Right now, though, I needed to talk to people. After our new additions had showers, we'd have to assess them, figure out just where they belonged in this new world, drag them out of denial, and hope they could help us fill this place up. We were at one hundred and twenty . . . no, one hundred and eighty-seven now. Almost twenty percent of the way there. We still had some days to do this.

I glanced around for Dale and couldn't see where he'd gone off to. The center was large. When trying to find someone, way *too* large. I almost took Dog with me and considered having him find Dale, but I didn't think the creature really cared for me. He shared a mutual over-protectiveness for my daughter. Keeping that truce was important.

"He's in the food court." Red was at my elbow so suddenly, I gasped.

"Don't do that," I snapped, and he returned a grin like he was glad he'd managed to rattle me.

The expression was gone in a flash—Red wasn't one to hold onto awkward situations. But it was nice to see him growing into his own now that he had a food plan of sorts.

That was so getting payback when I didn't have to worry about decomposing corpses potentially spreading disease and feeding mutated everything so much that they morphed beyond belief. I had no particular desire to see how big and fat the rodent population around here was getting off the recently dead.

"We need to figure out better food and supplies rationing when we can grab you for a moment," Red called after me as I headed into the food court to search for our one medic and hope he had some good news for me.

The upper floor food court probably sat around one hundred and fifty people. It was mostly full right now. Though Jana had just led the children off to one of the smaller restaurants near the courtyard so the thirty-or-so kids in the group were out of here.

Tables and chairs pulled into groups so people who knew each other could chat. Barry and Jules moved around through them, marking down names and talking to gatherings of people. Everyone seemed so tired, not that I could blame them. But Jules was good with people.

Barry too. Each of them had this ready manner about them. Barry was more boisterous, his manner disarming and friendly. People responded to him. Jules was just sweet and obviously caring. Her Class was perfect for her. I breathed in a sigh of relief, glad that we had people who could put others at ease.

Ray stood talking to Red over at what had been KFC with a couple of men I vaguely recognized.

They appeared to be discussing food, and I wasn't sure if it was going well, given all the hand gesturing.

I found Dale over near the restrooms, almost pointedly ignoring the discussion between Ray and Red.

"Are you hiding?" I asked.

He shook his head. "Not really, just trying to make sense of all this and figure out what to do."

Evelyn tapped me on the shoulder and stood, panting slightly next to me. "Sorry I bailed. I only have so many spoons for other human beings. Probably aliens too."

I could relate. Maybe I could cultivate and figure out the newly minted, partially alien plant life as it evolved and make a garden I could relax in.

I sighed and dragged myself into a seat just over from where Dale stood. He was drinking a can of soft drink, sipping it like it was the world's finest warm beverage.

"Either of you have a clue how we dispose of the sheer multitude of corpses that are starting to decay out there? It's really pongy out there—already drifting over to us. Baking in metal vehicles all day isn't doing any of that any good. And if we're not careful, disease will kill us before the aliens can manage it."

Dale sighed and put down his can. "Well, aren't you just a ray of fucking sunshine."

Evelyn snorted. Her button nose twitched like a rabbit's, and her pale blue eyes lit up with mischief.

I answered before she could chime in with something unflattering that I knew was sitting on her tongue. "Yes, yes I am. A ray of in-your-face-with-our-new-reality sunshine."

Dale sighed, and I could sympathize. I didn't want to go through any of this either. I just wanted to close my eyes and wake up from this nightmare, but considering I'd actually gotten several hours of sleep since this all started, I was certain waking up wasn't about to change anything. Survival, however, might.

"Those bodies out there are well into day three. They're going to be bloating and foaming . . . it's not going to be pretty." Dale shook his head and pushed his chair back, taking one last swig of cola before crunching the can. "I've dealt with pileups before, though not this long after the fact. Damn, am I glad Mike stepped up and took on organizing security."

"Yeah." Evelyn put her boots up on the table in front of her. "Perks of having worked security at the convention center, I guess. We'll need to get together soon enough and make sure we're collaborating properly. But I think we're lucky we have a few people who've transitioned over well."

Dale sighed. "Speaking of, I'll go see if we've got any other medical staff or other EMTs out there. I think Barry and Jules were making a list of everyone's pre-apocalypse occupations."

"I think there's a scrubs shop somewhere in here too," Evelyn added helpfully as she kept her butt firmly in her chair, refusing to move.

"Gee. Thanks for that contribution." Dale rolled his eyes. "This would be much easier if we had operational vehicles. Bicycles don't really count when we're trying to cart dead bodies."

Evelyn brightened up. "Hey, don't some of the stores have those weird little tent-hitch things for kids? So they can sit while you pedal? It would at least be something, right? Or else the department store should have those trolleys to place flat stuff on."

Dale frowned like he was trying to work out logistics in his head. "Maybe something we can use, or those loading bay hand-powered forklift things."

"Pallet Jacks." Evelyn interrupted.

Dale's frown disappeared and a smile escaped him. "Well. Let's get operation 'find a way to get rid of decomposing bodies' going."

I cringed at the name even if it was accurate, but at least I had some way to help. "And I'll go talk to our little tech geniuses in the making about how they can gather enough Mana to power a vehicle or refrigeration once they figure out how to wire them accordingly."

At least we had a plan. Sort of.

# Chapter Fifteen:
# Tech

## 60 Hours Post-System Onset

I could smell the singed wiring before I reached the knick-knack shop where the techy kids currently resided. Naturally, if they were soldering, there'd be a bit of a whiff, but this smelled stronger than I'd come to anticipate from that sort of work. I guess magical heat was more potent than a soldering iron.

However, as I crossed over the play area near my favorite coffee shop, I noticed several folded tables set up so that the techies could have stations there. Small, Mana-battery-powered soldering irons and pointed molten fingers fueled their work. All six of those kids, girls and boys, had grimaces of pure concentration on their faces as they worked.

I took a brief look at their stats with Analyze for kicks and was suitably impressed.

Level 9, Level 7, and three Level 5s. Another of them was a 6, but whatever that Class was, I couldn't pronounce it.

The batteries they'd created weren't attractive, but from what I could tell by the subtle blue lines leading to them, they'd managed to attract ambient Mana to the actual devices to continue to refuel them, as it were. Sure, it appeared they were using more power than they were gaining, but I couldn't believe what they'd achieved in such a short time.

I preened with a bit of mum pride right about then.

There were two women standing next to them, making comments and pointing to things they were doing. It seemed like they were giving advice. Their faces were vaguely familiar, but I couldn't place their names.

Jackson saw me and put down his soldering iron before running to grab my hand and drag me over.

"Mum. This is so cool. We only just figured this out like thirty minutes ago. Chris and Sarah figured out how we could attract some ambient Mana. Sort of like a lightning rod but for Mana. And they are helping us tweak the battery chambers so they can hold more of a charge. We're trying to make a larger power source right now. Hoping to power more essential things. Maybe save some of the food."

His smile lit up the whole level for me. Chris and Sarah's names sounded familiar, but all those people were starting to blend together into one big lump in my head. Something to do with engineering, maybe? I wasn't this person. This was what I needed Kyle for. That twin was getting a piece of my mind if I ever tracked him down in this post-apocalyptic wilderness.

Give me plants, the environment, anything, and I was all in. Hell, I was good at it. I was great at studying shit. Still, it wasn't that I couldn't be sociable, it was that I just preferred not to be.

Things every parent gets over as soon as their kids start school. Extrovert mode engaged.

"Hey. I'm Kira, Jackson's mum." I held out my hand, and instead, Sarah pulled me into a bear hug.

Not my preference for people I'd just met, but a good long hug had been scientifically proven to have healing properties, so I wasn't opposed to them.

"We've heard so much about you," she said as she pulled back and held me at arms' length. She reminded me of those gorgeous fifties pinup models. Buxom, delightful, with sparkling black eyes and manic red hair. She shone. "Jackson loves on his mum so much!"

I raised an eyebrow in the direction of my son, but he refused to make eye contact, his only telltale sign that he heard her being the reddening of his cheeks. That was good to know.

"Yeah, well, he's mostly happy with me right now, so they should have been fairly good rumors." I grinned at her. She was probably about seven or eight years younger than me and full of a zest for life.

"I'm Chris, this chatterbox is Sarah." The woman next to the pinup model held out her hand, far more comfortable than a hug for a first meeting.

Chris was the complete opposite of Sarah. Her short blonde hair cascaded down the left side of her head while the right side was shaved.

Her pantsuit was on point, and her protectiveness of Sarah was obvious even from this brief encounter. Not that I'd blame her. Her partner seemed like a treasure.

I nodded like my son hadn't already given me their names. "You know a thing or two about power sources?"

She nodded, but it was Sarah who took over with her exuberant air. "Yes! We met while studying electrical engineering. I diverged into sustainable power models when I entered my post graduate work, and Chris has been working on a solar adaption longevity model. Or something."

She laughed, like she only sort of understood it, and I had to think she might be used to pretending not to be as smart as she was.

That was okay. I knew on a personal level how handy pretending to be stupid could be. "Wow. We lucked out."

And we had.

If these guys were experts, or had at least studied sustainable alternate power sources, the odds were they'd be able to rig something up and combine it with the System-sponsored Mana magic. After all, the sun hadn't gone anywhere. It was still up there, shining like a total dick to send all of those corpses out there into the bloating phase as soon as possible.

"We'd love to help." Chris looked around. "Since these guys seem to have chosen Classes specifically for this. And frankly . . . I wish I'd have met them before I chose mine. Though mine will help, their Techzard and similar Classes are just smart, considering the circumstances."

"Do you think we could get solar power to work again? Running it through a different infrastructure, of course." We were going to need working power sooner than later.

Australia, Brisbane in particular, wasn't known for its mild heat. It was lucky this apocalypse decided to drop by in April. At least we had winter to get through first.

Chris hesitated. "Probably, but this Mana stuff, the way this whole Dungeon World seems to be initiating and building itself? I think our tech will need total realignment. Can we do it? Yes, I think we can, but we need more people who know what they're doing. And we need to know how the System works with these things."

Sarah smiled and jumped in, hugging Chris's arm. "It'll work, but I do know a few student housing areas we could check out and see if any of the students made it? They might even be able to help."

"Great. I'll get you to see Evelyn. She'll be arranging search groups." Now all I had to do was tell Evelyn what I'd signed her up for.

I also needed to check several things on the plants inside Garden City and outside of it. Everything was changing, nothing was staying the same, and the sooner I could figure out how the molecular structure of the plants was actually being altered, the faster I'd be able to adapt our plants and ourselves to it.

Chris seemed determined to go off in a search group. I used Analyze to check out her stats and Class. What I found was mildly surprising.

*Chris(tina) James*

*HP: 190*

*MP:220*

*Level 5 Energy Manipulator*

I had no idea what that did, but Level 5 was a decent start, even if the mobs out there were about to hit double figures. As long as we went in groups and allowed for healing and sufficient damage—we'd be fine.

And oh my gods, I'd just thought of the mutated creatures as mobs. I was so blaming Evelyn for that.

I couldn't micromanage the groups. My Skill didn't let me split into fifteen people so I could keep an eye on everything. Thus, Evelyn was going to spearhead the scouting groups. I was sure she'd love that.

I gave Jackson a hug, which I don't think he even noticed, and briefly waved at the two newcomers before heading over to Evelyn. She didn't need me to go about search and rescue with her every day.

Barry was a hefty Fire Mage, oddly enough. Considering his jovial personality and how busy he was cataloguing people, he'd end up staying in the complex.

Jules and her way of putting people at ease was perfect for healing. Gemma's assassin ways lent the perfect juxtaposition, and those two went hand in hand.

Molly and Sange were the perfect Tank and Healer combo. So right there was another starter group. Sange had displayed a willingness to lead earlier with the magpie fiasco, even if they were monosyllabic and curt.

Then there was Mark the Swashbuckler and Tasha the Fighter-Mage. Yeah, Evelyn had plenty of backup to choose from.

Kids. Kids. I knew there was something I was forgetting. Wait. I had

Jana willing to watch the kids. How had I already forgotten that?

"You"—Evelyn spoke up, stopping me short on my trek specifically to find her—"do not seem to be happy."

I sighed. "That obvious? I don't think anyone is *actually* happy right now. It's just that I'm concerned about all of the shit we have to organize. There's no manual, no guidelines, nowhere to figure out what it is we're supposed to do. It's infuriating."

She looked at me, or through me. "The main thing is that you're not alone in this. Breathe, we'll get through it. Don't take on more than you can handle. Delegate."

"Ah yes. Delegate." I dropped eye contact. "Speaking of which . . ."

"No. No, I didn't mean to me." Evelyn sounded mildly panicked, although that might have just been for show. "What have you signed me up for?"

"I need you to put together search parties that can withstand some damage. We need more survivors to come here. We need people to make a town. We need the town so we can get money and proper defenses. We need to make sure people are looting their kills. I know the kids were, and our original group know how to, but I feel like I've totally lost track. We all have personal storage. Have you noticed how weird that shit is?"

The Ranger laughed. "Yes. Yes, I have. Fine. I'll do it. Start gathering supplies and people. Loot everything we kill. Got it. Anything else?"

I paused for a moment. "Don't die. I've known you like two days, but right now it feels like a whole other lifetime. Try to stay alive and come bitch to me about how much you wish you could just stay put and do your own stuff. Right now, even if it's just for a few days, this semblance of normalcy is helping."

She nodded solemnly. "You got that right. Ditto, too. I know you're probably going to do something of your own. Let me know when I can include you in my patrols."

"Will do." Not sure how she was so observant, but at least she was mostly leader material, even if it was reluctant.

Not alone. Right. Got it.

"I'm off, then. Got to go round up my troops after all." She winked before leaving.

I rolled my eyes as she walked away. With Chris and Sarah working on other options for power generation, Evelyn organizing our recon parties, and Dale working on a way to get rid of corpses that were about to bloat and exude disease, I could finally get down to what I needed more than anything.

To understand what it was we were dealing with. To understand why I was like the only person who could see those damned blue lines. To understand how we could make it help us survive.

Scouring the suburb of Upper Mt. Gravatt wasn't easy or for the unfit. Hilly as fuck, windy, and full of mutations and what apparently were new-to-this-world creatures. But it was okay, because for some reason I couldn't quite figure out, we were apparently all a mite stronger. Fitter. Nothing had been noticeable at first, but now I swear I had more stamina. The System wanted us to play its game, so I guess it slowly started rejuvenating our entire bodies.

I guess I'd noticed it before, but now that I'd ventured into the parking areas so I could inspect the foliage, well, now I could really tell. At this rate I could probably hike for days. Thanks, System.

It wasn't like I was walking into a wilderness. Trees and plants were located at strategic points around the complex. Maybe it was to give its name credence. Garden City, right? Couldn't have something with "garden" in its name without having some sort of plant life.

I felt sorry for the trees, encased in concrete, their roots yearning for soil above them and not unforgiving concrete and bitumen. Still, we didn't lose leaves in this part of Australia. Brisbane was green all year round. It meant the leaves I could gather from the ground were sometimes fresh, and never autumnified.

My plan was to walk through the row of trees and take bark samples, earth samples, hell, any samples I could find. Then I'd make my way around to the courtyard where there was more greenery. The restaurants there had planters and could give me totally different samples from the gum trees out here.

Eerily silent. I couldn't hear any birds near me, not in the direct vicinity anyway. They were outside of the center's radius, might even have been scared off by yesterday's magpie fight.

Was that yesterday? I'd lost track of most of the days, only sort of resetting myself at night when our next day technically began at eleven.

The silence, even though the sun was up and beating down on me, even though the wind picked up now and then, whipping my hair around my face as if it totally ignored my ponytail. The silence just felt like the System was waiting.

And I had no idea for what.

I gathered the rest of my samples into the one kit I'd brought with me when we fled the university campus. No one was going on that hike after all. And I needed to know, to figure out something. Scientifically, there had to be a reason, method . . . anything.

The courtyard was empty too. No one sitting down and enjoying the outside in comfort. I could smell the rotten food coming from the multiple restaurants. But the vegetation at least, it smelled alive.

The restaurants would all have shut by the time the System intruded, but I did know a few staff who had been going over inventory when it hit. They were inside now. I wonder if the other workers survived.

Several leaves, and some more soil samples, and the silence got to me. I'd only been outside a couple of hours, but I needed to get back inside, under cover, where the Safe Zone we had felt, well, safer.

After my precarious trek outside to gather samples from trees and plants, I came inside to study them in what had once been a medical clinic downstairs in the complex and almost literally ran into Mike.

"Shit. Sorry." I was in full on plant mode and not really paying attention.

Mike laughed. He had that good-natured, grown-up vibe about him, but it still sounded strained enough that I perked up. Maybe it was Diviner activating, or maybe I was just less self-absorbed than I'd thought.

"Everything okay?"

He hesitated and frowned. "Trying to nail down security for something this big when we don't have any way to communicate with each other apart from sending runners? It's just a lot."

And it was a lot that I'd just haphazardly dumped in his lap. "Sorry. I reckon that's a lot of shit I lumped on you."

Mike held up his hands. "No. That's not what I meant at all. I've dealt with situations like this, where I need to have a lot done in a small amount of time. But that's not the problem—the problem is communication right now."

"Scooters? Could they grab scooters from Big W or maybe Kmart and just use those to speed up traversing the halls?" I mean, Jackson loved his damn scooter and had always begged for an electric one. Surely even without power they'd be faster than running.

Mike blinked at me and laughed again, his broad shoulders shaking. It was a loud sound and echoed through the empty lower level of the center. "Did not think of that, but it makes perfect sense. I just wasn't thinking outside of the walkie-talkie." He winked at me.

"Glad to help." I glanced down at all the stuff in my arms. "Now, if there's nothing else, I have to go check some things."

He eyed the pile of dirt and samples and didn't say a word about them. "We'll send someone for you if we need you. On a scooter."

The last was punctuated with a grin as he turned back the way he'd come. Probably heading to see if he could find a scooter to use.

If they needed me? Why on Earth would they need me? Then again, technically, this had all been my idea.

I moved to the small lab area. It was clear the Mana seeped into our bodies, correcting what was broken, repairing what was injured. Even if it happened years ago. In a way I felt younger even, rejuvenated. Did it expand our lifeline?

It made me wish I wasn't just a plant specialist. Where was my twin when I needed him to answer my bloody questions? He understood the human body like I did my plants. I was sure if we worked together, we could figure out how the System really affected the human body.

If he'd survived.

I shook my head in denial, forcing the tightness in my chest away. Of course he had. The bastard was too damn stubborn not to.

Two and a half days of this shit, and I was certain of one thing. It was going to get more difficult before it got easier. Figuring out how it worked, how Mana interacted with everything on this planet, meant we'd be able to harness the power more efficiently.

It had to.

I put my head down and got to work on all my samples. None of the results were making sense, and I wasn't entirely sure what I'd expected it to do, but each new test was just more flummoxing than the last. I wasn't even sure how long I'd been at this, but I did know I knew less now than I thought I did.

Sitting back, I pushed dirt-covered hands through my hair, wondering idly how long it would take for the plumbing to back up and how we could fix it before we had literal shit everywhere.

"You done?" Evelyn surprised me again. She was getting good at that.

I offered a tight smile in reply as I continued to concentrate on studying the stalk in front of me. Even the veins in the leaves of it were morphing, beginning mutations, making it less Earth-like and more System-affected.

I was as done as I was going to get without some good equipment, and maybe a manual on what the System did to convert our wildlife. Could have kicked myself for not thinking to bring something with me from the lab. Then again, the blue screens were freaking me out when they appeared.

"Yeah. Definitely done for now." What a frustrating waste of my entire afternoon.

"Good. You need to eat. Red says he hasn't seen you eat all day."

I blinked at her. "What time is it?"

"Night. It's nighttime."

Shit. I'd forgotten my kids for hours. At the first sign of panic entering my system, I had to clamp down. The System had me as their guardian. I got a strange feeling I would know if something happened to them.

"Food, then." I nodded, standing up and brushing myself off while reaching for a gang of wipes to sort out the dirt on my hands.

"What were you doing?" Evelyn asked as we walked back to our main gathering place upstairs.

"Just trying to make sense of what the System is doing to our world."

"Any answers?"

I laughed. "Nope. More questions."

"Perfect."

Evelyn was easy to walk next to. Not a lot of people got the companionable silence thing.

Barry walked up to me before we got past the tech kids' campout.

"There you are!" He waved from a shop away, his face bright and smiling.

I wondered how he did that all the time.

"Hey there." I acknowledged him, unable to keep from grinning in return.

"We have a lot of great people." His eagerness was contagious. "Mike has enough for security for now. Red has heaps of help with the food aspect. We even have a couple of nurses who can help Dale."

Ah, there it was. The hesitation.

"What is it, Barry?" I asked.

"Well, we just don't seem to have as many adventure Classes as I thought we would. Granted, we've only got like two hundred and thirty people, and a lot of them just got allocated . . ." He paused, looking at me. "What?"

"When did we hit that many people?"

Evelyn laughed. "You were in your dungeon all afternoon. We had two successful retrieving groups."

She preened a little, deservedly.

"Right. Ripper." I was shocked, and somehow oddly excited. "Well, maybe get someone to help you with the intakes, Barry. Someone who can't set shit on fire?"

He grinned. "Excellent. I was hoping you'd say that. I really want to go blow shit up."

Wisp ran up and barreled into me. "Mum!"

"I'm talking." She piped down, momentarily contrite, and I turned back to Barry. "Go get some Levels, help us get more people in. Just check on shit at night."

He nodded, his face still full of joy, and headed back the way he'd come. Polar opposite to his brother, but I couldn't imagine this small settlement without Red and Barry. I also didn't envy Red having to ration supplies.

"What's up, buttercup?" I asked her, raising her to sit on my hip and Dog followed our little procession as we crossed into the food court.

"I want to level too." She pouted.

"You can't level yet. You've still got growing to do." I hugged her tight and put her down as Red came up to me, momentarily met my eyes with a glare, and handed me a plate of food.

Damn it. I was starving.

"But I want to."

"You literally cannot. The System won't let *me* let you take a Class. So just stay alive and grow in here, okay?"

She looked at me for a good long minute, long enough for me to eat half of one sandwich. "Okay, but I get to keep Dog with me."

I nodded, my mouth full. That had never been a question. Somehow satisfied, she gave me a huge hug and ran off to where I could see Jackson and Darren deep in conversation.

"Tomorrow we ride at dawn!"

"What?" I almost choked at Evelyn's comment.

She laughed. "Tomorrow, we take separate groups out and start scouring for more survivors. It's been too long. We have to find more people."

"Tomorrow it is, then." I scarfed down the rest of my food, skulled a bottle of water, and stood up. "Sleep, gear up, kill shit, find survivors, level."

Evelyn nodded and I flashed her all a tight grin.

Kill shit. Level up. Learn more. Understand the new world. Survive.

That didn't sound too hard, right?

# Chapter Sixteen:
# Rescuing

## 4 Days, 9 Hours Post-System Onset

Sticky, black blood spattered me in the face.

Luckily, my reflexes were fast enough that I'd closed my eyes and mouth as its bludgeoned body exploded. At least I didn't get any of its innards in my insides. These globs looked entirely foreign and almost blended in with the bitumen and concrete of the streets around us.

The gelatinous globs were blob-like and reminded me of most creatures in any random game's starter zones. Except here, in what was now real life, blubber hid razor-like talons or feet. Hell, maybe they were toenails. All I knew was they hurt like buggery.

Here, in the suburban streets of MacGregor, just behind Garden City, these blobs had made their homes. Houses and duplexes, fenced yards and whatnot, these little buggers appeared to like this type of environment.

At least that's what we gathered over the last twenty-four hours of trying to find survivors.

Three more blobs died to our fantastically coordinated teamwork. My sarcasm was wasted on my inner monologue.

Molly and Sange were excellent at said teamwork though. The rest of us needed practice.

A loud screech attempted to explode my ear drums. I clutched my head, trying to drown it out, glancing up as a massive shadow passed over us. At first, I couldn't comprehend what I saw. It was huge and had wings, maybe feathers, but definitely a large beak. Probably reinforced if the effect Mana had on magpies was anything to go by. Yet it looked more like the dragons of make believe than a bird.

Even if it was black and white, like a magpie. Yeah, that's right, System. Cross a magpie with a dragon and let's doom the entire universe. Great plan there, I reckon.

Wait. Were dragons real? Fire dragons? Shadow dragons? Ice dragons? Maybe magpie-dragons weren't so bad.

Nah. They were worse.

"Is that—" Ray moved a little closer while my brain stuttered. "Is that a magpie dragon?"

The incredulity in his tone was palpable, and so in tune with what I'd thought that it was eerie.

"Apparently." Molly motioned along the street with her sword. I still wanted to know where it came from, damn it. I had to remember to ask her when I had time. "Those blob things have retreated. Maybe we're stupid not to."

"I don't think it sees us?" Jackson sounded unsure.

He was trying to be an adult, but he was still a kid. My kid. Shit.

I pulled him in with a light squeeze and let go, trying not to make a big deal of it. Teenagers could make big deals of everything. This time I lucked out. I actually got a grateful smile. Score one to me for still being a cool mum.

The Magon, as I'd dubbed it, kept flying to wherever it was headed, so at least it hadn't noticed us, or didn't consider us a worthy snack. I was okay with either of those. Breathing a sigh of relief, I spoke up.

"Let's see if we can find any other survivors while those damned globs aren't being a nuisance."

The group gave hasty nods, quickly looting the remnants—and ugh, sticking fingers into mush was no fun—before we were ready.

We moved through the streets. Eerily enough, back here, beyond the wreck that was Logan Road, it barely looked like the world had been touched.

MacGregor's streets seemed sleepy, like they would have been in the wee hours of any morning. Granted, it was mid-morning now, but still.

Houses were mostly upright, cars parked on the street like people had just returned from work. No crashes in sight. Birds I didn't want to look up at in case they were mutant versions still tweeted in the trees. If it wasn't for the presence of the globs and the occasional infected cat or dog that came out to attack us, I'd wonder if it had all been a nightmare.

Having to kill things every dozen or so steps disabused us of that notion at least.

There wasn't any sort of cooperation between the mutated creatures here. Perhaps they didn't band together to feed. Maybe their original temperaments had been more docile than our previous encounters.

Or. The other option.

You know, that one where everything is lulling you into a false sense of security so they can jump you at the last possible moment? Yeah. Should have gone with that one from the start.

Well-maintained hedges, brick fences, preserved Australian houses. Some two story with the underneath mostly open for flow of air, sometimes closed in with wooden paneling that still allowed the air to flow. Our tin roofs that never let you miss a downpour.

Not that you wanted to. Australia was one of the driest places on Earth.

Yep, this was a nice little neighborhood, except for the globs and mutated pets. Not another human in sight, just snarling dog- and cat-like creatures pushing in on us, shepherded by strange globs with their razor-like appendages.

Doone Street was proving to be less friendly than I'd anticipated. Then again, I'd almost face them than a white, suburban-football-mum late for dance class behind the wheel of an oversized petrol-machine.

But you know, to each their own.

Back to back in circular formation, Darren next to Dale, Jackson next to me, we maneuvered back the way we'd come. With Molly and Sange taking the front, Ray and I the rear, and everyone else in between. The Healer and Tank duo plowed through steadily and I made sure our rear was protected by throwing up the occasional Earth Barricade, worriedly gazing at my Mana consumption as we moved.

The dogs were the worst, and even though we could see they'd once been pets, four days in this Mana-active environment and they'd become something else. Something bigger, something nastier, something more savage. We had to take them out, and I couldn't bear to look at their broken bodies.

Memories of my childhood dog Lady lying broken on the sidewalk after being hit by a car tried to choke me. I had to swipe at my eyes once in a while, as the damn emotions threatened to take over.

I noticed I wasn't the only one. Molly teared up too but roared through her pain, taking it out on all the blobs in her path. Therapeutic.

A coordinated attack, with multiple targets coming at us, was the last thing I wanted, but I should have suspected it. They were pups, after all. A half-dozen of them snuck in low, using hedges and parked cars, stalking us before they attacked us all at once.

Great. Apparently, Mana gave them strategic brains too.

I cast, pulling out Earth Barricade and lengthening it. Bringing it up higher, but that only stopped a couple of our attackers. Using it as an offensive Skill required exact timing and wasn't easy. As it was, the barrier only completely deterred two of the creatures and forced them to go around the long way. I almost wished they'd jump—perhaps I could try the decapitation thing again.

Jackson and Dale tapped into their projectile spells, aiming at two globs that leapt at them from the sides. Their aim was precise, catching the two creatures mid-jump, sending them sprawling to the ground, legs scrambling as they shook off the shock. Not dead, only wounded.

Molly had three of them jump her at once from the front. She wielded her shield with aplomb, blocking one with the top, the others grabbing at an arm and leg, savaging it. Sange and Dale were on healing duty and made short work of her injuries, while Ray ice bolted the crap out of the creatures as they hung on. The one gripping her arm pulled away, allowing her to lay the smack down.

Then, I no longer had time to worry about the others.

Snarling came from my rear left, and I turned around in what felt like slow motion. I watched whatever that little fucker had once been launch itself in my direction. It was furry but looked like a glob, and its claws were razor sharp, like somewhere along the line it had become one with one of those alien things.

I raised my hand but knew it was too slow to fend off the little shit, and I could tell this one was going to hurt. Except it didn't.

It exploded in a blast of fur, goo, and guts that drenched not only me, but Ray and Jackson as well. The rest of what was left of it gave into gravity and splashed onto the ground at my feet, revealing a young woman standing behind it, her hand outstretched in our direction. She couldn't have been over twenty, and she was shaking like we had a hurricane I couldn't see.

The scent of singed whatever-the-creature-was reached my nostrils, and I scrunched my nose.

Fire. The girl used fire.

She looked up at me with a sigh of relief, and I belatedly realized she wasn't the only one. There'd been a fight going on outside our group that I'd totally missed, so caught up in keeping our group safe that I was. It made me a horrible fighter—but then again, I had like four days' worth of experience.

All the houses around us had people cautiously creeping out of them as well as those who'd come to our aid. Families who'd survived, who'd kept themselves safe and quiet in their houses, terrified behind their wooden or brick walls.

They'd come out to help.

Maybe the human race did have a hope in hell after all.

We brought back sixty-odd people with our party that night. Nothing bothered us on the way. Not with that much force on hand. We weren't the only group, either. Over a hundred people were found that afternoon. But in the scope of what we'd lost, it felt like we were holding onto ghosts.

Five nights had passed since the world stopped, since the System invaded us. Those five nights became a blur of organization, fighting, more organization and talking and even more fighting. Every day, more monsters, higher-Level monsters kept appearing, and we had to sweep further and further out from our Safe Zone.

Five nights and if you asked me what had happened on any one of them, all I could tell you was that I needed more coffee and to stop seeing the dead bodies behind my eyes. To stop smelling the death everywhere.

Now, I stood looking out at the carpark as the sun crested the horizon on our sixth day, while Evelyn gathered the troops behind me. All our most experienced people. All of twenty. Well, almost. I refused to let anyone under eighteen come anymore. Let's just say Jackson was glowering at me from a non-huggable distance. Cool mum status? Plummeting.

I had to. Right?

I preferred to be hated and overprotective than to outlive my child.

Red, in his quiet, knowledgeable way organized the foragers. We had a surprisingly large number of people who'd had backyard produce bins. We gathered food from houses that we passed, any sorts of fresh produce they might have in their gardens.

Our foragers slunk behind our fighters, like stealthy little thieves stealing potential sustenance.

Others were sent by Mike to find weapons of any sort, sweeping deserted residences and other shops—only after our fighters had cleared the areas. Any monsters they found there would be low in Levels and easy to kill.

From cricket bats to crossbows, and anything else they could find that might help us defend our positions. Our sports stores had given us a fantastic head start on an arsenal, but they weren't going to last forever. Mike thought ahead in ways I hadn't contemplated.

Barry, Jules, and Ray worked harmoniously to welcome and divide up all the newcomers. The jovial Fire Mage was always a friend to everyone, while Jules was sweetness personified. And Ray had just the right amount of humility to overlay the overconfidence he suffered from.

And still, I thought we were growing too fast, yet not fast enough.

I checked out the quest progress.

*Quest Progress: Gather Survivors*
*Survivors Gathered: 402/1000*

It wasn't enough. Five days gone. We'd never make it at this rate.
Shit.

The kids at least managed to level a good chunk when combining their crafting and gathering adventures outside, but I'd stopped those yesterday when one of our newer members got injured. Jackson wasn't happy with me. He was sitting at Level 12 and full of resentment. But we'd already lost eighteen people.

Eighteen people would have put us at 420. We needed every one of them. So we had to hedge our bets and do what we could to keep the kids safe. Humanity as a species needed our youth to survive. Maybe that was thinking too much like a biologist.

"Mum?" Wisp gave me a hug, pulling me out of the thoughts. "Do you want to take the bracer with you today? I'm not leaving the Safe Zone, and you might be able to use it more. It might save you?"

Damn it. I didn't want to cry. She was right. It could help me. Even if it wasn't the strongest thing in the world, that much protection could make the difference if it came to it. But what if something happened here? We weren't a real Safe Zone. This wasn't a town yet. Monsters might not be able to spawn, but they could still force their way in if they were determined enough. There was nothing in place that promised me my kids would survive while I was out there except my own wishful thinking.

I'd never forgive myself if something happened.

"Hey, it's yours. It's your Perk, and we got it to protect you," I started to say, but she stood back, giving me that "I'm not a kid anymore" look.

"Just like doing a back tuck in my floor routine was probably not a good idea for my safety, right?" She crossed her arms and locked eyes with me.

She had a point. This was totally a parent thing.

"Look. Please take it. Or else I'll worry about you so much I probably won't even be able to play." Her expression was solemn, but I could see from the way her eyes twinkled that she'd definitely be able to play.

I guess during all of this, having an eight-year-old who could still be a kid, even if just for a little while, was a bonus.

"Fine. I'll take it with me." I took it from her and snapped it onto my wrist with a sigh. "There, happy?"

"Nope. But I'm not as worried now."

She leaned in and gave me one of the tightest hugs I'd ever gotten from her. All that gymnast strength in one. Then she darted off to her brother. Maybe they'd both cooked the bracer thing up. But at least they were caring kids.

That was a good mum moment, right?

At least Jana was there to take care of the smaller kids.

"Okay." Evelyn cleared her throat next to me, pulling me out of my thoughts. "Everyone here? We leave in about ten minutes. I want to go over a few things first."

I glanced around at our makeshift vehicles. Bicycles and tricycles. The big tricycles. All human powered. At least it gave us a way to cover more ground together, especially now that we had to range much further out to find people.

Molly and Sange were coming with us, as well as Mark and Tasha. Gemma and Jules, Barry, not Red. He stayed here and oversaw all the rations and available food to feed us all. Plus, flinging capsicum wasn't exactly the best offensive Skill unless your opponent rubbed their eyes.

He'd managed to jimmy a couple of gas stoves into working properly, and the food had been good since the day before. I didn't envy him the amount of wasted food in those freezers he needed to dispose of, though. The stench would start to leak through those insulated doors soon enough.

Olfactory senses were overrated in the time of apocalypses . . . apocalypsi? Whatever. Don't think a plural was necessary anyway.

I glanced at the other people, all of them grouped up in tight little parties that started to stabilize already. Fighting and getting wounded and sometimes dying together seemed to have a bonding effect.

I recognized most of them. Ray from our first outing. A couple from the stories that had been told, late at night.

Az, who'd walked into a hoarder's house, only to be engulfed by what we can only call a newspaper slime. They'd pulled him out, but not before it stripped him of all his clothing. They'd burnt down that house. Lola with the high-pitched voice that had become a Perk-attack that made her incredibly effective against dogs.

Other, worse stories. We had way too many people for me to keep track of these days.

There had to be more out there. This couldn't be the only remnants of this area, could it? This was only like three percent its direct population, and we'd already ventured to MacGregor. I refused to believe there weren't more survivors out there. We just hadn't traveled far enough yet. But we were about to rectify that.

". . . and some of you have Class-given endurance. Which I get. Leave the cycles for those who don't." She gestured to the fourteen-odd "vehicles" we'd managed to put together. Most were more like large tricycles than bicycles, you know, since they had three wheels. Sturdier, able to carry a few spare things, a med kit, water, stuff like that.

I hoped Chris and Sarah could help Jackson and his little troupe with the batteries and power sources they were working on. Their tinkering was gathering momentum, but I couldn't help wanting the results sooner than later.

Evelyn continued and ushered everyone into their own groups. "I want us all to stay as close to one another as possible. Safety in numbers is our mantra, but should you get separated, try to stay in these smaller groups."

I scanned around the mass of people. Dale wasn't coming, which was a good thing since sometimes I got the feeling that he almost wanted to give up. Leaving him here with Darren would hopefully allow him to realize how much he was needed.

Still, I missed his presence. Only a couple of inches taller than me, he still had this calmness about him. Besides, he was like the first person I'd dragged with me.

Eventually, we were going to have to deal with the fallout of the onset, because none of us were okay, least of all anyone who lost someone in the first hours and had to push on and deal with it.

You know. Like. Everyone.

We had Sange and Jules and a couple of other Healer types. Or at least, I thought they were Healer types. I double checked my Mana Cloak, making sure it was charging. Eventually, if what I'd surmised about it was true, I'd be able to exponentially increase the Mana it could give me in a pinch.

A group of twenty of us riding through the carpark was conspicuous as hell. Hopefully, that chased off any smaller creatures looking to ambush us. Discouraging glob attacks was high on my list. Damn those little land piranhas.

The way was cleared out along Logan Road, anyway. At least for a bit. Several of the guys went with Dale yesterday to dispose of bodies. They'd found protective gear at one of the hardware stores and dealt with it all day yesterday. I wasn't sure how they'd managed it because I sure as hell couldn't have.

There were a lot of things going on, from taking care of shell-shocked kids to organizing food rotations and places to sleep that I couldn't do. Yet people still ran everything by me.

"You're being way too quiet today." Evelyn nudged me. "What's on your mind?"

I raised an eyebrow and gestured with my free hand to the world around us as I pedaled. "This?"

Evelyn laughed. She had this odd way about her, where she just took things in her stride. I wished I could muster that much ballsiness. I was more of a test, research, go-on-exact-data kind of person. Except when I found unexpected things, I guess.

"You two think we'll really find people?" Molly asked from my left-hand side, her brown hair pulled back in a no-nonsense ponytail.

"Hope so." Evelyn shrugged. "If not, maybe we can find things we can take back with us. Carts or maybe a trailer we could pull back. Anything that might help us be able to take care of all of that."

She gestured to the vehicles ahead of us. Logan Road hadn't been as hard hit as I'd imagined. Far fewer deaths, but again I attributed that to the time of night here. Death toll at seven in the morning with peak hour traffic would have been far worse than eleven at night. There were still some bodies in cars, as well as abandoned vehicles. We were still trying to figure out just what exactly happened to all our technological systems and why the initial Mana onset seemed to short everything out.

Up ahead, the cars were decently spaced and only had corpses in them every few vehicles. The bonus of that meant that if not all of them had bodies, then some people had survived at least the onset. Hopefully, anyway.

In which case this trip probably wouldn't return empty handed. It was a windy path that led down toward the center of Mt. Gravatt and then to Greenslopes, Stones' Corner . . . and beyond it, the city suburbs.

We'd see how far we got. This was only our first big group mission. We had more Levels, more confidence with our abilities, and we desperately needed to secure that damned Settlement Orb. Some of our lower-Level fighters remained behind. We kept the surrounding area pretty cleared out, so they could just wipe out low-Level spawns easily.

Only six hundred people to go. I didn't like the amount of panic that thought filled me with.

Every now and again I heard a loud caw from the trees. Like a magpie trying to distract us. It sent shivers down my back, yet I couldn't see the bird that made the sound. Everything around us appeared empty. No rats scuttling about, no cockroaches flying in my face, no mutant anythings anywhere. Not spiders, not dogs, not cats . . . nothing. And definitely no people, not even peeking out windows or anything.

"This isn't right, Evelyn," I said, trying to grab her attention from where she was chatting with Mark and Tasha.

We weren't going fast, maybe twelve kilometers an hour. Didn't want to hit something and wreck what little functioning transport we had.

"What?" She glanced at me and then frowned, looking back at the rest of our group still in tow behind us, formation still solid.

No spells or bats needed yet. My Mana Attunement had difficulties when I wasn't physically touching the ground, but I could still sense Mana welling and waiting. I could see the waves and flows of all the strands floating free and waiting for the right moment to engage something. The cloak made it all clearer, easier to interpret.

She looked at me, her brow furrowed. "Yeah. Way too quiet." But she said it like it didn't matter, like nothing was going to go wrong. "Gemma? Can you take Mark and maybe another of your lithe scout types and look around? See if there are any ambushes or gathering masses of mutated enemies anywhere?"

Evelyn made it sound lighthearted and routine, but that was just it. It wasn't. I could tell she was slightly rattled, her humor too forced. I guess it *did* matter to her.

"Sure thing, boss." Gemma laughed, gave her a half-hearted salute, and motioned to Mark the Swashbuckler, and someone whose name I didn't recall. Then they blended into the surroundings until I couldn't see them at all.

A ripple of Mana flowed through us, upsetting my stomach, and making me feel queasy. No one else seemed to be bothered by it. Joy to my affinity for the new nature through my cloak and abilities. A notification popped up.

**Mana Cloak**

*Please note due to excess ambient Mana, your cloak now holds a higher degree of Mana than normal at 102 Mana. Would you like to receive every notification or only important Mana milestones?*

*Please choose.*

*Every Notification OR Important Mana Milestones*

I chose the latter. If it was going to go up in two-Mana increments, it'd end up driving me crazy. Since getting the cloak I hadn't needed to use it yet.

I still couldn't place what it was that bugged me so much. We'd already gone through the intersection by Dawson Road and were moving up further to where Mt. Gravatt Plaza was.

There was a Red Rooster there. Which made me think of my favorite fries in the world, but I'd never be able to get them again because KFC was no more. That made me uniquely sad, actually. If you've never had KFC fries with extra salt and a dash of gravy, you don't know what you're missing. Though I should qualify that as *Australian* KFC fries. I remembered the excuse for fries we had back in the States from my years as a new teen before we moved, and just no.

"Hey. Kira!" Jules nudged me and smiled, her blonde hair braided like she was an ice princess. Her sweet nature always left me feeling cared for. "You seem a bit out of it."

"Sorry. Was thinking about never having KFC fries again."

And she got it because I saw this look of sadness wash over her face too. See? I wasn't alone in my weird obsession.

"Well, you had to go and ruin the mood, didn't you?" She fake pouted before brightening up. "But there isn't even a KFC here, right?"

"No, but we're almost to the Red Rooster, which I also love, but at the same time, the fries just aren't the same." I glanced around as we passed the showgrounds, starting to really worry about the lack of any type of monster around here.

This was Australia; we already had enough of the bloody things. How could it be so quiet?

Anyone scared of creepy crawlies avoided this country like a plague. So where had they gone, and what were they waiting for?

Jules smiled again, reassurance leaking through the expression. "It's okay. We will find those herbs and spices."

That made me laugh and really wish it was that simple. Everything could be solved by food, right? Good food and friends? Who was I kidding?

"So can you, like, sense any human life forms?" she asked, her eagerness showing.

Finding more people meant we weren't all alone.

The thing was, what I could sense wasn't the same anymore. It felt empty, but in a way I couldn't describe.

"Technically, I think? It's more like the Mana that runs everywhere around us and less like life forms themselves. Mana runs through everything now. It's changing all of us, living or not. Plants, humans, animals, even the earth . . . all of it. And it's the Mana I can sense. So I can tell when something is coming by the way the Mana moves." At least I thought that was how it worked.

"That is so cool." Jules's eyes sparkled. "I can just heal. And when the System already heals a lot of shit . . ." She shrugged.

"No, that's not true. Sometimes the System can't keep up with the damage. So we die. Some of us would already have died without you. Don't sell yourself short." I wasn't trying to make her feel better, just being realistic about the role she currently played, while being completely distracted at the lack of Mana gathering around us.

"Point. I'll take that boost of confidence and wander away now." She smiled at me, and the expression reached her eyes, giving them a twinkle.

I muttered an absentminded goodbye and kept a lookout for our stealthers. They hadn't come back to report to Evelyn yet and maybe half an hour had already passed. It was really bugging me. What should I do? Was it even a problem?

Cars. Houses. Apartment buildings. Nothing. Nothing stirred. Not even a mutated mouse.

As we came closer, we slowed down at the Creek Road intersection.

"Maybe people are hiding in that Woolies down there." Barry called out. And they could indeed be. His usual happy confidence felt a little forced. Maybe everyone could feel the unease.

The complex was a pretty popular shopping area with two grocery stores, a cafe, a butcher, and baker... It was a nice place, much smaller than Garden City, which some people preferred. Even had a liquor store. It would make sense for locals to congregate there, but not so much since it didn't have any inherent protections built in it.

Evelyn raised her voice so she could be heard as we all came to a standstill overlooking the complex. "Okay. We scout out the center really quick to see if anyone is here, and if they're not, we'll move on to the housing and apartments around this whole area and see if we can salvage anyone."

We left our tricycles stationed in the parking lot of the computer store across the way. A flat section of road was best for those rolling wheels. After that, we just made our way across the once-busy street. Wasn't like we had to watch out for traffic right now.

"Where is Gemma?" I asked Evelyn, trying to downplay the pit I felt in my stomach, like an abyss with no end. No Mana surges, everything far too quiet. This didn't bode well.

I really wanted to chew my nails.

Evelyn kept her determined smile in place and whispered out of the corner of her mouth. "I don't know, and I don't like it. I'm starting to not like any of this."

For all that Mt. Gravatt Plaza could have fit into Garden City about twenty times, right then I felt like it loomed over us. Ripples of blue spread out from it, past us, not touching us, like something was commanding it to do its bidding. Jules saw it first, and her gasp drew our attention.

Gemma stood there, clutching the white side of the building closest to the bank, leaving bloody trails from the wounds on her hands and body. A claw mark raked down her face, and her hair was matted with blood. She pitched forward as Jules ran to catch her, extending her healing shield over her best friend.

But Gemma fought to speak. "It's a trap . . . they're everywhere."

That was all she had left in her. She spluttered, and I hoped for Jules's sake that Gemma just passed out. Mark hadn't made it back, and I wasn't about to ask where he was. Tasha's eyes filled with tears, but she bit her lip and stood up straight.

"What did she mean by—" But Ray didn't get any further.

Now I could feel it. The building power pressing down on us, the malevolence, and the approaching stack of creatures in a circle all around us. Whatever it was, something had masked their approach from me, confusing both my cloak and my Mana Attunement. At least now we knew where all the wildlife had gone.

# Chapter Seventeen:

# Unexpectedly

I strained to see if I could feel the presence of those creatures now, and this time, if I looked for it, there was a different undercurrent. Like a hum hidden beneath the gentle roar of the propagating Mana. Now that I knew what to look for, I'd seek it the next time we thought something was odd.

That is, if we managed to stay alive and get back home.

I really hoped Gemma was still breathing. Jules acted like she was, but there was no trace of Mark or the other person I hadn't known. We were effectively down three of our people. Three of our highest damage dealers. If these mutations could see through stealth, then we couldn't use that to our advantage because we essentially had none right now.

"Shit." Evelyn breathed out the word, but she didn't sound panicked.

I could see her calculating something behind those eyes as she took in the surroundings. I looked with her, but my Mana Attunement coupled with the cloak told me more than I ever wanted to know.

There were creatures all around us, waiting in the shadows at the side of the building, peering at us from up in the trees. Waiting and watching like they were biding their time. I guess I should have been grateful we didn't go out at night.

All at once the cacophony of sound began. Magpies and kookaburras and Gods knew what else. It was everywhere, from all directions, above us, around us. It tingled my bones through my skin and set my teeth on edge. And then the growls started, forcing us back into a circle close to the Westpac Bank and yet just too far away from the entrance into the complex to make it undercover.

At least we managed to keep a wall on one side of us. Now they could only attack from above and not all sides. Mercies that were way too small.

If I squinted, I could tell where some of the ground-based creatures were. With their mottled brown and grey coats, the feral cats had grown with their mutations until they looked more like a lynx or, in the biggest cases, a mountain lion. They blended in perfectly with the mostly grey and concrete or bitumen surroundings. In some cases, I could swear shadows were shifting to keep them even more hidden. Either way, their urban camouflage was far too effective.

Seriously, System? You come to Australia and give our already awesomely diverse creatures the ability to camouflage on top of everything they can already do? Now that was some strange sort of irony, I swear. Let's make Australia a tad deadlier shall we? Said no one ever.

Evelyn was still taking in our surroundings. Nothing attacked us yet, but I could feel the anxiety around me emanating from the others in the group. Jules was beside herself, though trying to calm down. Tasha wasn't dealing well with Mark's absence, despite the brave face. Mana danced erratically around her like it was waiting for her to grasp on and use it. Molly, Sange, and Ray weren't doing much better either.

For the first time since I met him, Barry was at a loss for words and pale as a ghost.

"Hey." Sange moved over to Evelyn, eyes flitting everywhere but making contact with her. "We need to get to a safer area quickly and figure out a plan of attack."

"Already got the plan of attack," Evelyn murmured, barely loud enough for them to hear. "Don't die."

Sange laughed with a hint of panic but nodded in response and stood next to where Jules was finally righting herself. The thing was, we both knew Evelyn wasn't joking.

Someone behind me—Josh, I think his name was—hefted a cricket bat in his hand. Solid things those were. Damn near unbreakable and he looked like he knew how to swing one. "We're ready."

I was about to make a comment, but it was like the creatures had been waiting politely to be invited in or something, because they moved as one. Fluid in motion, even the bird mutations dropped from the trees at exactly the same time. If I'd had a moment, I might have felt like there was something fishy about that, but I didn't have the time to process anything other than being attacked.

I'd practiced a couple of times with the earth around me and using the barrier as a weapon and a defense. Earthen Barrier became denser when mixed with the concrete on top of it, and I managed to give both Evelyn and our two crossbow wielders some cover to shoot from. Barry and Tasha led the mages in defending us from the aerial assault. Fire, wind, ice . . . apparently, we'd picked up an Elsa.

But all I could do was defend and tell when things were coming toward us. There had to be more to this Class. Or did I just get it as a joke? Here is the possibility to understand what it is that Mana is, but ha-ha, there's nothing you can do with it anyway.

I activated my Level 11 Mana Transfer ability. Sure, it only helped me, but I knew I'd need all the Mana I could get.

### Mana Transfer (Level 1)

*Effect: Due to your devotion to understanding the world around you and how to preserve and bolster it, you can tap into the Mana saturation around you, bolstering your regeneration on a constant basis. Strength and capacity are dependent on spell and caster Level.*

*Mana Cost: 20 Mana – 30 seconds of regen increase.*

I could, at the very least for now, bolster my own supply of Mana.

I didn't have time to experiment with any of my other abilities, so I threw up Earth Barricades to tear apart the ground troops, smashing them with columns of stone, making them leap over them—and sometimes impaling themselves—or else to go around. I created a series of twisting roadblocks, forcing the ground-based monsters to move around the obstructions.

I anchored my last cast in front of the team, curving the barrier so that it could offer us as much protection from ankle biters as it could give us. I pumped more Mana into this one, twice what the other barriers had cost, and found myself almost tottering at the loss of Mana, but the added security was worth it.

All the while, the rest of the team was busy too.

Barry threw sheets of fire every twenty seconds or so. He must have had a cooldown on it. But it was barely enough to keep the MMNs from divebombing us.

Tasha tore through things with ice and wind magic practically leaping from her blades. Her Spellsword abilities appeared generically overpowered, but the desperation with which she fought bled out with her magic. Some part of her didn't care if she died, and still she pegged the birds to the trees with an accuracy that surprised me.

She was only Level 8 or so, if I recalled correctly. Channeling the anger at Mark not returning helped her accuracy, but it couldn't be healthy.

I didn't know the names of the other mages, but they were lower Levels too and picked off any of the overhead creatures that managed to escape Barry and Tasha. Still, they moved well together. Yesterday's leveling search parties had paid off.

From the birds to the feral house pets, from the rodents to the

214

cockroach mutations that I couldn't seem to escape. All the creatures moved with certainty. Like they knew everything they and each other were doing. A level of sentience I wouldn't have attributed to them.

That's when it hit me. These weren't suddenly genius-level animals. I didn't think the System worked that way. They were all being controlled by something. The way the patterns of Mana calmed around them all, weaving in and out of them, linking them together somehow.

"Mind control," I muttered, knowing Evelyn and probably Tasha would hear me.

But it was Sange who responded. "Shit. That makes so much more sense than the ridiculous theories my brain was coming up with."

They sounded relieved as they clubbed another mutant feral thing in the head, casting a heal over Molly at the same time.

There was no coordination to our assailants' attacks other than that they all went at once and just kept going until they couldn't.

Reinforcing my Earth Barricade took Mana dumps I didn't want to afford but had to. I watched as Evelyn took aim at incoming projectile kookaburras and magpies, picking them off in quick succession, her face contorted with concentration.

Sange worked in sync with Molly, while the little Tank viciously bashed anything that got near us with that shield of hers. Her rage lit her face up with an odd, unhinged light. All of us could do with a little of that right then.

The first Magpie Mutation Nightmare that made it through our firepower barrier only glanced off the side of my head because of Molly's quick thinking. Somehow, even though I knew it hit me, it was suddenly impaled on her sword, like she'd activated a rescue cooldown or something.

I could feel the blood trickling down the side of my face and sticking to my hair. It could have been a lethal hit had it made its mark, though at least now I had decent hit points. Goosebumps broke out all over me, but I didn't have the time to let fear freeze me.

Mana Regeneration wasn't the most generous of the System's gifts. Several minutes into the fight and our mages were already having to ration their power. Without Mana, we casters were left with melee weapons—our just-in-case backups. Bats, hatchets, even a fire axe.

Flailing around in the air near one another wasn't doing any of us favors, but it was all we had while we waited on Mana Regen. We did our best to deal with the flying monsters that made it over my Earthen Barrier, keeping our sides clear as best we could.

When we restored enough Mana, the mages cast destructive spells. Wait for Mana to regenerate, flail with bats at the overhead attackers while waiting. Replenish Mana. Rinse and repeat.

Magpies don't let go easily, and for the first time ever, I witnessed kookaburras attacking people with their massive fishing beaks. My first thought when seeing them had been dismissive.

You'd think I'd have learned by now. Though, to be fair, they only vaguely resembled their former selves. But all of them behaved mindlessly, diving in to draw blood and dashing back out, mechanical, clockwork-like.

Jules paled as a beak embedded in her arm. She howled in pain after a second that seemed to last an hour, realization finally making it from her pain receptors to her brain. The thing clawed at her arm, shredding her leather jacket and the flesh beneath, and flapped its wings about madly and attempted to open its beak within her arm, eliciting more screams from the traumatized healing mage the distinct ripping of flesh.

Someone I didn't recognize slapped her across the face and, while Jules was dazed from the action, yanked the bird out in one quick motion, smashing it against the ground with pure force. She was an older lady, maybe around fifty. Rugged in appearance, her silver hair almost regal, her matching eyes looked at Jules with sympathy.

"Sorry, love. You were flailing like a flaming galah. Had to do something to stun ya." She turned in time to smash a bat into an MMN that was about to hit her head. Scowling, she yelled at us. "Pay attention, kids. Don't gawk. Kill. Survive."

Simple words, yet she was right. With that one snapped command, we had no time to feel hopeless.

Enough Mana returned, I activated another fast Earth Barricade, like I had back outside Garden City when we first fought the MMNs. It shot up as a wave of the damned flying shitheads came zooming at us, taking out about a dozen because they were flying so closely together.

Blood and feathers spattered down onto us, along with a couple of screeching, partially decapitated surviving avian creatures that we squashed in quick succession. They were so much bigger now than they should have been.

The backline did their best to deal with the air with whilst our Tanks, Rangers, and Fighter-Mages dealt with the ground troops, but I couldn't protect those out there in the thick of it, and the floor behind my barrier looked like we'd been tarred and feathered.

Still, the creatures moved as one. Coming, never-ending, never stopping. They just ran and ran, dive-bombed and flew.

"We need to find the source. We need to find what's controlling them," Evelyn screamed over the noise.

It took all my self-control not to snap at her. I mean, "Nah, love, I was planning on just playing hit 'em for a six all day" was sitting right on the edge of my tongue.

Breathe, damn it. We all needed to calm the fuck down and breathe.

"Any ideas?" I asked, but as I gazed around where we stood, there weren't seventeen of us still standing.

Gemma lay prone on the ground, not having moved from where she dropped earlier. Was it bad that I was relieved to see that some of the blood on her seemed fresh? That would mean she was still alive, her heart still pumping.

That meant the System should heal her.

Three more of our number were nursing acute wounds our Healers couldn't fix, while still trying to flail around with a bat of some sort. Bloody gashes on their faces, arms, legs, through their shirts. Almost everyone was missing chunks of hair, and I was pretty sure one of the people I didn't know was missing most of one eyeball. I'd watched the strike, the rainbow fucking lorikeet scooping it out and making its way away, just before the victim fell to the ground, screaming and thrashing.

We were down to thirteen. We'd lose more as this fight continued.

Whatever was manipulating this wildlife was doing a bang-up job.

Jules still seemed pale, but she was healing others for all she was worth, and the massive wound in her arm had almost closed. Barry's blankets of fire provided more than just warmth, though charred wasn't the way I liked my meat.

Molly's fatigue was starting to show, but her stubbornness won out, and Sange was next to her every step of the way. Ray and the other mages had worked themselves into a rotation, and Evelyn's endless arrows were the godsend we needed.

We were holding on, and I kept looking, kept hunting for the problem, all the while swinging my bat at the damn mutated cats and dogs and fucking-hell-that's-a-massive-black-bellied-swamp snake. I hit that one twice as hard and twice as often to make sure it was down. What the fuck was one of those venomous fuckers doing here?

Suddenly, Barry screamed in agony, and it cut off even before I swiveled to look at him. I tried not to throw up as I blinked at his chest. Lodged, just off to the left of center was a mutated kookaburra. Its feathers rustled as it tried to free itself, feet unable to find a foothold in its victim's chest as the claws scrabbled at the flesh beneath it, slipping and sliding without gaining traction as it shredded what was left. Barry's mouth opened in a soft O just before blood bubbled out of the opening, and he crumpled to the ground.

The genuine, jovial friend to all who had done so much to make everyone feel welcome safe hadn't managed to save himself.

We'd all failed to save him.

Jules screamed and turned to him, but the older lady was there again, squeezing her hand and telling her to heal those she could still save.

*Those she could still save.*

Fuck this.

Time to gamble.

"Cover me!" I screamed to Evelyn and those around.

I stepped back from the Earth Barricade wall with one last smack of my bat and hoped they could help. The questions being shouted, I ignored.

I tapped into my cloak, trying to identify a larger-than-normal contributor to the Mana waves. Surely, there had to be a pool of power somewhere around here. The larger the Mana output or coalescence, the more likely it would be our target. I sorted through dozens of impressions, some false, some too deep in the earth, some too brief. I kept pushing, searching.

Because I was going to find and kill this mind-controlling, murderous creature if it was the last thing I did.

It took more concentration than I liked. More focus and time away from the fight than I could afford.

There, off to the left a ways, it was inside the shopping center. Was that why all the creatures circled it, keeping people away? Was it not so much a trap as a defense? So many bloody questions.

Still, it was using the creatures, and by doing so, had killed someone who'd become kind of a friend. And probably more because Mark and the other stealther still hadn't shown up.

"I need you to keep me covered when I make a run for it," I told Evelyn, coming out of my trance.

Tiredness showed around her eyes, and she looked at me like I had two heads.

"Can you or not?" I asked again, more impatiently, because time wasn't something we had right now.

"No. That's not it." She was looking behind me, like she'd seen a ghost or something.

About to turn, I didn't have to when a blanket of fire laid waste to the numerous birds still diving in to attack us. It wasn't Barry because Barry was dead. Which meant someone else had found us. I really hoped they were friendly. And then someone not in our tiny group spoke, and if felt like my world dropped out from under me.

"Is that you, Kira?"

# Chapter Eighteen:
# Bloody Hell

"Kyle"—I turned, not even realizing there were tears running down my face until my nose dripped— "Kyle . . ."

I'd known he was alive, because I could feel it, and I don't care what anyone says about twin connections. For us, we'd always been able to feel one another. Then I took a long, hard look at him and started to laugh. Not only was he surrounded by a gang with more people than I had with me, but they were firing weapons and spells and all sort of volatile shit at our attackers.

Kyle—well, I'd never seen him look so bedraggled in my entire life. Still a good four inches taller than me at six feet high, his shaggy black hair curled in ways my straight locks never could. His usually impeccably clean-shaven face was marred by stubble. It made him look a bit Indiana Jones-like, but I wasn't about to tell him that. The clothes he wore were torn and shredded in places with blood spatter strategically arranged around the holes, but even so I could tell they'd once been a pair of scrubs.

Not to mention he was alive.

I threw my arms around him, fighting back the tears of relief before pulling back and eyeing him seriously, the fight behind me all but forgotten. "You came here because of Dad, right?"

He laughed as his comrades slaughtered kookaburras and magpies by the dozen. Fireballs, slingshots of deadly something-or-others, people just diving into combat with what seemed to be glee. Could have been desperation too. But his smile gave me this sense of safety, like we could overcome anything. We'd always been the terrible two.

"Got me there. Dad's survival plan and all. Just be glad you didn't go to the city."

He said the latter somberly, never a default mood for my brother, so I knew it had to be bad. I wanted to ask just what had happened, but we were under attack, even if it was winding down. Right now, we had more immediate concerns.

"Something or some magic is controlling everything around us. All the non-human creatures, anyway. It's got to be close—as far as I can pinpoint, it's in the complex." I was rambling a little, still wrangling my feelings under control while trying to ascertain the ins and outs of my Mana Sense.

Joy didn't suit this atmosphere well.

Barry was still dead.

Kyle let out a low whistle. "We need to talk later, but dang it, what sort of fucking Class is that long-ass name?"

I laughed, but it rang hollow even to my ears. "Later. Let's go find this boss monster thing. It killed one of my friends."

A moment of silence followed my statement as my brother processed it, and I realized just how true it was.

"It's inside, then?" he asked, eyeing our exhausted group who'd gladly given over the fighting to the mass of people he'd brought along.

A wave of nausea threatened to bowl me over. I nodded, trying to ignore the bile in my throat, the sudden sense of enormity of what I'd been about to do, what was likely going to happen. If Kyle hadn't come along . . . I didn't even want to think what might have happened.

Even if I knew.

"Of course it is." Kyle didn't seem to notice my reaction. Or maybe he was ignoring it. He ran a hand through dirty hair and glanced at the large group he'd brought with him. "We're mostly worn out, but we're in a lot better condition than you all. We have several higher Levels. Like 10s, couple of 11s. Those should help flush this thing out."

Kyle smiled, and it was everything I remembered, instantly putting me at ease. Instantly enabling me to look at our situation from a calmer standpoint. He started calling orders to the others, talking about Mana and Stamina conservation and the people who followed him—well, they listened.

It was so easy to get wrapped up in a spiral of negatively geared thoughts. I needed to get better about that. Get better at leading people into combat.

Barry was dead. Gemma was only just sitting up and drinking water, the blood dried fast to her face. Only a few of her wounds were still closing. She didn't look good, but she was alive. I figured that put us in the what, seven to eight-minute mark since the start of all this.

Yet it felt like a small lifetime.

The guy whose name I didn't know had left us too, both of his eyes pecked out in the end. Gotta love mutated rainbow lorikeets. Sarcasm and its perfect storm of distracting me from the macabre.

Of the scouts, Mark and the other guy were still gone.

I didn't like their odds of returning.

It felt bad that I didn't know their names, but others did, and those others were mourning them. There was a numb spot in my chest for Barry. We'd found him that first night with Red. Oh no. Red wasn't going to take this well. And Mark . . . Tasha seemed lost now there was no one to focus on. I felt guilty, but really, I was grateful in a small part of me that our losses were so small.

And that I'd made Jackson stay behind.

Kyle's group helped to fix us all up and I glanced at my experience gain and . . . holy fuck. There was no way I'd tagged every one of those. It had to have something to do with the area effect of Mana Attunement, or perhaps the defensive capabilities of Earth Barricade.

*Your group has killed 323 lesser animal mutations. You have shared experience gain in 323 of these kills.*

*Experience gain for Level 7 mutated rat—27*

*Experience gain from Level 9 mutated cat—73*

*Experience gain from Level 4 mutated rat—18*

*Experience gain from Level 11 mutated (? Snake) – 176*

*…*

My eyes glazed over a little and instead of reading it all individually, I skipped to the end. I didn't need—didn't have time—to look up individual death notifications.

*Your Total experience gained: 28,073*

### *Level Up\*3*

*You have reached Level 14 as a Pest & Pathogens Unit: Microbiologist / Plant Pathologist / Entomologist / Hydrogeologist / Molecular Biologist —Abbreviated as: Ecological Chain Specialist*

*You have 2 Class Skill points and 9 Attribute points to distribute. A new Class Skill has become available. Would you like to choose this now?*

Leveling up wasn't enough to make the deaths worth it, to make the missing people come back. It felt like a hollow victory. I needed to figure out how best to use this Class for the benefit of all of us.

"Kira?" Kyle was there, at my elbow, his eyebrows knitting with concern like they always did when I wasn't handling something well. "Are you okay?"

224

Knew it. "Yeah. I'm okay. Just lost a couple of people I didn't think we were going to lose so early. That's all."

Yeah, maybe I put a little bit of woe-is-me into that last sentence. And really, that was the truth of it. We had spent less than ten minutes in this mid-morning fight for our lives and lost numerous people. I was doing abso-fucking-lutely fantastic, thank you very much.

And Kyle knew just how much bullshit I was spinning, too.

He stood there, watching while the rest of his people helped mine get back on their feet, giving me the silent treatment while his people arranged healing and checked that everyone was doing okay.

I watched as that older woman stood there with her arms crossed observing everything, a slight frown on her face. Her slapping Jules into coherence during that fight might have saved lives too. I really needed to talk to her.

Damn twins.

"Okay, I'm not fine, but neither are you, and neither are any of us." I glanced up at the approaching midday sun bringing the heat of fall with it and sighed. "We need to get in there and kill that mind control beast."

"Too right, mate. Too right," Kyle muttered.

I activated Analyze and checked out several of his group. They ranged all the way from Level 3 to Level 15. A good chunk of them were up there with Evelyn and me. Maybe I'd just been stupid thinking we could come out here and save people, but I got the distinct feeling that my brother had gathered some of these people on the way to find me.

Many of them were in scrubs too, with laden backpacks, now that I looked at it. It made me wonder just what all he'd salvaged that was medical in nature. Dale would be overjoyed.

"Okay," Kyle said. "Let's do this."

He clapped his hands together and turned around, starting to call out names.

In the end he gathered about twenty people Level 12 and above to him. We had about eight of our remaining sixteen members who were 11 or under, but the rest we pulled into the fighting group. Twenty-eight wasn't a little raid. That's what this was, right? Like a raid in a far-too-realistic, very deadly game.

Taking everyone would be a mistake. We couldn't leave the rest of the group behind with all the low Levels as their protectors.

Gods. I was thinking in Levels.

"Think this should be enough?" Kyle sounded almost eager to go into that center and kill something.

I shrugged.

"I don't know. You have a lot of people here. You planning to just zerg it to death? We don't get to respawn, you know. That's not going to work." I tried to crack a partial joke and I admit the laugh that broke free from my throat was tinged with hysteria.

Kyle frowned. "It's not a zerg. With your people and their Classes, and mine, we have ranged, close combat, magic users, Healers, Tanks, and from what I can tell of you, a utility Class that can sense incoming danger?"

He seemed genuinely baffled by my Class, and I suddenly felt guilty for not even checking his out.

Oops.

Thing was, if I did, I'd want to talk about it, and we all knew there wasn't time for that yet.

I shrugged, pulling my Mana Cloak in tighter, leaving no holes as I fiddled with my borrowed bracer. "Probably wise, just . . . let's down some tucker while we apply the new Skills and Attributes we got. Maybe we'll have a few surprises in our arsenal."

Red had salvaged and dehydrated meat before it went bad. He'd worked his ass off to make us rice and avocado balls and shit to take with us. Even with his newly acquired kitchen help, it still took him so much time. And now we had to go back and tell him his brother was dead.

Shit.

"Hey, Kira." Kyle leaned in, and I just wanted to give my big, three-minute-older brother a hug and collapse to the ground and have him tell me stupid jokes.

But instead, I swallowed the tears I wanted to shed, gave him a brief hug, and leaned back, smiling. "I'll be fine. After this is over, we can take your whole group back to the center and figure shit out."

He clapped his hands together. "Excellent. That's my pragmatic little sister talking." And then he leaned in as if it was one huge conspiracy. "I did kind of make everyone I met believe I had this amazing plan to make it to safety. Talked a lot of people into coming with me along the way . . ."

Kyle stopped as I stiffened.

Suddenly, the Mana began to fluctuate again. Blue strands slowly weaved out from around the shopping center, reaching out to find anything it could potentially manipulate. It wasn't the usual happy, hopping Mana doing its thing. You know, trying to find an outlet so it could mutate all the creatures and plants around it into deadly killing creatures.

More deadly, killing things.

This stuff was malevolent, full of nefarious purpose that made my skin crawl.

I held up my hand to forestall my brother from continuing to speak. "Chat later. I think we're out of time, and we have a monster to kill. And I don't know about you, but I haven't even looked at my new Skills yet."

# Chapter Nineteen:
# Skin Crawler

The inside of the center was remarkably cool. One of our new squad members picked the lock and saved us the trouble of announcing our intentions with a loud crash of glass.

It grated on me. I really didn't like being rescued. Time to fuck some shit up.

There was an odd scent to the chilly air. Not stale, not recycled, more like decay with a dash of mint. I wasn't sure if I should be scared or impressed by that. Waves of Mana moved everywhere, through the floor, around in the air, constantly, like they were checking on growth and evolution of the planet it had infected. I didn't think I'd ever get the hang of this.

I'd felt rushed choosing my Skills, but I think that was just my brain rebelling against circumstances. Water Siphon actually held some potential and was deliberately offensive.

The moment we entered, the group spread out, some of them throwing up their own light spells into the middle of the room. Pale blueish tile, white walls, and the chain-linked roller doors blocked off almost all the stores.

Nothing moved in here except for us.

We walked cautiously through the tiny mall. Even as we searched for this thing or creature, I found it odd that it wasn't in the places I'd assumed gave the greatest vantage points. Though my Attunement made me think we were standing on top of it and somehow weren't seeing—

"Damn it. It's in the rooftop parking area." I should have known. That's it, I wasn't sleeping tonight. If . . . no, *when* we made it back, I was sitting down and figuring out the intricate details of my Skills.

Twenty-eight of our highest Levels were in here with me, having left only a handful of them outside to guard the rest. I didn't like the pit forming in the bottom of my stomach, like we'd just made some terrible mistake. There were a lot of people out there waiting to be attacked once our mind controller found more tools to fight us with.

"Back out and around the driveway ramp?" Evelyn offered. "Might be better to avoid making more noise than necessary. Picking a lock even closer to where it is probably isn't the best idea."

"Good point," muttered a guy who looked like he had a gun slung over his back. I think his name was Morton or something.

"Let's go." I waved to everyone, as did Kyle, and got us moving.

We moved quietly back outside and passed the waiting group, holding our fingers to our lips to signify for them to remain silent. Trekked past the blood smeared all over the wall where Gemma had stumbled down. And then we ascended the ramp. What an idiot I was. Considering where the rogue had come stumbling down from, you'd have thought the ramp obvious.

Now. When you think apocalypse, the general person probably goes with zombies. Whether they're shambling, sprinting, falling apart, marginally intelligent . . . whatever. Or perhaps alien invasion with large tentacle-monster things razing the landscapes.

Personally, I'd always been curious about Mr. Blobby, the deep sea blobfish. Changes in water temperature, the sudden rising through the water elevation, lack of water to give it structural integrity—all those things added up to Mr. Blobby being quite the celebrity, even if his body wasn't nearly what it would have been had he been observed on the ocean floor where he belonged.

Which is all to say, I won? Sort of? Definitely weren't any zombies here. Only blobs.

230

In front of me, about the size of three elephants combined, sat the most similar, blobfish-looking creature I'd never wanted to encounter. Dead, blobby face with a parasite hanging out of the corner of its mouth? Sure— great food for plushies. A massive, squelching-with-unknown-liquid, obviously still-breathing, monstrous lookalike that could probably devour a modest-sized house? Nope.

This was the thing our Aussie apocalyptic nightmare was made of.

As we stood around, all just stunned by what we'd encountered, something dropped from its lipless mouth. It just slid out, taking forever to fall and bounce, making a kind of dull, hollow thunk on concrete. White and cracked and all too long and knobby at the end, it looked suspiciously like a human femur.

I guess we found Mark and the other guy. Or what was left of them.

I think someone made a gagging sound. Maybe it was me.

Pressure entered my head, pushing against my mind like it was trying to intrude, to convince me to let it in. Maybe humans were too sentient for it to exert control. No one around me appeared to have difficulty either, but the creature rippled in what I can only assume was irritation.

Great. We'd pissed off the giant blobfish.

It roared.

The gust of wind that exited its mouth threatened to push us all back, but luckily the three-foot barrier meant to stop cars from careening over the edge prevented us from falling off. The pressure in my mind felt like my skull was just shy of exploding.

*You have resisted Mind Blast.*

Great. There was little time to consider the ramifications of resisting an attack. Its breath made concentrating on anything else difficult.

Filled with the coppery tang of new blood and the old stench of decay, the pong wafted over me, threatening to empty my stomach of everything, including my intestines. I'd spent enough time around compost that I held onto my gag reflex. Most of the others were not so seasoned.

I glanced to the side; both Molly and Sange were with us, determination written all over their faces. They'd gotten on well with Barry and Mark. This was payback for them, a bit of it for all of us. At least, I could hope it was.

*Analyze engaged:*
*Mormaturian Blobnecked Rigoll—Elite, Level 18.*

I blinked at it, confused and somewhat worried. "It's Level 18," I muttered to my brother.

Kyle raised his voice as he spoke. "We've got this. Just do whatever you can to weaken it or to warn us of adds."

"Adze?" His Fire Thrower asked, confused. "What do we need a woodworking tool for?"

In the middle of an apocalypse, with people who might never have played a computer game, of course not everyone would know gaming terminology. I could see Kyle count to five before answering, trying not to yell at someone who didn't deserve it.

"Adds. Short for additional monsters."

"Oh." The Fire Thrower seemed to mull the word over. "Got it."

Kyle continued his comments. "Kira's abilities should let us know if we get adds. We'll get this bastard." He sounded confident, and even though I knew it was fake, it still helped me clamp down on my own fear.

How did I manage to turn into a quaking mess just because my brother appeared? Nope. Wasn't doing any of that damsel shit.

"Okay." I nodded, leaching off his bravado to boost myself.

There was no other option. The simple fact was that I refused to die, so it only stood to reason that Mister Rigoll over here was going to. It was time to show these invaders just how wrong it was to mess with Aussies, even those of us who were only fifty percent ridgy-didge.

Evelyn called for the charge. "Go!"

Both Molly and two other Tanks from my brother's entourage dashed into the fray, shields raised, abilities flying. The clash was less clangy and more squishy. Ranged attacks flew into the creature, but they sizzled out, didn't appear to have much effect. The thing was so soft, it kind of absorbed most of the impact. One disadvantage of giant monsters: there was a lot of them to hit.

This blobfish appeared to be made of mostly water, similar in appearance to the cute face the world had turned into a wacky internet sensation. I readied to use my new Skill, making sure no one else crossed in front of me. Wasn't entirely sure how this new Skill worked, but humans were made of a lot of water . . .

*Water Siphon engaged.*

I watched as I released the ability, and the liquid began to drain out of the creature in front of us. It was subtle to start. First it paled even more, and then it sort of lost its luster. Instead of glistening flesh, cracks began to appear in what passed for its skin, and a rumble of discontent emitted from it.

At this low Level of the spell, it took a lot of Mana to use Water Siphon. I'd been remiss not to pick more items or things that contributed to my Mana

Well. Mana Transfer, my Level 11 Skill, at this low Level was virtually useless.

### Water Siphon (Level 1)

*Effect: Moisture is in almost everything: humans, intergalactic species. This ability allows you to siphon the water out of anything that contains it. Level of effectiveness dependent on caster and spell Level.*

*Mana Cost: 60 Mana per Siphon. 25% water per application. Application duration—30 seconds.*

*Caution: Target will be immune to the effects of Water Siphon for 15 seconds after this application.*

Water Siphon was my one true offensive spell, but it was Mana intensive, and casting it every time it dropped meant I'd be out of Mana in no time.

Instead of chain casting it, I protected the Healers by raising the concrete through the ground around us. Given that we were on a rooftop, the task was significantly more difficult than when I stood on solid ground.

With Water Siphon still active on the target and the melee and ranged both doing great damage, we significantly chipped away at its health. Fascinatingly, its non-existent legs allowed faster movement than I'd anticipated in an environment where it didn't have water to support its bulk.

But there was slime around it, and it acted almost like a slip and slide.

It dashed forward, practically head-butting one of the Rangers who was standing next to Evelyn. I could hear the squelch of impact and watched the Ranger's health plummet from the blow even as he flew over the upstairs barrier to the driveway below. Mr. Rigoll over there appeared to have sucked up some of the Ranger's moisture, replenishing its own.

As soon as the creature's immunity to my Skill wore off, I was smacking it right back on there. If Mana allowed.

After the second dash, we realized it only mustered enough strength to execute that Skill every thirty seconds or so. Evelyn called out to all the ranged Classes to keep moving as they fought. If they weren't holding a fixed position, then nothing could focus in on them enough to count. Add in the few cars scattered around, even if some of the overhead sunshades had already crashed down, and there was decent cover if people weren't being stupid.

The entire fight was weird, a concrete battle with a massive, blob-creature that darted around, trying to hit us while we dodged behind Earth Barricades, abandoned cars, and one another, all while melee fighters lopped off what squishy bits they could.

Frankly, it felt like a temper tantrum from Rigoll over there because it couldn't mind control us.

Water Siphon wore off, and the creature slowly began to regenerate its sheen. As its hydration improved, our damage lessened. Like it was a sponge that otherwise absorbed everything you flung at it, dulling, and reducing the damage done to it.

Righteo, then—I'd keep doing that.

Thirty seconds on, fifteen-second immunity. Wham.

Its health kept dropping steadily but slowly as hell. Unable to contribute significantly with my own damage, I tried to make sure the Healers didn't need to keep me alive with their Mana. Blood Transfer was minimal, but it was something. Lessening the damage allowed the Healers to ration their Mana better.

This was way too game-like for me. So much of it brought me back to the old days of raiding as a group, all huddled up with our computers in our dorm rooms.

Rigoll's slimy coating seemed to exude a type of DoT onto those in melee range who came into contact with it. Another reason to continue sucking all the liquid I could out of it.

Replenishing Mana was easier for me than anyone else, but I still had to ration it. I was too low in Levels. We didn't have the experience, and with Levels from eleven through sixteen, we were so far below this thing that we were just chipping away constantly.

Elite in this world apparently meant exactly what it did in all the damned games out there: difficult.

It had to have a weakness other than when I pulled the moisture from it. Molly darted in, her massive shield taking the brunt of one of its Mind Blasts. At least I assumed that's what it was. The gust of air was concentrated toward her and rebounded off her shield, dissipating before it reached anything else.

At least this time we knew better, and it failed to push us back to the barrier, thanks to Molly's quick thinking.

We couldn't afford for it to breach any of our mental defenses and take control of us like it had those other creatures.

Rigoll squealed, its squishy body flailing as it opened too-huge eyes to gaze upon us. Garbled language spilled from its mouth like it thought we could understand it. And it wasn't until I realized what it said that I knew we could.

*Halt this insolence. I am life; I am what you breathe!*

"Hold your breath!" I yelled on instinct at the faintly disguised trigger word.

The faint, blue Mana waves were already pooling around it, rushing into its mouth as it inhaled it all, and I knew there was no way it'd come back out as Mana. Whatever was about to be spat all over us couldn't be something

236

good.

"Jules. Shield!" Sange yelled not a moment too soon.

The Healer was only a fraction too late, and the first three people on our frontline were hit by the spittle. It sizzled into their flesh through their makeshift armor, burning down to the bone like it specifically sought out the marrow. Flesh dripped from their bodies, faces elongating like one of those scream masks until they were no longer recognizable as human.

The rest of us were safe behind Jules's healing dome, cowering with relief. We didn't have the time to stare in horror like several of us were doing, but we did it anyway. The sheer gore of the scene in front of us was too much for some to look away from.

Not to mention the scent of melting bodies and the screams that no longer echoed because their voices were silenced.

Seconds passed, and the Mana around the Rigoll was sluggish. Like ambient Mana was reluctantly refilling its well. It acted a bit like a magnet pulling in all the surrounding metal, but that the magnet itself wasn't strong.

"Attack! While it's recovering!" I shouted and used Water Siphon again, not caring about Mana conservation anymore.

Molly rallied the rest, shaken more than most of us if the slight tremor in her hands was anything to go by. Couldn't blame her, really. She was about fifteen centimeters from one of those melted puddles of human.

"Attack! Attack! Attack!" Her repeated shout dragged everyone out of their daze. Such a massive voice for such a tiny powerhouse.

Our group began to attack with renewed zeal while I scanned the area with Mana Attunement, looking for more adds.

Water Siphon re-engaged, and my own Mana stores were becoming a problem.

"Use all of your Skills. Conserving Mana will get us killed faster here!"

I mean, what were we holding onto it for? To get the most out of your rotation in a game, you used Skills on cooldown, or timed them with the perfect moment. Right now, that stupid blob was taking a lot more damage than usual, so now was the time.

No matter how much we'd gamed, no matter how much we'd lived, nothing prepared us for this apocalypse. Sometimes, especially in a situation where, I don't know, the game becomes reality . . . we had to be reminded of things we already knew.

Molly led the way, her shield a shining beacon for everyone else. Sange remained behind, close to where I was, making sure she didn't take more damage than necessary, and keeping an eye on everyone else. Jules was spent; that shield must have been Mana intensive. Yet she kept Heal over Times on the other Healers, and the Tanks, helping where she could while preserving Mana just in case.

I didn't think we'd survive another one of those waves. We had to kill him quickly. Except our firepower just wasn't there yet. No mega-powerful spells.

Where was the overpowered chosen one, we were supposed to have? Or hell, a maniacal loner who had a death wish? Shit.

"It can't just pull those attacks out of its butt. It doesn't have the Mana to pull it off yet. Kill it before it can!" I made sure everyone could hear me.

"How do you know?" barked a newbie.

"You have your Class and I have mine." I bit my tongue and ran straight into the next bit before the guy could take offense. "Its Mana Regeneration is almost as limited as yours. Trust me. It doesn't have the power yet."

"Sure. Right." One of them laughed, joined shortly by another.

It was a nervous laugh, but dude, we were all feeling the anxiety here. We were all literally fighting for our lives.

Everyone single one of us had just seen three people melt down into a puddle.

I could see Kyle was going to jump to my rescue. But you know what? I didn't need that shit. I knew he cared, and it meant a lot to me. But I was an expert in my field, and I didn't require babying. Mana might not be plant life, but it was related to the earth, and thus I'd fight tooth and nail for that expert tag again.

"Either believe me and go all out and damage it, or you can wait and see which one of us is right and maybe you'll melt next time." I didn't put heat in my words; I made myself sound as reasonable as I could. As if I fought these massive blobfish creatures every single day.

Me? I was going all out. Sucking all its water out, tapping it for life and Mana Regen and everything I could. Smashing my trusty old Barrier into it. Hell, I even snatched a rock or two off the Earth Barricade to pitch at it. It still took a few precious seconds before my critics jumped in too, but at least they joined me.

"Forgot how tough you can be," Kyle muttered from his position next to me.

He was channeling something that ate his Mana like a piranha. Damn, I wanted to talk to him about his Class.

Right now, all I cared about was that he damaged Rigoll.

Every strike we put into it tore chunks of it off. The top part of it looked crispy and burnt, new flesh exposed when someone sent a shearing blade of wind that tore pieces away. Arrows kept sinking into the rubbery flesh, going all the way to the feathers. Fletching. Whatever.

It wasn't enough.

I wished I could cut off its supply of ambient Mana and thus halt its Mana Regen. If I was like Level 35, I'd be able to do that shit, but we weren't even a week in yet. How the hell was there a Level-18 elite in the middle of the suburbs?

"Speed it up. Do whatever you can." I used the "Mum Voice TM" I'd needed to use when the kids got too close to that hornet's nest a few years ago. Calm, all traces of panic subdued.

*Water Siphon unable to engage—insufficient Mana*

Shit. Okay, Cloak, do your stuff!

I activated the Cloak, refilling a chunk of my Mana bar, pulling with everything I could so I keep helping.

*Water Siphon engaged.*

Perfect timing.

As if the last cast was what did it, as if the multiple streams of water being pulled out of it and getting dumped aside made it reach a tipping point, Rigoll finally collapsed. It seemed to wither into itself as blades and bats hit harder, and the ranged fighters were forced to stop casting because they couldn't hit those in their line of sight.

Its health crept down further, hitting the twenty percent mark. The melee fighters kept whaling, but I refrained from casting anything else. To preserve my Mana. I wanted to have something in case the Water Siphons ran out before we finished killing it.

To aid with the killing, I hopped over to hit it with my bat a bit.

The sad thing was it no longer felt like a battle, but like we were just beating it to a pulp. Maybe that was a defense mechanism. My mental fortitude wasn't the best. I remembered that distinctly when choosing my

Class.

I frowned, noticing that everyone else apparently felt sorry for the poor little blob as well. Although Jules and Molly didn't appear to have fallen for it. Only my vague knowledge of carnivorous plants that lured in their victims helped me realize that this thing . . . it was playing us.

Fucker.

# Chapter Twenty:
# Reality Check

I wished I'd realized sooner. Maybe it was a last-ditch effort or something, perhaps a self-preservation method it could engage when its life got close to over. Whatever it was, the damned thing tried to play on our good nature. Plant knowledge to the rescue again.

"Guys." The word came out hoarse, more like a cough. Damn it. I couldn't express what I wanted to.

Jules glanced at me; her eyes rife with her own struggle. But she apparently was better at commanding her vocal cords. "Kill it! Don't let it trick you."

Molly let out a massive roar. If I hadn't witnessed it with my own ears, I'd never have believed it. "Fight it. We're so close. You saw what it did to us down there! What it did to us up here!"

I shook my head and gave it another go. "Payback!"

At least this time my words were audible. I'd take it. Our little tirade managed to drag the others out of that odd stupor. I could feel the Rigoll's anger as it allowed the last of its Mana to dissipate. That really *had* been its last-ditch effort, I guess.

Its Water Siphon resistance was almost up. With barely enough Mana, I had to time this exactly right to maintain the debuff on the creature.

Arrows and fireballs flew to strike the Rigoll from behind as the ranged casters finally got around its bulk to hammer away. As did icicles and other spells I couldn't recognize. Fighters couldn't use their swords very well; the jelly flesh caught them and sealed them into it. Instead, they used bludgeoning items like baseball and cricket bats. Each slug sounded like a hefty punch in the gut, deep and satisfying. It didn't so much ring through the air as thud.

The Rigoll began to dissolve like when jelly begins to liquify in the sun. Slowly at first, and then in a rush.

I could practically feel the Mana coalescing inside it, seeking an out so it could do its thing with something that wasn't dying. Nothing more than a dull glow to begin with as its health dipped under ten percent, but the more it melted, the more the Mana tried to escape.

In this short amount of time, I'd realized one thing. Mana—it didn't die. It just moved on. And here was a lot of Mana wanting to move on. That couldn't be good, right?

"I don't think it's going to die quietly," I said to Kyle as the creature's health ticked further and further down.

He gave me one of those I'll-talk-to-you-about-this-later looks and turned to someone I didn't know. "Get the melee to pull back and have ranged do whatever they can."

At the same time, Evelyn told those around her the same thing.

The Rigoll's health was plummeting now. Down to three percent and falling like it was gathering momentum. I backed away, but I didn't think it was going to work. I didn't think I could use shielding on myself, but I could use it on my brother. Only I didn't have enough Mana left to do so.

Shit.

It felt like everything moved in slow motion when the creature hit one percent. Blue strands of Mana wound through it, trying to escape from it. Those lines pulsed underneath the flagging skin. My head throbbed in time with it.

Mana migraine seemed like it might be a thing.

When Rigoll's health finally hit zero, Mana shot through its translucent skin—at least, that's how I saw it—erupting with the same acidic liquid that had already melted three of our damage dealers. It spurted out from the center, projecting toward us. Jules's shield slithered over my skin a split second before it hit us. I don't know how she'd managed to regenerate the Mana, but she had.

I could hear Molly screaming but didn't dare move while the acid was eating through the concrete right near my feet. The sound didn't cut off though, so at least she was still alive.

If the acid kept pouring, it was going to melt through to the center beneath us. Sange was next to Molly, and I couldn't hear anyone else screaming, but I also couldn't bring myself to look at why our Tank was freaking the fuck out.

We'd defeated it, finally. Jumping up, I touched a finger to the horrifically cold and clammy hunk of flesh that was left, accepted the loot without any thought, and told the blue screen notifications to fuck off. I glanced briefly over to see Molly sobbing and looked back over the whole group. At least she was alive.

Still though, it didn't feel like a victory to me.

Even though we'd been fighting for our lives, it didn't negate the fact that we needed to check for more survivors around the area. Even coming back the next day wasn't guaranteed to give us the same people. Mutations and strange creatures that had nothing to do with Earth were popping up everywhere.

It was a sorry group of us that returned to Garden City. Bedraggled perhaps, but over two hundred human lives accompanied us. Our train dragged out over a block, and most of them were only stepping one foot in front of the other, perfunctorily. The bikes carried the dead that still had solid form. Couldn't pick up melted goo that was further corroded by the giant blob explosion itself.

Ushering the survivors past us to file into Garden City, I really wished we could have just had a run-of-the-mill zombie apocalypse. I'd never been so down for an experimental drug gone wrong in my life.

Barry wasn't there to greet us. It wasn't until I walked through the doors and realized that his cheery face wasn't saying hi to everyone that it really hit me. I was surprised by how empty it felt in here even though it had only been a few days since we'd met. His jovial way, his bright beaming smile. Stolen by a fucking kookaburra projectile.

At least I didn't have to delegate the job to someone else. Jules volunteered to be the one to tell Red. I wasn't about to hold her back.

In my numb state of mind, Dolores—the woman who had slapped Jules across the face—and Ray stepped up to help get the newcomers organized. I liked Dolores. Not just for the fact that she stepped in and began to organize people, but because I didn't have to, and she was good at it—good with people.

Den Mother. Weirdest Class and title ever. What was she? A bear? I figured I'd ask her about that later.

Kyle flitted back and forth among the people he'd brought with him, anxiousness showing in his face. He checked on every person who'd accompanied him. So many of them were laden down by backpacks filled with supplies he'd commandeered from the hospital. It was so like him to think of others first and to take those thirty minutes that he needed to salvage items that might prove beneficial in the days to come.

Me? It all passed me by in this surreal, dream-like state. I was in shock, and I knew it. And I didn't care. I barely felt like myself, but more as if I was watching everything from outside of me like it didn't have anything to do with me.

Maybe I was tired, but I didn't feel sleepy, just worn out emotionally.

I sighed and sank into a seat at the edge of the food court, watching the bustle around me as if I wasn't a part of it.

I watched as new people entered, heaved a sigh of relief at seeing the Safe Zone notification pop-up, and got in line to talk to Ray and Dolores. Molly, her face pale, hovered around Sange as Dale grabbed healers to work on them.

Jules walked over after speaking to Red, inserting herself to do what she could too, her blonde hair tied up in a bun that made the lines of her face sterner than usual. Maybe it helped take her mind off how close Gemma had come to dying.

Red was nowhere to be seen. I couldn't blame him. Jules's face was still red from the tears she'd shed sharing the news with him. Now, she distracted herself.

I wished it were that easy for all of us.

Mana wove its way around and through the whole group. Its little strands of influence filled us up, watching us, healing Sange way too slowly. They weren't happy about it either. Apparently regrowing a limb, even with the System helping along merrily, wasn't something that was easy to do.

Well, not just System help. Kyle cast some sort of spell that helped, and from what I could tell took a lot of energy out of the caster and the receiver.

At least it was possible to grow limbs back.

Screams echoed through the shopping center, reverberating through the tiled and glass lined area like it was bouncing off canyon walls.

The people lining up to be accounted for shifted uncomfortably at the sound. Sange's healing process shared their pain with all our eardrums. From what I could gather of the hesitant people taking their turns talking to Jules and Ray, it seemed like only a third of people had adventure-type Classes, and those who didn't weren't comfortable around anything that reminded them of violence.

Especially the lost-limb type of reminder.

Part of me was certain they'd die first. Violence was an effective answer in our new little world.

"I knew you'd make it home." Wisp stood there right in front of me, pride in her eyes. Not just in me, but in herself for parting with her bracer. She pulled me out of my stupid downward spiral with her beautiful little soul.

I smiled at her and handed her bracer back while scooping her into a hug. She was eight; I was still allowed to do that. "Kept me safe. Now it needs to take care of you too."

She nodded solemnly, her eyes shifting over to the huge group of people still being sorted through.

"Is that really Uncle Kyle?" she asked, her tone wistful.

Her big eyes were wide with disbelief because, truth be told, he looked nothing like the uncle she remembered. His impeccable style and dress weren't present. He was a mess, his curly black hair disheveled and dirty, his face full of stubble he'd never worn before.

"That's really Uncle Kyle." Relief washed through me so sharply it took my breath for a second. He was here, he was alive, and he'd found me. One down, a few more to go.

Wisp glanced at me, then at her uncle, and I nodded. She ran so fast to him that I let out a bark of laughter, easing the tightness in my chest only slightly.

"You've got a good kid there, youngin'."

I turned, recognizing the voice, and felt relief wash over me again, although I hadn't even noticed that she'd left the check in line. She'd kept us alive by making sure that Jules didn't lose it all together while we were fighting.

"Dolores." I inclined my head, giving my attention back to my family as the older woman sat down.

I *really* liked her. There was this quiet, commanding confidence about her. Whether it came from her Class, Mana, or from life experience, I wasn't sure. But I was glad she was on our side.

Her silver-streaked hair lent her a distinguished aura, her strength obvious in the aged sinew visible beneath her sun-hardened skin. I realized belatedly that she was shorter than me, by maybe a couple of inches, making her five feet six, but when she moved, it was with an authority that made her appear six feet tall.

She sat next to me for a while without speaking, and it didn't feel uncomfortable, but it did make me wonder what she wanted to say. She'd insisted on helping gather the people and sort them into the "have a clue" and "no fucking idea" bunches. There was also now a registry of real-world-skilled people we might be able to find a use for.

Real world. Oh, this was real, all right.

I finally took my eyes off where my daughter chatted animatedly to my twin and tried to see if I could spy Gemma in our makeshift first aid area. Her sun-freckled face and sun-bleached hair appeared paler, and while I knew it was a trick of my mind, it also seemed fitting. She looked healed up, but her eyes were haunted, and I didn't think she'd be the same after this.

I knew I wouldn't be.

"So, we have us an apocalypse, and I think you've got some nifty type of ability the rest of us don't have." Dolores tone was low, but her words were pointed. She'd noticed me giving warnings when things were coming toward us, and she'd seen me locate the big fat shit we'd killed too. It wasn't like I tried to hide my Mana tracking abilities or anything. I didn't think it was something I should need to conceal. "I need to know more about it and what it can do if I'm going to help arrange these whippersnappers."

"Everyone knows about it." I shrugged.

She laughed and patted my hand like she was my mum. Technically, she was probably old enough to be, but still. "Not like that, love. Not the abilities that long-ass name thingamajig Class of yours calls ya. No, that Mana-sensing thing you do. The weaving of the Mana web you can see."

I turned to her, giving my full attention because that sounded way too much like what I could do to be coincidence. It'd be nice if I wasn't the only one. "What do you mean?"

She fiddled with her fingers a moment, letting her gaze span out and see everyone around us before speaking in a very quiet voice. "See. Not everyone can see Mana. My gran taught me about the life around us, about the way nature spreads and grows and evolves and becomes. You can see that too. It's how you knew what Tubby was going to do. Woulda taken us right with it. You can see the life of the earth. This System thing here? It categorizes it as Mana."

I blinked at her. I'd already come to the realization that not everyone else saw the strands of blue Mana that wove themselves everywhere around and into everything. But I didn't quite understand it, I guess.

"Well, yeah. I mean, the System even gave me a Skill for it. Did you get it too?"

She shook her head, and there was a hesitance to her response, like she wasn't sure how to say what she wanted to. "There's a difference in sensing Mana and seeing it. If you can do both, then we might just have a chance at making it through this whole shitfest."

Dolores grinned at me, and I knew instantly that she hated all of this just as much as the rest of us. But instead of getting down or desperate, this lady had decided to meet it head on. To do battle on her turf in her way.

Partner in crime it was. Shit yes. "Good. I mean, they ranked Australia as deadly. Maybe we should show this whole System Council thing just how deadly we are, right?"

Dolores laughed this time. It was a magical sound, light and free from constraint. Maybe we all needed a little bit more of Dolores in us. "Too right, mate. Let's show everyone just how dangerous Australians can be."

❖

696 people. We needed to find another 304 to be safe. Four more days until the quest timed out on us. We could find seventy-six people a day, right?

I sat in the dark close to the department store where Kylie and Wisp lay hand in hand, Kylie's short hair overshadowed by Wisp's billowing black locks. In her sleep, she seemed younger than eight. Small, sporty, and vulnerable. Her body didn't look like a gymnast's, not the way it did when she was awake and her muscles alert.

Right now, she just looked like my little girl, having a sleepover with her friend in a bed that almost swallowed the both of them.

Right now, they were sleeping like the children they deserved to be.

Fuck anything that tried to disrupt that.

I looked up at the ceiling, nursing my surprisingly not-horrible coffee in my hands. I didn't understand all the mechanics that were going on with the remnants of our old world. But I did know the tech team was growing and slowly making decent progress. They were still going at it, even now. Late at night, as we ticked over to the seventh day.

"You're thinking too much again." Kyle sat down next to me, a cup of coffee in his hand too, which he popped on my table. He didn't wait for me to answer but rested his head in his hands. "I can't believe I found you."

The relief in his voice, the pent-up doubt I knew so well rang through to me in each of those six words. Reaching out, I grabbed at one of his hands, and he swiveled his head slightly, smiling at me.

"I knew you weren't dead, but I didn't know . . . I just didn't know how else to go about finding you or Dad or Mum . . . or Mason." They were in a whole other city or state, and it wasn't like we could just hop on a train anymore. I refused to let myself admit that they were likely dead given the percentage of survivors.

By now, I was seriously missing my cell phone. I mean, technology was constantly attached to us, and now all I had was this built-in cerebral screen thing. No apps. Nothing. Not even any mindless candy-related games.

Kyle sighed, drawing my attention back to him, and continued to hold my hand even while he looked over at where Jackson and his friends were camped out in the store. They were still fiddling with minimal flickering light even though they really should be asleep. The sixth day was about to finish.

"You know," he started, surprising me somewhat, and then didn't even let me answer his rhetorical question. "I was on duty when it hit. In the middle of a surgery."

He pulled his hand away and looked at them, like he could still see blood even though they were scrubbed clean. There was no way his patient survived being open on a table when everything went down. I braced myself for his next words.

"All the electronics failed; no generators kicked back on. Nothing worked. Emergency lighting was out too." He shook his head. "All I could hear was Dad's voice telling me that when the end came, if we were still around, we needed to think clearly."

He gestured to the backpacks he and the others had been carrying. "Medicine. Antibiotics. One of them is a cooler pack that should hopefully still be holding it cold enough for the drips to be functional. I just grabbed so much, and other people who then grabbed more. And we left. Maybe being an ER surgeon helped us deal with mass hysteria and death. The city is . . . the city was burning. Literally. Nothing figurative about it."

"We saw the smoke from the freeway."

Kyle had to stop, and I just waited, patiently.

When he next spoke, it was in a rush. "Captain Cook Bridge is a goner. Totally destroyed. So is Victoria Bridge. Big chunks missing out of both of them. Black smoke so thick I couldn't even identify buildings anymore. We got out of there pretty fast."

I rubbed his back, trying to lend him support, trying to show I understood. Because I did to a certain extent, but at the same time, I really didn't. I hadn't witnessed it on that large a scale. But I had seen the freeways, and the dead, and the mutations. Plus, I could feel how he felt, and it wasn't pretty. It worried me.

"This is kind of nice here. That, back in the city, was more like what I'd imagined this would be. Destructive, obvious loss of life, uninhabitable. But out here, it's like nothing changed much. Until we ran into the mind-controlling monster."

"You're here now," I said softly, glad he was with me now. I was determined to make this a safe place and finish the fucking quest. Buy the bloody orb.

"Yeah. Wasn't sure we'd make it. We only started out with about twenty of us from the hospital. So many patients unable to make it out. All of us loaded down with supplies and food . . . and makeshift weapons." He sighed

253

and leaned back, and I let my hand fall away, knowing he didn't need it right now. "Thing is, we gathered over two hundred people on the way here. I can't even remember how. Just at crashes we came across, walking on the streets . . . we lost some along the way, too. Ended up ditching the freeway and came up Logan Road. Anyone in our direct path who needed help or was alone, we took them with us. But there's so many out there who . . ."

He faltered and I knew, as someone who had spent his life trying to save people, seeing so many die, so many deaths in those first twenty-four hours probably stabbed him through the heart.

"It's okay. We'll figure something out. Our little techies think they can convert ambient Mana into forms of power so we can use modified devices and even vehicles. It shouldn't be too long." Then I paused and let him know about the quest I was desperate to complete. "And once we have another three hundred or so people, I can buy the Settlement Orb and we can keep people properly safe."

He looked at me incredulously. "What do you mean 'Settlement Orb'?"

I shrugged. "Got a quest when I entered the information desk area up on this level. Told me that I needed to gather one thousand people, and then I would get a massive number of coins. Then it told me that for that same amount of coins—or similar—I could buy the Settlement Orb. Pretty sure the two are deliberately linked. Makes a crazy sort of apocalyptic sense."

Kyle chuckled, and I could hear how tired he was. There was little to no effort put into creating the sound. "So we have to go out there and find more people, bring them back here, and fortify ourselves?"

I considered his words for a moment. Apt description. "That's pretty much the plan."

"Great. Ripper, mate." He groaned this time. "Damn, I must be tired. Haven't used 'ripper, mate' in a while."

"Probably not the best thing for a surgeon to say to his patient as he wheels him through the ER. Don't worry, mate, it'll be a bloody ripper." I laughed, tiredness overwhelming me just as we ticked past 11 p.m. and past our sixth day in this fresh hell on Earth.

Even with the deaths, even with everything we'd been through today, I'd found my twin. Everything else might be in the shitter, but I had the bulk of my family with me. Now we just needed to load up on survivors. Then we'd begin to strengthen our stronghold and fight back against anyone or anything else that decided they wanted to take this from us.

# Chapter Twenty-One:
# Day 7 Post-System Onset

Almost a week. The seventh day in progress, the knowledge of which sank to the bottom of my stomach like a stone. We still needed so many people, though it hadn't specified where we got them from. We really didn't have that many choices, given lack of transport.

Dale and Kyle were chatting near the coffee shop when I walked down with the kids to find breakfast. There was a nasty smell underlying everything. Rotting fresh veggies and the like, with a whiff of decayed meat tossed in for good measure. Given the fact that we had a grocery store between where we slept and where we gathered, I was pretty sure it was the source of week-old food rot.

Red approached at the same time I did. The bags under his eyes told me he'd probably got less sleep than I did. His slender frame seemed positively gaunt, and his usual soft eagerness was absent. I couldn't imagine how he felt.

It was odd not to have Barry around. Though it may have been a short time, he'd been an integral part of this little team. Good with people, great at getting new folks settled, he put everyone at ease. Just a general all-around nice guy.

I could see why his brother would have trouble without him. Red was much more of an introvert.

Jackson enveloped his uncle in bear hugs as I looked over the main level now. With most of the shops opened to us, people began to congregate in groups. If they knew each other, it helped and they had someone to stay with, but if they didn't, it was almost a camaraderie of desperation. It was like they just needed to find someone they could share their loss with, even if it was silent.

"Food's rotting now the freezers' standby has been exhausted. They're chocka full of meat that's going to be rancid pretty soon. Not entirely sure how to manage that. We got rid of a lot of other stuff yesterday from the grocery stores, but not everything, so that's the smell. Not sure what to do now," Red said, and my brother frowned.

Bodies rotting to the left of me, food to the right. Here I was stuck in the middle of an alien invasion.

Evelyn tapped me on my shoulder and raised an eyebrow toward Kyle as my daughter attempted to use him as an uneven bar.

"He's used to it." He was, too. They always climbed on him. Jackson was too big now. But letting Wisp do her pull-ups on her uncle seemed like something they both enjoyed.

Evelyn smiled tightly, but Mike was suddenly at my other elbow and butted in before she could say anything.

"So, boss," he started, staring at a clipboard he'd wrangled from somewhere. "Security. Scooters were a great idea, but we're going to need some form of communication. Know anyone that can, like, telepathy orders around?"

I blinked at him. "First, not boss. Second, let's ask Dolores. Third, Jackson, come talk to Mike about walkie-talkies and what you need to make those work."

Mike opened his mouth to speak again, but Jackson stole his attention from me.

Which gave Evelyn the perfect opening. "We need to start scouting parties and hunting parties, and after . . . whatever it was yesterday, we need to make sure we're sending larger groups to patrol. Even five seems risky now."

Evelyn rarely made eye contact for long, head turning side-to-side, scouting out everything of her own accord, always watching. She must have been a wary game designer. An image of her stuck in an office cubicle, warily checking out her prey as she tapped away at code made me smile.

"Makes sense. Going to have to figure out new meats soon with everything going bad. And check out what the fruits are mutating into and what's edible, figure out nutrients. Not fun. Mutated food. That's all we need. They could have at least left us our diet. Why did they have to go screw that up?" I whined, knowing well that nutritional information was the least of our worries.

Red smiled wanly. "I'll gather some of our new additions to help me. Lots of potential cooking specialists—or food preparation. I'll send Dolores over for Mike."

I watched him leave, worried all over again.

Evelyn was obviously going over her own lists, paying no mind to anyone else. "You think ten people for hunting and leveling and maybe twenty-five for scouting for survivors is enough?" She asked the question hesitantly, and I knew the deaths from yesterday still weighed her down.

Still the numbers bothered me. "For hunting and leveling, if they're close to here, ten is great. Five if they're just doing the basic, baby monsters to level up. But I'd only send out the twenty-five groups looking for survivors as long as they come back or change routes if anything seems amiss. Especially if it suddenly seems like there's no wildlife anywhere around them."

Evelyn nodded. "Good point. We definitely don't want a repeat of yesterday anytime soon. We need food and these Credit things, I'm guessing? Do you think it's like, you know, RPGs? Do we have to gather pelts and skins and scales and stuff so we can craft?"

Yet another thing I hadn't thought of. "Probably? I mean, Jackson and his other tech buddies have been gaining experience just experimenting. I've been getting experience like that, loot from things we've killed. And this quest for the one hundred thousand Credits, which is incidentally enough to buy the core? It's all game-like. So, yeah, it's probably exactly like you're thinking."

"Anyone else find that weird?" Dolores said, suddenly beside us, obviously having been sent by Red. She wasn't alone. There were about ten other new additions with her from yesterday.

The round of incredulous looks Dolores got for that statement made it clear everyone did. But as much as we'd like to jaw about why, this wasn't the time.

Every single one of them looked at me like they expected me to solve for X. Instead, I started giving people orders, getting them moving.

Red had already headed back, but I was pretty sure he needed tarps, so I sent off a couple to raid the camping store.

A few of them appeared to be skilled adventurer Classes. A 15 and 12 among them. Needed those. Needed more people.

"Dolores, anyone in those listings from yesterday have a Class that includes long-distance telepathy?"

I don't think I've ever heard a bark of laughter as loud as the one the Den Mother snorted right then.

"Okay. Take that as a no." I should have known the System wasn't about to make shit easy for us. "Can you help Mike with some security tweaks?"

She nodded, raising an eyebrow at the busy people hanging on our every word. I glared at her as Evelyn grabbed a couple of the adventurers and headed off to find more.

Finally, I pushed my way into my brother's and Dale's apparently very medical discussion. I'd completely missed Dale's arrival.

"Want to move somewhere we won't be assaulted by the incoming stench from rotting food?" I asked pointedly.

It stopped their conversation as well as my daughter's acrobatics on Kyle's arm, and they walked with me back to our little coffee spot, beyond the rotting vegetable smell, to take in the coffee we required to rule the Garden City. I chuckled, remembering that movie from my childhood with a strange fondness.

Jackson ran off to his tech headquarters and started fiddling with something while Chris leaned over, frowning as if she wasn't entirely sure what they were supposed to accomplish. He chatted at her animatedly, but she still seemed confused.

My son stood up straight and put his hands on his hips, very obviously irritated by something, and if I was reading his body language correctly, it was the woman standing next to him. Mum pride tingled in my gut as a sense of relief washed over me. He could stand up for himself.

Dale cleared his throat to get my attention, but I kept a close eye on my son. He was a good kid, but he was going through puberty in the middle of an apocalypse. I had no clue if he was going to be able to keep his temper in check.

"We think we have medical staff covered for now. Kyle here, being a medical professional, gets to head that up. He's agreed to wrangle the several nurses and the couple of general practitioners and specialists he brought along," Dale said.

Kyle made a face but nodded. I knew how much he liked bureaucracy.

"Meanwhile, I can train people in field medicine and work at leveling up the Skills I get that pertain to medicines and healing." He ran a hand through his hair and glanced over to where Darren had now joined my son in what looked like a rather heated discussion over something technical. Didn't look like it was going to get physical, but I could be there in two shakes of a sheep's tail if it did.

Kyle nodded. "My Class will basically make sure my surgical skills don't go to waste, and I can do as much damage to something as I can healing. It's an odd Class. I took it because at first it seemed like being a doctor. But it's more of a give and take surgeon. If that makes sense?"

I shook my head. "Not really, but I'm sure you'll explain it to me another thirty-five times and I'll get it eventually."

Kyle glared at me. "Gee. Thanks."

"Very welcome," I retorted.

Mike beckoned to me from down near the supermarket. I bent down to give Kyle a brief hug. "Right, then. Let's go figure out all this security shit."

Apparently there was no escape from bureaucracy, even in an apocalypse.

# Chapter Twenty-Two:
# 20 Others

## 7 Days Post-System Onset: Late-Afternoon

We'd been at it for hours. Security details, food rations, organizing the plethora of shops with gear and clothes, food, and other sporting goods . . . we'd known for days now that the content wasn't going to last forever. But we had to make it last as long as possible.

Free-for-all grabbing wasn't going to fly.

I glanced at my newest Skill, frowning.

### Rock Slide (Level 1)

*Effect: Rocks are a strong part of the ecosystem around you. With the right level of encouragement, you might even be able to use them to attack or defend. The choice is yours. Strength and durability dependent on spell and caster Level.*

*Mana Cost: 30*

But I really couldn't let my head wander. I'd need to figure it out at some stage.

By the time we tried to figure out what monster meat was potentially edible, I felt like my head was turning into pumpkin guts. I put my head in my hands and would really have just enjoyed screaming a bit.

Night was already falling when a commotion echoed through to us from the courtyard, and I perked up for the first time in what felt like hours. Fantastic. A distraction.

The sounds of arguing bounced off the concrete walls, and we moved toward it. We'd stationed guards at every entrance. Some of the lower-level entrances had runners stationed with them so they could scooter to us with any urgent news.

I still patted myself on the back for that one.

By the time we got to the courtyard, the yelling had escalated into a complete standoff. Evelyn stood with one of her patrols, ushering a long line of people into the center. People pushed and shoved in their desperation to get inside. It was difficult to get a good look at them, but I saw enough of their expressions for it to make me angry at this Dungeon World shit all over again.

These people were scared. Tears cleared paths down grimy cheeks, and the fear in their eyes was palpable. Mana played over all of them, with weak strands and connections, like these people hadn't even activated their Perks. Or perhaps there wasn't much strength of Mana necessary for what they'd chosen.

If they'd never activated Perks, they were long gone now. We were hours away from a full week at this. Which really was a crock of shit. Not everyone possessed a clear head that would make sense of blue flashing screens. Although, I guess forty-eight hours . . . whatever.

It wasn't like this System cared, either. Not like it would have sympathy with people falling apart because their world was snatched out from under them, be understanding, and give them another chance.

Nope.

If you missed the window, I could guarantee any benefits it offered were gone for good.

The angry yelling continued, and I had to look beyond the in my face trudge of the hopeless to find the source. Finally, we managed to push through to join Evelyn and the rest of her patrol. The expression on her face said it all. Her lips pursed in a sign of grim determination I'd come to know over the last few days that basically said "fucking, try me, mate."

The rest of her patrol appeared to be in one piece. They stood, backing her up with a nice air of intimidation.

None of the newcomers appeared to be badly injured. But they were worn out and it might have only been a week, but I knew the System helped replenish our bodies constantly. So if they were tired and disheveled, someone or something had caused it.

It was the group of people standing off against Evelyn and her backup who didn't have a friendly air about them. Frankly, they looked like they'd been preparing for an apocalypse, any apocalypse, for a very long time.

They were geared up with cargo pants, bulging pockets, and had makeshift weapons slung over their backs. There were a good dozen of them in the courtyard. All of them tall, between about five-eight and six-three. Three women, a few men, and others who were languidly non-gendered, at least from where I stood.

Oddly enough, they wore matching uniforms, or at least, as matching as they could get. Black pants, maroon tops, probably remnants of Queensland pride right there. The air about them might have been imposing if I hadn't already encountered MMNs.

Four of the guys held bats as their primary weapon, hefting them like they'd either played baseball or cricket their entire lives. It was obvious they'd been strong even before the apocalypse hit, and my Analyze Skill showed me they'd picked Classes that complemented their former life skills.

Body Specialist was a Class that several of them had chosen, a handful of Level 14s. Damn, I wanted to know what a Body Specialist did, but I could assume it had something to do with hand-to-hand combat. Maybe.

Strength Enhancer—Levels 13 and 14—they had a few of those, too. Frankly, it appeared that they had a scattering of purely martial-based Strength Classes. Their Levels were so close, they had to have been hunting as a group.

It took me about thirty precious seconds to size them up, and during that time, the tension around us all only grew. My only questions were why they were here, and why they seemed to think they had a claim to the people who'd obviously just run away from them?

Before I could ask, Evelyn practically spat her next words at them, her eyes never leaving their group. "These people, and I use the word loosely, decided that their apartment complex was their property, including all other families and residents of it. They kept their 'charges' low Leveled and compliant, forcing them to choose menial and dependent Classes while they took the goods they produced as 'payment for protection' of them.

While not usually scientifically possible, I was sure my blood was boiling.

I could see the Mana lapping around them, but it wasn't as much as I'd seen around a lot of people, which would mean their affinity for magic was low. Probably. I really needed to talk to Dolores about the Mana Sensing thing again.

Dale and Kyle shifted behind me, not to mention Molly, Tasha, and Chris had come when they saw us running here. I wasn't sure what Chris could do, but I doubt she'd have stayed if she couldn't use her skills in combat.

It felt safer, having people stand with me who I felt strong with.

Humans generally took advantage of situations. By and large, we were a selfish group. Probably what started all this when the emissary was sent here.

This whole apocalypse thing? Wasn't an exception.

The tallest man stood about six-three and wasn't above using that height for intimidation. He crossed his arms and straightened while leaning forwards a little to try to loom, a scowl on his face.

He spoke in a voice so deep it couldn't be real. I almost burst out laughing. "Those fellas belong to us. We been protecting them since day one. Give 'em back and we won't have to hurt you."

An arrow landed between his feet, digging into the stone paving as soon as the words left his mouth. Evelyn's deadpan expression as she lowered her bow almost did me in.

This all felt a little too *Casablanca* to me. So surreal.

"I don't think it's us who has to worry." She said the words quietly, but they carried, echoing off the emptiness of the space.

The once-bustling gathering place with multiple bars and restaurants felt like a ghost town standoff.

Big Dude, who I thus named very appropriately, blanched ever so slightly, anger flashing over his face. He probably didn't like that Evelyn was telling him what to do.

Evelyn was shorter than me, but only by a few inches. Regardless of that, she had a massive presence. Self-assured, regal almost. I was getting ahead of myself.

Point was, he tried to pull himself up taller, and she was duly unimpressed.

Reflexes were all that saved me, and I'm not even sure when I developed them. There was a tingle in the Mana around me, and I shot Earth Barricade up in front of me as it turned into a cascade of Mana and catapulted my way. A crunch resounded through the area as the blue wave collided with my defenses and sent someone rolling to the ground. Releasing my spell, I spied a lithe, slinky guy decked all out in black, crouching and rubbing at his nose for all he was worth, a dagger hanging loosely from his other hand.

Irrational anger boiled underneath the surface of my patience, but I steeled my face and raised an eyebrow, doing my best to bluff my way through my next words. "Like she said. People aren't property, and we're not handing them over."

Slinky Guy stood up straight, and a wave of Mana flowed out from him, like he was testing waters. I wasn't so sure I'd be able to beat him with reflexes next time, not now he knew my abilities. He felt dangerous.

"Hand them over now. Or we'll come back and take them." He was well spoken and not lying. I could tell that even without my swanky Diviner Skill reinforcing it.

My brother stood back, observing, which was odd for Kyle, but maybe that was part of his Class now. Next thing on my list—talk to Kyle.

But Chris and all her engineering prowess stepped up. She had this quietly imposing aura around her, and I hadn't quite realized that she was almost as tall as Big Dude and towered over Slinky Guy since she'd never made me feel like I was short. "That's not going to change anything. Now or later, you're not taking any of them."

It was like she'd dropped the gauntlet.

Slinky and Big Dude rushed us, but this time with more coordination. They moved so smoothly that it took me aback, and I figured they had to have practiced these moves at some stage. Maybe they'd already slaughtered dozens of people—maybe the power from the System had gone to their heads.

Maybe they were just assholes.

I triggered Earth Barricade, slamming it up and decimating the beautiful brick formations that made up the courtyard patterns. The tiles crumbled and shattered, the noise rebounding off the shops that surrounded us as the earth pushed through from below. Slinky stumbled but regained his equilibrium faster than I hoped.

While I wanted to use Rock slide, I didn't think the close quarters of the courtyard were the best place to do so. Before I knew it, all of us, and all of these assholes were caught up in an all-out brawl. I blinked at the violence, at the raw primal urge ripping through people who were probably civilized a week ago.

Instinct alone saved me as Slinky blurred before my eyes with Mana flowing all around him showing me that he was about to shoot forward. I barely managed to sidestep in the same instant he moved. Suddenly he stood next to me, but not as close as I think he'd anticipated because the dagger at my side only scratched me instead of stabbing.

It still hurt like buggery, but the blade didn't get to enter my skin. Thank the whatever for small mercies.

I didn't like anything to do with this Apocalypse, but since we were stuck with it, I was super grateful for that damned Mana Sense. Even if I still had no idea how to properly interpret it.

Extending my Earth Barricade, it ripped with a crunching sound as rocks moved against each other and slammed into my opponent from the side. I don't think he was expecting a wall to move on him, at least from the glimpse of utter surprise on his face I got.

Slinky went flying, pinwheeling through the air. He arced overhead but regained his balance during the flight and landed lightly against one of the vertical walls of the movie theater before bouncing off and vanishing again.

Either I'd just made an enemy, or he was going to attack someone else. I couldn't sense his Mana flow this time, but I'd do my best to pick it out. For now, I turned to see how I could help with the mayhem surrounding the rest of us.

Chris and Sarah fought back-to-back with some strange kind of implements that I couldn't recognize. Sarah's red hair streamed out from static around them, and I realized she did have a combat Class, I just had no idea how it worked.

Together, they lit up with electrical pulses that flickered like lightning in a stormy sky. They formed a dome over the entirety of the area, around all of us who were fighting. It resembled the shield Jules had, yet I didn't think it was an ability. The rejuvenation it gave us appeared to be more contraption based.

Our opponents grew angry if the Big Dude's guttural roar was anything to go by.

His brows knotted in confusion when his punch connected with Molly's tower-shield and only drove her back a foot or so. He was obviously used to his punches packing more of a wallop if the cry of fury he let loose was anything to go by. Molly grinned from behind her shield and swung her own sword, the flat of it catching him in the side of the knee to his increasing anger.

Even in our defense of our base, of our people, killing other humans just wasn't our priority. We all knew our enemies weren't from Earth.

Spells flew around, Mana chasing and colliding with power as it was released. If I squinted properly, it almost looked like fireworks. Power clashed, making a rumble like thunder as it collided with the technological magic our two adult engineers had concocted.

Then Slinky was back. My Earth Barricade wasn't exactly like a puppy that could follow me around. I had to mentally target it and enable it. He was difficult to track, darting in and out of range, pushing me to try to hit him again with repeated casts of the Skill. While I couldn't quite track him, I could see traces of the Mana he used.

Frankly, I couldn't think about how close he came to stabbing me. But I could let my anger at it fuel me.

270

My Mana couldn't keep up with permanently reforming and dissipating my walls. My Mana Regen just wasn't there yet. Another Level or three. I just needed to get to Level 17, and I would get that self-Mana Regen Skill. I should have taken it instead of Rock Fall.

The punch hit my face out of left field.

Literally.

I'd completely lost track of my assailant as he blinked in and out quickly with whatever ability that was. His punch pancaked my face, my Mana Sense doing little to warn me of its approach. The blunt damage from the impact throbbed along one cheekbone. It sent me sailing over one of my own barriers and skidding along the torn-up ground.

If it had been an old-fashioned cartoon, I'd have had birds flying in a circle around my head. As it was, it felt like a stun-lock had grip over me. Possibly a Skill, possibly just pain.

Before I could get rid of the disorientation, Slinky tackled me, rolling me over and over. Random self-defense classes kicked in, but I was no martial artist. Not that they taught much about what to do when you were on the ground. Why was that, anyway?

Yeah, I was still a little woozy, and it didn't help that even after I got out of the stun-lock, he kept pounding into me with his fist, having lost the knife somewhere in the scuffle. All I had was the Mana around me, my knowledge of the earth, and in my rising panic, I pulled on my new Skill.

*Rockslide Activated*

*Warning: No immediate geologically sound area available. Calibrating adjustments now.*

Thing was, I hadn't had a chance to test it yet, and I had no idea how it activated or what it was trying to do by calibrating itself.

It was a surprise then when the clay earth that cluttered the ground bonded with the rocks and stone debris around me, climbed to the apex of one of my crumbling Earth Barricades, and showered down on us. Or more specifically, Slinky's back as he held me down.

He gaped at me in surprise and pain as multiple rocks smashed into his back from the top of one of my walls. With one of his hands braced against my body, I could feel the impact reverberating through my sternum, but much muted. Rather than rolling with the attack and giving up his position on top of me, he seemed to be tanking the attack.

Or maybe surprise just had him tensing. Who knows?

The final rock hit him in the back of the head, and he flopped down on top of me bonelessly. The rock rolled off his head down in front of my head, making me see the blood, hair, and bone it took with it. I was pretty sure he was still alive, but he was definitely unconscious.

Pushing with one hand and a propped-up leg, I managed to roll out from under him, all the while trying not to devolve into a panic attack. Somehow, unconscious, he was even heavier than before, and the fact that some strange dude who clearly wanted to kill me had me pinned down was a little gibbering monkey in the back of my head.

It wasn't like that. This wasn't that sort of thing. But it still did nothing for the stillness of my heart. I would deal with those nerves later.

Free at last, I cast my gaze around as I pushed myself up, I saw Ray caught in an Ice Lance battle with another mage. I didn't even remember him joining the fray. His opponent didn't appear to be as strong. It wasn't a Level thing, since Ray was lower in Level, but probably an exact Class or build thing.

Ray was literally an Ice Lancer, and the other guy was a Cold Weather Mage. Ray didn't need my help, but I wished I had enough time to sit and watch the battle. Cold wind swirled around them. It was fascinating.

My gaze fell on Tasha, who seemed to desperately need assistance, bleeding as she was from a couple of holes in her body.

I could see her left blade whirling as she drew a specific spell, barely holding her attacker at bay with her right. The sigils danced in the air and glowed brightly in silver for just a moment. Even though she was cornered, her Fighter-Mage Skills hampered by the fact that she'd been closed in on within striking distance, the spell wove its magic.

**_Into the Fray_**

_(Group Buff)_

_+10 to Physical Damage Resistance._

_Duration: 60 seconds_

It was a small buff, but it helped everyone around her. Even in such confines, she'd buffed her group at the same time as herself. Of course, the fact that she was helping others meant that her opponent took her to the ground in that moment of distraction, driving the air out of her as he then proceeded to climb on top of her.

Maybe it was an instinctive thing. Maybe it was a guy thing. But they all seemed to want to mount their prey and then punch downwards. Leverage from up top. Made sense, but it was a brute force thing that I wouldn't think of as a first resort.

Tasha was all the way over the other side of the courtyard, and there was no way I'd get there in time to help. Still, I had to try.

Before I could arrive, something flashed in front of me, hitting her square in the chest. Light, so bright that it made me squint and turn away, exploded from her chest.

I stumbled to a stop, gasping.

Not another one. I couldn't lose another one.

When the light dimmed, Ray stood over Tasha, his hand held out before him and his face pale. Like he hadn't been sure whatever he just did would work. Icicles clattered slowly to the ground from the barrier they'd formed in front of the Fighter-Mage.

Her assailant lay stunned, groggy and barely coming to—as did others who'd been close. They shook their heads, obviously trying to clear them.

My brother grabbed hold of Tasha, hauling the still-living woman—and let me tell you, my heart started beating again when I realized she was still alive—to her feet. Together, the pair regrouped with the rest of the team, facing our assailants, who were reforming their own line too.

Air rushed back into my lungs in a cold, gulping breath. She really was okay.

Since we had a moment, I tapped into Big Dude with my Blood Transfer and started leaching his life to heal myself so that our Healers didn't need to bother with me. He barely even glanced at me.

While that went on, I was looking over the fight details, trying to figure out what Ray had just done. I don't think I was the only one, since no one was starting up the fight again, not even Molly and Big Dude.

They all just appeared to be shocked. All of us were. A temporary, complete twenty-second lull in combat—like no one knew how to start up again after the blinding ice flash.

Which is why, when Slinky crept up behind me, close enough to touch, his dagger back in hand, it was the channeling of Mana through his body that alerted me.

Damn the System sometimes. It woke him up earlier than it should have. With that head trauma, he should have been out for like an hour at least.

I spun around and shoved at him with my hands, activating Water Siphon as I did so. The effect was instantaneous and disgusting, and I felt bile rise in my throat.

Slinky's skin greyed immediately, lending him the appearance of a wrung-out sponge. I pulled my hands away, but since I'd activated it, the spell didn't stop. My opponent fell to his knees, gasping for breath, one hand steadying himself on the ground while the other clutched at his chest, as his skin paled further. I considered casting again, even if it meant killing him.

I wasn't about to let this fucker take me away from my kids, even if he *was* human.

And then another flash descended over us, but it wasn't ice this time, more like a gentle coalescing light. My skin tingled, and I looked around for the source.

**Den Barrier Activated.**

*While within this barrier you are under the stewardship of the Den Mother. The more under her protection, the better the temporary buff.*
*Currently: +74 armor*
*+ 5 Mana and Health Regen per 30 seconds in combat.*
*Duration: 60 seconds*

The Den Barrier and Slinky's predicament distracted the rest of their team when none of us had really recovered yet anyway. Still gasping in pain, Slinky rolled on the floor feebly, and I gagged at the sight of him again.

Big Dude glanced over at me, then to Dolores, and back to Ray. His eyes narrowed at the ten-odd left of his team that weren't rolling around on the floor in agony. They were all in a ready pose, but even he could feel the hesitation in the courtyard now.

Evelyn raised an eyebrow as our eyes briefly met, and I knew we'd have to talk about Skills and this fight in particular soon. Not to mention I really had to talk to Dolores about this whole Den Mother thing.

I couldn't wrap my head around how close I'd come to killing another human being. How much I wanted to. Maybe the apocalypse was changing all of us.

"See?" Chris flicked strands of blonde hair out of her eyes and crossed her arm. I pretended not to notice how much her voice shook. "We aren't giving you those people back. And we're not leaving anyone else you've screwed over behind."

"Do you not realize how fucked up it is that you did this?" Dolores asked, butting into the middle in all her Level 12 glory. The scowl on her face could have turned milk sour . . . if we'd had any that survived the blackouts.

The older woman had this presence, this motherly countenance that just demanded respect and attention. She was scolding them. "We are human. We were in-fucking-vaded, goddamn it. And the first thing you do is try to enslave your fellow humans and take advantage of them? Shame on you!"

The ability to inflict a wave of guilt that large was impressive. Our visitors were squirming under her gaze, none of them meeting it. Their feet shifted, and one of them even wrung his hands. Hell, even I felt guilty.

Big Dude's eyes seemed troubled for the first time since we'd caught them trying to break into our little village and take "their people" back.

Slinky still rolled on the ground gasping for air. My stomach lurched again, and I decided to do some more trial and error with that Skill before I used it on another human. I hadn't even given it a second thought and somehow, I'd drained most of his moisture . . . whatever it was that made him turn grey and left a husk of a man.

"This is not remotely acceptable. We were assured you are mostly civilized." That was a new voice. Light and airy, conceited and not quite . . . human. Like a South African and French accent had a baby.

Seriously. What the fuck was this? Not only had they shut our country down, killed like forty percent of our population inside of twenty-four hours . . . and now they were in our fucking city?

I turned, feeling my face fall flat and stern as I raised my eyebrow. The kind of face my kids called "momma bear," and crossed my arms.

"And just who the fuck are you?"

# Chapter Twenty-Three:
# First Contact

## 7 Days Post-System Onset—10:45 p.m.

The moment the words were out of my mouth, I wished I hadn't been so rash. Losing my temper was never a good thing, especially considering this was quite literally the first conversational alien I'd met.

The . . . creature in front of me only vaguely resembled a human. I couldn't place a gender, but the more I stared at them, the less I cared. They stood about six feet tall and had what I could only describe as a lithe body, with four toned arms that hung gracefully down their side and four total digits on the end of each hand. But there was a transparency to the ribbon-like flesh that lent a serenity to the courtyard.

Their body flowed like the ribbons on a maypole that had been left out in the wind. Languid. Lulling.

The feet were wide and flat, yet like the rest of this speech-capable alien, delicately perfect. With the way their feet splayed out, resembling a full-blooming hibiscus flower placed upside down, I wondered just how surefooted it could be.

Our unwelcome visitor appeared taken aback by my outburst. And from the horror on all our assailants faces, I finally realized that this . . . being wasn't with them but had walked in on our little human love spat.

"I am Dequasha of the Intergalactic Rare Species Hunter's Association, here to inform you that our hunters will arrive in"—they paused to check, as if they too had an interface they needed to interact with—"Nine Earth days. Please vacate this . . . Terra Australis . . . before that period. It would be best if you take your . . . *things* with you."

The almost hypnotic clicking in the undertones of how they spoke reminded me of the metronome from my nightmare violin lessons as a child. The sound lulled me, making me almost forget the words they'd spoken.

"Vacate?" Evelyn said quietly, with an angry edge to her voice.

Dequasha blinked, like a nictitating membrane, somewhat like crocodiles and some birds and other creatures. Their membranes blinked and blinked as they sought to move on. "Vacate. Leave. Abandon. Vamoose. This is no longer your home."

Even as I felt the anger of my human companions begin to rise, I couldn't help Analyzing Dequasha.

**Dequasha Mitoi'riya**

*Direct Descendent, Prominatia of the Mitoi Clan*

*Mitoi-Aral offshoot.*

*Hunter-Ranked Magi*

*Level: ???*

I blinked, having no idea what the hell I'd just read meant.

"I beg to differ." Ray took a small step forward, his hands still firmly aimed at Big Dude, just in case the guy got any ideas. "This is Australia, mate. As long as there's a chance for us to survive, we'll take it. We're not handing over anything to you."

Dequasha waved their hand dismissively as if swatting a fly, and a low-rumbled bark emanated from their throat. Maybe it was a derisive laugh or code or something. "Your thoughts are not of our concern. No Settlement Orb has been claimed within a significant distance. You will fail, as it has been predicted, and we will take over your exotic-wildlife-populated landmass."

They paused, looked at myself, and sort of through Ray before doing that weird blinking thing again that made my skin crawl. Clapping their hands so loudly it made every single one of us jump, they spoke once more.

"Enough! Vacate. You have nine Earth days."

And then Dequasha was gone.

That was how we slid past eleven at night and into our eighth day of this System Apocalypse.

After that encounter, the wind went out of all our sails. It was obvious we had the upper hand and many more people we could pull out of Garden City. Our opponents, perhaps sobered by the experience of an ethereal, plant-like alien coming and talking to us in the middle of a fucking skirmish, wilted and surrendered.

I still hadn't picked my jaw off the floor. We had nine days to vacate Garden City? No, no. What we had to do was get these people in here and accounted for so we could finish that damned quest and get the orb. No Settlement Orb claimed? We'd see about that.

We just got here. I wasn't going to let them take the only Safe Zone I'd found for my children out from under me.

"Try and take our base. I don't think so," I mumbled, more to myself than anything else. But Evelyn and Ray were standing close enough to me to hear.

Slinky, healed enough by the System that he was able to make a wobbly stand, spoke in a gravelly voice like he hadn't had a drink in weeks. Oops. "What do we need to do, for this to become a . . . settlement?"

I eyed him thoughtfully. We had the upper hand, and I was pretty sure, even without speaking to Mike, that we were fully capable of keeping them in check. Should I give him the answer? Could I afford not to? Between a bunch of asshole thugs and losing Garden City, did I have a choice?

"We need to gather another three hundred people. Wait." I mentally calculated those who had already funneled in when they ran to us for protection.

I couldn't be sure, but it seemed to be a bedraggled fifty or so who'd streamed past me.

"Probably need another two hundred and fifty survivors." I amended the number, making sure we would have the bare minimum. And then, I swear to the gods of whatever, I would figure out how to fortify what we had. "Once we do that, we can access the settlement interface. Right now, we're just not enough survivors to be considered one."

Seven hundred and fifty people, and they wouldn't consider that a settlement. I didn't like these beings who had taken over our world. I didn't like the circumstances they'd placed us in, nor the rules we needed to abide by. But they had Buckley's chance of me rolling over and taking this.

Kyle placed his hand on my shoulder, just a touch. Like I'd said, I didn't lose my temper much, but when I did, I boiled.

"Um." Slinky pushed himself completely upright now, without the aid of the post he'd been leaning against. It looked like he didn't want to say what he was about to, as if he knew how the words would sound when he spoke them, but he swallowed visibly and came out with it anyway. "We have two apartment blocks under guard up a ways. Some of our group are keeping watch over them. There's about a hundred people in each, give or take. Should help with those numbers."

Breathe. I just had to breathe, or I was going to knock out his teeth. Violence never got us anywhere, right? Even if it really fucking felt like an answer. Evelyn beat me to a response.

"Two hundred people that you're . . . guarding?"

Slinky ran a hand through his hair. He seemed uncomfortable. Good. Let him be. What an arse. Who did they think they were kidding?

"Look. We didn't know what to do, we didn't know what this was. We picked Classes, figured out ways to benefit our group of friends and just went for it. We didn't think . . ." his voice trailed away, and then he whispered a little more. "I didn't think . . ."

Looked like our words were beginning to sink in. With the others too, if their defeated postures and bewildered gazes were anything to go by. Maybe they'd thought it was a game after all. Storing up resources and NPCs.

Hell, the damn aliens had called us that too, hadn't they?

Having an alien drop into the middle of your argument with other players was a great way to disabuse you of the "this is a game" notion. If we died here, we didn't suddenly respawn like in a computer game. Dead here was dead everywhere.

Dead. Dead. Dead.

As if to punctuate my rather morbid thoughts, one of those strangely magpie-influenced dragons flew far overhead, squawking like it agreed with every thought in my head and would gladly put me out of my misery. Only its shadow passed through the meager moonlight, coating us just for a second.

A hush fell over the group as it flew languidly away, not having noticed us. Could have been calling for a mate, for all we knew. I did not want to encounter two of those.

Big Dude looked up. "I'm Gary. The assassin over there is Drake. We didn't mean to be—"

"Arseholes? Drongos? Jackasses? Yobbos?" Ray supplied, his arms crossed as he fought off whatever instincts seemed to be trying to jump out of his body.

Ice mage or not, I think he ran hot. We'd have to keep an eye on him.

"Enough talk." Evelyn shook her head. "Gary. Drake. We'll come with you to escort your people over. The rest of this group will stay here in custody of some of our members." She shot a glance at me.

I sighed. "We'll need to travel in smaller groups. How far did you hamper these people with their leveling?"

I needed to know if they'd be able to do anything that could help us while we retrieved them, or if they were going to be dead weight. At least we'd kept the immediate circumference around Garden City well cleared of monsters and mutations. It would be hard pressed for anything close to us to exceed Level Ten right now.

Pushing down my anger, I grabbed at my logic so I could focus on getting this quest finished and our position secured. Give my kids as safe a place as possible to continue living.

Drake spoke up, his voice stronger now. I hadn't realized how long it would take him to recover. I really needed to double check that Water Siphon spell; there might have been some fine print I didn't see. "The highest is Level 7, maybe 8 by now. They're mostly crafting Classes. Majority will be around Level 6. I think."

I pinched the bridge of my nose, glad that I no longer needed my prescription glasses, thanks to the System. Even if I missed being able to push them up my nose and look down at idiots. It could have been much worse. "Okay. Let's get this organized."

I shot a note to my son, so he would know I was heading out.

*Really? Without me again?*

Just as I'd suspected, he wasn't happy about it. If he was just a little older, I think it would be easier, but this wasn't our world anymore. I'd adapt to this new way of life sooner or later, just now I was going to push it as late as I could.

*K: Take care of your sister for me.*

*J: Dog is doing that.*

*K: Dog is?*

*J: You'll see what I mean later.*

Great, now I had something else to worry about. But instead of lashing out like my mum might have when she was stressed, I just took a deep breath, thanked the System for the first time that this was a chat and not voice interface, and replied. *Okay. Keep working on energy upgrades. We are going to need them sooner than later.*

*J: Oh?*

*K: Later. Chris and Sarah should be back with you soon. I promise, once I feel like I can protect you better, I'll start taking you out with me.*

*J: That's SOON, right?*

I laughed as I typed *Yeah* with my mind and turned to gather this motley crew into some form of rescue operation.

# Chapter Twenty-Four:
# Goddamn Quests

*Quest Update—Quest: Gather Survivors*

*Current Population: 988*

*Quest Time Remaining: 66 hours*

I sat down on the floor, this time pushing myself back against one of the dividers upstairs. It was plexiglass and would hold. My gaze drifted to the ceiling of the center and the skylights strategically placed over the opening.

It was starting to get crowded in here, at least on this top level where everyone seemed to gather. It wasn't even the whole top level. Garden City wasn't some tiny shopping center. Think like ten massive football fields. We were about to hit that thousand people mark, and we had plenty of room for all of them.

It was that I think they preferred to feel like they were surrounded by a heap of other humans. Maybe that was this could be less real.

We still kept Drake and Gary in their own little section with their other "protectors." I couldn't tell if they were truly contrite or not, even though my Skill seemed to insist they were. I had no idea what they might have picked as Skills that could disable or trick my ability.

Twelve people. That's all we needed. Just twelve more.

"Mum." Wisp stood over me, Dog at her side, his tongue lolling out of his mouth as he eyed me. I think he was laughing.

"Yes?" I asked, wishing I could just close my eyes and sleep on the cold, tiled floor. She was up early, it had only just hit five in the morning, and I hadn't slept.

"Are you okay? Dog and I are worried." She sounded like my little girl, but I suddenly realized just how much she'd been through in the last week. On impulse, I pushed myself up and enveloped her in a hug.

She hadn't hit that age yet where she was embarrassed, though I knew she was getting close, and she hugged me back. Hard. Maybe we both needed it. Dog pushed his nose in on the hug too, and I could have sworn the animal had grown since this morning. Yesterday morning. Whatever time. An entire week since the shit hit the fan.

"I'm fine, love. Just knackered. You know how it goes." I grimaced, trying to make her smile, but she just stood and stared at me, arms crossed. She'd always been observant, and I could never pull one over her.

"Mum." She sat down and patted the ground for me to sit like she hadn't just made me stand up. "You pretend not to like people, and then you work behind the scenes to try and make things better for them. And you use all your energy and have none left for you."

"I know, love," I said and gave her another squeeze.

Not that interrupting her made Wisp happy with me. "After that . . . you're tired for a while. Grumpy with me and Jackson and everyone else."

I winced in reflexive parental guilt. The type you get when you know you screwed up, even if you screwed up because you were tired and fed up and they'd been bugging you for days on end for more TV, more sweets, more gymnastic practice, more computer parts . . .

"So just . . . there are lots of people here. And me. I'm not as old as Jackson, but I'll be nine before Christmas." She winked at me. Loved to remind me that she got two lots of presents in close succession. "I'm okay. In here, with the other kids and Jana, and with Dog to watch out for me. Don't worry about me. Besides." And she flashed her bracer. "I'll be okay."

I couldn't tell whether she was being brave or really believed it. Sometimes my littlest was a bit of an enigma. "Maybe we'll make you the adult. You're taking this awfully well."

She shrugged. "Maybe? But really. If I try to throw a tantrum, what's that going to change? I'll dirty my shirt and hurt my throat, and I really don't want to look silly in front of some of the other kids."

I laughed and I realized then, she'd been trying to get me to do that. Not just a little laugh, one of those full-throated ones that does good for the soul. She'd never thrown a tantrum in her life; she just wasn't that sort of kid. Some kids needed that. Some didn't. Wisp was one hundred percent herself.

"Thank you," I said to her, locking gazes.

She grinned hugely and reached in to give me another hug. "Always, Mum."

I smiled as she walked away, her black hair flying out behind her, the dog trailing in her wake. They grew up so fast, and this new world was going to make it that much faster, that much more necessary.

There were so many parents around who just weren't parents anymore. It was testament to how brutal things were. More than one of them watched Wisp and the other kids with the kind of hunger and loss and desperation that made me quail.

More than one ex-parent watched them like they'd do anything, just about anything, to bring their kids back, to keep the rest of the kids alive.

Had to admit, I knew that feeling all too well.

I sighed and pushed myself up because I needed a damn nap. Surely, I could squeeze in a couple of hours. Sun wasn't due up for a while yet. Later, I had to get those dozen people.

❖

The thing was, sleep and I weren't really on speaking terms, and neither, apparently, was this new world. I don't know what I was expecting.

I woke in the early morning to noise out the front of the Harvey Norman's where most of us still slept because we hadn't been bothered to move the mattresses or beds out yet.

Except it wasn't commotion, it was Ray trying to be subtle and quiet and accidentally tripping over some of the toys the younger children had left out on the tiles. I cringed at the loud cacophony of sound, but somehow, the kids who were still asleep didn't wake up.

Oh, to be a child and nap on any surface, anywhere, at any time. That should have been a superpower. It was just about five and the sun was still asleep. I'd managed maybe ninety minutes. I leveraged myself out of the way-too-comfortable mattress and walked to the front where he was picking up the toys he'd scattered everywhere.

"What is it?" I asked, arms crossed and a sudden chill breezing through the center that made me shiver.

That was odd. It's not like it had windows that opened. Maybe it was Ray's ability.

He looked up, smiling. His face lit up with excitement, and I found myself not minding as much that his racket had woken me way before I wanted to be.

"Kira. There are people approaching. A decent-sized group who look tired and just done with the world." He grinned even more. "They should fill our quest quota!"

I wasn't sure he should be that happy that they looked like they were done with the world, and I paused my own rejoicing for a moment. It was still mostly dark outside, and these people were walking in it. We'd noticed so far that the dark housed some of the worst creatures and mutations. So how had those people gotten here in the first place?

"Okay," I said, trying to think about it rationally. "Are we sure they're not like, you know . . . zombies?"

Ray blinked at me like I'd just punched a hole in him, even if it was only in his excitement. "I didn't think about that. I mean, they could be, right?"

I nodded, even though I thought it highly unlikely, I just felt squeamish about people who'd traveled through the dark. "Let's just go take a look then."

Ray's gaze darted around constantly as we met up with Jules, who'd picked up Evelyn. I glanced at the two of them, wondering why they didn't just wake Evelyn and I up at the same time. Though I guess Evelyn was a heavier sleeper, else she'd not have slept through that noise.

Moments later, Dolores sidled up to us in that quiet, grandmotherly way that stopped the moment she opened her mouth. "Them's gonna be some trouble?"

I shrugged, not having the foggiest. "Guess we'll find out."

We didn't have to walk to the courtyard this time. Instead, we pushed open the doors to the outside parking area where we'd gone out on our adventure of the blubber fish of doom.

There, just beyond the glass doors, I could see them. Maybe around twenty-five or so people at first, but there were shadows behind them I couldn't make out.

They weren't shambling at all, and none of their body parts appeared to be dropping off from what I could see.

In fact, they seemed to be trudging onward regardless of everything else. Some of them were women, and two of those clutched small children. The fathers appeared to pull wagons behind them.

Every single one of them looked totally beat up. As though this System

291

world had chewed all their newly reborn hopes and dreams up and shat them out.

I realized in the slowly, dawning light that there weren't just the couple of dozen or so people Ray had initially estimated. The straggling train of people spread out for quite a ways, like they just couldn't all stick together. Maybe a hundred, or even more, I couldn't tell.

It must have been agony trying to travel together when they were so spread out.

Somehow, even knowing my quest was going to be more than complete, I could just see trouble coming.

# Chapter Twenty-Five:
# Quest Complete

## 8 Days Post-System Onset—11 a.m.

People streamed by me and into the center for hours, long surpassing the thousand mark we needed. Even as they began streaming in, I sent Jules and Gemma to grab people and start expanding the potential shops for habitation. Everything down here in the vicinity of the food court was taken.

People had begun to drift toward their own homes, for want of a better word. Here and there, groups occupied former shops instead of just crashing in a department store or on the hallways outside.

I mentally swiped the quest completion notification away when I received it while I helped usher people in.

Mike's security force was everywhere, their matching baseball caps the only way to tell them apart. Simple but effective, at least until now. We were going to need more than the stock the shops had soon.

One woman sobbed into her hands while Dale checked the abrasions on her back, and someone I didn't know knelt in front of her, trying to calm her down. Times like this we could have used a Bard. Something soothing and lulling would help these people and their overwhelming sense of exhaustion.

Damn, I wished Mason had been with us.

The relief on everyone's faces as we took them in and made them comfortable was reward enough. But the Mana that danced around their feet wasn't what I'd come to expect from a group of people this huge.

Maybe they'd chosen crafting or teaching Classes.

I wasn't entirely sure what I should be looking for, but I knew something was off. Not with them. No, these people gave me an overwhelming sense of honesty, of being genuinely relieved that they'd found sanctuary. Standing back, I crossed my arms. Only a few stragglers were still incoming. Sure, there was a lot more to be done. Ray and Dolores flitted around gathering everyone's information so we could maybe form a functional self-sustaining society.

Dale and Kyle, along with a few nurses and other general practitioners from before this influx were checking everyone over for nutrition and dehydration, not to mention double checking the System had healed wounds correctly.

Red and his small team of cooks and gatherers ran around making sure everyone who came had some water and sustenance. Shit. Water. Plumbing was another of those things we had to think of.

"I wonder how far they trekked to be here," I muttered quietly.

Jackson's response from next to me answered my rhetorical question so suddenly that I jumped. Maybe I was just used to him being near me, so his Mana signature didn't alert me or something.

"Someone mentioned that they passed through Eight Mile Plains, picking up stragglers as they went." His voice caught on the last word, and I could see how much paler he looked than usual.

Reaching over, I gave his shoulders a squeeze, and he let me, sagging into my side just a little in a way that told me how much he needed that physical contact. My little boy had grown up, but he was still a kid in many ways. It was a warm feeling, something that made me glad he was mine. To know that he still needed his mum, even if it was because of this world we found ourselves in now.

"Thanks," he said, standing back up straight after a few seconds, pulling himself up almost to my height.

When had that happened? Had he seriously grown in a week? Thanks,

System.

"'Course. Gotta keep you healthy at least until you're eighteen or I fail as a parent, you know. And I do hate to fail."

Jackson laughed. "Thanks, Mum. Seriously. You've taken this a lot better than I thought you would."

I raised an eyebrow at my son for thinking the same about me as I did about him. Although his acceptance made sense. He'd been playing with that damned VR rig his father got him for ages. So this . . . his father.

Damn it.

Mason was probably dead already. He'd never been the most pragmatic of people—such a dreamer. Part of our attraction to each other, and definitely contributed to our growing apart. Still, I hoped he was alive, for the kids' sake if nothing else.

I suppressed a sigh and nodded at Jackson. "Run along. Go build us tech things we can use to, I don't know, communicate or something. Go play with gadgets and make them shine, so we can show these aliens they chose the wrong country and planet to fuck with."

"Mum!" he mock scolded. "Language."

I laughed, but it sounded empty even to me. Mana danced around my fingers, like it was attaching itself to me, like I had something it needed. And then I noticed Wisp. She stood by the woman I'd seen crying earlier, her hand on Dog's back. The pup nuzzled the woman's hands, and her breathing had slowed back to a normal rate. Wisp scratched his back, an odd little smile on her face. Now, that was interesting.

"Are you going to get that settlement card thing or whatever it is, or are you just going to stand there and watch your daughter and her quasi-therapy dog work their own brand of magic?" Evelyn sounded impatient, even if still delightfully blunt.

She had a point. I cracked my neck from side to side. "Yeah. I think we're good here now."

My once-quiet haven was now bustling with traffic as we expanded our presence through the center. No longer did I have my little favorite coffee shop spot. People were just everywhere. I was pretty sure we could probably hold around ten thousand people in a pinch, but that would be seriously the most.

It looked like the library was my new headquarters, I guessed.

Evelyn followed me as I led the way. Somewhere along the line we picked up Ray, Chris, Kyle, and Dolores. Entering the library, it suddenly seemed so small with so many people. It was in a good spot though, and it made me think we'd be able to defend the orb if someone decided to try and take it.

You know. Like evil plant-looking alien buggers.

Still. This was quiet, out of the way, a repository of knowledge. It fit, right? And we only had eight days left to prepare to rebuff the aliens who wanted us to clear out before they got here.

Fat chance of compliance there, mates.

Taking a deep breath, I activated the notifications with my mind.


***Quest Update—Quest: Gather Survivors***
*Current Population: 1,142*


***Congratulations! Quest: Gather Survivors Completed***
*You have successfully gathered more than 1,000 survivors into a defensible position and surprisingly helped increase the overall survival rate of the Dungeon Continent Australia. Welcome to the beginning stages of society!*
*Requirements: Gather 1,000 Survivors within the bounds of the temporary Safe Zone*

296

*Time Limit: For completing this momentous task more than 48 hours before the deadline (62, to be precise), you have a completion bonus of 12% increased reward.*

*Rewards: 112,000 Credits*

**Quest: Obtain Settlement Orb**

*Cost: 100,000 Credits*

*Do you wish to purchase this Settlement Orb?*

*Yes or No?*

This System was such a shit. If we'd kept it down to the line, we would have had no extra money left over. Of course, I wanted the damned Settlement Orb. I motioned for the YES.

**Congratulations! You have become the Settlement Owner of Garden City Township—Brisbane Australia.**

*You have successfully upgraded your village to a town.*

*Due to the unique nature of your town's make up and being located in Australia, you own the area demarcated as Garden City Township. Additional areas that fall within the control of the Settlement Orb are currently unowned and thus not within the Safe Zone until 80% purchased.*

*You gain one Advanced Military Building, one Scientific/Production Building Spot, and one Special Spot. Your defensible position is now marked on the map, and you may purchase upgrades for defenses. The current location (Garden City Shopping Center and included carpark) is a Safe Zone. Mana flow is stabilized, and random spawning is neutralized in Safe Zones. Areas outside of Safe Zone continue to experience fluctuating Mana flows and increased spawn rates. Full access to administrative controls are now granted.*

*Current options available include:*

*- Access to the Shop Feature*

*- Land Purchases by Individuals*

*- Settlement Defenses*

*- Utility Upgrades*

*- Tax Rates*

*Next Level attainable is a Large Town and must meet the following requirements:*

*1.   Minimum Population of 20,000.*

*2.   100% of Land Purchased*

*3.   Minimum Tax Revenue Level*

I blinked at all the information in front of me. Shit. Taxes? I reflexively chose the default option for that. Could always come back later.

But wait—there were more notifications blinking at me like they might die if I didn't open them.

### Quest Completed: Trade Hub Creation

*The Coefficient Crafting Cartel have lifted the Trade Lock Skill, locking the Settlement Orb of the Garden City Township from utilization of the Shop functions until a trade hub around the Settlement Orb is created.*

*You now have:*

*Shop 20% discount for 5 years for all contributors to the quest*

*Galactic Trade Hub\**

> *\* Please note that a representative will be sent to you as soon as possible to assist in managing and setting up of your Galactic Trade Hub.*

*Meanwhile, please find the Shop Transportation Orb in the most convenient space within your settlement.*

"Well," I said, still taking in the plethora of information. "We have a shop. We have been storing everything, right? Like all the stuff we loot?"

Considering our inventories expanded very conveniently every five Levels or so, I thought we had been. Another notification flashed at me, but I minimized it while we continued the discussion.

Evelyn nodded, tapping her fingers against her crossed arms. "Yeah, we have multiple inventories completely full. Not the crafting stuff, though—there are crafting Classes that need some of those items. We've already had people start using what they can. Why?"

I grinned at her. "Well, now we get access to the shop—and eventually or soon, a Crafting Cartel. People sell all their stuff and get money. Credits. Whatever. If I can figure out where it's put the entrance."

"What does it say?" Dolores asked, standing close to my shoulder like she was hoping for a peek over it.

"Most convenient place in the settlement . . ." I pursed my lips.

"Info desk," Kyle butted in. "Willing to bet that's the info desk. Know how it works?"

I was about to shake my head when my brain kicked me. "Well, it's called a Shop Transportation Orb. So I'm guessing it's like an orb that . . . transports you?"

He laughed. "I'll get on that. If it's already there, we might have people milling about who are confused."

I waved him away and concentrated on the rest of the information. First things first.

Crafting was going to have its own spot if this Cartel was what I thought it was. Good. Didn't need to worry about that much for now. People could keep going the way they'd been up to now.

Shop was sorted, sort of. I'd figure out the rest of the information as I went. Time to check that notification.

*Quest Granted:*

*A Habitable Safe Zone*

*Part One - Plumbing*

*It looks like you've survived so much that you've established a Safe Zone. Since you're on a continent that wasn't deemed survivable by local inhabitants, it looks like you're going to need to make that Safe Zone habitable.*

*First of all, there are a lot of you, so raw sewage is probably not a good thing.*

*Task: Use the Shop and/or local resources to complement the options in your town administration interface to establish a working plumbing system within the confines of what you previously had.*

*Reward: 12,000 Credits for the town treasury and Part Two of this Quest.*

*Time Limit: 4 days*

"Plumbing, we'll need to address plumbing." I spoke my thoughts out loud. This whole interface was complex and encompassing. There were so many things to consider, menus. Dolores was still trying to peek over my shoulder, and I grinned, feeling a little evil.

"Soooo, Dolores," I asked in my sweetest hey-would-you-totally-do-me-a-favor type of voice.

She raised an eyebrow at me skeptically, but to her credit, she didn't take a step back.

"What?"

"You're good at smacking people out of stupors, want to help me organize the town?" I grinned at her. It would be far less overwhelming when I had someone to chat about things with.

Dolores narrowed her eyes, and then smiled. "Sure thing, kiddo. I think this Den Mother Class thing will probably help me access things too. Some of my Skills might be just right for this."

"Perfect!" At a quick glance, there was just so much. Security elements, defensive elements, building and creation. Food stores and rationing and it went on and on. So much it made me giddy. We'd have to get Red and Mike and Dale . . . and several others in on this so we could get our little town working like it needed to.

We could have all of our divisions running smoothly and working together to not take shit from anyone.

So much for no settlements having been claimed. Ha! Take that, aliens.

"Thanks, Dolores." I took a breath. So much shit to consider. Not that I set out to do this, but it needed to be done. And stepping up just meant I could make sure my kids survived, to spite this alien invasion.

Access given to Dolores, I watched the older woman's eyes open wide as she took in the pure scope of what having a town actually meant. A part of me cackled evilly. Served her right for being so eager.

"Plumbing. We have a quest to make sure it's taken care of. I think there are others after it." I motioned for her to look for it, and she nodded, already immersed in the information before her. "Make it so," I quipped at Dolores as Jules came running up to us, panting, and breathing hard.

Girl needed to get some cardio in if that short run was killing her that much, or the System needed to do better. "Finally got to the last guy, the one ushering them all through the door. He mumbled something about a there being a massive magpie out there. They've been moving in short bursts for days, trying to keep everyone together. You should talk to him."

I took a deep breath and got my get-shit-done pants back on. I'd almost swapped them out for my sleep-for-a-while pants. Silly me, getting ahead of myself.

With Kyle off manning the shopfront and ushering people in or out of it or whatever he'd decided to do, it was up to me to have human interaction with strangers. Seemed like the apocalypse was a lot of that. A lot of the unexpected.

Still, there was this sense of urgency hanging over my head. Like we needed more people in charge, more people doing more things. More of everything. And that it still wouldn't be enough.

Everything had changed, and the doom I felt ticking above us had nothing to do with the initial burst of this Mana Dungeon stuff. Not anymore. No, it was now all about those damned aliens who were coming to try and take our country away from us.

Fuck them and the ships they'd ride in on.

# Chapter Twenty-Six:
# The Shop

The Shop wasn't what I expected. First, after touching the damn orb, I was asked if I wanted to access the main System Shop or my default trade Shop. Whatever the fuck that was. Selecting the first option meant I got a bunch of blue screens.

And I just wasn't going through more of those right now.

Rather than deal with that, I decided to try the second option. And ended up here. In an entirely different location. After some quick experimenting—meaning turning around and running back through the doorway that was behind me—I realized it was just teleporting me places.

Now, here I was with myself, the kids, and of course, Dog. I didn't even want to know why the System had decided Dog was part of my familial unit now.

Whatever.

In many ways it seemed like a sort of mini-mall. Super mini. A hallway painted a nice and soothing pale blue with low lighting that accentuated how calm the place was. A strange scent lingered, as if vanilla and cypress had copulated. Our inventories were full, and we still needed to go back for more.

We stood in a hallway with a tiny little host podium at the front where a . . . fox person stood? I inspected them.

**Name: Shi'enah**
*Species: Kitsuisha*
*Level: ???*
*Shop Host*

All righty, then.

Shi'enah looked up at us, a delicate fox eyebrow raised. "Welcome, traveler. I am Shi'enah."

The fox gestured to either side at the different shopfronts there.

The hallway ran maybe fifty meters, maybe a bit less. There were doors at distinct intervals along either side of it, each of them a subtle different shade of blue.

"Are you after anything specific?" Shi'enah asked politely, a slight purr emanating behind the words.

I shook my head, and Wisp spoke up. "No, thanks. We just want to have a bit of a look and sell some stuff."

Shi'enah perked up a bit. "If you would like to sell, please step into one of the first two shops and our sellers will take care of you. Afterward, feel free to browse. I warn you to be careful—sometimes you can get lost in all the choices."

The next smile was a little sly, but I didn't think the fox was trying to put one over on us. It was likely true. We didn't have days to spend in here. We needed to be very specific about how we spent our money. What about haggling? Damn it. I hadn't thought about that. Surely they weren't going to offer us the best prices out the gate.

"Let's go into the one on the left." Wisp led the way before I could say a word, Dog trailing behind her like he was ready to kill anything that looked at her sideways.

Jackson and I followed her in. His curiosity had taken over, and he was drinking in the surroundings, quietly observing everything and committing it to memory.

I'd never been sure if he had a photographic memory, but if it wasn't, it was damned close.

"Hi." Wisp spoke brightly. "I'd like to sell my inventory, and I'd like your best prices."

She smiled so sweetly, the creature behind the counter smiled back. His eyes were slit like a cat's, and there was an odd, scaly pattern to his skin. The name plate on the counter in front of him clearly let us know his name was Chjaveen. He seemed rather exotic, even in comparison to the fox out front. He'd also made the fatal mistake of one hundred percent underestimating my daughter.

She had this cuteness about her that made people just want to give her things. Sort of like the vast majority of under-ten-year-olds. Difficult to stay mad at them, difficult not to buy them the world.

Damned kids.

We'd been very careful not to take items with us that had potential for crafting or that might actually be useful. Like meats and other food items, pristine and well-preserved skins and horns and things like that. Even then, we had a plethora of odds and ends that just had no purpose that we could see.

Wisp crossed her arms and smiled at Chjaveen. "Well, then, let's take a gander."

Chjaveen's skin turned a lighter color, something I was surprised to note. I wondered if it was the same for aliens as humans, but then the haggling began in earnest. Wisp didn't have a Class yet, but she was a kid, a cute kid who knew how to wrap adults around her little finger. And bloody oath was she good at it.

Chjaveen didn't appear to mind in the slightest. He almost seemed eager as he leaned over the counter going over the items with Wisp. Over a week of not being able to sell anything, and we'd accumulated quite a lot. Fifty-seven thousand Credits after two trips. Not huge considering we were three people, but it wasn't bad. Guess I didn't need to save for college anymore.

Wait. Did the Galactic Council or System have college? Oh, god. Something else to worry about.

I gave each of the kids two thousand Credits and with the twelve thousand I already had that technically wasn't mine; that made it sixty-five thousand Credits left. And I had no idea how to spend them on anything.

There were so many possibilities, so many things I wanted to know, that we needed to know. I was sure there were Skills too and armor and . . . whoa. Take a breath, Kira. To be honest, it was a galactic mall. How could I not be excited about everything they could potentially have here?

We walked back out to the beginning of the hallway where Shi'enah greeted us once again. "I see you sold many things."

I wasn't sure if the fox was happy, mad, or amused—and decided it didn't really matter. Getting straight to the point, my words came out a little harsher than I'd intended.

"Are there guides? Like is there a beginner's guide to what the hell it means when your world becomes a Dungeon World?" I forcibly calmed myself, seeing the look on the fox's face. "Sorry for being abrupt. I'm a little on edge. Is there such a thing? Please?"

Shi'enah relaxed and smiled. "Yes. *Smasher's Guide to the Apocalypse*. You can find it three doors down and to the right, along with other informational and Skill texts."

I nodded a thank you and ushered the kids down the hall with me, Dog trailing my daughter like he'd chosen to be her personal bodyguard, and I could see what Jackson meant. That was fine by me; the more protection Wisp got, the better I'd feel about our entire situation.

❖

*Guides to the Apocalypse* were just the tip of the iceberg. Costing a little under fifty Credits when Wisp finally decided to buy it, the book had introductions and several chapters we'd already gotten through—like Class choices and Perk assistance. Might have been nice to have a while ago, but it was what it was. The other chapters, however, they'd be useful.

We spent some time in there browsing the books. Jackson wanted one to help with Mana-to-home-planet technology conversion. He flipped through it, his eyes growing wider by the page. Of course, if he hadn't known what he was looking at, it wouldn't have made much sense, because it was seriously all gobbledygook to me when I tried to glance at it. Plants, just give me plants any day.

"Four thousand Creditsssss," the creature behind the counter said, his S intonations sibilant.

The naga—because yes, it was a naga—just sat there, staring at us. Annoyingly, after a minute, any book we picked up disappeared from our hands, and we couldn't pick it up again till either he agreed that we could look at another page, or we bought one.

I guess they had a lot fewer problems with shoplifters this way. Though, I bet the stupid System had Shoplifters as a Class or something.

Wisp walked up, a pout on her face, and I looked away while she began to haggle. I couldn't keep a straight face while she did that. Did kids get a boost to their Charisma stat or something? Three and a half thousand Credits later, Jackson had his book. I really needed to keep an eye on how much we were spending.

Wisp seemed happy to just look at what she could. There was nothing that particularly caught her interest except the whole Shop phenomena.

Maybe some more armor, maybe . . . I had no idea. What we needed to do was know more about the . . . exactly.

I walked up to the counter, activating the purchasing interface and searched for Intergalactic Rare Species Hunter's Alliance or IRSHA, as it was abbreviated. The number of books available made me cringe. I needed to narrow them down.

Maybe something like a history of IRSHA and the rules that governed them or something? So I scanned through the list coming out with a couple of them. Two books. Five thousand Credits I considered well spent.

The shopkeepers didn't need to know how much I needed these. Knowing your enemy was always half the battle. And the shop wasn't about to disappear. I'd be back for a lot more once I figured out exactly what I wanted to know.

After I went over more of the settlement shit with Dor, roped the others into the System admin, and after I figured out how we were going to prepare everyone. But mostly after I had a damned coffee.

Not wanting to risk spending any more of our money before I fully understood what we might be needing, we left the Shop. Neither Wisp nor Jackson protested. I think they wanted to save their money for bigger things.

Once we blipped back out, the handy little clock in my upper sight showed we'd spent a lot less time in there than I thought we had. I looked around. The store orb was already attracting people, and with Kyle having set himself up to explain things to those who wanted to know and to stop the panic when people kept disappearing and reappearing, it appeared to be going smoothly.

It was a pity we couldn't bring any wealth from our world with us. So much for my superannuation. I didn't think retirement in this world was going to be an option anyway.

Jackson gave me a quick squeeze, clutching his book instead of putting it in inventory, and dashed off toward where his group of tinkerers were, well, tinkering. Dog nosed my hand and trotted deliberately after Wisp, who was walking toward Jana and some of the other kids her age.

I turned away to find somewhere I could sit. The evil coffee corporation had several seats empty, and I decided it was better than nothing. After all, I really needed that damned coffee.

Ray had three people set up there behind the counter. They were making food items, it appeared, and working with gas-powered stoves to heat up water. There were powdered creamers for us to use. Frankly, it was more than the coffee shop I'd expected in this dystopian-level future.

I grabbed a . . . whatever wrap they'd made me and a coffee with a dash of non-sweet creamer and plopped myself down at an open table near the front of the shop. Stats. I needed to check my stats. With everything going on, I kept forgetting I possessed a stat sheet. Pretty soon, it'd be second nature.

Before I could though, a shadow fell over my table. I looked up, automatically engaging Analyze.

**Leena**

*Level: 12*

*Street Smartist*

Ah, it was Ray's sister. "Hey, Leena. What's up?"

She fidgeted, and a few people milled behind her, obviously there to lend her moral support. Her bright hair was pulled over to one side, and she twirled one loose strand around her fingers as she spoke. "So. Those signs like worked, right?"

I nodded, recalling the signs telling people to come here were her idea.

"We made a couple of huge banners and hung them around the center down from the roof. You know, so people can see them from farther away," she continued, getting into what she was saying now.

"Yep." I knew. I'd seen them.

"Do you think we could, you know, like go out with some of the hunting parties and drape some more big banners over apartment buildings and whatnot? Directing them to come here, maybe?" The hesitation was back, but she didn't give up. She was keen on this idea.

I mulled it over, swirling the coffee in the cup in my hands. "Sure. I don't see why not. I'll talk to Evelyn and see what we can do, but on one condition."

Her eyes opened wide as she waited.

"You do what you're told no matter what group you go with. Only three of you at a time, and only when the leader of the patrol says you're safe to hang the banner. Got it?" I thought that would do. Evelyn could always add more stuff to the list.

"Got it. You won't regret it, Kira!" Leena's eyes lit up as she dashed across the way to where her brother was directing a group of people.

I chuckled, sipped my not-absolutely-disgusting instant coffee and pulled up my damned status screen.

| Status Screen | | | |
|---|---|---|---|
| Name | Kira Kent | Class | Ecological Chain Specialist |
| Race | Human (Female) | Level | 17 (4578 XP to next Level) |

| Titles | | | |
|---|---|---|---|
| Diviner | | | |
| Health | 260 | Stamina | 260 |
| Mana | 550 | Mana Regeneration | 40 / minute |
| **Attributes** | | | |
| Strength | 18 | Agility | 25 |
| Constitution | 26 | Perception | 51 |
| Intelligence | 55 | Willpower | 40 |
| Charisma | 25 | Luck | 18 |
| **Class Skills** | | | |
| Mana Attunement | 2 | Earth Barricade | 2 |
| Blood Transfer | 1 | Rockslide | 1 |
| Water Siphon | 2 | Mana Transfer | 1 |
| **Skills** | | | |
| Leadership | 1 | Mana Sense | 2 |
| **Combat Spells** | | | |
| Shield of Power* | | | |
| **Perks** | | | |
| Diviner | | Mana Cloak 2 | |

My Skills steadily increased, but I wasn't exactly sure how I was supposed to apply all of them. It would be nice if the apocalypse came with a little fairy that sat on my shoulder and held my hand like a tutorial.

I laughed. Like they'd make it that easy.

I'd put another point into Water Siphon since it was so useful. As my best combat-effective Class Skill, it stood a solid chance of doing damage at range. I still didn't like what it did to humans, but it was better than nothing.

Mana Transfer still sucked, but at least I could help others as long as I had Mana to help with. And, of course, Mana Attunement worked well with my Mana Sense, so while I needed points in it, I didn't feel too compelled to make it my one and only thing. Though it increased in range with each point and meant I'd have an extended early warning system, right now it was enough. It was easy for me to spot squirrelly people trying to creep up on me. Or groups of mutations flying our way.

Other than that, I kept most of my other Attributes pretty spread out. Intelligence based for the Mana. I did like having higher physical stats, just because of how often I ended up having to hit things with a bat, but my role while fighting with people was fast becoming more utility support. I liked that. It was so me. Like plants, I lived in the background—Plant Girl!

Stats distributed, everything up to date, I was glad I hadn't looked longer at the stuff in the Shop. I could see myself falling down a rabbit hole of spell upgrade books and becoming broke. Maybe their whole idea was to get us addicted to the Shop and all its offerings. Sell an organ, a body part . . . nope. Not my thing.

I wasn't the highest Level we had, but I was up there with the main group.

Sipping on my coffee at my little table, I pulled out a notebook and started jotting down the adventurers I could remember and their Levels. Writing them down by hand always seemed to cement them in my mind. Which was a good thing—I needed to know this.

I knew someone had stopped in front of my table even without looking up; hell, even without using my Mana Senses. The shadow told me it all. Maybe this coffee shop wasn't the best place to get thinking things done.

Schooling my expression as the person in front of me cleared their throat, I looked up.

"Kira?" an elderly lady said, and I immediately regretted my impatience and activated Analyze.

**Ethel Dorchester**

*Level: 11*

*Weaver of Traps*

Ooooh, I liked her Class and immediately wanted to know more about it.

"That's me. What can I do for you, Ethel?" She wasn't even phased by the fact that I knew her name.

Instead, she just smiled at me like I vaguely remembered my grandmother doing when I was much younger. "Is there anything I could do to help?"

I blinked at her. I mean, sure, I'd had the Settlement Orb quest. I guess I'd completed it and owned it. Damn it. I was in charge. Oops. So I smiled. "There is so much you could do to help, it isn't funny. Are you any good with little kids?"

Ethel smiled, and it lit up the whole Shop. "I used to be a primary school teacher before I retired . . . twenty years ago. But I feel younger than I did then! So yes. I'd love to help."

"Great." I craned my neck to try and locate the group of kids. I could see them down the way in the wing opposite the one to the busway. "Jana will be down that way with all those kids. Just tell her I sent you."

Ethel reached down and patted my arm, her expression soft. "You're doing great, dear. Thank you. For doing all of this."

"I'm not doing it alone." Compliments! The bane of my existence. I took a swig of my now-lukewarm coffee. "But thank you."

She nodded like she knew better and headed out toward where I'd indicated while I gulped down the rest of my coffee, determined to go and find Dolores before anyone else stopped me. Right after I finished my notes and this not-too-bad wrap of indeterminate ingredients I was downing.

While I could manage a lot of things, and trust me, multiple many-leveled experiments could attest to this—I knew my limits, and playing armchair general had never appealed to me. Anyway, this was no game of RISK.

This was reality now.

Whoa.

What a concept. Like I knew it was real, but at the same time, sitting here in the middle of Garden City where I'd been coming most of my life since our move to Australia . . . it felt surreal.

All the little blue strands wove in and out of people, through people, around people. The Mana was alive, like the rest of our planet, like an extension of life. It pulsed and beat with a drum-like resonance when I closed my eyes. It resembled a bass beat only I could feel, and I think that was the most magnetic part of this. I'd gotten so used to how the Mana felt even in the space of this week, how it looked, how it reacted, that I could tell when something was changing.

And when people were approaching me.

Kyle's hand on my shoulder didn't alarm me, but I did realize that I needed to just get up and leave from this bustling spot.

"I can hear your brain working overtime from the Shop orb," Kyle said quietly as he sat next to me.

"You left your post," I said, half-accusingly.

He shrugged. "It's okay. Someone else took over. Arvin or something. I didn't quite catch the name. Not like it's difficult to direct new shoppers." He winked at me and leaned back against the divider in the chair he'd commandeered.

I glanced down at my Level list in my notebook and gave Kyle his answer. "My brain isn't working overtime; it just feels capable of so much more. Could be all this Intelligence stuff."

We had about a hundred and ten people from Level 12 through 19. It wasn't much at all. Slightly less than ten percent of the people we now housed.

"We have a week to get prepared. To get our higher Levels higher, more functional, to regain some of our amenities—like making sure the plumbing doesn't end up blowing up in our faces. We need money to up our defenses so we can show these IRSHA guys that we aren't giving up any portion of our country in any way that could be considered easy."

Tension built in my gut. It was a lot, but I knew we could do it. And I felt like Jackson and Darren and Chris and Sarah were a huge part of how we'd make it happen. That Mana energy conversion was vitally important to our survival here. I just wasn't sure how I knew—other than Mana sort of coaxed me into that mentality.

Kyle nodded, his thoughtful face running through all the logical rigmarole he usually went through to reach conclusions. "So less than ten percent of us are adventurers?"

I nodded, and he sighed. "Not uncommon, you know. Still need people to teach, cook, make things, and mind kids, run the city, patrol the city. It's still the world, just much changed now."

I tapped the IRSHA book and went to take another swig of coffee only to realize it was empty. Damn it. Not like it was amazing, but it'd been something. "Digging into the town interface is going to give us a lot of options once we understand them all. Then we just need to level all our combat Classes up. As well as any that have a combat Class but haven't been leveling."

Kyle frowned thoughtfully. I knew there was something he wasn't telling me, because I could just sense it; I could feel it. When it was important enough, he'd tell me in time. Still, I worried.

"I'll go talk to Evelyn and sort out some leveling areas that can double with scouting for survivors?" He asked more than told me, which meant he was having major issues right now with whatever was in his head.

"Yep, and the lower Levels can stay in the areas just outside the Safe Zone and get a few more Levels too," I added in, scribbling things down. I didn't care what anyone said—typing it just wasn't the same.

"We've got this."

I nodded, and he leaned forward, giving me a kiss on the forehead like he'd done since I could remember before he headed off to find our archer.

Dor was downstairs in what used to be the 8 Street Eatery. Alone. She sat there, puffing on a cigarette, making smoke rings with her mouth and watching as each of them floated into the darkness above her. A melancholy air hung around her, and she didn't move a muscle except to inhale and exhale. It reminded me of some of those sixties-era black-and-white photographs, and she seemed so sad it broke my heart.

I wasn't even sure why.

"Stop staring. Sit down. Talk to me." Her tone wasn't as commanding as usual. Maybe this was the her she reveled in when by herself. Perhaps what I'd seen so far was just her persona, the person we become when we are needed.

It was like a mum power.

No matter how shitty your day, no matter what your mood when you wake up or get home, you have this total ability to just shut it all off and be there for the kids. It's not even a task; it's just something we do.

Maybe it's in our genes, maybe it's just in our heads. But being a mum was a superpower I was proud of, even if I did sometimes just wish I could sleep in. On any other day, that is, than Mother's Day and my birthday.

"What's the Den Mother Class all about?" I asked, getting right to the point and desperately hoping that it would do what I was needed it to.

She raised an eyebrow. "Direct. I like that." Then she sighed, stubbed out her cigarette, and steepled her fingers.

"Strange thing, this System. Keeps me healthier the longer its active. I swear I can feel the chronic lung issues vanishing. You'd think they wouldn't want an old Sheila like me hanging around too long." She grinned as she stood and stretched. "Den Mother appears to give me the ability to enhance protections around people who are in my group or designated family, or those who are in close proximity. If I go through the Skill tree, it lets me see some sort of management prospects along one of my lines. Like Haggling and the ability to town build." She shrugged and gestured around at the center. "Seems pretty built to me."

I laughed, couldn't help it. Dolores was pretty great. Take no shit, tell you to fuck off as soon as look at you . . . and she got this whole Mana fuckery thing.

"So you've got access to the town shit, but I need you to help me figure out the rest of it, and who might be best for us to put in certain positions—grant access for things." I held my breath for a moment. While I could do this myself, there was a lot of other stuff I had to do too. If she said no, it wasn't the end of the world. Nope. Been there, done that.

"Fair dinkum, mate?" she asked, half-hesitantly, ready to make it a joke in the blink of an eye.

I nodded. "Ridgy-didge."

This time, Dor laughed, and her shoulders relaxed. "All right. I guess you're on the up and up. I'll help. But don't go dumping all this shit into my lap, okay? I know you've got two little ones to take care of. But there's a lot more to this world now, and I won't have you chickening out."

It made me wonder, just for a moment, what she'd been through. What had happened to her and her family to make her make a comment like that? Had she been previously abandoned? There was so much we didn't know about one another, and I was taking blind leaps of faith every other hour. You had to when the world ended. Still didn't mean that every time I did, my belly didn't flop a little.

Eventually, I just nodded at her. It didn't matter what she'd been through before. She was here now. And we were all going through some megashit together.

"You're right, though. From everything I've seen of it, we're going to need more than just you or I." Dor sounded thoughtful. "That brother of yours? He a doctor, right?"

"Yeah, surgeon," I added, realizing that the fridges down here were quite pongy, too. Red hadn't thought to tend to the rest of the center yet. We'd be expanding down here soon enough . . . I made a note to let him know.

Did we have enough beds? Surely there were mattresses backed up in

318

the stock rooms at least, right?

"Kira?" Dor's tone was gentle, and she was close enough to me now to touch my arm lightly. "Let me look at this and get some ideas too, then we can talk. Go take care of your kids, and for all our sanity, go get some decent sleep for once."

# Chapter Twenty-Seven:
# Level Up

## 9 Days Post-System Onset—10 a.m.

Almost ten days since the invasion or takeover or Mana saturation began. Right on a week before our lovely hunter friends from IRSHA wanted to evict us. What we needed in the remaining time was Levels. As many Levels as we could possibly wrangle.

It's what we'd done for the remainder of the day yesterday and what we'd undertake for the foreseeable future.

I checked everything I had with me, using an old-fashioned backpack from one of the stores to keep food and hydration inside. The System didn't convert old stuff to its own storage. I kind of liked having a backpack. Ten groups of twelve people. We were no longer in danger of falling anywhere below the population threshold for a town . . . unless we had another apocalypse.

"So we're doing this, Mum?" Jackson's voice held a slight tremor.

I could tell he was scared. Which was good since I was terrified. Taking my kid out with me was a different level of dangerous.

I nodded. "We need Levels. The crafting aspects of your Class help you a bit, but the more Skills you have, the more you can defend yourself or help power up items we need. Frankly, we need you guys to develop those power ups. It's okay, you're coming with your uncle and me."

Kyle insisted on going with me. It was a twin thing, or perhaps our thing. Not that we'd mention it out loud, but right now I needed that proximity. The familiar helped me focus. I also knew that if anything happened to me, he'd do his best to get Jackson to safety.

If anything happened to me . . . not even contemplating that.

Mana flared briefly around me and then flocked to me like it didn't want me to be upset. Because of course, the blue stuff was sentient or something. Not really . . . but perhaps it was sensitive to me at any rate. There'd eventually be places I needed to go where having a Level advantage would be super helpful. That's what I had to focus on. All I had to do was level and work on the rest instead of sleeping.

Daisy Hill Koala Sanctuary was high on my list of places I desperately wanted to visit to see just how Mana had affected our ecosystem. But it would take far too long to get there. A multi-day trip maybe, unless we figured out some moving vehicles. Right now, I just wasn't comfortable with leaving my kiddo alone back here for too long.

"Bet you we get more Levels." Evelyn suddenly stood beside me, a big grin on her face.

One I knew was all bravado. She wasn't nearly as confident as she acted. I don't think anyone was.

Damn, I really wished she was going with our group, but she was one of the highest Levels too, and we couldn't just group everyone I wanted with me into my group. The whole reason was to level the lower ones up as far and fast as we could. To practice using these abilities and Skills as a cohesive group so we could take whatever the System threw at us.

A part of me wondered how much it mattered. The book I'd read about the IRSHA talked about Advanced and Master Classes, compared to our Basic Classes. A whole new concept introduced by *Smasher's Guide*, which...

Whatever.

Point was, they had people with more Levels than us. A lot more. All this running around might mean jack if they brought one of the big boys. But what else were going to do? Roll over and call it a day?

No.

Instead, we split everyone. Evelyn with her own group. Gemma, now mostly recovered from her injuries, with Evelyn. Not that physical injuries took a lot of time to heal. No, I was talking about the mental trauma from the near-death experience she'd had. Jules went with Gemma and took that group together.

Apart from flitting around and helping settle newcomers, the Healer had barely strayed from her friend's side since the huge fight. It seemed so long ago now.

Dale took Darren and went with another group, one without a Healer otherwise. Tasha was with him too. Sange and Molly led another group, though I wasn't sure how Sange would go. Since the battle with the Rigoll, their confidence had taken a hit. There was this haunted look in their eyes now. I added regrowing a limb to the list of things I never wanted to experience. But apparently, we'd been lucky that Kyle had the healing Class he did, or Sange would have lost the appendage completely.

Had to hope more of our residents could get that ability or spell— couldn't just rely on one person for it.

We were taking Chris and Sarah with our group. Level 12 wasn't going to help them survive if push came to shove, and while their offensive Skills were good, it was their technology-based abilities we needed to bolster.

So many names, so many people . . . it was becoming a headache.

"We're going to kick your arses," I said to Evelyn, raising an eyebrow.

She clapped me on the back, her false bravado in full swing for everyone around us to see. "Want to make a wager?"

"Sure." I glanced around, not one hundred percent paying attention to what she was saying. But instead of continuing her charade, she leaned in close, her hand suddenly warm on my shoulder and whispered in my ear.

"If I win, I get to take you out on a date."

Her breath tickled the hair around my ear, sending unexpected shivers through my body. I was about to open my mouth and reply that I didn't date, because I hadn't since the divorce—always putting the kids and my work ahead of anything else. I wasn't unhappy that way, but sometimes I did get lonely.

She pulled back, a brief expression of uncertainty crossing her face like she'd read me wrong. Thing was, she hadn't, I just wasn't expecting her to ask. Not in these circumstances, but I guess the Apocalypse wasn't going away any time soon.

"Why not." I grinned at her, watching her face flood with relief even if she only showed it briefly.

"In that case," she said, with an evil glint to her gaze, "there is no way you're winning."

I grinned back but suddenly wasn't entirely sure this was the best idea. Still, if we could take an evening out of this crazy shit happening around us to find a bit of enjoyment . . . what the hell. I'd give it a go.

She *was* independent and strong, after all.

Blood exploded all over me in goopy masses of sticky, green alien remains. Who knew it really was a different color, right? These creatures were one hundred percent not from here, nor did they appear to be a mutation of any type of Australian creature I'd ever seen.

Note to self: do not use Blood Transfer when a creature is about to explode. Sure, it healed me up, but it also seemed to take it literally and exploded purely in my direction. How did you target a damn explosion that perfectly?

My son, so helpful, couldn't stop laughing. I glared at him, but I didn't think the quickly coagulating blood was doing any of us favors. The sense of urgency took any mirth out of the situation for me.

I turned quickly, ignoring my sticky predicament, and shot out one of my Earth Barricades right underneath an approaching group of . . . I had no idea what these things were.

*Analyze engaged.*
*Eeshiriatmels*
*Level 16*

Their beady little eyes stood atop thick stalks on top of a rounded head positioned over what looked like a badly made ghost costume. If that costume had already been drenched in blood and left to rot in the sun for a few days. They only stood around four feet tall, but the eyes moved on a three hundred-sixty-degree turning basis, and it freaked me the fuck out.

These guys hadn't been here at the beginning when the System initiated. Coming back to the same area we'd started in felt necessary. A just-in-case thing. While Toohey Forest wasn't too far from our safe haven, it was far enough that I'd just wanted to reach here and turn around.

We hadn't seen survivors on the way, but we'd moved along the freeway again, nor turning down University Road. We even traversed down James Toohey Avenue a little, but the neighborhood was like a trashed ghost town. Houses leveled, crumbling, with plant life doing things I'd never seen it do.

I itched to examine it.

But when we exited the neighborhood again, we were attacked from the tree line. Running in after them seemed like a good idea at the time?

There were masses of these creatures scattered all through the forest.

Slightly phosphorescent, they lit up in the dimness of the canopy.

Another exploded with a blast of light from Jackson. This time, without my ill-timed Blood Transfer spell, the liquid just splashed randomly in a huge arc, spraying a bit on most of our party like war paint. I felt strangely vindicated.

The experience just rolled in. Not in a huge way, nothing like that, but a slow build that didn't stop. Sarah and Chris needed Jackson's back up more than I cared to admit, but it got us all experience. Slow and steady and not horrifically or mind-numbingly dangerous.

While I wouldn't call the Toohey Forest safe by any stretch of the imagination, we had grown enough that those damned cockbats didn't pose as much of a threat to us anymore. They were still here, being flying mutations. But now the ground was infested with these Eeshiriatmels.

The cockbats weren't so difficult to take out anymore, not with the Levels we'd gained. We encountered rodents of ridiculous bloody size all over the place. I hadn't even realized we had that many types of wild rodent near us.

And then there were the Eeshiriatmels. Levels 15 to 18, and they moved in sync with one another, like they were a team, maybe even a hive mind. Great for leveling but not so much fun to fight.

Kyle fought his way over to where I stood with a few of our under-15s, or at least, upon engaging Analyze, they'd been under 15 before we started this hours long trek.

"Mana management is going to be a problem if we have prolonged fights," he commented to me as he lobbed what seemed like an anodized ball of blood.

Analyze revealed his Class to me as a Regeneration Specialist. From what I understood, he could both heal for obvious reasons and reverse the healing process to kill. Most of his spells appeared to have a switch one way or another.

Not exactly what I think he'd have chosen had he had more time to choose. I could already see its effect on him. Killing wasn't really in my brother's nature.

"If I can get my Level up to forty, I can help with that." Forty seemed impossibly far away, what with every Level taking more experience and every spell requiring more Mana. I was closing in on nineteen now that we'd been at this a few hours, but I felt as if experience trickled in like molasses.

Maybe the Shop had Mana potions. I kicked myself for not checking for the mundane things present in every game I'd ever played.

"We're not going to hit 40 before these hunters come at us." Kyle grimaced, like he was trying to figure something out and the calculations weren't doing what he wanted them to. That was the problem with math; there were no grey areas.

The next group of Eeshiriatmels came running straight for me. These were slightly different, with what looked like false gold eyelashes outlining the tops of their eyes. Not freaky at all.

Their Level read 20, and I got a sudden twist in the pit of my stomach. They weren't like the ones we'd just finished facing. The Mana emanating from them felt stronger.

"These ones are more dangerous," I called out, dodging the trees in my way as I raced to the other side of our group. Dead leaves crunched under my feet, and the sun didn't quite make it through the canopy, leaving us in a weird sort of twilight of our own.

I made it just in time, sliding in like I'd just stolen second base to erect an Earth Barricade. Tapping into my cloak refilled my Mana just shy of full, allowing for the item to begin replenishing immediately. My gut told me I'd need all the Mana I could get.

These higher-Leveled ones were stronger; they broke through my wall with almost no effort at all, making me wonder if the smaller ones had been there to lull us into a false sense of security, or maybe as a test. Pity for them we'd been practicing.

Something flew over the top of my head, falling into the center of the Eeshiriatmels. It made a resounding thud as it landed drawing all their attention momentarily as Chris yelled out "DUCK!"

Pushing myself back, I threw an arm around Jackson, the other around Kyle, and jumped us as far and fast as I could away from the incoming group. Even if it turned into more of a stumble. As the rest of our team dove away too, I used a massive chunk of Mana to throw up another Earth Barricade.

I barely made it in time. Even though Chris had lobbed one of her Mana-fueled ball bombs at the creatures, we couldn't tell how much damage it did. The Earth Barricade only stayed upright for a few moments before the new Eeshiriatmels' bodies plummeted through it as if it were paper.

I glanced over at the Engineer, and she shrugged. These new versions of our opponents didn't seem easy to take down, but as the dust cleared, I gasped. Beyond my now rubble remnants of a Barricade were seven corpses of the higher-Leveled Eyestalks.

They hadn't pushed through; they'd fallen through it. Torn apart like fleshy mushrooms, they gleamed with some sort of enchantment. They looked like mushrooms gone bad. Rotten. As if their cores had been eaten from the inside.

The forest around us was eerily quiet now, and I couldn't help but hope it wasn't the calm before the storm. Kyle was helping two of our lower Levels who'd gotten hit by some of the debris in all the commotion. I wished I could remember their names, but information overload was giving me headaches.

Looting the corpses, I scanned around with Mana Attunement for disturbances anywhere around us, making sure we didn't have more incoming. Nothing showed up. Not even a cockbat or three. Silence and calm. Since encountering that previous mind-controlling bastard, silence and calm made me uneasy.

**Congratulations! You have received an Eeshiriatmel Life Stone.**

*This stone grants the wielder the power to imbue a weapon with Life Leech. 3/3 charges.*

*Warning: weapon must be freshly crafted. Will not function if applied to an existing weapon.*

I raised an eyebrow, wondering whether it would be better to sell or keep these. I'd looted four of them. A gut feeling told me keeping them was the best option. After all, it didn't appear as if the world was going to revert to its former glory. Eventually, I'd have a weapon of some sort, right?

That was all the interesting stuff I got from the corpses. Otherwise just some flesh and skin and a few eyeballs. Trying not to gag, I closed my inventory and checked on the rest of the group. 19, super close to 20. I could deal with that. Jackson had just hit the milestone himself. I walked over and gave him a brief mum shoulder squeeze. He glanced up at me gratefully as I did so. Go me and my restraint in wanting to wrap him up in a hug he'd never escape from and thus never be hurt.

I could control myself.

Kyle walked over after having attended to the injuries I'd noticed earlier. "Nothing life-threatening. Well, I should rephrase that. Nothing life-threatening now that the System doesn't want us to die and ruin its fun."

He sounded . . . angry at it. I could get that. After all, what the fuck, universe? I mean, here we were minding our own business, getting work done way too late for normal, and we were blindsided. I got the anger, really I did, especially having to juggle raising two lucky-to-be-alive kids during it.

But what I didn't get was holding onto that anger. Why not just turn it into determination? The will to just say fuck you, you're not getting our planet that easily. That's what I'd done, or at least it was what I was trying to do.

"Kyle, we'll get through this." I used my gentle, calm-the-seething-giant tone, but it didn't seem to work.

Something flashed through his eyes as he glanced at me, but I didn't get to see it for long when he looked away. "That's not the point anymore, K. Don't you see? This System thing has taken our world and our accomplishments and just zeroed them out. They don't care about our culture, about the things we've fought for. Their only concern is this Dungeon World, which I'm slowly beginning to realize is all about entertainment for other species."

He wasn't wrong. I knew that, I could feel it. But being angry about it didn't change it. Only actions could do that.

Making my voice as soothing as possible, I grimaced. "I see it all, every single bit of it. How it took from me, my kids, and the rest of us. I've watched several people I'd begun to like get torn apart. But there's something almost magical about the ambient Mana. It's always there, always present, always waiting . . . and it's waiting as much for us as it is for them. Waiting for us to take it, harness it, and master it."

He locked eyes with me, surprise showing in his expression, like he hadn't expected me to have given this so much thought. Thing was, I didn't realize I had.

"You always surprise me," he said, smiled briefly, and set off to help lead us back home.

I sighed, contemplating how much truth was in what I'd said. It was starting to get dark, and we needed to head back, see if we could salvage any people along the way. Even as I stood in thought, blue waves lapped at my fingertips like a seal trying to get a fish. Sometimes I surprised myself.

# Chapter Twenty-Eight:
# Township

## 9 Days Post-System Onset—10 p.m.

I'd leveled up to 20 on the way home. Sort of anti-climactic. We'd only managed to find a handful of survivors on the way, who were surprisingly doing quite well for themselves. Dragging a bunch of Level 15s into Garden City with us late at night, we'd finally made it home.

I didn't like being outside at night, and now I curled up in the back of the coffee shop Ray had set up in the old corporate one's shell, on a bench, with my daughter snuggled up next to me and Dog on the floor at our feet.

We had a bunch of us 20 and above now. Initially, when the System mentioned I'd get experience for being the Settlement Owner, I'd been elated.

Twenty-odd experience a day was nothing when my next Levels required fifteen thousand.

Still. Level 20 gave me a whole new tier of Skills and a hybrid ability. I found myself oddly excited as I sat down to look over my choices. Only to realize that at Level 20, I only actually had one choice, although that expanded once I hit 21.

### Tier Two Hybrid Ability (20)
### Mudslide

*Effect: Proficiency with Water Siphoning and coaxing the ground to do what you want enables you to pull forth a mudslide. Usable twice per day. Usage, severity, and impact dependent on caster and Skill Level.*

*Caution: Make sure you understand the lay of the land before engaging this ability.*

*Mana Cost: 65*

*Area of Effect: 3-meter radius from targeted casting. Damage minimum 2x caster Level per target.*

### Tier Three (21-29)

### Treesong

*Effect: Your affinity with Nature and the Mana around you lends you a unique affinity with the plant life. Incantations can bring out the most in these familiar life forms. Sung like a soothing lullaby, even the plants can rise to your bidding, if you approach them correctly.*

*Caution: Don't piss off the trees.*

*Mana Cost: 35 Mana per 5 seconds. Channeled.*

### Topsoil

*Effect: The top layer of ground is always the most fragile. Using your Mana proficiency, you can coax strength out of this to entrap, ensnare, or protect those around you.*

*Caution: Use wisely. Topsoil doesn't distinguish well between friend and foe. It only recognizes blood.*

*Mana Cost: 65 per directed action*

### Implantation

*Not every Skill does damage immediately. Some Skills take skill and experience to make use of, and Implantation is one of them. Implant a seed of power and growth within an opponent, leeching Mana and damage from attacks cast at the opponent. When the seed blossoms, a portion of damage and health is returned to those surrounding and is dealt as damage.*

*Duration: 10 seconds*

*Effect: Implant a seed of Mana into the chest of your enemy. During the duration of Implantation, the seed will absorb a portion of damage done to the enemy. The absorbed Mana will be reverted once seed has fully grown in an explosion with a maximum of 5-meter radius around enemy. Explosion will return Health, Mana, and Stamina to those affected.*

*Should the target die before the bomb seed can complete its countdown, all benefits are forfeit. Use this wisely.*

*Mana, Stamina, and Health equaling 75% of the absorbed amount of damage is returned to all targets within a 5 meter diameter. 25% of absorbed amount is dealt as damage to initial target.*

*Caution: Target cannot be effect by this spell more than once per minute.*

Oh, wow, I couldn't wait to get to Implantation. Did I have to get all my Skills? I'd received a spare Skill point at Level 19 while we'd been leveling, so technically I could get Mudslide, and I'd get another at 21 for Implantation, but . . .

I frowned.

"Hey!" Evelyn dropped into the bench on the other side of me and leaned her head against my shoulder, carefully so as not to wake Wisp. The archer was spattered in blood from head to toe, bits of it already so dry it was cracking and peeling off in places. "I don't think I beat you."

The tone of her voice was sad, sort of defeated. In total, we'd lost four people out there trying to level. Four people. Dead.

Maybe I was becoming numb to all the death, but I didn't feel the same emptiness anymore. It could also have been that I hadn't personally known those people well.

"How many?" I asked, still mulling over possibilities for Mudslide in my head. Hadn't it been a delicious, non-alcoholic-tasting alcoholic beverage?

"Two." She muttered the word so softly I almost didn't hear it.

Not thinking, I reached over and ruffled her hair.

"Not your fault. None of this is any of our fault," I whispered, leaning back in against the bench padding and fighting back a sudden urge to sob loudly. Emotions, man. Fuckers, all of them.

"Not our fault. Just whoever greeted that emissary in typical torturous fashion." She chuckled, but it was dry, not humorous at all. "Still, I was looking forward to claiming my reward."

We were silent for a bit, and I wasn't quite sure how to take her comment. After all, right now, with everything going on, dating was a stupid concept, even if it was flattering. Ready for it? Not by a long shot. I nudged her with my knee.

"Let's just rain check that. Too much going on right now. Let's concentrate on surviving past this damned invasion." I stopped uneasily as a fluctuation in the sea of Mana around us and the center rippled through to me. Nausea swept over me, like I'd just become seasick.

"Kira?" The concern in Evelyn's voice reached me more than my name, and I just nodded, trying to regain my bearings and figure out just what was going on.

The fluid way Mana worked reminded me of water, but there was far more to it than that. The swell subsided, and I found my mind coming back into myself, resetting, and losing the feeling of bile in my throat.

"I'm fine." There had to be a book on the theory behind Mana, right? I needed that book. "I'm just not sure if IRSHA is going to give us those nine days they said we'd have to vacate the country, planet, whatever they meant."

"What makes you think that?" Ray asked quietly, pulling up a chair on the opposite side of my table.

He fell into it, exhaustion written all over him. This little area was becoming crowded, but they were people I'd grown accustomed to. Wisp moved slightly in her sleep.

He splayed his hands out, tiny bits of ice hanging on the ends as he watched them.

I shrugged. It was more than just a gut feeling—it went through my entire body, into the bones, and down into the ground, anchoring in the earth like it wanted me to grow roots. "Just a feeling."

He looked at me for a long moment, his gaze sizing up everything he knew about me from the week he'd known me. Had that only been a week? Then he nodded. "There's so much that we have to do. Figure out everyone's abilities. Build defenses."

He eyed me pointedly as he pushed himself back up.

"Dolores is looking into just what that takes." It was an effort not to feel affronted, but I knew he was worried, and getting uppity wasn't going to help anyone.

"Great. We'll show those bastards just what we're made of."

"Too right, mate," I muttered as he walked away. "Too bloody right."

"Rain check, then?" Evelyn asked, and I couldn't tell if she was miffed or not.

The way my head was still trying to process too much around me made reading who I was speaking with difficult.

I tried to make my nod decisive and punctuated it with words for good measure. "Rain checked as fuck."

Evelyn laughed. "That made no sense, and yet somehow, all the sense. I'll leave it to you."

She pushed herself up and walked back toward the food court and the shop entrance, hefting her bow as she went.

"She likes you, Mum." Wisp's voice made me jump.

I hadn't expected her to wake up. Narrowing my eyes, I looked her over, and the blue waves around her confused me. They didn't seem to be around many of the other kids, just her and a few of the others. Had she even been asleep?

"Does she, now?" I asked, raising an eyebrow. To my surprise, Dog wuffed at me, pushing his head onto my knee. Glancing away, I grinned at Wisp. "Okay. Right now, there are more important things, buttercup. Right now, we've got to make sure we're all going to be around for many moons to come, okay?"

Wisp crossed her arms. When she went into serious mode, my kid was ridiculously astute. She saw everything, picked up on things even I didn't notice, and always remembered what had happened. "I know it's not easy, Mum. I'm sorry I'm still so little."

Crying was not something Wisp did often unless she was seriously hurt, overtired, or a combination of both. The almost-crying tinge to her voice likely stemmed from her wanting to do so much more and being restricted by the System.

I drew her into my side, giving her a huge hug. I'm not sure how long we remained like that. Her skin was warm to the touch, her breathing heavy, like she was trying to hold back great gulping sobs or something, and her tiny body was just filled with muscles from four years of daredevil practice.

When she pulled back, she had that resolute expression on her face. Like when she couldn't do back handsprings and spent hours upon hours almost getting them until she finally did. Damn, she could be stubborn. "We can do this, Mum. We are smart and we are strong. And Jackson is cool too. You. Me. And Jackson."

Now I got it. Way to go, dense Mum. She didn't want anything upsetting our precarious balance right now. I couldn't argue with her.

I grinned at her and ruffled her black hair. "Yeah. We're Kents. We've got this. Although you need a shower."

She wrinkled her nose at me, and Dog backed off a few steps as if unsure whether I meant the both of them. "But Mum, do we really need to keep clean? It's the apocalypse. I'll just get dirty again."

"Showers. Now." It took all my willpower not to laugh at her comment.

She glared at me before darting off with Dog in the direction of the showers, but the glare was halfhearted at best. Part of me wanted to go after her, but the rudimentary defenses of our town still needed tending to. It was time to shower, sleep, and then find Dolores when my brain was working better.

❖

## 10 Days Post-System Onset—6:30 a.m.

"I wish everyone would stop calling me Dolores. You're the only one who calls me Dor," grumbled the older woman as we sat down in the library going over all the controls and ins and outs of the Settlement Orb controls. "Dolores just makes me feel old."

I glanced at her, a half-smile forming despite my intentions. Dor just had this way about her that made me feel ten times calmer than I'd thought I'd be able to when I woke up this morning. "We're sitting at thirteen hundred people now, then?" I asked to distract myself.

"Give or take," she murmured, running through some lists she could understand and I couldn't.

"That's good. Soon around thirteen hundred people will be calling you

Dor," I quipped, and she looked at me for a moment before bursting out laughing.

"Bet your mother loved that mouth." She half-grinned, half-glared at me.

I laughed this time. "Yeah. Mum does. Did."

Suddenly, I didn't want to think about whether my parents were alive or dead. I mean, statistically, probably not, but they'd been preppers for as long as I could remember, and everything about them and how they lived told me they would have been better prepared than almost anyone for this to happen.

But they lived down the Gold Coast Hinterlands, off near Mt. Tamborine. One of these days, I'd try to get down there and see if they'd survived. Right now, I couldn't afford the emotions it took for me to think about them.

Too many feelings and I was going to stop functioning. None of that. I couldn't afford that. My focus needed to be on the kids and Kyle. A bit of Evelyn and maybe Ray, Gemma, and Jules. Sange and Molly—the people who'd been with me since the start.

"Just breathe, kiddo," Dor said quietly. "I didn't think. Won't bring up that shit again, right?"

I nodded, my focus back on everything in front of me.

### Summarized Settlement Status

*Current Population: 1342 (Town)*

*Combined Settlement Treasury: 102,300 Credits (+1.76k per day)*

*Combined Town Mana: 1,205 Mana Points (+22 Mana per day)*

*Taxes: 10% Sales Tax on Shop*

*Facilities of Note: Still forming—being determined*

*Enchantments of Note: Basic Collection fields (Upgrade Levels available once sufficient pre-requisites have been reached)*

*Defenses of Note: Basic Settlement Shield Level 1—Upgrade Levels available: 1*

Looking at the numbers, I got the feeling our little town was starting off dirt poor. "Do you understand what the shield upgrade levels are? Or maybe what we need to upgrade enchantments—or perhaps what others are available?"

It was confusing, but damn it. We were getting this done.

Dor seemed a bit perplexed. "I'm no planning major. I only picked Den Mother so I could protect people, and I don't have the Levels yet to hit some of the more helpful Skills. I need to go out with you again."

Dor was Level 16 now and got a bit more experience being an admin of the settlement than I did because of her Class. But she was far from being as high as we needed.

"Have we done the plumbing yet?" I asked because we had to make sure we finished that quest if we wanted the next leg of it.

Dolores brightened at that. "Yes! I saw that just before you got here. It's not too pricey to activate. The nice quest basically gives back to us what we'll spend. Which is good. But we did have to make a few Shop purchases first. Easy enough. Just took me a while to find it. I should be able to activate it . . ."

**Congratulations! Quest Completion**

*A Habitable Safe Zone*

*Part One: Plumbing*

*You've finished the quest with three days to spare. You gain a ten percent bonus.*

*Reward: 13,200 Credits for the town treasury*

***New Quest Granted:***

***A Habitable Safe Zone***

*Part Two: Power*

*It's starting to get colder and darker earlier on this continent. Light sure would be handy. Since you insist on surviving, how about putting your Technomancers, Techzards, Energy Manipulators, and whatnot to work?*

*Task: Develop the casing needed to attract Mana to power your town, enabling the amenities you've lost.*

*This must be developed by your own town's members with not more than 25% of the apparatus pieces obtained through the Shop.*

*Reward: 20,000 Credits and the ability to power your city. Access to the third and final Part of this Quest.*

*Time Limit: 6 days*

*Note: This quest may be shared with people of the appropriate Classes for completing this quest if they do not already have a form of admin access.*

"Whoa." I let out a long breath, and Dolores paused as she received the same notification.

She paused. "Well, I guess we're doing that next."

"Yeah. Good thing Jackson, Chris, and Sarah and the rest are already on this. Just need to . . . give them a deadline now." Guess we weren't affording some of those more expensive upgrades for a bit.

Kyle was about to walk into the room; I could feel him approaching. His Mana aura had a weird resonance about it, like a life-and-death marker. It preceded him and trailed behind him too. His moods had changed since this apocalypse landed on our doorstep, and I wasn't entirely sure the world coming to an end was the only reason. Some of it, and it was just a suspicion right now, but some of it stemmed from the Class he'd chosen—from the things he could do with it and the weight it carried with it.

"Got any amazing insight into the admin controls?" I asked as he walked into the room.

Nothing in his facial expression told me that I'd surprised him, but there was an almost-imperceptible hitch in his gait that meant I'd scored a point.

"No, but I believe one of the ladies who came back with us last night might be able to help. She worked in one of the Brisbane City Planning Offices before the apocalypse hit, and when it flashed up with Classes, she said she panicked and just took its recommendation." He shrugged and sat down, accessing the planning information too.

"Why isn't she here, then, son?" Dolores asked, and I was pretty sure she was trying not to yell at him. She seemed so matter-of-fact and common-sensical that I think my brother's strange, floating awareness was something she wasn't sure how to deal with.

He blinked at her. "What? Oh, sorry. So much going on, and despite the increases in Intelligence so far, my brain just hasn't gotten used to all the different thought processes I can follow right now. Seems like a dream most of the—"

"Kyle!" I called out, keeping hold of my temper as he rambled off yet again. "Why isn't she here? What is her name?"

"Oh. Her name is Sienna. She's taking care of her two kids first." He raised an eyebrow at me like I should understand that at least, and I suppressed the scowl that attempted to jump off my face at him. "She'll be here shortly."

I wanted to glance at my wrist, where until recently, my now-rather-useless, Wi-Fi-connected watch had sat. Not having a clock sucked. Everyone not having clocks or mobile phones sucked even more. How were you supposed to check on anyone when they were running late? And everyone had to arrange for meetings beforehand. It was like living in the '90s again.

Now all we had to tell the time was the bloody interface in our heads, and we had to work forward from US time because the damned clock was in US Eastern Standard Time. Money—much better to focus on the money all this was going to take us.

"Any taxes or tithes go immediately into the city account. Like taxes from sales and maybe purchases at the Shop?" At least that's how it looked to me, otherwise I couldn't tell how our tiny town could already have so many Credits.

Dor narrowed her eyes and gestured in a swiping motion a couple of times before nodding. "Yeah, it is. This initial number of sales made is from the first, what . . . ten to eleven days? Like, usually, this is probably a weekly income or less. We'd been hoarding stuff until we had somewhere to offload it. Then again, with higher Level monsters coming, that means higher value loot so . . ." She shrugged. "But we're going to need to save a lot if we want to extend our borders past the center and its carpark."

I scrolled through a few options. Like expanding to include physical walls. Then there were fences, iron fences, stone walls, metal walls . . . all of them more expensive than the other, and even just to place them around the town as it was now would drain what we had now and then some.

Sleep. I just wanted to go back to sleep, but I wasn't actually tired. It's just that sleep allowed me not to think, and right now I had numbers up to my eyeballs and not plants.

"Do we want to upgrade existing defenses and then extend them when we've begun expanding?" I asked, biting my lip as I did so.

Kyle shook his head. "I don't think so. From what I can tell, this township thing comes with, like, occupancy and ownership Levels. People appear to be able to save up and buy their own places, but if they don't buy them, and if the city can't afford to buy them and do them up, then we must be careful not to overextend ourselves. I think?"

Sarah poked her head in, her red hair unmistakable.

"Am I interrupting?" she asked, practically skipping in anyway.

"No," I lied a little, but I liked Sarah. She was good people. "What's up?"

"The plumbing is back! The smells are gone, and it's glorious, and I kind of wanted to say thank you." She blushed slightly, but I knew she wasn't shy in any way. It was just reflex.

Dolores got up and gave Sarah's shoulder a squeeze. "Well. Since you're here. We have a bit of a job for you."

I laughed as Sarah's face took on a stricken expression and Dolores began to explain the power quest. Turning back to Kyle, I stopped.

Footsteps preceded even the Mana wave that warned me of the incoming young woman. Sienna arrived at the doorway, her thick brown hair hanging in gorgeous, bouncy curls around her face.

"Sorry for being late. Kids would not stop asking me for things." She smiled, more genuinely this time, with her apology behind it. She was much shorter than me, almost as petite as Molly, maybe around five feet and two inches. I think my heart almost stopped.

"It's fine," I managed to grind out, wondering when I'd lost the use of the English language.

Kyle glanced at me, his eyes in a daze, like something had smacked him upside the head too. "Basically, your Class should help us interpret the town interface to its full extent. We've managed a few things, but . . ."

I marveled at my brother, unsure how he'd managed to keep words in an actual, sentence-like structure.

"Excellent. Give me a bit and I'll be able to make heads and tails of this. We'll get our walls sorted out in time to show those hunters exactly what they're dealing with." Sienna's voice held a lilt that I thought might lull me to sleep, and she busied herself as I gave her access to the administration options. Sienna's eyes were like a bronzed amber, vibrant and beautiful.

But when she looked away and spoke to Dor, some of that strange pressure eased up in my mind. Long enough for me to realize just what it was.

Charisma. Whatever her Class did, whatever it meant for all of us, her Charisma had to be incredibly high. All I'd wanted was to worship the ground she walked on. And she was gorgeous, but that magical air about her, now that I could recognize it, it was fucking dangerous.

Great. We even had to be careful of each other.

*Way to fuck things up, Galactic Council,* I thought at the voices in my head. Sadly, they were silent.

From the plumbing infrastructure we'd enabled to miniscule details on how our walled defenses would work, I preferred us to have something solid for people to traverse, but Mike, who'd arrived somewhat later, and Kyle weren't so enthusiastic for it. They were more in favor of a fence like an invisible one that kept dogs in.

We spent the rest of the day wasting leveling time and worrying about city defenses instead. It was more involved than I'd ever thought it would be.

But Garden City needed its walls, needed defenses, because there was no way we were vacating anything without a fight.

❖

It took time for the walls to be put in place, and all we could do for a couple of days was watch as they emerged. Well, at least as we traversed in and out of them anyway.

Our Levels weren't going to climb by themselves, and having hit 20, it took so much more effort now. Mike was busy placing guards on the walls. I stood at the bottom, looking up at one of the three towers, marveling at how tall it was. I'd never hated stairs so much as I did right then. Just a blocky tower with a simple gate and an overlook up about five stories that could get a good view of the land approaching our town.

Garden City was huge, like one hundred and forty thousand square meters, something like one and a half million square feet. I'd have liked more gates, but this felt safer.

Still, it was a town, now surrounded by a stone wall we could defend, where people could patrol the tops of them, thus keeping our little place safe.

The walls rose about twelve feet, not particularly high yet, but it was something. The gates were placed at three spots around the perimeter and guarded heavily. Well, as much as we could guard heavily anyway. Against monsters and the occasional human. Though we were willing to let survivors in as long as they didn't plan to attack us.

Inside, the atmosphere had changed slightly. Less subdued and sprinkled with a tiny bit of hope. Our people talked, and the children inside played, filling the tiled halls with their laughter and screams of joy.

Wisp even seemed to have made a friend. Another girl that appeared to be around her age, but I hadn't caught her name yet. The girls stood, guarded by Dog, as they spoke to the rest of the children around their age. All of them watched the younger kids playing in the indoor playground, a holdover from the mall. In fact, they'd expanded the little area with help from some

347

of the department stores. The original coffee place I'd liked was no more.

Worth it.

All in all, we had dozens of children. Not an entire generation, but a start.

A lot more than I expected, truth be told. This environment wasn't exactly conducive to surviving at all, especially if you were small.

"They really hit it off."

Sienna stood next to me suddenly. Did she know the effect she had on people? I was lucky that my Perception and Willpower belatedly allowed me to realize what it was she was doing, even if inadvertently. Otherwise, I'm not entirely sure what might have happened.

I guessed town planners were almost politicians and probably required the Charisma to get their way. "Yeah. Wisp was already forthrightly outgoing. She's very good at speaking her mind."

Sienna smiled and a shadow passed over her face. "Aisha needs people like that. She keeps to herself until she gets to know you. Now all I have to worry about is my son."

"Son?"

"Rolo."

"How old is he?" I asked, trying to be polite.

That Charisma, even though I could tell, and even though I knew, was still difficult to fend off. If my Attributes hadn't been as high as they were, I think I'd have been done for. Not that she seemed devious, not really. But . . .

Damn.

I needed more mental resistance.

"Rolo is twelve, but he's not . . ." She paused, and I could see now where the pain in her shadows came from. "He sees the world in bright colors, through his sister, through me. I'm not sure if this new age will be something he can manage."

I wasn't sure how best to approach the matter, but I could practically feel the worry pouring off her in waves.

"The System, the ability to quantify and explain, elaborate . . . he'll probably work well with it." I watched as Rolo looked over an area I couldn't see anything in, like he was watching magic dance. The sense of wonderment on his face though, it told me he could see so much more than he was probably supposed to.

"You think he'll be safe?" Sienna hesitated, like she hadn't yet dared herself to hope.

I nodded, suddenly pretty damn sure of it myself. "Once we get this city and its defenses locked down and have enough people to stand up for ourselves? I think he's going to be a huge part of keeping us safe."

She stared at me for a while before nodding slowly. Maybe she didn't believe me, but right then the Mana around me felt like I was being licked by five puppy dogs who were very glad to see me.

I figured I was on the right track. And if not, well, I'd take the delusion for today anyway.

# Chapter Twenty-Nine:
# Dungeon World

## 12 Days Post-System Onset—7 a.m.

"It doesn't matter how many defenses we have up. If we're all cowering behind them and unable to use their full potential because our own Levels are stagnating around the 20s? Nothing is going to matter."

It wasn't the first time I wished Ray's Ice Lancer Class leaked over to his hot-headed personality. He was being testy, not that I could blame him.

We'd had two days of navigating the System menu, of sending out small leveling parties, of getting some sort of system working to make us stronger. I got the feeling Ray felt cooped up.

Sienna worked quietly in a corner with Dor, their heads down. Mike stood with them, crouching down to the table height every now and again to talk to them. Security, building, taxes, rationing . . .

The world had ended, but the bureaucracy stayed the same.

The guidebook we'd gotten was stupidly rudimentary. So much so that it was almost useless now that we had gained some Levels.

We had a dozen or so of us 20 and over now, but no one past 22, and we'd just got done with day twelve. We only had five days left. I didn't think we could suddenly hit Level 50 and become amazing superheroes, but I'd been hoping we could maybe hit the mid-20s.

I wasn't sure how we were supposed to make a difference to our situation in only five days.

"We need quasi-safe leveling areas," Kyle mused, thinking out loud.

Everyone looked at him. Sitting at Level 21, he was one of the ones who'd stagnated first. After 20, every experience point felt like we were pulling teeth.

He cleared his throat and continued. "I don't mean it like that. I'm fully aware that nowhere except the area immediately surrounding us is safe."

Chris laughed and gave Sarah a squeeze. "It's just because we've been killing the fresh spawns, the new mutants, before they've had enough time to fight between themselves and level up. The moment we step out of this safe area we've created, I'm actually worried for us." Chris shrugged, and the mood filled with uneasiness.

"That's a damned good point." Dale's tone held no hint of mirth. "Sure, we've headed out a couple of hours, but we've had twelve to fifteen groups going. Now we're fighting things that are so easy, we're barely getting experience."

"Like they've greyed out to us, you know, like they do in games," Jackson added in. He was only half-heartedly taking part in the conversation. His hands were busy fiddling with some device he'd created for testing ambient Mana flow.

Frankly, brainstorming the power device had taken most of Jackson's, Chris's, and Sarah's time. Not to mention the other kids like Darren. But we needed it. For so many reasons, not the least of wanting a decent bloody coffee.

"We have to expand our leveling areas, then." Evelyn sighed, crossing her arms. "Go out further. Leave younger Levels and smaller teams back toward here in the safer area so they can level through to maybe 16. Then they graduate and move on while the more experienced of us keep pushing our Levels by expanding our controlled territory."

It made sense, but something about it sent the hairs on the back of my neck screaming. Walking into danger had never been on my radar before this. "Sounds like a plan. Every major group needs to take two smaller ones to litter the way toward wherever we're going. Levels up to 15, and then 16 to 18, then 19 and up."

The area beyond where we'd been clearing was bound to have higher opponents considering they'd been fighting amongst themselves the whole time. But how high was too high?

We couldn't take a jump of ten Levels. The higher up these creatures got in their Levels, the more wallop they packed, and the more dangerous they became. Hell, I'd got the impression that we weren't supposed to survive Australia's apocalypse at all.

My brother was being more silent than usual. He had been ever since we'd found them on day seven, almost a full week into our nightmare. We'd grown, we'd begun to form a small civilization right here in our teenage stomping grounds.

So why was I feeling so trepidatious?

Evelyn moved forward, like she was going to say something, and then halted, pressed her hand against her ear, and looked up at everyone. "Scouts are out in the field now, trying to get a gauge on just what we're looking at Level-wise if we pass the thresholds of where we've been keeping the wildlife mostly under control."

I nodded. "How long will it take to get us a few destinations going?"

The Ranger shrugged. "I have a group of scouts out right now—"

But she stopped in the middle of the sentence, and her face went pale, giving her usual olive tones a grey overlay. She held up a hand and worried at her lip. I hadn't contemplated panicking before, but now I did. Whatever she was about to tell us, we weren't going to like any of it.

The library, or headquarters as we'd now dubbed it, was oddly balanced. Quiet, yet somehow not. Neither Dor nor Sienna seemed affected. They kept chattering while the tension grew.

Finally, Evelyn raised her head and looked everyone in the eyes as she did so.

"The idea is sound, and most areas have a great amount of space where the creatures we'll want to level on start around Level 21 and continue into the mid- to high-20s." Evelyn took a breath and squared her jaw.

Whatever was coming was particularly difficult for her. I resisted the urge to go and pat her shoulder or squeeze her hand while she weathered this. After all, she knew how to be strong.

"It seems we have a Dungeon forming not eight hundred meters away from us. It's not a hundred percent confirmed—that's what the scouts are doing right now." She let the statement drop like a sack of rocks.

I brushed my fingers over her shoulder, letting her know I was there should she need me. She glanced at me gratefully before squeezing my hand and pushing it off her shoulder.

"Where?" I'd not even noticed when Jules walked into the room. Perhaps she'd been there the whole time.

Evelyn paused and then let the words spill out in a rush. "MacGregor High School, just back and over the freeway."

MacGregor High School was bloody close. Like a stone's throw close.

Ray shrugged, seemingly unimpressed. "Didn't they say this was a Dungeon World? Wasn't that one of the many notifications we got at the start? They were bored with the nine or twelve or who knows how many they already had. So I guess Dungeons are going to open up all around us."

I mean, it was still almost a kilometer away. Probably stood to reason that I didn't feel Mana rushing to it. Perhaps I did need to extend Mana Attunement. Surely a Dungeon would require a mass of Mana. Time. I needed more time to be able to do all of this, to make sense of everything.

This wasn't like some TV show I could skip and catch up on my studies. Missing something here could lead to complications like death, demise, and, oh right, dying.

"So? That's the plan then? We go and look at the Dungeon, right?" Gemma's spirit had mostly recovered since her partial flaying at the hands of the Rigoll we'd encountered.

Her eyes shone brightly, almost too much, and I wondered if she'd found some fantastic drug to help her deal mentally with it all in such a short amount of time.

"I mean, it makes sense." Kyle spoke up, and I could tell from his tone that he wasn't completely into the conversation, even if he should be. Again, a tingle ran down my back. Was he really okay? Later. After everything went down, we'd have time then. He continued like my eyes weren't trying to bore holes through him. "Probably take about what? A group of us? Two?"

This time he was looking directly between Evelyn and I, as if we had all the gaming answers. Just because he went ahead and became a surgeon didn't mean I wasted all my nights in games when I should have been studying harder.

It was only some of them.

Stupid sibling guilt trips.

I cleared my throat. "Two. I'd prefer to go in with too much firepower and defenses than to risk being overrun by going with too few."

"Solid strategy." Evelyn glanced my way and winked, which, for some obscure reason made me blush furiously. "Molly and Sange . . . my only concern is I would like another Tank. We have four dedicated Healers, but we need more people who can take a hit."

Chris raised her hand. "I've been working on some of the options in my Class. Not quite there yet, but I think I've adapted enough tech that I can help. I've got what I need for the power device, just waiting on a few other things to click for that first. But once I hit 20, I'll be able to tank more effectively."

Evelyn raised an eyebrow, and I noticed how nervous Sarah appeared to be, as if she didn't agree with what her partner said at all. She twisted a long strand of her bright red hair furiously around her pointer finger, released, and repeated.

The archer ended up lowering her gaze and shaking her head while she crossed her arms. "Fine. If you know what you're doing, I'll take your word for it."

Mulling over the groups in my head, I concluded that we probably had too many people and that leaving the boys back made more sense because otherwise I'd be trying to protect Darren and Jackson above all else. Which could get myself and any number of other people killed.

"Jackson, Darren," I called out, but before I could finish what I was going to say, they rolled their eyes and glared at me.

"Fine. We know what you're going to say. Don't want us to be a midnight snack." Jackson's sullenness came through loud and clear, especially since he wasn't trying to hide it.

Darren nudged him softly before speaking up. "We get it. Parental instinct and all. We won't make it more difficult for any of you."

It was probably the longest string of words I'd heard Darren utter since meeting him almost two weeks ago. He had a slight lilt to his voice, probably inherited from his mother. His quiet and unassuming nature had blinded me to the fact that he was pretty tall, maybe close to six feet already. Jackson was probably jealous—all five feet five of him. He hadn't caught me. Yet.

I was glad he'd met Darren.

"Thanks. Now for what we really need." I moved closer to them, beckoning to Chris and Sarah too. "How is the tech going? Are we on track to make the deadline? Like, not trying to be a dick, but we have just under four days left."

Chris chimed in. "We've basically got it, just having to wait for Jackson and Darren to level up a certain skillset they have. Not to mention Sarah's finesse levels for her intricate work require—"

Sarah cut her partner off, unable to contain her enthusiasm. "Yes! I've got the plans written down, but we have to make almost all of it or we won't get credit for finishing the quest. There are several tweaks I came up with instead of sleeping last night."

Then she stopped, a sheepish expression suddenly crossing her face as she realized she'd just been raving about all the science-based energy things.

"Sorry. It's just that we're getting really close to a few different breakthroughs. Or else I think they're breakthroughs, anyway. The thing is, we need to get through those steps so we can supplement the items I found in the Shop and really get things going!" Then she looked up at Chris and stopped short, her cheeks blushing almost as red as her hair.

I looked between them. "So, basically, you think we can make the deadline?"

Chris nodded emphatically and then turned to Sarah. "You stay here. Work with the kids and make sure they don't screw up all the hard work we've achieved. We're so close to giving ourselves a form of power again."

Jackson and Darren's disappointment washed away, eagerness taking its place. I think talking tech with Sarah suddenly triumphed over Dungeon diving and potential imminent death. I suddenly missed my best friend Aria. She'd understood my plant obsession like no one else, but she'd moved away last year. All the way over to Perth. I could only hope she'd survived.

"That's settled, then." Evelyn glanced around and I could see her doing a quick calculation of who we had with us and just what defenses and offenses we had.

My Class was a conundrum: a support Class with a weird ability to tell when there was an incoming mob, creature, invasion, and to be able to shove a wall into something, et cetera. Utility at its finest.

In the end, we narrowed it down to Kyle, me, Chris, Dale, Molly, Sange, Evelyn, Ray, Tasha, Jules, and Gemma. Evelyn frowned though. "That's not two full groups of us."

"We have time, don't we?" Tasha asked, her confidence still not having returned since Mark had disappeared. We'd never truly found his body. Maybe she was pretending he was still alive.

Evelyn shook her head. "No time like the present. Dor and Sienna will direct the lower Levels who've been playing in the sand to branch out a bit. We're still getting the rest of our non-combat Classes organized and productive. But as for the Dungeon, we need to be going soon, if not now."

"Oh." Tasha seemed reluctant, her eyes haunted.

Dor spoke up. "We have roughly thirty percent combat Classes, seventy percent not. Almost four hundred combatants is a decent amount, but only a small percentage of you are around the Level-20 mark. So go see what this Dungeon has to offer. It's a baby Dungeon. It's still forming, right? Or just formed. It'll still have Mana weirdness, but you've got Kira with you. You'll be fine."

She smiled at me, like that was the best answer in all the world, that everyone was going to be fine with me along.

No pressure or anything.

# Chapter Thirty:
# MacGregor Dungeon

## 12 Days Post-System Onset—10 a.m.

MacGregor High School looked just like I remembered it from my days of interschool sports. Sort of, anyway. There were no high schoolers running around in green shorts and green polo tops hemmed in red that my regional rivals wore. In fact, it was deserted. Of humans, that is.

Given the twisted and mutating, goblin-resembling creatures that ambled around in the carpark, I couldn't blame people.

I'm not sure what made me think goblin. These creatures didn't have green, warty skin; it was a sickly grey instead. Almost like they were zombified versions or something. They also didn't have an adorable little protruding jawline or big brown eyes that made you want to pick them up and hug them. So they weren't either type of goblin I'd ever encountered in mythology before.

No, these had rough, blemished, greyed skin. It seemed tough, and their almost-lifeless grey eyes bled back into their face in ways that made it look like they didn't have eyes from some angles. It was good to know that not all the creatures we'd encounter began their lives here on Earth, because these things would have had to be some badly mutated fuckers for that to happen.

Analyzing them gave me little to less info. It was only more confusing.

### Level 19 Orbtralon Guard
*Elite*

Guess they weren't goblins after all. And these guys were harder than the normal monsters. I got that. I hadn't actually seen any creatures like this guard before. Rigoll had been an elite boss. But these were elite guards. It felt intimidating to be faced with an elite mob, but we did have twelve people, including the new one Evelyn grabbed. I had no idea what their name was, but I was happy they weren't wearing a red shirt. No one should tempt the fates like that.

Two guards stood on either side of the high school entrance. Flames shot out of stone urns that hadn't been there when the apocalypse hit, and I was certain that whatever waited for us inside, it hadn't been there before either.

Evelyn motioned for us to follow her directions, and I was only too happy to. Fighting? It wasn't my thing.

Kyle, however—my sweet, serious, studious, lifesaving Kyle—he seemed to be enjoying all this in a way I'd never imagined he would. Apocalypses apparently changed everything and potentially everyone.

The first Orbtralon Guard took an icicle to the brain through his right eye. In moments, it swayed from side to side and then plummeted to the ground, alerting all its nearby friends. Out of the corner of my eye, I could see Ray blinking like he hadn't expected that shot to hit so hard. It was the same Skill he'd used way back when he first chose his Class, and I knew it took a chunk of Mana. Being able to kill that efficiently without having to regen Mana could be catastrophic for his state of mind.

Three more Orbtralon Guards screamed at the top of their lungs and ran in to fight with us. Chris slammed what looked like a piece of metal onto the ground. The moment it made contact, the sides folded out to become a metallic shield, like a larger version of riot shields seen on television. Magic extended from it to wrap around us, making it possible for us to hit things out there but reducing the possible magic damage it did to us in here.

"Nice," I said to Chris and got busy figuring out how to do damage without wasting all my Mana.

Blood Transfer here, Mana Drain there. All of it worked toward weakening our opponents. Of course, the latter only worked on magic-based mobs.

The Mana around me felt turbulent, like it was irritated by our intrusion. After all, it was trying to build a Dungeon right here.

Mana was real, it was everywhere, and I kept thinking that it had something very important to tell me.

**Congratulations! You have been granted a Quest.**
**Just what the hell is Mana?**

*Objectives: Figure out what it is that Mana actually is. It's been here for as long as anyone can remember. Always there, fueling, waiting, watching, judging, deciding. Mana is and was and has always been, but something inside of you sparks its curiosity, never mind your own.*

*Find out what Mana is and unlock the key to the universe.*

*Reward: Knowledge is Power, didn't you know?*

What a weird fucking notification. Glancing around at my friends, I couldn't help but wonder if one of them had somehow figured out how to hack into someone's head for shits and giggles.

But they were busy, and I knew in the gravity of this situation no one else would have played that sort of practical joke. I was also pretty sure no one else got that notification.

A flash of Mana twinkled at me from the corner of my eye, like it was waving at me, telling me to do this Quest. Not that I could say no. After all, it had just given it to me. System Quest perhaps?

And then there was no time to think about weird Quests anymore.

❖

I leaned on what was left of my second baseball bat. Trusty old metal thing. I wasn't as short of breath as I should have been. But the System had changed a lot about my Constitution and Stamina, literally, including taking away the aches in my knees from years of netball.

These mobs in MacGregor High were horrible. No solo content here.

Fortunately, we'd brought more people than we absolutely needed. That safety in numbers thing was a fact.

"Kira! Left!"

I couldn't even tell whose voice was whose anymore. But I reacted, swinging my bat around to my left and thudding satisfyingly with whatever it was that had been about to chomp down on me. Bat was no longer my first choice of weapon. I desperately needed something better than this. Maybe the shop had something. Perhaps IRSHA would come bearing gifts. Who knew?

Apparently, I was going to make everything happen after IRSHA. Talking to my teen, making sure my other kid was okay with her strange dog for a companion, talking to Evelyn about this whole date thing she'd brought up, finding more information about the System and how we could use it . . .

The list never fucking ended. But learning how to use a weapon that wasn't made for close-contact crushing things' heads in? That was high on my list.

Thoughts ran through my head at nineteen to the dozen, even while casting Earth Barricade, Water Siphoning where possible, and trying to figure out when Mudslide was an option. Mechanical, almost. We were in such a dance of repetitive movement, it let me think about things I probably shouldn't be doing during a fight.

Cockroaches the size of my entire lower body crawled through the Orbtralon ranks too, their carapaces thicker due to their unusual size. Even their eyes were highly visible and held a strange sentience to them now. I shuddered every time I had to beat at one until the goo started oozing out of it.

Those carapaces were hard to crack.

More of those Orbtralon Guards added into the mix, screaming at us when we crunched down on what appeared to be their pets. More than twelve days into this and goblin-like creatures having pets shouldn't have fazed me, but it still did. Probably wasn't going to change anytime soon.

We'd fought our way down so far, but there was no getting beyond this goblin city. Instead, we just had to dive into it. The halls no longer resembled a school but instead were made of rock structures, all properly interconnected, and the classrooms were reduced to caves. Creatures hid in those rooms, waiting to jump us, but we were prepared as we made our way down through the halls. No fewer than four of us ever ventured into a cave at once.

Healer. Tank. Backup.

All for one and one for all, and all of us pummeled these things beyond recognition. Maybe some of it was taking out our fears and frustrations. Nightmares didn't last long, but now . . . we'd be living one for the rest of our lives unless we took control.

Unless we took back our dignity.

I smashed another Orbtralonion in the side of its skull. Only this time I realized it wasn't a Guard, but an Officer. Rather than crumple from the hit like an Orbtralonion or even flinch backwards long enough for me to swing again, the Officer just grinned at me and swung a fist directly at me since I'd managed to get caught up in my thoughts and let it get that little bit too close.

I got my bat up in time so that it just pushed me back and bruised my arm, wrenching something in my hand at the same time. Then he took another step, his eyes gleaming with malevolence and spite.

Shit.

"Help! Have an Officer," I shouted.

I assumed he was going to be harder than the Guards, and damn it, I was right. He hefted a huge, spiked hammer, or maybe it was a warhammer? I couldn't be sure. Despite the size of it, he wielded it with finesse. It didn't matter that his skin was coarse and rough, grey and warty. The Officer was a master at his weapon choice.

My baseball bat and rudimentary skills were useless, which I found out in the worst of ways when the hammer came crashing down against the back of my calf. He'd swung up high and then twisted the entire thing around when I brought my arms up to defend. The hammer moved faster than I'd thought possible.

I heard the bone crunch as it snapped beneath the pressure. The blinding pain almost closed my eyes, and I screamed in a voice that didn't even sound like myself.

I hit the ground hard, not even feeling the pain of the impact. Another swing, a return one, caught me on the way down but only grazed me, making my hip and body tremble in pain. Then he stopped, dealing with a blast or two from my friends. Then, his hammer was high up in the air, and he was over me.

Flashes of my kids sped before my eyes. The thought of leaving them without any parent in this fucking nightmare fueled my rage. I kicked out blindly with my good leg, the tug dislodging the already-mending bone in the other. But blindly kicking worked. It made contact with the Officer.

I'd caught him by surprise, disrupting his balance for a split second. Enough that the hammer came crashing down beside my head instead of on it, shattering stone and pelting me with shards. One cut open my cheek; another lodged in my neck.

Broken bones in a game world that began to auto fix you quicker than you could say "oh my god, I need a doctor"—they were nothing. This creature was nothing, and there was no way it was coming between me and my kids.

"Fuck you!" I screamed as my hand latched onto his thigh, and I activated Water Siphon, fueling it with as much fury and as much anger as I could summon. At the same time, I triggered Blood Transfer too and watched in fascination as the Officer's body drained of liquid and filled me with healing. His eyes bulged hard as he exsanguinated before me, exploding into a shower of eyeball fluid and blood.

He fell to the floor as my calf stopped hurting, the bonecracking back into place, and the warhammer's haft barely missed me as it clattered down from his lifeless hands.

Only then did I realize I'd never stopped screaming.

# Chapter Thirty-One:
# Loot Restrictions

## 12 Days Post-System Onset—2 p.m.

### *Warhammer of the Orbtralon Chiefs*

*Congratulations! You have gained the Warhammer of the Orbtralon Chiefs. In order to access this item, an Orbtralon Chief, also known as an Officer, must undergo several punishing trials which include besting his seven training officers in combat.*

*Weapon Stats Modifiers:*

*+10% Strength*

*+5% Constitution*

*+10% Mental Resistance*

### *Weapon requirements:*

*Strength: 26*

*Intelligence: 60*

*Perception: 50*

*Warning: You have not met the requirements to use this weapon.*

*Warning: As you have not met the requirements, you are barred from seeing the full potential of this weapon.*

"Damn it." I growled as I left the hammer in my inventory. Like how many people had all those Attributes up that high? It seemed like a far-fetched set of requirements, so I vindictively wanted to use this specific hammer.

Paranoia made me hesitate about putting points into Strength so I could wield it since, well, it had almost smashed my head. Maybe that was an omen. Strength was the only gateway keeping me from using it. I'd met all the other prerequisites.

I couldn't help but ask, was it a trap? If it looked too good to be true, that usually meant it was.

Then again, could we—I—turn down any advantage? No matter how trapped? I shook my head after a second, putting it off for now and storing the entire thing in inventory.

Later.

Level 21. We'd retrieved some decent loot and gained a few Levels among us. I really wanted to use the weapon. I wanted to be able to defend myself and my kids. That fight had really stung with how close I came to being dead. Deaded.

I couldn't afford for that to happen. I couldn't afford for my kids to be without a mother.

And damn it, I didn't fucking want to die.

I'd survived along with only forty percent of this Earth's population after the first freaking day. They were not going to beat me. Australians lived in one of the deadliest places on Earth anyway. I wasn't going down without a fight.

"K?" Kyle stood in front of me, concern on his face. He was still covered in Orbtralon blood, its grey sheen only too obvious.

"I'm okay. Just. That was close." I knew he'd know what I meant.

He knelt in front of me as I gulped in the cleaner air of the city, fighting back a tiny bit of hysteria.

"K. The kids are fine, and you are alive. And if you hone those Skills you used in there to defend yourself and kill the named mob? Nothing is going to touch that." He leaned forward and gave my forehead a gentle kiss. "Besides, I'll always be here to back you up."

"Even though there's something you're not telling me, right?" The words shot out of my mouth before I could hold them back, and I knew it was better out than in.

Still though, shadows crossed his face as he blatantly fought a response. "Later. Just . . . later."

Then, I watched as he turned to check on the rest of the party, leaving me.

I kicked myself, hoping I didn't make him lose concentration he might need to save a life. Having not spent my extra Attribute points since I hit 17, I had twelve lying around. I mean, I could totally get my Strength up and use that damned hammer.

I could also totally use the Attributes to make death not such a close thing as it had just been.

The thought hung at the back of my mind while we all readied ourselves to continue on through this Dungeon. I bet the Shop sold everything. I hadn't taken the time out yet to really investigate just how far we could go with the Shop. But damn, did I need to get stronger.

The cavern was empty, except for our group looting Orbtralon corpses and righting ourselves again.

Evelyn nudged me in the ribs, catching me by surprise considering I'd been uselessly wallowing in self-reproach.

"You look glum." She paused, and when I looked up, she nodded. "Yes. I'd say *glum* is the correct term for your face right now."

"I'll glum your face in a minute," I muttered petulantly.

Evelyn burst out laughing, the sound echoing off the stone walls around us. Sure, it probably alerted the entire rest of the monster population in here, but it was a beautiful sound.

"Glum my face. Suuuure you will. Mind telling me what that entails?" She asked the last with a whisper of sultriness to her tone and succeeded in making me blush.

"Shut it. We have monsters to kill." I pushed myself up, not making eye contact with her again.

It felt strange to have such flirty reactions amidst adrenaline-fueled hikes into monster lairs. Maybe part of it was the fear and anticipation trying to strangle me. Still, Evelyn had been with me from almost the beginning. I think part of our thing was that. There was a surety in having someone by your side throughout the first two weeks who hadn't died yet.

A loud screech echoed through the halls, and I looked up in time to see a bat-like human creature launch itself from what had once been the top of a staircase. Then a lot more followed it.

Many Australian schools were outside schools, though some had changed since I attended way back when. They were separate buildings with outside verandas and two to three staircases at difference spacings along the building. It was kinda cool.

MacGregor had been, or was being, transformed into one huge Dungeon, which required the rock to grow through and over what had once been mostly wood and brick buildings, though halls were often made from metal siding. Here and there, the rock layers hadn't solidified completely, and a portion of sky could be glimpsed.

It seemed though, that the Officer we'd fought had only been in the first building's cave, leaving more entrances behind it. And these bat-like monkeys appeared to have made a home in the next cave.

Those ten seconds would have been better spent readying myself for the onslaught of flying bat-monkey things. One of them stood at the back, at the top of where a staircase landing would have been. I examined him.

*Wingridemu Sire*
*Level 18 Elite*
*Pack Leader*

Oh great. Just what we needed. Evelyn moved to the back with Kyle and Ray, all of them having some sort of ranged weapon or Skill or spell.

I shook my head, focusing on the creatures surrounding us. The warhammer felt heavy in my inventory, lulling me into temptation like it was saying: *Hey, I can make mincemeat out of these guys. Use me, you know you want to.*

Nope. Right now, I needed to use my trusty, old, almost-broken baseball bat. That and all the Mana abilities at my disposal.

The bat creatures rose, their wings unable to hold them aloft for too long, yet still long enough to mix their weight with the gravity weighing them down for a dive attack. They swooped at us, almost crashing into me, and crashing directly into the shield Chris threw up again.

I could feel the shielding around us reverberate and crack. It wasn't going to hold for long, so damage reduction would go with it. Kyle had regeneration buffs on all of us but Ray and Evelyn, given they generally stayed out of direct damage areas. I could feel the life pulsing from his spells.

Sange and Molly's teamwork was breathtakingly deadly. Molly's tower shield could take on more forms now, extending with spears all around it, extending into a little tank for her to seek refuge behind when attacked by too many, whirling blades on occasion from each side.

Sange might have been knocked down fighting the Rigoll, but now they shone. There was a slight desperation to their moves now, like they had something to prove. And Molly's health never dipped.

And then I had my own Wingridemu to deal with. The thud as my bat connected with the midsection of one of the pack members reverberated through my arms to my body, making me nauseated. The creature doubled over, its wings folding in as the air whooshed out of its lungs. One of Evelyn's arrows caught it directly through the eye socket, but the thing still didn't fall down dead. Valiantly trying to flail its wings at us, it screeched in such a way that my ears felt like they were bleeding.

The only one who didn't follow was that damned Pack Leader, who was fully focused on Molly. It made me glad, yet again, that I wasn't a Tank. The hits she took every time that thing beat on her? Not my thing.

Tasha took on her whirlwind stance. Not sure if that was the actual Skill, but that's what it looked like, and since she'd dumped all her points into Dexterity and Strength, not to mention leveled up, she was that much stronger. Her blades whirled around her in intricate patterns I couldn't quite follow but whose effects I could see. She danced through the pack as they swooped around us, gliding towards me.

Since losing Mark, her focus had been lax, but now it came back tenfold. Determination underwritten by sheer willpower. Her blades bit through wing membrane and cartilage like they were butter, and the flick of blood as she spun coated us all.

Once the creatures were maimed and grounded, the rest of us could do our things. It was easier to target a creature that wasn't flitting just out of reach through the air.

Tasha made it look easy. I couldn't help wondering if part of her was cutting these things up in the mild hope that perhaps one of them would accidentally take her out, even as my bat crushed in the side of a Wingridemu's skull.

Evelyn's arrows picked out everything with an accuracy that made my skin tingle. I was glad she was on our side. Her blow flashed with runes I'd not noticed before. Perhaps an upgrade, but it flared every time her accuracy homed in.

We plowed through the pack. Ray's Ice Lances. Kyle's reverse healing. Jules's protective shielding. Chris's shield wall. Molly and Sange's perfect unity. Gemma's damage and Tasha's whirling blades.

All of us, just a pack of surviving humans.

With the last of the easier Wingridemus dead, we turned to help out Sange and Molly, who'd been fighting off the Pack Leader with Gemma's backstabbing help. It was almost dead and not quite a boss, so we made short work of what was left of it.

Gasping for air as the thing hit the ground, I noticed that my experience barely moved. I mean, I knew the experience needed to level had increased once I hit 20, but damn it. I'd foolishly thought the mobs might be worth exponentially more. I might have just scraped into 21, but 22 was still far away.

We looted the corpses, but nothing special popped up. Not that I expected it to. After all, these were just what we'd have called group trash mobs in games years ago. Still, it felt like I was missing something.

I was tired as we went through what we'd got. It wasn't until my brother approached me and knelt where I'd collapsed on the floor to recuperate, that I realized I was still sitting. "So. What did you get with your new Skill point?"

I blinked at him. New Skill . . . oh shit.

I could feel myself blushing under the question, and Kyle chuckled. "You forgot, didn't you?"

"Shut up. I'm too old for this!" I retorted.

He laughed again, and I wanted to smack him and hug him at the same time. Still, we weren't in pre-apocalyptic, Earth-world high school. We were technically fighting for our lives. So, instead, I grumbled and activated my blue screens of annoyance to go through my information. Even though we'd effectively cleared this courtyard area, I knew I didn't have all the time in the world.

The mutations knew we were here. They'd come seeking us out eventually.

I pulled up the Skill Tree and checked out the new tier of Skills that I could finally buy. Which idiot released Skill sections at Level 20 but didn't give Skill points till 21? What kind of buggy System was it that did things like that?

Shaking my head, I peered at the Skills available.

Treesong, Topsoil, and Implantation.

I did a double take. Implantation, if used correctly, was kind of awesome. Maybe? Unless I was misreading something.

### Implantation

*Not every Skill does damage immediately. Some Skills take skill and experience to make use of, and Implantation is one of them. Implant a seed of power and growth within an opponent, leaching Mana and damage from attacks cast at the opponent. When the seed blossoms, a portion of damage and health is returned to those surrounding and is dealt as damage.*

*Duration: 10 seconds*

*Effect: Implant a seed of Mana into the chest of your enemy. During the duration of implantation, the seed will absorb a portion of damage done to the enemy. The absorbed Mana will be reverted once seed has fully grown in an explosion with a maximum of 5-meter radius around enemy.*

*Explosion will return Health, Mana and Stamina to those affected.*

*Should the target die before the bomb seed can complete its countdown, all benefits are forfeit. Use this wisely.*

*Mana, Stamina, and Health equaling 75% of the absorbed amount of damage is returned to all targets within a 5 meter diameter. 25% of absorbed amount is dealt as damage to initial target.*

*Caution: Target cannot be effect by this spell more than once per minute.*

*Mana Cost: 90*

Yeah. That was a definite yes. Selecting it, I felt a chill slide over me briefly, like I'd activated something or other. I guess I had.

Pushing myself upright with my now almost-defunct baseball bat, I was glad to know I had a spare in my inventory, even though I knew it wasn't the best weapon. Once we were done here, I needed to sit down and figure out exactly what the best course of action was for me and that hammer.

Such a pretty hammer.

"Hey." Ray jogged up to me from where he'd been backing up Gemma's scouting.

I was surprised the rogue wanted to *keep* scouting after all the shit we'd run into when she went last time, but I guessed it was do or die.

Literally.

"Horses eat hay. What can I do for you?" I cringed as I heard the echo of my mother coming out of my mouth.

It made me wonder how much else of her had rubbed off on me over the years. Not that it was a bad thing. She was a great person. Loving, supportive, caring, adventurous, and stern when she needed to be. Most of the time, anyway.

And in all that recollection, I'd managed to miss what it was he said. Shaking my head, I stopped him.

"Sorry. Brain fart. What did you say?"

He laughed this time, and I'm not sure why. "This Dungeon seems a lot bigger than we first thought. How deep do you think we should go before we turn back?"

I blinked at him. Why were they asking me? Maybe because I had kids back at the center and they wanted to know if I was okay staying away from them for too long. Which I wasn't, but for now I knew they were safe.

"Well, until we get an idea of how all this works, right? We have no idea if they respawn. We're not entirely sure what the angle or the reason for the Dungeon is. And as of now, no one has been seriously hurt. The System takes care of most of that shit anyway."

"So we keep going until we get a better idea of how the Dungeons on this Dungeon World work?" Ray's eyes sparkled, and not with laughter.

I could practically see his brain working calculations in anticipation of what they might discover. He was eager to know, to figure out this puzzle.

And to my complete and utter astonishment, I found that I was looking forward to it too. "Yeah. Let's do that."

# Chapter Thirty-Two:
# Eye of the Beholder

## 12 Days Post-System Onset—4 p.m.

My least favorite thing about Dungeon MacGregor was the reminders that until very recently, it had been a high school. Desks jutted out of the now-stone floors and walls, their meager contents spilling from the inside like the lifeblood of our youth.

Hmm. That felt more melancholy than . . . well, I felt. "Hey, guys, wait a few. Something isn't right here."

Because just like back with Sienna, I wasn't acting like myself. Something was off.

I had enough Perception to understand it, but not enough understanding of this world to know why.

Jules spoke up for the first time since entering the Dungeon. Her blonde hair had goops of green blood still stuck in it from the Orbtralon fights, but it made her look oddly like a battle princess. All her concentration was usually spent on healing, on preserving us and making sure we didn't all end up dead. Commendable. "Yeah, I'm upset, but I don't know about what."

"Well." Evelyn spoke bluntly. "What do we do about it?"

I could almost hear Dale thinking that he didn't feel vulnerable—what a crock of shit—when his facial expression changed. "Shit. I think you're right. This is bringing back memories of childhood and how vulnerable children are. It's the school desks, the remnants and memories around this place."

He paled, and I knew he was thinking about Darren.

"So how do we find this manipulator?" Sange spoke softly, eyes darting all around us. Some of their quiet confidence had returned. "It's obviously aware that we're not falling for it now."

"Extra caution sounds like a plan." Gemma's voice trembled as she glanced around, a soft blue glow emanating from her, coating her like a non-stick pan. "This feels so similar. Almost like that mind-control Blobby again, just not quite. A little different, not as pushy. More like it wants us to agree of our own accord. To fall into its trap."

Her words tapered off, and all I could think was that what she said sounded too perfect. Even and reasoned despite the obvious fear on her face.

Fog began to swirl at our feet, lifting the spilled books and pens, tablets and rulers, whiteboard markers and dust. They twirled around in the air, faster and faster until they finally formed, well . . .

A blob of school materials.

I looked at it and blinked. Everyone except Gemma seemed more confused than interested. She, however, appeared absolutely terrified.

The books made up this creature, assisted by pens and tablets here and there. Almost like it was trying to be a marshmallow-puff man and failing miserably. Then it opened its mouth and screamed at us.

It sounded like that T-rex in the movie scene where they had to run from it in the car. It was loud and enveloping, casing us all in the noise so much that my brain felt suddenly mush-like.

Asshole stun-locked us.

I could see a timer at the corner of my vision. It wouldn't even allow me to access Analyze. A tiny circle counted down my stun timer. Five seconds. In the grand scheme of things, five seconds was nothing.

In an emerging battle, it was forever.

Mana billowed around my feet, like it was trying to reach out and help me. But I had no Skills I could use while stunned, and the blue wave around me shimmered with irritation as the tiny counter hit four.

The creature lumbered forward, moving slowly toward its target. Gemma couldn't move. Her face was contorted in terror, and I knew memories flashed in front of her eyes. Though I had no clue what she'd seen, I knew it had to be terrible.

Three seconds, and I couldn't do anything as what appeared now to be massive jaws—not made out of the things in this room—opened and began to close down over her entire upper body.

No.

We were not going to lose her. I refused to let this happen. I tried to will the Mana to help me, to will my body to move, but nothing listened. All I could do was watch.

Two seconds remained, and the mouth was almost closed. I could envision it already, the blood and the remaining body parts just squirting all over the room, over us. Anger boiled inside me. This wasn't going to happen.

Out of the corner of my eye, I saw movement and feared the worst, knowing that we were probably being attacked from all sides now. But it wasn't the enemy. It was Chris. I'd never really understood her Class or just what it could do. But whatever it was had allowed her to break the stun early and dash, sprinting toward Gemma.

All in slow motion as my timer ticked past the two second mark, making its way down to one, I watched when Chris catapulted into Gemma, moving frame by frame in front of my eyes as she whisked our Rogue literally from death's jaws and slowly smashed into the wall on the other side. Blood erupted and sprayed over the entire room, but it was only part of her appendages, ripped open as the creature chomped down.

Another second, that's all there was, but it was enough for more blood to pump out, for Gemma's eyes to close and her face to pale, and for the creature to begin moving again, opening its giant maw for yet another scream.

The stun-lock ended.

"Cut its vocal cords!" I screamed as at least three heal spells slammed into Gemma's body, trying to stem the flow of blood from limb loss until the System fixed her. Death was only death if you lost your head (literally and figuratively) in this new world. And I'd be damned if I was letting anything take her now.

I watched as Kyle took a little longer to cast his limb regrowth spell. Just to be on the safe side. No time like the present to start.

Ray shot icicles at the creature, aiming for its throat while Evelyn embedded arrow after arrow in the same spots lower down.

The strangely alive creature screamed in annoyance as the small objects interrupted it constantly, never letting it use its best power. While we didn't cut its throat, we managed to prevent it from using its scream immediately.

Rather than just continue its failed attacks, the damn thing started swinging.

Molly grunted with each hit she took, that massive tower shield slowly gaining more dents than a Honda Civic. I took the chance and shot Implantation at it. There was no way the creature was going down in the next ten seconds anyway.

Its eyes opened wide as the Mana seed hit into the middle and burrowed in. It didn't seem to do any real damage when it entered—not that it was supposed to—but it must have been uncomfortable, for it screamed again. This time, no stun effect was evident.

I refused to look at Gemma; I was angry enough already, and I pushed it all into pummeling the shit out of this mutated alien with everything I had.

380

Damn it all. No one else on my watch.

Then I didn't have time to give it any thought, as I started swinging my bat. I couldn't get too close, but the thing jutted out enough that there was always something to hit. Pencils and tables and chairs broke apart, sent spinning away into the darkness of the cave with each wallop. My hands hurt, my breathing came ragged, but I didn't stop swinging and counting.

Eight seconds until detonation, and I called out. "Burn it with everything you have and damage the hell out of this bastard!"

And they did.

Arrows rained down, Evelyn's face grim. Ray powered up that huge ice lance and landed two of them, Kyle did whatever Kyle does, while I fired Water Siphon at the monster. My spell had little to no effect. This creature wasn't like others we'd encountered who had similar physiology to humans. Or most biologicals.

No, this was a nightmare creation that appeared to feed on fear and confusion. Well, I wasn't confused about bashing the fuck out of it, and I refused to live in fear anymore. Water wasn't what held it together, and I sadly didn't have a happiness bomb on me.

Tasha attacked it with a flurry of weapon strikes that I couldn't track visually, and book pages, cracked tablet screens, and severed pens began to litter the floor around her.

I Analyzed it briefly, just wanting a name for the thing. We needed to make notes about this Dungeon, give information so people knew what to expect. If it worked like in games, that was.

**Kratika Nightmare**

*Level 22 Elite*

*Your worst nightmares ignited.*

Just great. Way to be literal.

Ten seconds later and my Mana seed birthed. I'm not entirely sure what I was expecting, but the creature's life jumped down about thirty percent in the ten seconds it was implanted. It was a low-Level type of boss monster at the most. But that thirty percent ended up meaning when my bomb went off, another three percent of its hit points vanished.

It screamed in pain while the Healers' and casters' Mana was replenished, the Tanks' hit points received a nice refill, and Evelyn and Tasha received full Stamina refills.

Nice! Expensive but damn a good spell.

While I could have used it again, the creature would be immune for another minute, so it would be a waste of a chunk of Mana. Instead, I smashed Earth Barricades into it and tumbled rocks down from the wall and onto its head.

Eventually, with joint effort on Tasha, Ray, and Evelyn's behalf, the creature's book-lined neck finally ripped open, leaking out glugs of what appeared to be paper mâché onto the floor. The blood of the school monster. Poetic.

Attacking was easier after that. No throat meant no scream, and no scream meant no danger for stun-lock.

Mana transfer might not be powerful yet, but it really helped maintain Mana levels for myself. Considering the way I was throwing around my abilities, I was lucky to have that Cloak and Mana as a friend. And it clearly was. It sparkled around myself and my friends, but it appeared disgruntled by the creature formed largely out of Mana for reasons I couldn't explain.

Perhaps it was upset with the way it treated the new world this Mana had infused. Maybe it had to do with imbalance occurring already in the wilderness. Australia was bound to do that. We had so many variations of wildlife only found here, of course Mana mutations were bound to go haywire.

I swear it rippled reproachfully.

When the Nightmare fell to the floor after five minutes of fighting, give or take a few since I'd not been able to access my interface while stun-locked, I felt like we'd been at it for days. My entire body ached, my Mana bar and Cloak were empty, and I wanted to run to Gemma and hug her. But Jules was doing a fine job of that herself. Not that I could blame her.

I looted the thing, too numb to check what it had on it. We'd have to sort through all of that later. Right now, we needed to get Gemma back to our little town.

"Call it," I mumbled and didn't think anyone heard me. I was more tired than I'd realized.

Kyle draped an arm over me and pulled me tight. His gaze was haunted, but I'd seen him like that before—over a beer while we sat on my couch after he'd lost a patient. He always took it hard, always blamed himself for not being able to do more.

"Yeah, let's call it." He spoke clearly, like he was in the ER.

And I half expected him to follow the with "time of death, 3:21 p.m." Or something like that. But he didn't. He just held onto me. We both needed a little support right then.

It was a somber group who returned to Garden City that night—with loot and tales of how you'd better hit Level 20 and go with at least two full groups if you wanted to have a hope of not dying prematurely in that Dungeon. Not all of it was bad news in my eyes. The Dungeon was most definitely not a safe place for our people to level, but once groups got over 20 and could go in with twelve people, there might be some good bolstering loot to be had.

Rather than go straight in, I detoured to walk the supermarket shelves. A lot of it was going bare, the vegetable, dairy, and meat sections stripped. Still, not everything was gone.

Once our population hit the five hundreds, Ray had taken it upon himself to ration the remaining stocks. A good thing, too—storerooms were full as well. And he had multiple groups working the stores now, ensuring no one tried to hog things.

Wisp clung to my waist as we wandered around the store, picking out her favorite chips, grabbing a few of those packaged cupcakes, and my favorite mint chocolate bars. They were amazing, with this gooey cream center. Couldn't get this stuff anywhere else in the world. And right now, I needed it.

I grabbed some actual food too. Evelyn, Kyle, Dale, Darren, me, and the kids were all going to take one of the small shops as our home. While we'd been out trying not to get ourselves killed, the people back home had been busy remodeling the non-essential shops, those that didn't stock clothing or non-perishable food, sporting, or outdoor goods, into little apartments. They'd been through all the camping things, and we had a lot of little gas stoves, beds, cots, air mattresses, blankets.

We were well set up for here for a while.

Gemma was still being healed.

She hadn't even woken up as Dale carried her back. She'd seemed so small, so young with her eyes closed, her hair escaping the tight braid at her back, and missing half her limbs. Healing had stopped the bleeding, and Kyle's spell was slowly kicking in like it had with Sange. We'd decided perhaps the best thing to do was to leave her as out of it as we could while she healed.

Sange assured us it was the humane thing to do. And I couldn't help but agree. I remembered those screams, and Sange had only lost half an arm.

"Fuck, I'm tired," I said as Wisp and I entered what had once been the Body Shop store. Which was supposedly our new home.

Counters had been moved, and we had enough little beds in there now. With the middle sections pushed back along the walls, there was surprisingly a lot of room. Couple of beds in the back too. Running cold water since Dolores had completed the plumbing upgrade portion of the quest. At least I didn't have to worry about sewage back up anymore. And we had a little two-burner camping stove set up with a gas cylinder attached to it.

"Mum," Wisp admonished me a bit belatedly. "Language."

I laughed, and the laughter wouldn't stop. It fell out of me like a waterfall, accompanied by tears I hadn't shed yet. My little girl hugged my waist tightly, and I could feel her own body trembling. Dog snuffled his nose in between us and I felt this strange calm take over. But right then, I didn't want to question it. Right then I just wanted to stand with my little girl and be thankful that the two people I loved most in the world were with me.

I was lucky, and I knew it.

Dale patted Darren on the back, and I could see the tears in his eyes. Blue waves danced around him, but I couldn't tell why.

Nothing could fix that sort of hole, not even time.

"Mum!"

I looked down to see Wisp tugging at me with that petulant look on her face. The one that told me I'd missed something vital. "Sorry. Mind is a million miles away."

She frowned, and then perked up. "I said Dog listens to what I say. It's like he knows."

That statement made me pause, and I looked closer at Dog. Mana danced around him, in and out of him, like a conduit or something, strangely energized as it passed through. A notification pinged, but I ignored it in favor of Analyzing the dog in detail.

**Species: Canine**
*Designation: Dog*
*Companion mode activated*
*Protection capacity 85%*

What the actual hell? An idea popped into my head, like one I didn't want to happen. I mean, after all, I had control over her Classes and Skills until she was old enough to make the choice, right?

Analyzing Wisp, I suppressed the urge to curse loudly.

**Species: Human Child**
*Designation: Wisp*
*Affinity: Animal Companion—Whisperer*
*Warning: This is not a Class. This is a bond triggered with certain like-minded creatures.*

Well, then. At least she hadn't somehow got an actual Class. But what the hell was an affinity, and was I going to have to spend another five thousand Credits to get a book that would tell me about five points I probably could have surmised myself?

"So Dog is your protector now, then?" I asked, crouching down a bit so I could talk to her and the pet on their eye level.

She nodded, her eyes shining. "I finally have a dog that no one can tell me I can't have."

Her voice was smug. She'd wanted a puppy for years.

I guess the System won that point. It had given my kid a dog. At least it was one that would protect her. I could roll with that.

If I got my way, we weren't just going to survive. We were going to thrive.

# Chapter Thirty-Three: Countdown

**12 Days Post-System Onset—7 p.m.**

I was busy in my makeshift lab when my brother walked in. The way the vegetation around the center had morphed and mutated was simply fascinating. I was tracking mutations of plants, just little samples, but still, even with the ambient Mana in the center under control, it was fascinating.

"What you doing?" Kyle asked, leaning up against the counter with his arms crossed.

Ah, he was ready to talk. "I'm trying to figure out just what this Mana stuff is."

He blinked at me, like he hadn't contemplated things that deeply yet.

"You can see it?" he asked, his tone somewhat incredulous.

"You can't?" I poked back, not really thinking about it.

"No, actually. I haven't had time to look." His eyes flashed with a rare expression of annoyance.

Putting down my pen, I stood and looked at him. He was taller than me by his few inches but had such similar bone structure. We shared the same nose, chin, and eyebrow ridges. Mine were just a tad more delicate. But right now, he was scowling, and that meant there was something wrong.

"Spill. What is it?" I tried hard not to let too much concern enter my voice, tried to sound partially bored.

He sighed and rubbed his neck. Eventually, he chose to look at me directly. Those eyes held a haunted look I hadn't seen in years. Not since our childhood cat died and he blamed himself.

"This." He held out his hands and I looked at them.

Long, delicate fingers, perfect for piano or surgery. He'd excelled in both areas. They were still fine-tuned instruments, and I couldn't understand what he was trying to tell me.

"Sometimes, I don't know what you're saying, so you'll just have to use words." I spoke quietly, trying to soothe him because he was in obvious distress.

"I chose my Class because it seemed perfect. Healing and helping. Everything I've always lived for, always done. But . . ."

The struggle in his mind was obvious. His shoulders hunched, and his voice cracked on that last word. I inched closer, offering comfort in being present, forgetting my own work in lieu of helping my twin.

"Kira. It's not just healing. It's the opposite. My hands, this power, this Mana that you speak of—I can extract life too. Extract it to heal myself and others or just to destroy—to revert a thing to nothingness, to a lack of life." He tried to smile, but the expression came off wan and forced. "It's played havoc with my head, wrapping my mind around this."

"This?"

"Killing and healing. My oath."

"Oh."

"I can heal while intentionally harming. And if I'm not careful, I can harm without a second thought. This isn't an actual game. I can't go and respec or reroll my Class. This is what I'm stuck with. This is what I am. And the Class Skill choices I have to make further down the line . . ." He paused, his face ashen now. "I don't know if I can make them."

Without seeing his Class specifics, I couldn't help much, but I could do what sisters do. Be there for him.

"You can make them because you have to. And you can choose when or if you use those Skills. There's nothing to worry about. I have faith in you. We all do. Those Skills aren't evil or malicious unless they're in the hands of someone who wants to use them with those intentions."

He smiled, his color back to more normal levels. "I forgot how pragmatic you can be. Making sense while I stress myself into a corner."

I hugged him. Long and fierce, like I'd never let him go. Hugs are beneficial when they last for twenty seconds, and I swear this one lasted for about a minute, rejuvenating both of us a little.

"I just don't want this world to change me, for this Class to do so. I don't want it to bring out a darker side of me." He was thinking too much. Something he always did, hell, something both of us did. Imaginations running wild were just part of how we grew up.

The thing was, I couldn't promise him that those Skills and abilities wouldn't change him, but I could promise him one thing. "If you promise me that you'll always listen to me when I talk to you, I'll promise to pull you up if I notice anything strange about your behavior."

Kyle contemplated that for a moment, and I could see him taking the offer seriously. "Done. I will listen. You can also always tell me that I said I'd listen in case I pretend that I didn't."

"Don't you know it," I teased.

The tension that surrounded him like a rain cloud lightened up a bit, and he leaned in for one last hug. "We got this, little sis."

"We do indeed."

The rumbling started a few hours later and jiggled our beds, mattresses, and cots so violently that many tumbled to the floor. Garden City wasn't carpeted as a rule, so a lot of those upsets ended up in bruises and sore heads.

Me? Having studied some measure of geology and being in the process of understanding just what Mana was and how it came to infuse our continent, I was alarmed to say the least. Australia wasn't known for earthquakes of any sort. It wasn't anywhere near a fault line. What just happened, despite the panic around me, was nothing of the kind.

No, I instinctively knew that whatever that was, it came from tunneling. Not directly under us—it wasn't disruptive enough for that—but near us.

I leapt up from my chair where I'd apparently dozed off whilst studying my Mana and plant samples and ran to the library to pull up the settlement plans. Dolores and Sienna beat me to it, but then, they'd been closer to start with.

"How do we check where that came from?" I asked.

Dor frowned as she leafed through something, and it turned into a scowl when she stood up straight. "It's not underneath us. We extended our shielding to make sure tunneling under our gates wasn't a possibility. You know, the old 'if you can't go head on, drop in or dig up'? Couldn't have that happening."

"So that's not possible within our town." Sienna was making motions to pull up shit I couldn't see. "It's coming from outside the Center but close. It's not like we've been able to expand yet. It's under Logan Road, like it's trying to get through to us but failing." Sienna paused, confusion crossing her face. "It doesn't even make sense. It's coming from around us."

Great. How did we stop a giant mole from tunneling through to us? An idea hit me. "Wait, you don't think it's IRSHA trying to tunnel through to ambush us, do you?"

Dor shook her head. "They might have been deliberately tried to misdirect us. I mean, this apocalypse is invasion like."

"Because they're not human and they don't give two fucks about us and would probably shoot us on sight if it means they can get to their exotic kills?" I muttered, trying to recall everything I'd read about them.

The others didn't say anything after that as they checked in on reinforcements for our security systems, doubling down in a couple of areas. I could practically feel the town's bank account draining of the tiny amount of cash it had.

But that was why we had it, right? City planning was all about keeping the city safe and accessible. Defenses might be a new thing due to our former age of technology, but we needed them now.

Dale voice cracked as he spoke to me. "Kira, you have to come now."

I blinked at the panic in his voice. Something must have happened to Darren. Surely the shaking hadn't dislodged any of those damned Mana-charged appliances the kids had been working on.

"It's okay," I said in my best soothing voice, trying to calm him down before he lost it. "We're protected, and the Center is safe, we're just reinforcing things before we go and check out what the hell is making all of that noise."

He stuttered through the words, trying to get out what he wanted to say.

"Shit. Dale. Breathe. What is wrong?"

He took a breath I could hear, and I watched other people behind him sprinting to the entrance.

"The kids. They've already gone outside."

"Say what now?" My heart tried to jump up into my throat and choke me, but I pushed past it and forced myself to breathe. He couldn't be saying what I think he was saying.

"Jackson, Darren, and Wisp. With a few others. They've gone outside." He was practically sobbing now, like he could remember seeing his wife and other child dead next to him in the car. Like he was recalling just how wrong this could all go.

I didn't blame him, but I wouldn't let I stop me.

There was a part of me screaming, angry that the kids had been so stupid. But there had to be more to it than that, and if I could just manage to let my logic win out for another minute, I was sure I'd find out what that was.

"Why? Do you know why they went? Did they say anything?" My words came out rather measured.

"It was Wisp. She said she had to go out and check if everything was okay, that Dog knew something was happening out there, and we had to help."

He took another breath while I tried to wrap my very in-denial brain around what he'd just said as I started moving toward the exit and a gate.

"Jackson jumped to go with her, and Darren followed. A few of the other kids. When Ray ran out after them. I don't understand." Then he paused, and I could practically feel him calming down. "Kira. We can't lose them."

If he lost Darren, Dale was a goner too. His son was all he was currently alive for. The only reason. I got it. I so totally got it that I was already halfway out to the gate. In the middle of the bloody night.

"We've got this," I said and wrapped one hand around his arm as I dragged him toward the tower with me.

I didn't completely believe my words, but I'd make sure I did soon enough. All I knew was that my kids had headed out into imminent danger, and I wasn't about to let them die. If Dog led Wisp there, I'd either misunderstood something about their bond, or else there was a damned good reason she needed to be out there in the first place.

# Chapter Thirty-Four:
# Mutations

## 13 Days Post-System Onset—12 a.m.

The moon shone brighter than I'd thought it could, or maybe that was because all the city lights no longer existed. It could be one or the other. Either way, the carpark was bathed in soft light that accentuated the tiny figures standing at the wall and peering down below it.

At least they hadn't jumped the wall and ventured straight out into the streets yet.

Saving graces, right?

Even as I approached, I watched Wisp lead the way, racing down the stairs and to the arched gateway that led out to the road. There was no way I'd make it in time to reach her before she left the confines of our town.

So I did what any protective parent would do, I slammed an Earth Barricade at my maximum range just before she could open the gates, effectively barring her. Giving me enough time to make it to her side. When I spun her by the shoulders to face me, I hadn't realized I was already crying. My fear seeped into my veins and just exploded.

"What the hell are you doing? Are you trying to kill yourself?" And I rounded on Dog, who stood there, judging me silently with those big, brown eyes. "And you? What the hell are you doing taking my kid into danger like that? At least fucking tell me that you're going! Explain to me, let me know."

My energy left as quickly as the anger had come over me, and I felt like the worst parent in the world for yelling at my kid. But the worry, the fear, they gripped me in that instant where we'd all lost so much, where my kids— my entire reason for being alive, for fighting this shit tooth and nail—were in danger.

Jackson made it down to hear the tail end of my tirade, but I held up a hand to stop what I knew was coming. I wanted Wisp to tell me herself, to let me understand why she would do such a thing when she was usually so logical.

"Mum, I don't have time. There's a baby out there that needs to be saved. Its mum is injured."

The plea in her voice, the desperation sounding through every single word undid me.

I released my hold on the barrier and let it collapse. "Fine. But I'm coming with you. We all are." I gestured behind us at the trail of people. Dale and Evelyn, Ray and Tasha, even Jules was there, though without Gemma for now.

Sange and Molly were running across the carpark too. My dread left me. Strength returned. We had this.

I'm not sure what I'd been expecting, but the completely destroyed sight of Logan Road wasn't it. I mean, there were usually six lanes, a medium strip, and a whole parking lane section there. But now they were gone, and in its place was an explosion of asphalt. Cars were tossed aside negligibly, some of them precariously balanced against others.

Massive, winged creatures surrounded that explosion, firing what seemed to be barbs down on their target. It was too dark to make out much, but they looked like a magpie crossed with some sort of humanoid demon. Almost like harpies in nature, without opposable thumbs. There were maybe three dozen of them, flying in circles, swooping down to attack their target with their claws and beaks.

The creature in the middle of the explosion made me stop to take it in. About the size of a Brisbane city bus and brown, with close-cut fur and tiny, stubby legs, she screeched in rage at the plethora of mutants aiming themselves at her burrow. The shriek was high-pitched and squeal-like, setting my teeth on edge, as though it wasn't really meant to be heard by humans.

Maybe it wasn't and it was my high Perception.

When her attackers came in close, she about-faced and scurried deeper into her burrow before sticking her butt back at them, luring them into her nest. Stupidly aggressive like most monsters in this new world were, they charged right in, sometimes knocking one another out of the air to get in close.

Now, because most of her blocked the entrance to the burrow, once they were lodged and trapped inside, scratching, and tearing at her, she'd lower herself down a little, getting them deeper, leaving them more space. Then a simple and sudden push upwards into reinforced ground, and she smashed her butt up against the rim to crush the living daylights out of her attackers.

Of course, she couldn't get that many of them at a time, leaving the magpie-harpies to scream at her and climb into the air. The rest squawked and tried to attack again, only to meet the same fate.

It was the particular attack, the literal bum rush that told me what she was.

That poor momma was a freaking wombat.

A massively mutated giant wombat, but a wombat, nevertheless. And even though she defended that burrow with all her might, the compounding wounds from her attackers were growing as much as her desperation to protect the young in her den.

"Shit." I calmed down a bit, no longer as upset with Dog and my daughter. Because they were trying to save innocent creatures, and it looked like the wombat mum had had enough Intelligence to seek out humans to help her.

Or to help her save at least her babies.

The Mana flow around these creatures pulsated with each use of their power, undeniably unstable. It fed into them, fueled them, changed them all, and it made the mother roar in pain every time those harpies attacked.

I didn't have anything to lose. Dragging my kids away now would be heartless, and I'd always taught them to be kind.

Guess it was time to swallow my worries and lead by example, right? Being a parent. I tell you, best and worst decision ever.

When the next harpy attack started, I sprinted from my crouched position, launching myself toward the mother, and activated a gigantic Earthen Barrier right in the path of those stupid flying monsters. They flew smack-bang right into the center of the massive wall I'd erected. As I heard the resounding thud of contact, I felt smugly justified with my choice.

Having braced herself for impact, the wombat mother, or Wombutant as the inspection notice stated, backed herself back out of her den to turn toward me. I'm not sure why I didn't cower in fear. This Wombutant stood about a story tall. Think hippo-ified and bus-sized but longer and furrier without the chomping teeth.

And trust me, up close, it seemed a hell of a lot larger.

Instead of fear, her wounds upset me, made me angry. I kept a strong façade up and petted the nose she offered. Those harpies had raked their claws into and along both of her sides, even as she'd smashed their heads in against the bitumen encasing her burrow. The relief from her washed over me, as she finally managed to find protection for the young I could now hear below me.

There were still a dozen or so of her attackers in the air. Ray shot his signature Ice Lance, Evelyn riddled them with arrows, and I knew the others were helping too. This Wombutant momma was tired, and she'd fought, despite everything that had happened to her and her babies. She'd defended and kept them safe until she just couldn't anymore.

Wisp suddenly stood next to me and reached forward to touch her nose. Mana rushed in between them, cementing whatever message they'd shared and understood. Instant sparks of recognition, of calmness in the wake of violence.

Above us, Ray and Evelyn continued their assault, with Molly and Sange fighting off those who dared get in close. Amidst it all, the feeling of loss and calm, acceptance, and solace ran through me. Dale appeared by my side and placed a hand lightly on the creature's side, pushing life-force into her, and her eyes lit up in surprise, before closing as she fell into a slumber.

All around me the harpies fell from the sky as Ray and Chris, Kyle and Dale, Evelyn, Darren, and Jackson all played their part in bringing down the remainder of the three dozen of those damned flying menaces. Jules's and Chris's shielding protected us, and I realized that had the harpies been organized and not a screeching mess, we'd all probably have died out here.

Instead, we took them down with little effort. I even pitched in, when the smarter harpy or two swung around the barrier and came in sideways. Water Siphon seemed to really wreck their balance at flying, a horrible thing to happen when you're gliding in for a face peck.

After that, a lot of stomping and bat smacking ended that problem.

Even so, Momma Wombutant was exhausted from the fight and the energy it took to heal those wounds. Lying above ground, protected by the humans she'd found, she slept. Deep below, her babies continued to cry out.

It wasn't any surprise to me at all that my tiny daughter lowered herself into the hole with her brother to retrieve the babies.

So what if I threw a Shield of Power over her before she went in? No one else needed to know.

❖

I'd been wrong. You see, I was a plant life expert, not an actual wildlife expert. Apparently, wombats only had one joey at a time. All that wailing noise came from one—singular—wombat child. And, oh boy, was it vocal.

It was also about the size of Wisp's torso, and its little eyes were still bleary. The thing clung pitifully to my daughter like a lifeline, but its wailing didn't seem to bother her or Dog. Nope, the smile on her face woke one of my worst fears.

Mana danced around her, through her, through the joey, like it was tying them together in an inextricable pattern of complexity. First up, she already had Dog, and I wasn't sure how that animal was going to like having another one take up attention. But more importantly, I wasn't sure how the massive momma wombat was going to take her tiny child bonding with mine.

I did not feel like being buttocks-slammed into oblivion.

Brushing himself off to dislodge the dust and dirt of the massive burrow at our feet, Jackson elbowed me. "You realize she's not letting that go, right?"

I sighed, not wanting to admit anything of the sort. "It's not even up to her. I don't think we could extricate those tiny claws from her even if we tried."

Glancing around, I realized we'd drawn a rather massive crowd. Evelyn stood at the head of the mother, stroking down the line of her nose and mumbling soothing words to the creature. Even in the moonlight, the archer's face seemed peaceful. She seemed to fit nicely in the crook of this world's insanity, and she was blossoming.

Maybe it was my thoughts—perhaps I'd made a noise—but she looked over at me and grinned. Smiling back, I let the warmth suffuse me. Sure. I was standing outside in the middle of the night where Logan Road had been torn up by an elephant-sized wombat digging a burrow.

Whatever. Time to embrace my new normal.

Wisp stood in front of me now, her clothing ripped and muddied and the biggest smile on her face. Her eyes gleamed in the moonlight as she held the medium-dog-sized baby wombat to her chest. I didn't like the size it would turn into, but right then I didn't have the heart to take it away from her.

"Mum. I think she likes me."

In all this darkness, she could still find wonder. And by finding it, she gave some back to me. The way kids did even before the apocalypse arrived. That pretty much sealed its—and my—fate.

Wisp really was smitten, and the thing mewled into her neck like it never wanted to leave. I had to wonder how old it was, how desperate the mother had been to protect her child, and a chill washed over me.

Knowing exactly how this intelligent marsupial felt, how protective, bewildered, and fierce she had to be as she dug that burrow to escape her attackers. I totally got her.

Like she could hear my thoughts, the momma wombat cracked open an eye and fixed her gaze on me. There was no threat there, more of an understanding. Recognition flushed over her face as she saw her baby snuggling with mine and realized she was safe. Enough intelligence remained in her, or perhaps she'd gained it, to realize that we'd helped her. That we would also help her child.

Right then, I knew we'd gained an ally, and my daughter a new pet wombat baby. Maybe keeping an eye on her companions would keep her out of trouble.

Yeah, right. Nothing *ever* kept her out of trouble.

# Chapter Thirty-Five:
# Ambient Flow

Not sure about anyone else, but I sure as hell didn't get back to sleep easily. After all the excitement, I managed to sleep around 3 a.m., but I was up with the sun. Again.

By the time I truly woke up though, I'd been sitting nursing a very bad excuse for a coffee for about forty minutes and staring off into space.

Evelyn and the others had finished maneuvering the momma wombat into the center carpark so she could stay behind protective lines while recovering. And my daughter . . .

I don't think she'd put the baby down since she'd picked it up. It didn't appear to mind, nor did it look like it was about to leave any time soon. It really was adorable. Little stub nose, furry whiskers, the beginnings of an armored butt plate of doom. She could have done worse, and the momma didn't seem to mind that Wisp had brought it inside to snuggle while she slept.

All in all, that thirteenth morning dawned nicely. Even if we'd all been up most of the night. I knew we weren't about to have down time—that was more of a myth for now.

So much had happened in the last twenty-four hours. From our Dungeon trek to my samples, to my brother and the fact that I had to go scour the Shop. I groaned, pulling out my notebook and pen to make notes about the Dungeon area first.

The Mana saturation of that area made the respawning Dungeon not only a great place for potential experience, but also for death. The worse fact was, the way my Mana Sense felt, it seemed to be growing stronger each damn moment.

But with caution, we could send mid-Level 20s groups there as we progressed. The opportunity for good loot was there too.

We still had three-ish days before our friendly neighborhood IRSHA said they'd arrive.

I looked up at the unexpected sudden tension flooding toward me. Only it wasn't that. Instead, it was an underlying excitement that I swear came from my son and Darren tearing through the shopping center to my coffee shop near the info desk.

They stood breathlessly in front of the little table I'd sequestered, their faces so bright I was quite sure they hadn't tried to sleep yet. Another all-nighter.

"Jackson?" I knew my tone told him enough, and he at least had the decency to blush.

"Mum. I promise this is amazing. Here." He handed me what looked like one of those long-range, super-expensive walkie-talkies. The device glowed a subtle blue like it was hugging a ball of Mana.

I glanced at him, and he gestured erratically, all excited. Darren ended up piping in even though I swear I'd barely ever heard the kid speak. "He wants you to turn them on. We've got wall communications up and running. Rudimentary but effective enough until someone develops mind speech or rediscovers electricity."

I blinked at him and realized just why he got along so well with my kid. Good. At least in this wacky wilderness, they had each other to help make sense of things and to fiddle with things and, hell, to be majorly useful.

Then I looked down at the walkie-talkie in my hands. Who'd have thought this little thing was an amazing advancement? But we'd essentially just enabled our security division to have easier communication.

This—this would be groundbreaking. We'd only been back from the Dungeon for like twelve hours, had a massive burrowing wombat fiasco, and they'd still managed this?

"Thanks, boys." I meant it, but Jackson butted in somewhat sheepishly.

"Well, it wasn't just us. Sarah found Mana-harnessing balls in the shop and then bought some after your trip out yesterday." He was bursting with excitement.

Sarah joined us, her red hair up in a bun for once, and put her hands on her hips, smiling like she hadn't slept in days either. "I found them. It was getting them to work with the differing abilities we have that was the trick. I'd only been able to afford a few of them before Chris got in last night and sold to the store."

"How many do we have?" I asked.

"Fifteen. Enough for each wall patrol and the gates. So that's nine of them out there. We also have six of them in here. One is in the library for Dor and Sienna, one with Red for rationing, one with Jules and Ray for refugee intake. Mike has another, and a spare one for you." Sarah handed one of them over to me, and I blinked at her.

For me, eh? Okay, I could do that. "Thanks. Now you don't need to run all the way here to talk to me."

Sarah laughed. "I'm sure you'll still get your fair share of inquiries. Besides, don't worry. We'll get more working. It's the frequencies we must work on. Those are the hard ones."

Evelyn had sauntered over and was looking at the one Sarah had handed me. I could tell from the half-smile on her face that she was suitably impressed. "Nice work. There's barely any bulk of difference from the original. How much did you need to modify it?"

"Well . . ." Jackson went off on a long and detailed discussion with her of exactly what they'd had to do to make all this possible.

I laughed but sobered up quickly as Sarah and then Chris sat down next to me.

"What's up?" I asked. Their vibes were telling me they had some news to drop.

"At least there aren't zombies." Chris sat down next to me, and Sarah moved off to talk to Evelyn and Jackson.

"Yet," I added, taking another sip of my old, sock-tasting coffee. "Let's stay nice and pragmatic, shall we?"

"Pragmatic it is, then. No zombies yet." She paused for a while, sipping on one of the fancy instant coffees. Swirling it around in her cup for a few moments, she sniffed at it and cringed. "Really need some better stuff."

"Maybe I could find something in the Shop. Or maybe, when they finally send us our Crafting Cartel Representative, there'll be a coffee roaster."

"We would be that lucky."

I laughed, and she did too. Yeah, somehow, I didn't think aliens did bean juice.

It was all mundane chatter, like a calm before the storm. I could feel the Mana gathering all around our area. If I closed my eyes, I could map it out in my head. Something was brewing; something was coming. Maybe it wasn't Mana itself but Mana that let me sense it? So many bloody questions.

Maybe Chris could feel it too, because she turned the conversation serious.

"Your kid. Jackson. He's damn smart. And I don't just mean made smart by the System. He's levels of intuitive smart that I'm glad survived the human culling."

There was bitterness in her voice, and I realized how much Sarah tempered Chris's personality when they were together. The softer edge was missing, and here was the real personality, the one who analyzed shit and prepared for the worst.

I nodded and waited for her to continue, knowing something was coming.

"Would you mind if I taught him some engineering aspects we can apply to this world?"

It was a strange question to ask in the aftermath of everything we'd been through, especially the walkie-talkie advent, but I appreciated the sentiment. "Sure, if that's something he wants then I have no reason to stand in the way. What exactly are you thinking about?"

Relief crossed her face, closely followed by excitement. Such a tiny thing, bringing joy in such dire circumstances. I smiled in what I hoped was an encouraging way.

"So I get why they gave us this Quest."

I waited.

"The power generator through the Shop is insanely expensive, at least for where we are right now. There are parts, however, that can be bought to give us the beginning of an ambient Mana gatherer. That's what we've been working with. All of us, piecing it together."

Chris paused for a moment, like she was gathering thoughts. "If I've got my Class right, and if Sarah has done her calculations correctly, which of course she has, I think the Techzard-type Classes can help us trigger the ambient Mana flow needed to fill the . . . well I guess you could call them batteries. They're just huge."

My eyes narrowed. There was something she wasn't mentioning.

Thank you, Diviner ability for kicking in.

"Okay, so now I know all the good things, what's the downside?"

Chris hesitated and ran a hand through her short hair. "We're going to have to go outside of the Safe Zone."

Truth. But there was still something missing. I considered her words, mulling them over in my mind as I fixed my gaze on her until she broke.

"Damn, you're good at this," she said. "Okay, so, I want you to understand I'm not trying to pull the wool over your eyes or to have a go at you, but I need you to listen and hear me out before you veto what I think might make this work. And to be honest, it's the only way I see us finishing the quest on time."

"I'm listening."

"I know we've kept the surrounding areas pretty clear as we've been scouting for survivors."

She was right; we had. By now, the monsters roaming the streets within a two-ish-kilometer radius were generally in the 15-and-under Level range.

Except for the Dungeon, of course.

Fucking Dungeon.

"The Mana around here isn't ideal. It moves too slowly and has mostly settled, at least sort of. There's no way we'll fill these generators in the time we have left, considering we also need to finish building the last one. Anyway. The closest place I can perform this experiment is the outskirts of that still-forming dungeon." Chris raised her head for a moment, meeting my eyes with determination.

I knew she'd never deliberately endanger my boy, but I also didn't feel like letting him wander off with a group of people I'd barely known two weeks to a place that almost killed us the last time we were there.

I debated my options, but really, the answer was fast in coming.

"Well, I'm not sending the bunch of you off alone. I'll come with you." Not that I was Wonder Woman or anything, but if something happened, I'd much prefer to be with them and know there was nothing I could do than to always be second guessing what happened.

Chris breathed in what I could only assume was a sigh of relief.

"Excellent. I'd like to go as soon as possible. Maybe later today if you're up to it. I'll be bringing Darren, Dale, Jackson, Sarah, and Miller and Sean." At my questioning glance, Chris continued. "The other two boys who have a similar Class that can harness and apply the energy."

Chris seemed a bit perturbed that I didn't recall their names. Honestly, I'd never been able to remember Jackson's friends' names. Faces, sure. Names? Hell no. Give me a platycerium, better known as a staghorn, anyway. Those were names I could rattle off in a heartbeat.

"You're an odd one, Kira," Chris said, her voice thoughtful now. "I think in another life we would have been friends if we'd ever met. It's nice to know I have people around me who aren't just someone I have to get along with."

The statement surprised me, but at the same time, it gave me this warm feeling. That here, in the middle of this entire clusterfuck of an apocalypse, we had people we could mesh with. It gave me hope, however minuscule. Provided, of course, that we could maintain it. Considering the current rate of the decline of the human species, I wasn't entirely sure we had any type of future.

"Ditto," I said before she got up and left.

For a few moments I just sat there, watching her walk away and join Sarah, Chris placing a kiss on her partner's forehead as they locked arms around each other. Solace in such a time of need.

I missed Mason, just a little, and only very briefly. Apocalypse and all, but I really did miss my ex's sense of humor.

❖

The utility belt I buckled around my waist felt heavier than I'd anticipated. Weight of the world and all. Sienna and Dor had run over all this information they'd discovered when putting up the protections for Garden City with me, and my head was spinning. Lack of sleep didn't appear to be interfering with my cognitive functions nearly as much as it used to pre-apoc.

I just hated that kind of bureaucracy, even if I did need to know it. It was my settlement. For now, at least.

And really, I was loath to give it up. The lack of control over where my kids would stay . . . let's just say that's the kind of thing that gave a mum nightmares.

Tonight at eleven marked the start of the fourteenth day, though I was willing to start just referring to the full twenty-four-hour thing as one now. We weren't there yet. Not quite at two weeks, even if I could barely remember our lives as they'd been before that.

Our group gathered outside, and Wisp hugged me tightly, or at least as tightly as she could. She was still holding that baby wombat, who was currently bleating quietly and snuffling its nose. I didn't want to think how big this thing was going to get. One glance at the momma wombat gave me a starting point but . . . well. We were all just starting, weren't we?

Dog stood there by her side as always, stoic, and protective. Nearly up to her shoulders now.

I petted his head. Good dog.

"Keep safe, Mum," Wisp said.

Leaving her at the center was starting to wear on me, but what I left to do, it was important. For her survival, our survival . . . maybe for everyone.

We needed air filtration and, hell, air conditioning when it came to it, food refrigeration. These were things that would help us live on and prosper.

Leaning down, I gathered her and her massive pet into a hug. The soft bleats quieted for just a moment, and I smiled. "Take care of each other. You too, Dog."

Dog wuffed, and I regretted not giving him a better name. Still, he didn't seem to care, so who was I to judge?

Evelyn chose that moment to whack me on the back with a mischievous grin and ruffle Wisp's hair. "You take care of momma for me? She's going to need a little bit of help getting back on her feet. I've got some people fetching food for her already."

Wisp nodded, her little jaw jutting out at being given a grown-up responsibility.

Evelyn turned to me next without missing a beat. "Thanks for inviting me. Makes me feel loved."

She wiggled her eyebrows, and while I blushed, something had me internally frowning. Maybe it was the psychology classes I'd taken in college. Maybe it was the Diviner ability. There was something in the way and words that she spoke that worried me slightly. Not for myself, but for her well-being.

Maybe she wasn't as well-adjusted as I'd thought. Maybe I needed to keep an eye on that.

"Of course. Can't go into imminent danger without my Ranger, right?"

"Of course you can't."

The edge around her vanished, and I chalked it up to something I needed to watch. Evelyn was an amazing Archer, or whatever her Class was, but this world was trying us all, and she was excellent at bravado.

Jackson and Darren stood speaking with their two friends Chris had mentioned. Miller? And Simon, Sean . . . something or other.

One of the boys had to be about seventeen. Tall and lanky and doing that definite slowly turning-into-a-man thing with broader shoulders and a little more confidence in his stance. His voice was deep and carried farther than the others. He sounded respectful, and his words weren't bossy. I immediately found respect for the kid, because if my vague recollections were anything to go by, I was fairly certain he'd come here without any parental assistance whatsoever.

Jackson deferred to him, standing close but not in front, acknowledging everything he said, agreeing with a lot of it, but obviously discussing things he didn't. His shoulders never hunched into that defensive position they took when his father tried to discuss sports with him. Jackson just wasn't the sports kid. That was all Wisp.

After this, I'd check on how that kid was faring.

**_Miller Danson_**

_Level 19_

_Technomancer_

Miller it was.

My toolbelt held water bottles, some beef jerky. Nothing like the American kind, but good enough, and some first aid supplies. Not that we needed them with the System being the way it was. It would repair anything short of a death blow. But just making sure I had disinfectant, making sure I had something to do anything, made me feel more prepared.

Chris and Sarah stood off to the side with Dale, frowning as they loaded backpacks with devices that appeared to be made of glass. Curious, I walked over with Evelyn trailing behind me. "What's that?"

Even as I asked, I realized the thing in front of me was far more than just pieces of glass put together. However they'd done it, it appeared to be some sort of ambient-Mana-vacuum bottle that would accumulate and maintain a store of the stuff within its confines.

Maybe.

Sarah sighed. "It's a prototype. We have three different ones. The idea is that we fill these with the most potent Mana we can find once we set them up and activate them, which next to a forming Dungeon is bound to be the most potent kind. I think. If Mana even cares."

I nodded encouragingly. I got it. We were all kind of running around in the dark, and even if the Shop sold stuff like this, buying things to keep us alive, to improve our personal Classes and abilities was more important. Probably.

"Once we have it filled, we can adjust the flows from outside by using a Skill called Ambient Mana Attraction that a couple of us have. Then, well, it just self-recharges. That's the whole idea, anyway."

She shrugged self-deprecatingly, and I could see that she *wanted* this to work more than she was certain that it would. Thing was that all of these Skills and abilities, we didn't know if they'd work how we thought they would until we tried.

"So . . . it's a Mana battery?" I said, after parsing it all together.

There were more than a few frowns, but Sarah cut in before anyone could object with a "Sure. Yes and no. Sort of a Mana battery and gatherer."

Hey, I was a plant person. Dumbed down engineering was what I did.

Sange and Molly walked up, interrupting what I'd been about to say next.

"Sorry. Took us a bit to get our stuff together." Molly smiled at me while Sange stood stoically behind her, and Jules came to stand with them too, her blonde hair braided tightly down her back.

Chris was confused, staring at the others. "I didn't think—"

"No, you didn't. There's no way we can approach a forming Dungeon and hope we don't run into any trouble. Tank and Healers are the least we can do," Evelyn said. "Especially since you'll be busy manning the Mana things."

Chris flushed slightly and nodded. "I got ahead of myself. Everyone got supplies? Ready to go?"

Jules placed a hand lightly on Chris's, her calming smile doing its thing. "It's okay. I think sometimes we just . . . we need to reassess."

It's why she was so good at welcoming survivors. She was one of the sweetest people I'd ever met.

Crossing through the gate though, I had an awful feeling we'd forgotten something. While it was almost a kilometer away, I could see the swell of Mana rippling across the skyline in the warming afternoon. Blues of all different varieties shot up and into the sky, sparks flying, waves bouncing.

Mana enjoyed making Dungeons, it seemed.

The insides of that thing were still forming, changing, and shaping. MacGregor High School wasn't one anymore. We'd only faced the first few encounters, and from the rampant Mana releases around the thing, I wasn't sure we were ready for anything it spat out at us while we conducted this experiment.

Then again, in most games, Dungeons were isolated. So long as we didn't go in, we should be safe. If the world followed game logic. Which it did.

Half the time.

The other half, well, that's what the team was here for.

At Level 21 my inventory was now a grid of nine by nine. Eighty-one slots. And still that hammer weighed me down. Before leaving, I pulled up the statistics on it and frowned, weighing the pros and cons that I could see, and yet still, again, I was sure I was missing something.

### Warhammer of the Orbtralon Chiefs

*Congratulations! You have gained the Warhammer of the Orbtralon Chiefs. In order to access this item, an Orbtralon Chief, also known as Officer, must undergo several punishing trials which include besting his seven training officers in combat. Weapon Stats Modifiers:*

*+10% of Strength*

*+5% of Constitution*

*+12% Mental Resistance*

### Weapon Requirements:

*Strength: 26*

*Intelligence: 60*

*Perception: 50*

*Warning: You have not met the requirements to use this weapon.*

*Warning: As you have not met the requirements, you are barred from seeing the full potential of this weapon.*

The others were still ironing out the final details as we stood in front of the gate, so I took the brief respite to pull up my stats. I knew my Strength was close. I should only have to use eight of the twelve points I needed to allocate for my strength.

| Status Screen | | | |
|---|---|---|---|
| Name | Kira Kent | Class | Ecological Chain Specialist |
| Race | Human (Female) | Level | 21 (9472 XP to next Level) |
| Titles | | | |
| Diviner | | | |
| Health | 300 | Stamina | 300 |
| Mana | 650 | Mana Regeneration | 44 / minute |
| Attributes | | | |
| Strength | 26 | Agility | 27 |
| Constitution | 30 | Perception | 55 |
| Intelligence | 65 | Willpower | 44 |
| Charisma | 25 | Luck | 18 |
| Class Skills | | | |
| Mana Attunement | 2 | Earth Barricade | 2 |
| Blood Transfer | 1 | Mudslide | 1 |
| Water Siphon | 2 | Mana Transfer | 1 |
| Rockslide | 1 | Implantation | 1 |

| Skills | | | |
|---|---|---|---|
| Leadership | 3 | Mana Sense | 4 |
| Blunt Weapons | 4 | | |
| **Combat Spells** | | | |
| Shield of Power* | | | |
| **Perks** | | | |
| Diviner | | Analyze | |
| Mana Cloak 2 | | | |

Well, I guess I'd done it now. Couple of those remaining extra points into Intelligence and Agility. If I was going to wield that massive thing, I was going to need way more fitness with it. Keeping points back was good planning, but too many held was just going to get me killed. And I had a reason to apply them now.

My Constitution jumped up a whopping one point, thanks to the weapon's boost. Apparently, it didn't round up when there were halves. My Strength sat at 28 now. It was my Mental Resistance that caused me to heave a sigh of relief. It sat at thirty-four percent, and I could already feel how much less noise there was around my head.

As for my Skills, I was seriously considering hiding the entire thing. I'd hidden most of the random tiny skill ups that I got—things like walking or cooking (for coffee)—or the like and kept the ones that felt important. Like Leadership or Mana Sense.

Stupid UI management. I swear, next thing the System was going to be selling skins for my Status Screens.

Damn. I hoped I hadn't just given it ideas.

I glanced back down at the hammer in my hand and tossed my partially destroyed baseball bat down in the process. Gasps went off around me as I drew the large and intricately carved steel weapon out of seemingly nowhere. There was a dull, ethereal glow surrounding it.

Mana.

Suddenly, I suspected what the hidden features were and should have been able to guess it beforehand. Inspecting the weapon, I was greeted with an additional ability that I'd been unable to see before now. The name had changed too. Only slightly, but it was enough.

### Warhammer of the Orbtralon Chiefs' Ancestors

*Weapon Ability*

*Note: Weapon must be actively equipped for this ability to be available.*

*Mana Forge*

*This hammer was forged in the Mana fires of the Orbtralon Ancestors longer ago than your piddly planet has existed. How a lowly Orbtralon Chief got a hold of it is a testament to how far they, as a species, have fallen.*

*This Warhammer blesses its wielder with the ability to take the Mana flow they can see and mold it directly into physical elements that this Warhammer will then utilize as it is wielded.*

*Warning: Be aware of the lure of Mana. It can grant you great power but demands a high cost in the process. Most Mana Forgers lose their minds.*

Yeah. It sounded great. I wondered if having Mana Sense made this better or worse. Now all I had to do was to not let Mana drive me insane.

I'd get right on that.

# Chapter Thirty-Six:
# Power Source

## 13 Days Post-System Onset—6 p.m.

The area around the Dungeon seemed far more sinister than I remembered the last time we visited it, but the Mana was thicker, pungent even. It got into the back of my nose like the stench of raw sewage, and I choked a little as we ventured closer to it.

Chris spoke softly, almost reverently, like she wasn't sure she should be speaking at all. Couldn't say I blamed her.

"We need to set these down with their tendrils splayed so we can absorb from different streams of Mana." Chris crept forwards, and I had to keep reminding myself that while she could use her Class for combat, it wasn't necessarily always *meant* for combat.

The oval had me on edge. It wasn't technically part of the high school building complexes that had been taken over by the Dungeon transformation, but it was still a part of the school. Mana hovered over it, into the ground and above it, like gentle fog or clouds that weren't up high enough.

It didn't move frantically like some of it I'd seen but simply waited there. Perhaps it was absorbing all the power around it or helping the Mana take over the vegetation, but for that brief instant of watching the calming fog of Mana, I almost forgot the dangerous changes it forced on our world.

And still, all I wanted to do was understand exactly what it was.

*Congratulations!*

*You have still been granted a Quest. We got it already. You're curious about Mana and why you can sense it. So here, as a reminder:*

### *What is Mana?*

*Level of Quest: Unnecessary*

*Reward: Knowledge*

*Warnings: Curiosity killed lots of cats. Will you be satisfied?*

I blinked the notification out of my way. Now the System was just being a dick. Maybe it was being more observant because I used Implantation and got my damned hammer. Maybe we weren't dying quickly enough for it or something.

The Mana power storage-system-battery-thing didn't operate how I'd expected, but once they had it set up, I could see how the tendrils allowed the Mana to begin filling the repository instead of spreading out to the forming Dungeon.

Jackson, Darren, Miller, and Sean assisted Sarah and Chris in gently laying them all out at the same time. Chris took the bulb, while Sarah and the kids positioned the tendrils on each of the devices.

Then, as they anchored the tendrils, each of them glowed, casting some type of spell. Slowly but surely, shortly afterward, the devices began to glow. Well, they did, at least for me. For the others, there was a small indicator Sarah built into it that would tell them when it was full.

While I wasn't sure how she'd been able to create such a thing if she couldn't see Mana like I could, I just assumed she'd received it from some Level of Skills she'd gained from leveling her Class.

Or the Shop. There was always that option now.

Glancing around me, I decided I didn't like the quiet, nor our location. Considering the amount of times, I'd gotten distracted while running laps in school and then got in trouble because I'd be playing with plants, ovals weren't my favorite place in the world.

Besides that, the wildlife around us was doing that thing again. The no-noise, no-presence thing began to set off all my alarms even as I watched the Mana Repository fill up. Yeah, that was a much better name.

Closing my eyes, I wondered just what it was out there that kept things so silent. What was waiting for us? I couldn't feel any pressure against my mind.

Power radiated all around us, difficult to pinpoint with the current developing Dungeon so close to us. It rippled like the ocean in the calm before a storm, like it was readying itself to prepare for a violent monsoon.

Suddenly, my eyes flew open like someone had just sucker punched me a split second before the ground beneath us began to subtly shake. More like the rumble of a passing train if you lived a couple of blocks away, but that wasn't what this was.

"What the—" Jackson looked up at me, his eyes wide with sudden fear.

But even as I took a step toward him, I knew I wasn't going to make it before whatever this was happened.

"Get down!" I screamed while the rush of Mana pushed through so fast that it blindsided me.

This massive, bulbous, octopus-like creature shot through the ground to the right of where one repository was merrily filling up on Mana. Like a catapult, it launched the Healer who stood over where it erupted up high into the air, maybe twelve stories or so.

Its tentacles flailed around, knocking a few more of us off our feet, sending Molly flying so far she had to use her dash to get back to it in time.

All I could do, half-kneeling on the ground, was watch as Jules plummeted back down to Earth, her blonde hair ripping free of her braid, dropping with a sickening, final thud back onto the ground below.

❖

Mine wasn't the only scream that tore through the area. I think Jackson's was the loudest. Out of the corner of my eye, I could see him, shocked, pale. Surely someone else could have cast his portion of the spell.

There wasn't time for grief, there wasn't time to acknowledge the death, there was only time to compensate for it.

"Clear the middle," I called out, my voice barely sounding like my own.

Apparently, grief didn't care about my plans or time; it was smacking me in the face anyway. Hefting my Warhammer, I grimaced at the weight.

"Clear and rally behind Molly." It was all I had left, and we had to preserve those damned repositories or else Jules's sacrifice was in vain.

Chris and Sarah, Jackson and Darren, Dale, Evelyn . . . everyone. We moved like clockwork, stilted, and controlled by necessity rather than anything else.

Molly screamed loudly, using a Skill to taunt the monster to her, so loudly I was glad I wasn't the person in front of her. Analyzing the creature quickly, I got its species.

**Mollecupai**
*Level 25 Elite*
*HP: 4,200*
*MP: 2,100*

Well, that was helpful. Not.

Even though perhaps a tad ironic, it almost had the same name as our Tank. Still. Molly had distracted it enough with her scream.

Either way, the thing was massive, and we weren't really equipped to deal with it. We hadn't taken a full fighting force out with us. What a fucking stupid thing to do.

Yet Jackson and Darren stepped up. They flung bolts at the monster, fire and light, anything that could hurt it. I'd almost forgotten they had combat Skills, it'd been so long since we needed them.

Molly stayed in front, keeping its attention with her own sword, frequently dodging incoming damage only barely as the thing threatened to take her head off. She staggered back whenever it did hit her, the poor shield—even after repairs in the Shop—looking like it had been through the wringer. Still, she was determined, though I noticed tears streaming down her face as she fought.

Chris backed Molly up, activating her shield orb, diminishing the damage we took from the tentacles.

Dale took over the healing that used to be Jules's job. I could see the sadness in his face, how pale his features were, and how scared to death he was. But he didn't stop healing, and that was all I could ask of him.

I knew how he felt.

Remaining close to Jackson, I did what I could, casting Water Siphon at it. Implantation worked well in such a situation, but the massive creature didn't react well to the explosions that took it down a couple of percent at a time. It just got more upset, swinging harder at Molly and Chris when they got too close. Even Evelyn had to duck and jump aside occasionally, dodging the swinging tentacles.

Not a game, not at all where Molly could keep the creature's aggro on her entirely. She had most of its attention, but we all still had to be on our toes. Chris didn't appear to have taunts other than the fact that she diminished damage, and no mob liked that.

Implantation did great damage; it pulled Molly back and kept her in fighting shape, but it was so Mana intensive I found it difficult to keep up every minute without allowing myself room for emergencies.

Jackson and Dale were stable, smart enough to keep retreating so that they were never in danger of getting hit. I was just about to leave and dive in with my massive Warhammer when I saw a sudden twist in the Mana flow inside the monster.

"Ability incoming!" I shouted.

It gave them but a fraction of a second to react, and luckily it was all they needed.

Molly and Sange retreated, able to jump over the tentacle sweep that threatened to bowl them over instead. Another tentacle reached out, doing the same at head level all around it, focused mainly on the ranged casters and fighters. A dark light blossomed around its tentacles as it swept, a little lingering flame that stayed in the air even after its tentacles flew by for a few seconds before it disappeared.

We all managed to dodge it or back off far enough that we weren't in danger. But if we hadn't had that small portion of warning, it could have been serious for a lot of us. Those flames weren't the only problem, since I'd only just realized its damned tentacles were lined in tiny, razor-sharp blades.

Even with the ground vibrating, melee weapons clashing and impacting and spells firing, I could still see Jules's body out of the corner of my vision, limply rebounding off the ground with every bit of impact, blood squishing out further.

I didn't get it, didn't understand why her enhanced Constitution didn't save her. Did she not put enough points into it? Was she unconscious as she flew into the air or something and couldn't activate the shield that had saved so many of us before?

Did the Mollecupai use a Skill when it first attacked?

Considering its Mana, probably.

I'd known her for a short while only. Two weeks that seemed like a lifetime. And now she was gone.

I was too busy, too distracted at watching numbers and stats and my own implanted seed. The shout caught me by surprise.

"Kira!"

I looked up in time to see my twin motion with his hands at the tentacle that was about to hit me square in the face. I watched as the severed limb sprayed greenish blue blood all over me in slow motion, watched blood pump out. Then time sped up and my brother's face turned ashen as he stared at me, at his hands.

"Thank you!" I called out, knowing he needed something to take his mind off the destruction he'd caused.

We really needed to sit down and have a long talk about a lot of things.

We needed a therapist. We *all* needed a therapist.

Later.

After we finished surviving this.

My hammer tingled, jolting up my arms and reverberating through me. I glanced down at it and realized the head was glowing and the rivets of the hammer had soft strands of Mana drifting through them.

All righty, then. Bit bonkers, but you know. Hadn't eaten any mushrooms lately, so it was probably real.

The ground reverberated, sprays of earth showering all of us as the remaining tentacles operated independently of each other. My weapon thrummed in my hand with each Mana surge. Begging me to use it, almost.

Power flooded me through the haft, and before I could think or reason with myself, I charged that damned creature full on. I heard a scream tear from my throat, primal in nature as I did so.

Stupid, Kira. Stupid.

Even as I swung my weapon, I could feel my shoulders straining beneath the force. The deep, sickening thunk as it tore into flesh just out from the base of the body, ripping through with its might like it was cutting through butter.

The Mollecupai squealed like the ear-piercing shriek of a tantruming toddler, but I'd been through far worse than that. Grimacing, I drew back my gavel of tentacle mashing, attracting all sorts of fine strands of Mana to it as I did so, and slammed it back home, successfully severing off another of the creature's tentacles.

It was like some sort of rage fueled me, gripped me tightly, took over and demanded that I use the Mana around me to forge a new world. To take away those that would stand in my way.

Some part of me realized that these feelings, this whole sentiment, stemmed largely from the weapon I wielded. Mana could make me crazy? Sure thing.

Right now, I'd take the strength it offered me and grind my tentacled enemy into a fine and sloppy paste. There'd be plenty of time to psychoanalyze my actions later. In that instant though, all that mattered was shattering it like it had broken Jules.

I was still cognizant enough to recognize my team working with me. Sange, burning giant chunks of tentacles and targeting eyes to keep it distracted, while topping their tank up constantly. Molly, on my other side, kept that side of me safe. Kept the monstrous tentacles away, even as she threw Skill after Skill into play, burning through Mana and Stamina like crazy to keep me alive.

Chris, with her shield that shot little floating darts when she spun it, hammering into the body of the creature, drilling in and shocking. Working independently and together with my brother to take up more space, more focus.

And, of course, Dale. Because even with all that, the Mollecupai had its own little tricks. Something shot out at me, tore into my legs, my stomach. My blood coated the ground, but I was on my feet seconds later when Dale hit me with a healing spell.

Pain, sure, but I could deal with pain.

After a few moments, even the knowledge my friends, my team, was keeping me alive faded. All that remained in my awareness was the thrashing tentacles, Mana pumping through me, guts and gore covering me from head to toe, and the frantic beating of my own heart.

Nothing.

Not this fucking Mollecupai, not the lack of power, not IRSHA, not the damned System itself was going to take anything else from me or those I cared about. And I'd raise my kids to do the same. The System was in for generations of Kents out to destroy it.

Yeah. That was my new motto.

Fuck the System.

# Chapter Thirty-Seven:
# Turn the Power On

## 13 Days Post-System Onset—9 p.m.

I don't know how long I'd been beating on that thing, but by the time I let myself stop, it was long dead. Standing in a pool of pulped flesh, I blinked down at the hammer, all sparkling in its apparent self-cleaning abilities, and shoved it in my inventory. The last thing I needed right then was more of this pinpoint-focused destruction.

The others were busy gathering the now-full repositories, clamping down on the items they needed to get it home, hooked up, and working. They were quiet as they worked, whispering and shooting glances my way once in a while. It didn't stop them working, though. Nothing would, not if we wanted to make sure that Jules's sacrifice didn't go to waste.

A notification flashed in front of my face, and I only took a brief moment to acknowledge it before willing it away.

*Mana Cloak*

*Please note, due to overwhelming saturation of ambient Mana you just hung around in, your Cloak's Mana capacity has increased to 175. This announcement was brought to you by an important Mana milestone.*

Important my arse. Important was the body lying over there, pushed to the edge of the oval, some of the pulp sticking to her delicate face. Even as I walked over, I could tell how crumpled her form was, every bone in her body had to have shattered from that height, or at least broken numerous times. Not my area of expertise.

Her blonde hair was filled with her own blood and that of the

Mollecupai, stealing some of her innocence.

But Jules, she'd been one of the good ones. Kyle stopped next to me, remaining silent as he lent me strength I desperately needed. There were words vying for attention in my brain, things I wanted to say, needed to express. But nothing was going to bring her back, and even if we'd had a necromancer, we all know how that would have worked out.

We'd avoided zombies so far.

"It's not your fault." Kyle spoke softly, giving me as much comfort as he could with those empty words. We both knew I'd beat myself up about it anyway.

He bent down and scooped her up so we could head back to the center before some other cunt of a monster decided to burst out of the ground. I felt my tears catch in my throat. Be damned if I was going to cry. I needed to push that to the side and use that energy to just . . .

Apparently not even my tears listened to me.

I forced myself to breathe, to think.

Silver lining, that's what I needed. To look on the bright side of it, to see the light even through the gloom.

It was an apocalypse—death went hand in hand with it. Our little tech Classes had managed to engineer three power sources. We'd have light again, instead of the low-glowing, eye-hurting little lights we'd been making do with.

We might be able to get some of the refrigerators working, give us back some of our comforts. At least, maybe after a bit of tinkering. Slow steps to regaining our civilization. Weren't all empires built on the sacrifice of the few?

Somehow, I had a feeling those sacrificed didn't take acceptance as well as those who survived and benefited.

Fuck it.

I made a scan of my mental list.

*Settlement Orb Gained: Check*

*Official Safety Zone Initiated: Check*

*Administrators Instated and Organized: Check*

*Defenses and Security Patrols in Place and Being Reinforced as Money Allowed: Check*

*Alternate Power Sources to Power All Our Human Tech Shit: In Definite Progress*

In another three days, I was pretty sure we'd have to fight for our home, the new one we'd built after the old one was taken away from us. I wanted to show this Intergalactic Administration just how resilient humans were, kind of like the cockroaches I was slowly growing to respect.

We were going to be ready. I'd make sure of it.

It was a somber group that made its way back through the streets toward the center again. Twilight approached, just like winter was coming. We traipsed—there was really no other word for it—toward our destination when suddenly Jackson reached his hand for mine.

"You okay, mate?" I asked, realizing belatedly that I hadn't given him a hug or any reassurance since Jules fell from the sky. I'd simply been walking along next to my twin while he carried a body.

Jackson's huge eyes watched me for a few seconds before he leant in and gave me a huge hug. "You kinda went berserk back there, Mum."

He was right. I'd have to watch that. It wasn't me, and I couldn't let abilities, weapons, or this damned intrusive Dungeon Worlding of our planet change the me I rather liked. "Yeah. Next time, you have my permission to pinch me and pull me out of that."

Jackson paused. "Okay. But only if warranted. I liked Jules. She was kind to all of us younger kids. I think you went berserk at exactly the right moment."

I side-hugged him whether he wanted it or not, but took the fact that he didn't pull away from me as a good sign. We walked for about a block in silence before he spoke again.

"So, you know, I'm okay with not going out on the bigger patrols for a while." He said the words like he was being nice to me, but I could sense deep down that today had scared him. And that was okay. He was only thirteen, for fuck's sake.

Squeezing him again, I smiled. "Okay. I'll have you work on those power sources instead. What do you say?"

"It's a deal."

His grin lit up my whole world.

He and his sister really were it though, and through everything that we'd been through these last two weeks, they'd survived.

Bloody oath. This was *our* world. Whatever happened, whether it was IRSHA coming to make us vacate, or more insanely powerful monsters or mutated flaming koalas, we'd handle it.

We had power now, were gaining more Levels every day and building our fighting force. To top it all off, we had a community.

Everything else would fall into place because that's what Aussies do.

Fuck the System and anyone else who thought they could take my home or family.

# Epilogue

Gemma didn't cry. She barely even blinked when I told her about Jules. Instead, she sort of gulped back a response, nodded curtly, turned, and walked away. Her shoulders were full of tension, and everything about her told me she just wanted to be left alone.

I did. Wisp didn't. Or more precisely, Dog didn't, who trailed after the girl, dragging my kid with him.

Chris and Sarah were busy working with Jackson and his crew to install the three Mana batteries that could give us back our power. It was proving a lot more complicated than I'd imagined, and I just hoped we could make it before the Quest deadline. We still had almost two days. Should be good.

"How you holdin' up?" Dolores sat down next to me in my little coffee shop setup. I'd started coming down to the good ole Raybucks—yeah, that suited it much better now—and taking up the same table near the front.

I took a moment to just analyze how I was truly feeling.

"I'm holding up pretty shit right now." It was the truth, and it felt good to say it out loud. But there was so much more to it. "Don't get me wrong. We did what we set out to do, and we will finally get this place on track to be a real base we can reinforce. For now, we are safe. The kids are safe. It just would have been nice if we hadn't had to sacrifice for it. That's all."

Dor narrowed her eyes at me, like she was trying to look into my mind. "That's it? Isn't that a bit too pragmatic?"

I shook my head. "How? What else can we be? Move forward. Don't dwell on what's happened because we can't change it. Keep the survivors alive." I could feel the sadness still in my throat, but there was a strength from that. Jules was dead—it was a sad fact, but a fact nevertheless.

"Okay. I'll go along with it. So what are we doing next?"

That acceptance was all I needed. About to list off the things we needed to do, I stopped when my Walkie crackled.

"Kira?"

Kyle's voice crackled, but I still recognized it. He'd gone to the gate to talk to Mike about patrols. "We have a problem . . . a big problem."

Shit.

I knew what this was with sudden impeccable clarity. Call it twintuition or whatever you want. "Fuck."

Dolores looked at me, immediately alert. "What?"

"Outside." I left my notepad, grabbed my Walkie and sprinted outside.

Gusts of wind began to blow my hair in every direction at once, as soon as I stepped out of the center. But it wasn't the sort of wind I was used to, not here in Brisbane. South-easterlies were always harsh winds, but they didn't alternate directions like this.

Dolores followed me, and I'd seen Evelyn coming behind us as well. I squinted up at the sky, but it was dark now, and I couldn't see as well as usual. Sure enough, there was something there. Flat and sort of opaquely cloud-colored, it hung there. It didn't seem like any alien spaceship I'd ever seen on any intergalactic television series.

Evelyn caught up to me as we ran out to join Mike and Kyle. "Is that a fucking spaceship?"

Urgency bit at my heels like a herding corgi, and I needed to make it through. I took the stairs two at a time. Not like my knees would notice. The System left no old aches and pain behind.

"Yeah. It's a fucking spaceship. And I think there's more than one of them." The weight of the statement dragged me down. If this was what I thought it was, and I was certain I was right, then it didn't matter how well we'd prepared or what we'd done to be ready in time.

We finally reached the top, Dolores still a ways back. Scanning the sky, I glanced at my brother, his face deathly white. I could now make out three more craft, four in total.

No, no, no. They were the only words coming to me, and they weren't helpful at all. This couldn't be happening, right? This only happened with unwanted family members who invited themselves over all the time and then turned up without anything to bring to the barbecue.

Or hell, those people you'd explicitly told to fuck off or not made plans with who came anyway.

Kyle's voice shook. "They're here, Kira."

"Al-fucking-ready."

Dolores caught up to us, panting slightly. "But it's IRSHA isn't it?"

All I could do was nod.

Mike tapped his foot impatiently, and his shoulders had a slight twitch. He was nervous. "They're not supposed to be here for another three days."

Evelyn crossed her arms. "Well, apparently IRSHA can't tell the time, or they're just rude fucks."

"But we're not ready." Evelyn's voice sounded small for the first time since I'd known her. "Not yet."

I gripped the railing, leaning over to see if I anyone or anything had disembarked. "Well, fuck me dead."

I had nothing else constructive at that moment.

Damn it. Sometimes, I hated being right.

**Follow Kira and her journey in Australia in:**
**Flat Out (Book 2 of the System Apocalypse: Australia)**
https://readerlinks.com/l/2289535

# Authors' Note

Hi there! K.T. Hanna here.

I want to thank you for reading *The System Apocalypse: Australia - Town Under*. Brisbane is where I was born and raised (for the most part), and I have loved being able to include it in this series. There are mutant koalas, emus, and platypus yet to come. If you enjoyed this one, then you're going to love the next books. Writing in Tao's world has been a fantastic experience and I can't wait to show everyone else just how amazing Kira can be.

If you enjoyed the book, I ask you, please take a moment to leave a review. **Reviews** are an author's lifesblood. Without them, our books sink into obscurity. With them, most algorithms allow well reviewed books to self-promote in some way.

Want to find out more about my books? Here is how you can keep in contact with me:

- Sign up for my **Reader's Group** and get a short story for free: http://login.somnia-online.c/
- If you'd like to contact me, my email is: kthannaauthor@gmail.com I'll do my very best to get back to you.
- If you'd like previews of what I'm writing, or art I'm commissioning then join my **Patreon**: https://www.patreon.com/KTHanna
- I can be found in my FB reader group fairly often (https://www.facebook.com/groups/worldsofkthanna/), and also on Twitter (https://twitter.com/KTHanna) & Instagram (https://www.instagram.com/kt_hanna).

*-KT*

Australia has always been a continent I wanted to write about, but having neither visited or done much research on the country beyond memes, I knew little of it. It was serendipity then, that KT was just finishing up on Somnia Online and we got chatting. Knowing that I enjoyed her writing, I asked her if she'd be willing to indulge me in writing a version of the System Apocalypse set in Australia and she agreed to my delight.

Discussing with her what she wanted made me even more excited for the series, for we have not seen a character like Kira. A mother, an Australian, someone whose focus is going to be very much Earth-bound because that's where her children are. It appealed to me, as a reader and an author, and I have to say, reading the notes of book 2, I can't wait to show you all what is about to come.

*-Tao*

# About the Authors

## KT Hanna

KT Hanna has such a love for words, a single one can spark entire worlds.

Born in Australia, she met her husband in a computer game, moved to the U.S.A. and went into culture shock. Bonus? Not as many creatures specifically designed to kill you.

KT creates science-fiction, fantasy, and LitRPG like it's going out of style, with a dash of horror for fun! She plays computer games, and ferries her daughter everywhere, all while looking after her cats, dogs, and her husband.

No, she doesn't sleep. She is entirely powered by caffeine, Chipotle, and sarcasm.

To find out more information about the author's other series, visit their website: https://www.kthanna.com/

## Tao Wong

Tao Wong is an avid fantasy and sci-fi reader who spends his time working and writing in the North of Canada. He's spent way too many years doing martial arts of many forms, and having broken himself too often, he now spends his time writing about fantasy worlds.

For updates on the series and other books written by Tao Wong (and special one-shot stories), please visit the author's website: http://www.mylife-mytao.com

Or visit his Facebook Page: https://www.facebook.com/taowongauthor/

Subscribe to Tao's mailing list to receive **exclusive access to short stories in the Thousand Li and System Apocalypse universes.**

# Acknowledgements
# from KT Hanna

I have a lot of people to thank. Even those who don't contribute directly through the writing craft keep me going and help me write my best stories.

Love of my life, Trevor, and my little Bria. It's his fault I found the genre, and her fault I never give up on writing.

I wouldn't be here without the following friends:
Jami Nord & Owen Littman
Amanda W.
Quinton Shyn
Dawn Chapman
Bonnie Price
Andrea Parseneau
Cait Greer
M Evan Matyas
Dave Willmarth
Charles Dean
Daniel Schinhofen
Jay Boyce
Michael Chatfield
Luke Chmilenko
Tao Wong

And of course my family:
Mumskin & Papilie, Tracey, Bev, & Robbie.

The entire Rainbow Room.

Kristen, Everlosst, Hydrael, Kai

And every one of my Patrons, not to mention my FB Group. You all help me maintain a level of sanity.

# About the Publisher

Starlit Publishing is wholly owned and operated by Tao Wong. It is a science fiction and fantasy publisher focused on the LitRPG & cultivation genres. Their focus is on promoting new, upcoming authors in the genre whose writing challenges the existing stereotypes while giving a rip-roaring good read.

For more information about latest releases and new, exciting authors from Starlit Publishing, visit our website or sign up to our newsletter list:

https://www.starlitpublishing.com/

For more great information about LitRPG series, check out these Facebook groups:

- GameLit Society

https://www.facebook.com/groups/LitRPGsociety/

- LitRPG Books

https://www.facebook.com/groups/LitRPG.books/

# Glossary

## Ecological Chain Specialist Skill Tree

*Basic Class: Pest & Pathogens Unit: Microbiologist / Plant Pathologist / Entomologist / Hydrogeologist / Molecular Biologist - Abbreviated as: Ecological Chain Specialist*

| | | | | | |
|---|---|---|---|---|---|
| Earth Barricade | | Mana Attunement | | Blood Transfer | |
| Water Siphon | Mud Slide | Rockslide | | Mana Transfer | |
| Treesong | | Top Soil | Planted in Place | Implantation | |
| Vine Defense | | Stone's Throw | | Blood Dispersion | |
| Cocoon | | Ecological Outreach | | Mana Dispersion | |

## Ecological Chain Specialist Skills

### Mana Attunement (Level 2)

Using your affinity for the world around you, you can tap into the earth and coax it to warn you of any incoming threats. Radius and specific information increases with Skill Level and Level of caster's awareness. Mana Regeneration reduced by 5 Mana per second permanently. This is a passive Skill.

Effect: Adds an additional seismic sense to user which can detect ground-based movement. Degree of sensitivity dependent on distance and degree of earth disruption.

Range: 200 meters

**Earth Barricade (Level 2)**

Earth Barricade allows you to command the earth beneath your feet for the purpose of defending yourself and your allies.

Effect: 100 HP shield created, within a 3m x 2.5m region (shapeable).

Mana Cost: 20 Mana

**Blood Transfer (Level 1)**

Due to your devotion to understanding the world and mechanics of biological evolution, you are able to tap into the blood of your opponents and redirect that damage to heal yourself. Beneficial effects only usable on self.

Caution: Best targeted on enemies. Self-heal only.

Effect: Drains and transfers 5 HP per second. Target must have blood.

Mana Cost: 5 Mana per second

**Mudslide (Level 1)**

Effect: Proficiency with Water Siphoning and coaxing the ground to do what you want enables you to pull forth a mudslide. Usable twice per day. Usage, severity, and impact dependent on caster and Skill Level.

Caution: Make sure you understand the lay of the land before engaging this ability.

Mana Cost: 65

Area of Effect: 3-meter radius from targeted casting. Damage minimum 2x caster Level per target.

444

**Water Siphon (Level 2)**

Effect: Moisture is in almost everything: humans, intergalactic species. This ability allows you to siphon the water out of anything that contains it. Level of effectiveness dependent on caster and spell Level.

Mana Cost: 60 Mana per Siphon. 25% water per application. Application duration—30 seconds.

Caution: Target will be immune to the effects of Water Siphon for 15 seconds after this application.

**Mana Transfer (Level 1)**

Effect: Due to your devotion to understanding the world around you and how to preserve and bolster it, you can tap into the Mana saturation around you, bolstering your regeneration on a constant basis. Strength and capacity are dependent on spell and caster Level.

Mana Cost: 20 Mana – 30 seconds of regen increase.

**Rockslide (Level 1)**

Effect: Rocks are a strong part of the ecosystem around you. With the right level of encouragement, you might even be able to use them to attack or defend. The choice is yours. Strength and durability dependent on spell and caster Level.

Mana Cost: 30

**Implantation (Level 1)**

Not every Skill does damage immediately. Some Skills take skill and experience to make use of, and Implantation is one of them. Implant a seed of power and growth within an opponent, leeching Mana and damage from attacks cast at the opponent. When the seed blossoms, a portion of damage and health is returned to those surrounding and is dealt as damage.

Duration: 10 seconds

Effect: Implant a seed of Mana into the chest of your enemy. During the duration of Implantation, the seed will absorb a portion of damage done to the enemy. The absorbed Mana will be reverted once seed has fully grown in an explosion with a maximum of 5-meter radius around enemy. Explosion will return Health, Mana, and Stamina to those affected.

Should the target die before the bomb seed can complete its countdown, all benefits are forfeit. Use this wisely.

Mana, Stamina, and Health equaling 75% of the absorbed amount of damage is returned to all targets within a 5 meter diameter. 25% of absorbed amount is dealt as damage to initial target.

Caution: Target cannot be effect by this spell more than once per minute.

**Treesong**

Effect: Your affinity with Nature and the Mana around you lends you a unique affinity with the plant life. Incantations can bring out the most in these familiar life forms. Sung like a soothing lullaby, even the plants can rise to your bidding, if you approach them correctly.

Caution: Don't piss off the trees.

Mana Cost: 35 Mana per 5 seconds. Channeled.

## Topsoil

Effect: The top layer of ground is always the most fragile. Using your Mana proficiency, you can coax strength out of this to entrap, ensnare, or protect those around you.

Caution: Use wisely. Topsoil doesn't distinguish well between friend and foe. It only recognizes blood.

Mana Cost: 65 per directed action

# Other Class Skills

### Leadership (Level 3)

### Mana Sense (Level 4)

Due to your natural affinity for, and your innate sense with Mana, you can see all Mana flows within your immediate vicinity. The more you access this ability, the more information it will give you, and the higher it will level. This is a passive Skill.

### Blunt Weapons (Level 4)

# Spells

### Shield of Power

This shield can be activated on a family member regardless of distance between them. It can absorb up to ten times the caster's hit points trading each hit point for ten shield points. Castable once per hour.

While active the ally is locked inside and cannot disperse the shield before the caster allows it, or the caster dies.

Cost: 25 Mana + Hit Points traded for Shield

Note: Shield of Power is limited to a maximum of 200 Hit Points at current level of Skill

# Equipment

### Warhammer of the Orbtralon Chiefs

In order to access this item, an Orbtralon Chief, also known as Officer, must undergo several punishing trials which include besting his seven training officers in combat.

### Weapon Stats Modifiers:

+10% of Strength

+5% of Constitution

+12% Mental Resistance

### Weapon Requirements:

Strength: 26

Intelligence: 60

Perception: 50

### Warhammer of the Orbtralon Chiefs' Ancestors

Weapon Ability

Note: Weapon must be actively equipped for this ability to be available.

### *Mana Forge*

This hammer was forged in the Mana fires of the Orbtralon Ancestors longer ago than your piddly planet has existed. How a lowly Orbtralon Chief got a hold of it is a testament to how far they, as a species, have fallen.

This Warhammer blesses its wielder with the ability to take the Mana flow they can see and mold it directly into physical elements that this Warhammer will then utilize as it is wielded.

Warning: Be aware of the lure of Mana. It can grant you great power but demands a high cost in the process. Most Mana Forgers lose their minds.

# Perks

### Diviner

Permanent Passive ability. All Perception-based Skills increase 75% faster. Perception gains a 20-point boost, and you gain the Skill—Sense Motive—at Level 24. This will provide a contested chance (approximately a 50% chance using human subterfuge Skill-Level norms) to know when people are attempting to deceive you. Chance to divine increases with each Skill Level gained.

### Analyze (Skill)

Enables the ability to see another being's name, statistics, Class, and abilities to certain extents. May conflict with other Skills and abilities.

*Note:* Medium Perk may be used to allow Perk to be offered on a familial level.

### Mana Cloak (Level 2)

This is a passive ability that covers the body with a thin layer of ambient Mana, allowing the ability to sense surrounding Mana surges and mutations with greater accuracy. Works well in conjunction with Mana Attunement. Can serve as a secondary Mana pool (100) if necessary. Full charge requires 2 hours of ambient Mana flow.

*Note:* This Cloak may be modified by the user and have a percentage of Mana regeneration from the user applied to it. The Cloak will upgrade accordingly.

449

# Preview Tao Wong's other series:

# The System Apocalypse

## Life in the North (The System Apocalypse Book 1)

## Chapter One

*Greetings citizen. As a peaceful and organised immersion into the Galactic Council has been declined (extensively and painfully we might add), your world has been declared a Dungeon World. Thank you. We were getting bored with the 12 that we had previously.*

*Please note that the process of developing a Dungeon World can be difficult for current inhabitants. We recommend leaving the planet till the process is completed in 373 days, 2 hours, 14 minutes and 12 seconds.*

*For those of you unable or unwilling to leave, do note that new Dungeons and wandering monsters will spawn intermittently throughout the integration process. All new Dungeons and zones will receive recommended minimum levels, however, during the transition period expect there to be significant volatility in the levels and types of monsters in each Dungeon and zone.*

*As a new Dungeon World, your planet has been designated a free-immigration location. Undeveloped worlds in the Galactic Council may take advantage of this new immigration policy. Please try not to greet all new visitors the same way as you did our Emissary, you humans could do with some friends.*

*As part of the transition, all sentient subjects will have access to new classes and skills as well as the traditional user interface adopted by the Galactic Council in 119 GC.*

*Thank you for your co-operation and good luck! We look forward to meeting you soon.*

*Time to System initiation: 59 minutes 23 seconds*

I groan, freeing my hand enough to swipe at the blue box in front of my face as I crank my eyes open. Weird dream. It's not as if I had drunk that much either, just a few shots of whiskey before I went to bed. Almost as soon as the box disappears, another appears, obscuring the small 2-person tent that I'm sleeping in.

*Congratulations! You have been spawned in the Kluane National Park (Level 110+) zone.*
*You have received 7,500 XP (Delayed)*

*As per Dungeon World Development Schedule 124.3.2.1, inhabitants assigned to a region with a recommended Level 25 or more above the inhabitants' current Level will receive one Small perk.*

*As per Dungeon World Development Schedule 124.3.2.2, inhabitants assigned to a region with a recommended Level 50 or more above the inhabitants' current Level will receive one Medium perk.*

*As per Dungeon World Development Schedule 124.3.2.3, inhabitants assigned to a region with a recommended Level 75 or more above the inhabitants' current Level will receive one Large perk.*

*As per Dungeon World Development Schedule 124.3.2.4, inhabitants assigned to a region with a recommended Level 100 or more above the inhabitants' current Level will receive one Greater perk.*

What the hell? I jerk forwards and almost fall immediately backwards, the sleeping bag tangling me up. I scramble out, pulling my 5' 8" frame into a sitting position as I swipe black hair out of my eyes to stare at the taunting blue message. Alright, I'm awake and this is not a dream.

This can't be happening, I mean, sure it's happening, but it can't be. It must be a dream, things like this didn't happen in real life. However, considering the rather realistic aches and pains that encompass my body from yesterday's hike, it's really not a dream. Still, this can't be happening.

When I reach out, attempting to touch the screen itself and for a moment, nothing happens until I move my hand when the screen seems to 'stick' to it, swinging with my hand. It's almost like a window in a touchscreen which makes no sense, since this is the real world and there's no tablet. Now that I'm concentrating, I can even feel how the screen has a slight tactile sensation to it, like touching plastic wrap stretched too tight except with the added tingle of static electricity. I stare at my hand and the window and then flick it away watching the window shrink. This makes no sense.

Just yesterday I had hiked up the King's Throne Peak with all my gear to overlook the lake. Early April in the Yukon means that the peak itself was still covered with snow but I'd packed for that, though the final couple of kilometers had been tougher than I had expected. Still, being out and about at least cleared my mind of the dismal state of my life after moving to White-horse. No job, barely enough money to pay next month's rent and having just broken up with my girlfriend, leaving on a Tuesday on my junker of a

Tao Wong and KT Hanna

car was just what the doctor ordered. As bad as my life had been, I'm pretty sure I wasn't even close to breaking down, at least not enough to see things.

I shut my eyes, forcing them to stay shut for a count of three before I open them again. The blue box stays, taunting me with its reality. I can feel my breathing shorten, my thoughts splitting in a thousand different directions as I try to make sense of what's happening.

**Stop.**

I force my eyes close again and old training, old habits come into play. I bottle up the feelings of panic that encroach on my mind, force my scattered thoughts to stop swirling and compartmentalise my feelings. This is not the time or place for all this. I shove it all into a box and close the lid, pushing my emotions down until all there is a comforting, familiar, numbness.

A therapist once said my emotional detachment is a learned self-defence mechanism, one that was useful during my youth but somewhat unnecessary now that I'm an adult with more control over my surroundings. My girlfriend, my ex-girlfriend, just called me an emotionless dick. I've been taught better coping mechanisms but when push comes to shove, I go with what works. If there's an environment which I can't control, I'm going to call floating blue boxes in the real world one of them.

Calmer now, I open my eyes and re-read the information. First rule – what is, is. No more arguing or screaming or worrying about why or how or if I'm insane. What is, is. So. I have perks. And there's a system providing the perks and assigning levels. There's also going to be dungeons and monsters. I'm in a frigging MMO without a damn manual it looks like, which means that at least some of my misspent youth is going to be useful. I wonder what my dad would say. I push the familiar flash of anger down at the thought of him, focusing instead on my current problems.

My first requirement is information. Or better yet, a guide. I'm working on instinct here, going by what feels right rather than what I think is right since the thinking part of me is busy putting its fingers in its ears and going 'na-na-na-na-na'.

"Status?" I query and a new screen blooms.

| Status Screen | | | |
|---|---|---|---|
| Name | John Lee | Class | None |
| Race | Human (Male) | Level | 0 |
| **Titles** | | | |
| None | | | |
| Health | 100 | Stamina | 100 |
| Mana | 100 | | |
| **Status** | | | |
| Twisted ankle (-5% movement speed) | | | |
| Tendinitis (-10% Manual Agility) | | | |
| **Attributes** | | | |
| Strength | 11 | Agility | 10 |
| Constitution | 11 | Perception | 14 |
| Intelligence | 16 | Willpower | 18 |
| Charisma | 8 | Luck | 7 |
| **Skills** | | | |
| None | | | |
| **Class Skills** | | | |
| None | | | |

| Spells |
| --- |
| None |

**Unassigned Attributes:**

*1 Small, 1 Medium, 1 Large, 1 Greater Perk*

*Would you like to assign these attributes? (Y/N)*

The second window pop's up almost immediately on top of the first. I want more time to look over my Status but the information seems mostly self-explanatory and it's better to get this over with. It's not as if I have a lot of time. Almost as soon as I think that, the Y depresses and a giant list of Perks flashes up.

Oh, I do **not** have time for this. I definitely don't have time to get stuck in character creation. Being stuck in a zone that is way out of my Level when the System initializes is a one-way ticket to chowville. The giant list of perks before me is way too much to even begin sorting through, especially with names that don't necessarily make sense. What the hell does Adaptive Coloring actually mean? Right, this system seems to work via thought, reacting to what I think so, perhaps I can sort by perk type – narrow it down to small perks for a guide or companion of some form?

Almost as soon as I think of it, the system flashes out and only the word Companion appears. I nod slightly to myself and further details appear, providing two options.

*AI*                    *Spirit*

I select AI but a new notice flashes up

***AI Selection unavailable.*** *Minimum requirements of:*
*Mark IV Processing Unit not met*

I grunt. Yeah, no shit. I don't have a computer on me. Or... in me? No cyberpunk world for me. Not yet at least, though how cool would that be with a computer for a brain and metallic arms that don't hurt from being on the computer too much. Not the time for this, so I pick Spirit next and I acknowledge the query.

***System Companion Spirit gained***

*Congratulations! World Fourth. As the fourth individual to gain a Companion Spirit, your companion is now (Linked). Linked Companions will grow and develop with you.*

As I dismiss the notifications, I can see a light begin to glow to my right. I twist around, wondering who or what my new companion is going to be.

"Run, hide or fight. Ain't hard to make a choice boy-o."

Look, I'm no pervert. I didn't need a cute, beautiful fairy as my System Companion Spirit. Sure, a part of me hoped for it, I'm a red-blooded male who wouldn't mind staring at something pretty. Still, practically speaking, I would have settled for a Genderless automaton that was efficient and answered my questions with a minimum of lip. Instead, I get... him.

I stare at my new Companion and sigh mentally. Barely a foot tall, he's built like a linebacker with a full, curly brown beard. Brown hair, brown eyes and olive skin in a body-hugging orange jumpsuit that's tight in all the wrong places completes the ensemble. Ali my new companion has been here for all of 10 minutes giving me the lowdown and I'm already partly regretting my choice.

Partly, because for all of his berating, he's actually quite useful.

"Run," I finally decide, pulling apart the chocolate bar and taking another bite. No use fighting, nothing in the store that could scratch a Level 110 monster is going to be usable by me according to Ali and while there's no guarantee one of them will spawn immediately, even the lower level monsters that will make up its dinner would be too tough for me.

Hiding just delays things, so I have to get the hell out of the park which really, shouldn't be that hard. It took me half-a-day of hard hiking to get up this far in the mountain from the parking lot and the parking lot is just inside the new zone. At a good pace, I should be down in a few hours which if I understand things properly means there aren't that many monsters. Once I'm out, it seems Whitehorse has a Safe Zone, which means I can hunker down and figure out what the hell is going on.

"About damn time," grouses Ali. A wave of his hands and a series of new windows appear in front of me. Shortly after appearing he demanded full access to my System which has allowed him to manipulate the information I can see and receive. It's going a lot faster this way since he just pushes the information to me, letting me read through things while he does the deeper search. The new blue windows - System messages according to him - are his picks for medium and large perks respectively.

### Prodigy: Subterfuge

*You're a natural born spy. Intrepid would hire you immediately.*

*Effect: All Subterfuge skills are gained 100% quicker. +50% Skill Level increase for all Subterfuge skills.*

"Why this?" I frown, poking at the Subterfuge side. I'm not exactly the spying kind, more direct in most of my interactions. I've never really felt the need to lie too much and I certainly don't see myself creeping around breaking into buildings.

"Stealth skills. It gives a direct bonus to all of them which means you'll gain them faster. A small perk would allow us to directly affect the base Stealth skill but at this level, we've got to go up to its main category." Ali replies and continues, "If you manage to survive, it'll probably be useful in the future anyway."

### Quantum Stealth Manipulator (QSM)

*The QSM allows its bearer to phase-shift, placing himself adjacent to the current dimension*

*Effect: While active, user is rendered invisible and undetectable to normal and magical means as long as the QSM is active. Solid objects may be passed through but will drain charge at a higher rate. Charge lasts 5 minutes under normal conditions.*

"The QSM – how do I recharge it?"

"It uses a Type III Crystal Manipulator. The Crystal draws upon ambient and line specific..." Ali stares at my face for a moment before waving his hand. "It recharges automatically. It'll be fully charged in a day under normal conditions."

"No Level requirements on these?"

"None."

I picked Ali because he knows the System better than I do, so I can either accept what he's saying or I can do it myself. Put that way, there's really not much of a choice. It's what we talked about, though that Perk Subterfuge isn't really going to be that useful for me. On the other hand, any bonuses to staying out of sight would be great and the QSM would let me run away if I was found out. Which just left my Greater Perk.

### Advanced Class: Erethran Honor Guard

*The Erethran Honor Guard are Elite Members of the Erethran Armed Forces.*

*Class Abilities: +2 Per Level in Strength. + 4 Per Level in Constitution and Agility. +3 Per Level in Intelligence and Willpower. Additional 3 Free Attributes per Level. +90% Mental Resistance. +40% Elemental Resistance*

*May designate a Personal Weapon. Personal Weapon is Soulbound and upgradeable. Honor Guard members may have up to 4 Hard Point Links before Essence Penalties apply.*

*Warning! Minimum Attribute Requirements for the Erethran Honor Guard Class not met. Class Skills Locked till minimum requirements met.*

### Advanced Class: Dragon Knight

*Groomed before birth, Dragon Knights are the Elite Warriors of the Kingdom of Xylargh.*

*Class Abilities: +3 Per Level in Strength and Agility. + 4 Per Level in Constitution. +3 Per Level Intelligence and Willpower. + 1 in Charisma. Additional 2 Free Attributes per Level.*

*+80% Mental Resistance. +50% Elemental Resistance*

*Gain One Greater and One Lesser Elemental Affinity*

*Warning! Minimum Attribute Requirements for the Dragon Knight Class not met. Class Skills Locked till minimum requirements met.*

"That's it?"

"No, you could get this too."

### Class: Demi-God

*You sexy looking human, you'll be a demi-god. Smart, strong, handsome. What more could you want?*

*Class Abilities: +100 to all Attributes*

*All Greater Affinities Gained*

*Super Sexiness Trait*

"That's not a thing."

"It really ain't," smirking, Ali waves and the last screen dismisses. "You wanted a class that helps you survive? That means mental resistances. Otherwise, you'll be pissing those pretty little Pac-Man boxers the moment you see a Level 50 monster. You wanted an end-game? The Honor Guard are some mean motherfuckers. They combine magic and tech making them one of the most versatile groups around, and their Master class advancements are truly scary. The Dragon Knights fight Dragons. One on one and they sometimes even win. Oh, and neither, and I quote 'makes me into a monster'.

"If these are Advanced Classes, what other classes are there?" I prod at Ali, still hesitating. This seems like a big choice.

"Basic, Advance, Master, Grandmaster, Heroic, Legendary," lists Ali and he shrugs. "I could get you a Master Class with your perk, but you'd be locked out of your Class Skills forever. You'd also take forever to level because of the higher minimum experience level gains. Instead, I've got you a rare Advanced Class - it'll give you a better base stat gain per level and you won't have to wait forever to gain access to your Class Skills. Getting a Basic Class, even a rarer Basic Class would be a waste of the Greater Perk. So, what's it going to be?"

As cool as punching a dragon in the face would be, I know which way I'm going the moment he called it up. I mentally select the Guard and light fills me. At first, it just forces me to squint but it begins to dig in, pushing into my body and mind, sending electric, hot claws into my cells. The pain is worse than anything I've felt and I've broken bones, shattered ribs and even managed to electrocute myself before. I know I'm screaming but the pain keeps coming, swarming over me and tearing at my mind, my control. Luckily, darkness claims me before my mind shatters.

**Read Life in the North**
**https://readerlinks.com/l/1340826**

# Preview KT Hanna's other series:

# Somnia Online (Completed)

## Initializing (Somnia Online Book 1)

## Chapter One: The Gift

Storm Corp

Storm Technologies Division - Theoretical Neuroscience Arm

Countdown: Five years before Somnia Online implementation

Doctor Michael Jeffries was, again, impressed with his own genius. He ran his hands over his precious prototype. The headset wasn't as streamlined as he wanted of course, with its sharp edges and slipshod adjustments, but these were only the early stages. A thin graphite band held its arms in place, which reached out to tangle fingers into the hair of the wearer, digging down to secure themselves to the scalp and allow for deeper immersion than ever before. While it dug a little more than he liked at the moment, he'd been focused on what it could do rather than how it looked.

If everything went right, he knew Storm Corp would lavish rewards on him. After all, obtaining military research grants and the benefits that came with them were the epitome of success.

He leaned back and looked out of his window, still cradling his prototype like it might shatter at any moment. It was the key to everything he'd been working toward his whole life. Knowing a person, not only as a person, but as an infinitely complex set of neurons and synapses firing back and forth and creating the individual.

To know a person better than they knew themselves? It was the culmination of decades of devotion. Dr. Jeffries smiled and stood up, resting the headset on its podium with a reverence reserved only for it.

All they had to do was get the grant, and then begin the testing phase. The AIs he'd been using would be perfect for implementing the first stages, but then they'd have to widen the test.

They'd need more power, but that could wait until later.

There was still so much to do. He turned toward his office door, anxiousness simmering at the edge of his frayed nerves.

"Still no word..." he muttered. "How can that be?"

Jeffries walked to the window and looked out over the view of the parking lot. No view in sight, just a small office in the back of the building, but at least he did have a window, facing more buildings which showed the wear of time.

The knock on his door barely reached his ears before the door flew open with a bang.

"Michael!" His assistant, Jessa, yelled his name, waving a piece of paper in the air. "We got the grant! You did it!"

Michael stepped forward slowly, and then faster, and grabbed her hands, whirling her around before letting go and dancing a little jig himself.

"Thank you, Jessa. Let's get this started!"

"You've got it!" She closed the door in a whirlwind, and Michael watched her go, wondering just how his headset would read Jessa. She wasn't really the assistant type...

Walking over to where his prototype rested on its perch he stroked the rough carbon fiber surface and stared out of his window again. It was time to move on up in the world.

Time to know everyone better than they knew themselves.

❖

Summer Residence

Home of Laria, David, and Wren

Two Months Prior to Somnia Online Launch


Running over the percentages in her head, Wren frowned as she navigated the staircase to the lower level. If she'd done her calculations right, she'd taken all the pre-requisites she needed to tackle her neuro-engineering degree in the fall. Even though sonogenetics was still tickling at the back of her mind, neuro-engineering was where the future lay. Biting back a disgruntled sigh, she made her way into the kitchen. After exams she could dive back into her virtual worlds with Harlow and execute a bit of therapeutic violence.

Her parents stood behind the kitchen table, ridiculously excited grins on their faces, and she blinked her notes away, disabling her augmented vision with a thought. It made multitasking in life so much easier to just have the internet right there in your eyes all the time.

"Mom, Dad... you're not at work?" Seriously, if they'd gotten themselves fired, there was no way she could afford to go to college regardless of how many scholarships she managed to Tetris together. They never covered full tuition these days, so amassing a few scholarships would still only work if her parents helped.

Her mother laughed. Laria Sommers never failed to be bright and cheerful, something Wren had not inherited from her.

"Sweetheart! We have a present for you." Her mother's grin was so wide she could rival a Cheshire Cat for the part. "Open it, open it!"

Only then did Wren's eyes fall on the box sitting neatly wrapped on top of the table. It was quite large, a nice silver wrapped cube a little over a foot high. The thing was, her parents weren't the most observant of people. They were sweet, worked long hours, and even though they made it a rule to eat

465

dinner together five nights a week, they were often vague. Since they were MMORPG sweethearts though, they'd encouraged her love of virtual worlds. Not to mention they both worked in the industry. It was the one escape she had from an otherwise dull existence.

Approaching the package cautiously, Wren raised an eyebrow at her parents. "What's the occasion?"

"You!" Even her father seemed excited. His stoic IT professor personality was obviously on vacation. Or else they'd been drinking. Maybe they'd pulled an all-nighter. It wouldn't be the first time.

"Stop looking at us like that." He chided her, his brown eyes filled with a warmth only he ever exuded. It calmed Wren, making her smile despite her best efforts. "You've been working so hard, you've got acceptances from five colleges with as close to a full scholarship as possible, and you've refused to take part in the after graduation trip. You deserve this."

Wren didn't have the heart to mention that her invite to the graduation trip hadn't been entirely on the up and up—she didn't have much, if anything, in common with her classmates—still, why spoil things for him? He was obviously trying hard, and considering they both seemed to think she'd love it, curiosity got the better of her.

With a hint of childish abandon, she ripped the paper off the box and turned it over in her hands, barely daring to blink, just in case it disappeared.

*Storm Entertainment Presents:*

*SOMNIA ONLINE*

*"Experience the class you were born to play!"*

*Recommended headgear for best virtual immersion.*

"Seriously?" She blinked up at them, and could feel her face cracking into a grin even wider than her mother's. "Are you fucking serious?"

"Yes! I finally got my hands on it. You've got it earlier than most. It's not exactly the one people will get from the stores." Her mother practically shone with excitement. She'd been working on the development of Somnia Online for years. It was the biggest title she'd ever been in charge of, but it was so hush-hush, even Wren knew little about it. This headset cost a pretty penny. For her mom to have gotten her hands on one two months before release, even though she was lead designer on the game—it was probably courtesy of the design team.

"Can I..." She hesitated, unsure of herself. It was one thing to constantly pretend she knew exactly what she was doing, and it was another entirely to actually be confident. "Can I take it out of the box?"

"Of course." Her mother sidled over, and stood shoulder to shoulder with Wren. Their hair was nearly identical, smooth black waves that hung down to the middle of their backs, both in a no-nonsense ponytail. Together they opened the box, and Wren reached in with delicate fingers to retrieve the headset. It was glorious.

The arms of the connections gave it a fragile appearance but she knew from the online specifications that it was made of tough carbon fiber. The sleek silver design fit easily over the head, sort of like a headband. Small branches shot off the main piece and settled over her forehead, tracing back through her hair like an intricate headpiece. It was beautiful, if a little delicate.

"But you can't play with it until your finals are done. Your suit won't arrive for another few weeks." Her mother kissed her cheek and dashed over to pick up her purse.

"Wait..." Wren was shell-shocked. "You got me the suit too?"

"Of course! Except that's just standard issue." Her mother beamed another smile. "I have to go, or I'll be late for a meeting. Love you! I know you'll ace those finals."

Wren blinked as the whirlwind that was her mother slammed the door in her wake. It was still early, and the lightweight headset in her hands had a surreal quality to it, so unlike the bulky glasses contraption she had upstairs in her room. "Thanks Dad." She whispered, knowing he'd probably helped pull the strings too.

Nothing was cheap. Even public schooling cost money, and so many kids didn't seem to care. It was the bone of contention that didn't exactly make her popular with her peers. Somehow she'd inherited a sense of responsibility from her parents. Even though the world had largely gone to shit in the last sixty years, her parents were still ridiculously optimistic.

Her father enveloped her in a warm hug, pulling her back to the days before her mother got so busy, when they'd all curl up in the living room together and play stupid games. "Just approach the finals like you always do. Maybe we can let you scan early as added incentive! I'll talk to your mother."

Wren smiled, suddenly a little emotional. Just wait until she told Harlow!

"Kiddo, I've got a class to teach." Her Dad's voice suddenly took on a somber tone. "Just remember, you have to tell me if this game is worth your old Dad trying his hand at it."

His grin disarmed Wren, and she smiled. "Don't worry Dad, I'll be your guinea pig any day."

❖

"No way!"

Harlow's voice echoed so loudly through the earpiece, that Wren had to dial down the volume for a moment.

"Yes way. You've preordered it, what are you so jealous of?" It was difficult to keep the resentment out of her own voice, which wasn't fair since Harlow had paid for most of hers herself. Harlow was what people called a go-getter. She put her mind to something, and fucking did it. Be it school, a part time job with a goal, or playing her ranger or hunter characters in any given massively multiplayer roleplaying game and kicking everyone's ass at it.

"But I don't have mine, yet. I won't get it for ages!"

The whine in her tone made Wren chuckle. It's not like they lived far apart, but hopping into their games was just easy... well, not until finals were over. Good thing they'd already defeated all the content available in their last adventure.

"You'll get yours when I get my suit." Wren paused, preemptively dialing down for the squeal she knew was coming.

"You're getting a freaking suit?"

There it was.

"Yeah. Mom and Dad said it's because I studied my ass off. I guess being the pariah of my grade finally paid off." She couldn't keep the bitterness from her tone. It wasn't like she was bullied as such, just constantly snubbed, and selectively ridiculed. It helped to have online worlds to escape into every night. She continued before Harlow could sympathize. "Still though, two more months and we're done!"

"Forever! Well, until the fall and college anyway. Can you believe we're going to get to play with full immersion gear, Wren? Can you?" Harlow's excitement was contagious, and Wren found herself bouncing on her ball chair as she searched through sites, her contact monitors allowing her to multitask while talking.

"Dad's trying to get mom to let me try the headset out as an incentive, but when I get my suit, want to meet up so we can undergo the full scan?" Wren thought it would be that much more fun if it was both of them. After all, she did have a king sized bed. She frowned at an article that popped up in relation to the full immersion experience and Somnia Online, and bookmarked it for later reference.

"You bet. It's a date! I've got to go now. My brother's home."

"Ciao." Wren laughed as she disconnected the conversation. She pulled up the articles she'd found and perused them again. Just the same old warnings about how suits and chairs couldn't be guaranteed to keep your body from degradation while spending unhealthy amounts of time in virtual worlds. The headgear was also highlighted for producing irregular neural activity. Groups were up in arms about them... but gaming had always been a pretty convenient target.

Wren smiled. At least, despite the absent mindedness and forgotten occasions, her mom didn't try to stop her from gaming. Wren flipped through several pages, before she came to the promotional footage of Somnia Online.

She activated it and watched the familiar interaction with the Storm Entertainment Logo proudly front and center. The voiceover began.

*Imagine a world where you can be everything you've ever wanted to be. Where you can taste the food, smell the air, and feel the pain that keeps us alive! Befriend or repel a dragon. Build your guild's reputation and establish a base. Wage wars with other guilds, or other species. Find the twelve keys and unlock the secrets they hold.*

*Every choice you make will shape the world. Give in to your deepest desires.*

*Rip away your masks, your fears, and everything that's holding you back... Discover the class you were born to play.*

Mist swirled around snow-covered mountains, through dark dungeons with savage looking beasts whose eyes held far too much intelligence in their eyes for a game. Bustling cities flashed by, NPCs changed their expression based on directional conversation, rare spawns beat the living shit out of poor newbies.

The music thundered, swords clashed, mages threw fireballs, while rogues assassinated. Lively footage with a raw dose of reality. Ending with the sigil for Somnia Online. *Pre-order now!*

Wren smiled. She couldn't wait to play the game, to be what she was born to be.

**Read the completed series: Somnia Online!**
**https://readerlinks.com/l/2114331**

To learn more about LitRPG, talk to authors including myself, and just have an awesome time, please join the LitRPG Group:

https://www.facebook.com/groups/LitRPGGroup/

Made in United States
North Haven, CT
01 May 2022

18760514R00290